THE
BOOK
OF
MYSTERIES

JONATHAN CAHN

FRONT
LINE

Most CHARISMA HOUSE BOOK GROUP products are available at special quantity discounts for bulk purchase for sales promotions, premiums, fund-raising, and educational needs. For details, write Charisma House Book Group, 600 Rinehart Road, Lake Mary, Florida 32746, or telephone (407) 333-0600.

THE BOOK OF MYSTERIES by Jonathan Cahn
Published by FrontLine
Charisma Media/Charisma House Book Group
600 Rinehart Road
Lake Mary, Florida 32746
www.charismahouse.com

Scripture quotations are either the author's own translation or are taken from the New King James Version®. Copyright © 1982 by Thomas Nelson. Used by permission. All rights reserved.

Quotations from the Talmud are from the Babylonian Talmud, Tractate Yoma 39b; Babylonian Talmud, Sanhedrin 98b; Babylonian Talmud, Chapter 4, Folio 37; Jerusalem Talmud, Sanhedrin, Folio 24.

AUTHOR'S NOTE: At the bottom of every mystery is a title that identifies the full teaching or message that goes deeper into the mystery or gives more information than can be given on one page. You can find information on ordering these teachings or messages in the back of this book.

Cover design by Justin Evans

Visit the author's website at www.jonathancahn.com.

Library of Congress Control Number: 2016946282
International Standard Book Number: 978-1-62998-941-9
E-book ISBN: 978-1-62998-942-6

While the author has made every effort to provide accurate Internet addresses at the time of publication, neither the publisher nor the author assumes any responsibility for errors or for changes that occur after publication.

First edition

16 17 18 19 20 — 987654321
Printed in the United States of America

To Renata, my beloved and treasure, for her love, her encouragement, her patience, and her faithfulness, without which this book would not have been written.

To Eliel and Dael, the precious jewels and the surprise joy of our lives.

To my mother and father, for the gift of life, and for all their blessings given.

And to Him who is the Mystery of all mysteries, the Giver of all gifts, and the Gift behind them all.

CONTENTS

THE BEGINNING

WHO ARE YOU?" I asked.

"A teacher," he replied.

"A teacher of what?"

"Mysteries."

"And where do you teach?"

"Here."

"In the desert?"

"What better place to find the truth with no distractions?"

"In a school?"

"Some would call it that," he replied.

"And who are your students?"

"Seekers of truth."

"How do they know to come...to the desert?"

"Word of mouth...an encounter, if it's meant to be. It just happens in the encounter...as in this one."

"As in this encounter?"

"If it's meant to be."

"And where do your students live?"

"There are many accommodations."

"Dorms?"

"That might be stretching it," he replied. "Rooms, dwelling places, chambers."

"And how much does it cost to..."

"Attend?"

"Yes."

"It doesn't."

"How is that possible?"

"If one is truly seeking, it's provided for."

"Really?"

"Come," he said.

"To the school?"

"Come and you'll see."

"I can't," I said. "I'm in the middle of a kind of journey."

"Through a Middle Eastern desert?" he said.

"Yes."

"And what exactly were you expecting to find?"

"Nothing just..."

"You're on a journey to find nothing?"

"I like to travel."

INFINITY IN A JAR

IT WAS MORNING. The teacher came to my room holding a little clay jar.

"A question," he said. "Can that which is little contain that which is big?"

"No," I answered.

"Can that which is finite encompass that which is infinite?"

"No," I said again.

"But it can," he replied.

"How?"

He lifted the jar and removed the cap from its top.

"It can," he said. "It can if it's an open vessel. A closed vessel can never contain anything larger than its own size. But an open vessel has no limitations. It now can contain the blowing of the wind or the outpouring of the rain. It could even contain the flowing of a river."

"It would take a long time to contain a river."

"It could take forever, but the principle is the same."

"And the reason you're showing me this ..."

"Which is larger, that which you know or that which you don't know?"

"That which I don't know, I would think."

"So then, it's only wise that you seek that which you don't know."

"I guess."

"But how do you contain that which is bigger than you ... that which is bigger than your ability to comprehend?"

"By becoming an open vessel," I said.

"Yes," said the teacher. "Only by opening yourself up can you come to know that which you don't already know. And only by becoming an open vessel can you contain that which is greater than yourself. The truth is always greater than our knowing. Your mind and heart are finite, clay jars. But the truth has no end. God has no end. The Eternal is infinite ... always flowing."

"Like the river," I said.

"Yes," he said, "but when the jar opens itself, it becomes unlimited. It can contain the waters of the river ... So open now your mind, your heart, and your life. For it is only the open vessel and an open heart that can contain the infinity of God."

The Mission: Today, open your mind, your heart, and your life to that which you don't yet know, that you might contain that which is greater than yourself.

Isaiah 55:1–9; Jeremiah 33:3; 2 Corinthians 4:7

Filled Up With the Fullness

THE I AM OF ALL I AMS

IT WAS BY the second day that I realized that there would be no set time for the teacher's coming. He came in the afternoon.

"Do you know the Name of God?" asked the teacher.

"I don't know that I do."

It's made up of four Hebrew letters, the *yud*, the *heh*, the *vav*, and the *heh*: YHVH. It's the most sacred of names, so sacred some refuse to say it. And yet you say it all the time."

"The sacred Name of God?" I replied. "How could I when I never knew it?"

"When you speak of yourself, you say the Name."

"I don't understand."

"When you feel happy, you say, '*I am* happy.' And when you're not, you say '*I am* sad.' When you tell others who you are, you say, 'I am' followed by your name.

"*YHVH* means 'I Am.' It's the Name of the Eternal, the Name of God. His Name is *I Am*.

"Then we all say His Name."

"Yes. And you have always said it. It is woven into the fabric of existence that when you speak of yourself, you must say His Name."

"Why is that?"

"It's because your existence comes from His existence. He is the I Am of all existence…the I Am of all I ams. Your *I am* only exists because of His *I Am*. And as you exist from Him, so it is only from Him that you can find the reason and purpose of your existence. Therefore, when you say your name, you must always speak His Name. And you must always speak His Name first."

"Because…"

"Because His existence is first and your existence flows forth from His. That's the flow of existence. Therefore, you must put Him first and then let everything flow from that. Let everything begin with Him and flow forth from Him. That's the secret of life. To not only live *for* Him, but to live your life *from Him,* to live from His living, to move from His moving, to act from His actions, to feel from His heart, to be from His being, and to become who you are from who He is…I am."

The Mission: Today, learn the secret of living each moment from His life, doing from His doing, loving from His love, and being from His being.

Exodus 3:14–15; Acts 17:28

The I Am Mysteries

"With no destination?"

"Not in particular."

"But what if there was a destination?"

"What do you mean?"

"What if there was something you were meant to find?"

"Like what?"

"Come and you'll see. The new year's about to begin. It's a good time to start."

"To start?"

"The new course. The course I teach starts with the new year and ends at the year's end."

"I can't."

"Of course you can," he said.

"I mean, I don't know that I would."

"You will," he said, "if it's meant to be."

That's how it all began, an unplanned encounter in the middle of a desert. I don't know which was more absurd, what he told me about his "school" or the fact that I actually ended up there as one of his students. And I can't say exactly what it was that led me to take that step. Perhaps it was the thought that if I didn't do it, I would always wonder what it would have been like to have done so and regret having not taken the chance.

Nothing about the school was ordinary. The accommodations were sparse as one would expect considering the location. And yet it didn't seem to matter, not to any of the students. They came from all walks of life and from a wide variety of places.

It wasn't entirely barren. There were carefully maintained gardens of trees, plants, vines, and flowers. And then there were the people who lived in the surrounding region, the nomads, the shepherds, the many desert dwellers who lived in the tent encampments or tent villages that dotted the arid landscape. About an hour's walk from the school was a small city. On occasion I would go there, as would others from the school, to purchase goods, to observe, and, when appropriate, to seek to apply the lessons given.

The school had other classes and teachers, but he was clearly preeminent and the one who oversaw everything else. He was so preeminent that he was known simply as "the teacher." All the more reason I could never understand why he chose me as one of his students.

He lived a simple, ascetic life, as did everyone at the school. It was in keeping with the goal of eliminating all distractions. We drew our water from a well, and at night the school was lit up with candles and oil lamps. It was as if we were all transported back to ancient times. And yet, at the same time, the teacher seemed very much aware of what was going on in the larger world from which the school seemed so cut off. Nor was he averse to making use of any tool or service of the modern world that would serve the purposes of the teachings.

As for the teachings themselves, they were no less ordinary than the school in which they were given. Most of the classes I was given consisted of just me and the teacher. There was no set time or place. They could take place early in the morning, in the middle of the day, or late at night and in desert plains, on mountaintops, on hills, in oil-lit chambers, while overlooking one of the tent villages, or while journeying through the desert on camels. There were times when the teaching would be triggered or initiated by the surroundings or by something we happened to see, or at least it seemed that way. I could never quite tell if the teaching was based on the surroundings or the surroundings on the teaching. And there were some teachings that came about in response to one of my questions. Each teaching would impart a mystery or truth. Some mysteries would build upon other mysteries or together form a larger mystery. At the end of each teaching he would give me an assignment, a mission to apply what I learned to my life that day.

I kept a journal in which I wrote down what he taught me and our conversations as best I could remember them—the teachings, the mysteries, the questions and answers, and the references I was able to find later on that matched up with what he shared. So by the end of the course and the year I had recorded three hundred sixty-five mysteries, one for each day of the year, a teaching, a mystery, and a mission.

The following is the record of what I was shown by the teacher, the mysteries he imparted, as I received them in the year I dwelt in the desert.

————◆————

THE SHANNAH

H E CAME TO me at night.

"What is a year?" asked the teacher.

"Three hundred sixty-five days," I answered.

"But in the holy language of Scripture it's more than that. It's called the *shannah*...and it contains a secret. The word *shannah* is linked to the number two."

"I don't get the connection."

"*Shannah* can mean the second, the duplicate, or the repeat. In the course of nature the year is the repeating of what has already been...the winter, the spring, the summer, and the fall, the blossoming of flowers and their withering away, the rebirth of nature and its dying, the same progression, the same replaying of what already was. So a year is a shannah, a repetition. And now you have a new year before you. And what kind of year will it be?"

"What do you mean?"

"The nature of nature is to repeat, just as we live, by nature, as creatures of habit. We gravitate toward doing that which we've done before, the same routines and courses, even when those routines and courses are harmful to us. So what will the shannah, this new year, be for you?"

"Well if the year means the repeat, I guess I don't have much of a choice. It will be mostly the same as the one before."

"But you do have a choice," he said. "You see, *shannah* has a double meaning. It not only means the repeat...it also means the change."

"How can the same word mean the opposite?"

"The same way the year ahead of you can be either. The way of the world is to repeat—but the way of God is the way of newness and change. You can't know God and not be changed by knowing Him. And His will is that the year, the shannah ahead, be not a time of repetition but of change, of new beginnings, new steps, of breaking out of the old. And if you want to experience a year of new things, you must choose to live not in the repetition of the natural, but in the newness of the supernatural. Choose to walk not in your will but in the will of Him who is beyond the natural and beyond all that is old. As it is written, He makes all things new. Open up your life to the newness of His will, and you will walk in the newness of life and in the shannah of change."

The Mission: Today, step out of your old ways, habits, and steps. Do what you've never done before but should have. Walk in the newness of the Spirit.

Isaiah 43:19; Romans 6:4; 2 Corinthians 5:17

The Shannah

THE RUACH

HE TOOK ME to an open desert plain. It was a windy day, so windy it was almost violent.

"Come," said the teacher. He was asking me to walk against the wind's blowing. So I did.

"What is it like to walk against the wind?" he asked.

"It's a struggle," I replied.

"In the language of Scripture," he said, "the word for *wind* is *ruach*. But it has another meaning; it also means the Spirit. In Hebrew, the Holy Spirit is the Holy Wind. So what happens if you walk against the wind?"

"It creates drag. It becomes harder to walk and you get tired."

"In the same way," he said, "when you walk against the Spirit, it creates a drag on your life. Everything you do becomes harder. It takes more energy to do less. So when you go against His Spirit, you're fighting against the Wind. And you can't walk against the direction of the Wind without getting weary and worn out."

"And what way is the direction of the Wind, the Spirit?"

"The Spirit is the *Holy* Spirit. Therefore, it blows in the direction of the holy, and blows against the direction of the unholy. Now try something else. Turn around and walk back, the same way you came."

So I did. I was now walking in the direction of the wind's blowing.

"And what was that like?" he asked.

"It was much easier," I said.

"That's because there was no drag," he said. "You were walking in the direction of the wind. And the wind helped you walk. It moved you ahead. It made your walking easier. So when you walk against the wind, it creates drag. But if you turn around, then the wind gives you power. So it is with the Spirit. If you turn, if you change your course, if you repent, if you walk in the Spirit, then the drag will disappear. Then the Spirit will empower you and will move you forward. And then everything you do, that you must do, will become easier."

"So if you walk in the Spirit," I said, "life will go from being a drag to a breeze."

"Yes," said the teacher. "For those who walk in the Spirit, the Wind is at their back."

The Mission: What part of your life is against the direction of the Spirit? Today, turn it around and start walking with the Wind at your back.

John 3:8; Acts 2:2; Galatians 5:16–17

Ruach

APPOINTING YOUR DAYS

WE'VE SPOKEN OF the year before you," said the teacher. "Today we will speak of the days before you. What will the days yet to come bring to your life?"

"How could I know that?" I replied. "I don't really have a say in the matter."

"But what if you did?"

"How?"

"It is written, 'Teach us to number our days.' What does that mean?"

"That our days are limited, and so it's wise to number them."

"That's correct," he said. "And it's the first meaning of the Scripture. But in the original language is a secret. And this secret can change your life, the days of your life. In the Hebrew it says, 'Teach us to *manah* our days.' The same word, *manah,* appears in the Book of Jonah where it is written that God manahs a fish, a worm, and a wind."

"Then *manah* must mean more than number."

"It does. It means to prepare and to appoint. So you must not only *number* your days, you must learn to *prepare* your days, to *appoint* your days."

"What does that mean?"

"It means that you're not just to watch and wait passively to see what your days will bring. You're to prepare them."

"How can I prepare my days before they happen?"

"How did the first days happen in the beginning? They didn't just happen. Before they existed, God prepared them. He appointed them. He purposed them. So if you're a child of God, you must do likewise."

"How?"

"Prayer."

"Praying for days that don't yet exist?"

"Prayer isn't only for what is, but for what is not yet."

"But I can't determine what will happen."

"It doesn't matter what happens. You appoint your days in God to bring what is good. You consecrate them for the purposes of God. And then you use your days to accomplish those purposes. Don't let your days determine your life. Let your life determine your days. And don't just let your days go by. Prepare them, that they might become vessels of blessing and life. Appoint your days."

The Mission: Prepare the days ahead. Set them apart. Commit them into God's hands and appoint them for the fulfilling of His purposes.

Psalm 90:12; Acts 19:21

The Shannah and the Manah

THE MYSTERY OF THE BRIDE

O N OUR JOURNEY to the city, we stopped on a nearby hill.

"Look," said the teacher, pointing to an event at the city's edge.

"It looks like a wedding," I replied, "or the preparation for a wedding." The bride, in a white gown, was standing in a garden with her bridesmaids.

"You're watching a cosmic mystery, the shadow of a mystery. Existence," he said, "is a love story...or was meant to be a love story. The bride is a picture of what we each were created to be."

"I don't understand."

"We were each created to be the bride. That's why we can never be complete in ourselves. That's why, deep down, in the center of our being, in the deepest part of our heart, we seek to be filled. For the bride is made to be married. So we can never find our completion until we are joined to Him who is beyond us. And that is why we go through our lives trying to join ourselves..."

"Join ourselves to what?"

"To that which we think will fill the longing of our hearts—to people, success, possessions, achievements, money, comfort, acceptance, beauty, romance, family, power, a movement, a goal, and any multitude of things. For the bride was created to be married, and she can never rest until she is."

"So none of the other things can work?"

"No. None of the other things are the Bridegroom."

"And who is the Bridegroom?"

"The Bridegroom is God, the One for whom we were created."

"So we have to find Him."

"More than that," he said. "A bride doesn't just find the Bridegroom; she *marries* Him. So it's not enough to find God; you must *marry Him*."

"Marry God? How?"

"By joining every part of your life and being—your deepest parts, your heart, your soul, your wounds, your longings, your desires, everything—to God. Only then can you be complete. Only then can your deepest needs and longings be fulfilled. For the mystery of our hearts is the mystery of the bride. And the bride can only find her completion in the Bridegroom. And the Bridegroom of our souls...is God."

The Mission: Put away anything that substitutes for His presence, and join all that you are, your deepest parts, to your Bridegroom.

Deuteronomy 6:5; Song of Solomon 1:1–4; Ephesians 5:28–32

The Mystery of the Calah

THE POWER OF THE YUD

THE TEACHER LED me out into the desert ravine where we sat down in the sand, face-to-face. He picked up a stick and, with the slightest of movements, created the smallest of marks in the sand.

"This can change your life," he said.

"An apostrophe?"

"A *yud.*"

"What's a yud?"

"A yud is a letter, the smallest of Hebrew letters…barely more than a dot, so small you could miss it. From the yud came the Roman letters *I* and *J*. And from the yud came the Greek letter *iota.*"

"As in 'not one iota.'"

"Yes, or as in 'not one jot.' It all comes from the same tiny letter."

"So it's the smallest of letters. Why is it significant?"

"That's the point…as the smallest of letters, it is most significant. It is the yud that begins the greatest and most sacred of Hebrew words: The sacred Name of God, *YHVH*, begins with a yud. The land of God, *Israel*, begins with a yud. The City of God, *Jerusalem*, begins with the yud. And the name *Jesus*, in Hebrew, begins, as well, with a yud."

"And what does it all mean?"

"The greatest of words begin with the smallest of letters. In the same way, the greatest works of God begin with the smallest of strokes. Life itself begins on a scale so small, it can't even be seen. It's the secret of the yud."

"And how does one apply it?"

"We are called to the new and to change. But by nature we avoid both newness and change. So how do you change? How do you go from a life of failure to a life of victory? It's an overwhelming prospect. How do you do it? With the yud. You start by taking the yud of steps, the smallest of steps but toward the greatest of changes. You don't start out with a great victory, but you take the yud, one small action, one little step toward that great victory. You take that one step, that yud of courage, that iota of change, that smallest stroke of new beginnings, the yud of the life you're called to live. You begin the greatest of things with the smallest of strokes. You begin by applying the secret of the yud."

The Mission: Today, take the smallest of actions, but in a new direction, the first step toward the life of victory you're called to live—the yud of a new journey.

Job 8:7; Acts 3:4–9

The First Step

THE MIDBAR

HE TOOK ME out in the desert to an immense valley surrounded by reddish mountains, which turned increasingly purple and blue as they extended out into the far distance.

"What words come to your mind," said the teacher, "when you look at the desert wilderness?"

"Dry...barren...hot...austere...severe...hard...forbidding..."

"And when people go through hard times—times of loss, crisis, tragedy, loneliness, conflict, hardship, problems, separation, tears—they speak of going through the wilderness. And yet the wilderness is a holy place. It was in a desert wilderness that God gave His Law, His Word, and where He revealed His presence. The wilderness is holy."

"So the hard times in our lives are holy?"

"For those who are His children, yes."

"How so?"

"In Hebrew, the wilderness is called the *midbar. Midbar* comes from the root word *dabar.* And *dabar* means to speak. What is the wilderness? It is the midbar. And what is the midbar? It is the place of God's speaking, the place of His voice. It's where God especially talks to us. Why did He bring His people into wilderness, into the midbar? So He could speak to them. He brought Moses into the midbar to speak to him through a burning bush. He brought Elijah to the midbar to speak to him in a still, small voice. So too He brings us into the wilderness that He might speak to us."

"What is it about the wilderness that makes it the place of God's speaking?"

"Look around you," he said. "What do you see?"

"Rock, sand, mountains—not much."

"That's why," said the teacher. "God speaks, but we don't hear. We have too many distractions. But in the wilderness the distractions are gone. So God brings us to the wilderness that we might hear His voice. Therefore, do not fear or despise the wildernesses of your life, and don't despise His removing of the distractions. Rather embrace it. Draw closer to Him. And listen to what He is saying. Seek to hear His voice, and you will hear Him. For the wilderness in your life is not just a wilderness. It is holy ground...the midbar...the place of His voice."

The Mission: Put away the distractions, those things that keep you from hearing. And go into the wilderness, the midbar, and seek the voice of God.

Deuteronomy 8:2–16; Psalm 46:10; Jeremiah 29:12–13; Luke 3:2

THE SHAMAYIM AND THE ARETZ

HE LED ME out in the darkness of the night to a sandy expanse. There we lay down and gazed up into the star-filled skies.

"It's so vast," said the teacher, without turning from his upward gaze.

"The sky?" I answered. "I would think it is."

"In Hebrew, the word for *heaven* is *shamayim*. The word for *earth* is *aretz*. When you hear a Hebrew word that ends with *im*, it's a sign that word is plural. So what does this tell you?"

"The word for heaven is plural...but the word for earth is not."

"Correct. *Shamayim*, heaven, is plural, but *aretz*, earth, is not. And it's not just the words; it's what the words represent."

"Which is..."

"That which is earthly is singular. That which belongs to the physical realm is finite. Everything that is physical is limited. That's why, no matter how much of the earthly realm you get, no matter how many earthly possessions you possess, it can never fill you or bring you completion."

"Because they're limited," I said, "because they're finite."

"And so a life focused on the physical..."

"Is a life filled with limitations."

"But if you empty your heart of physical things..."

"Then you empty yourself of limitations."

"So the things of earth are finite," he said, "but the things of heaven are infinite. The physical is limited, but the spiritual is unlimited. Only that which is spiritual, the infinite, can fill the heart."

"But how does one get away from living in the earthly realm?"

"One doesn't," said the teacher. "You can't escape living *in* the earthly realm—but you don't have to live *of* the earthly realm. You must deal with earthly things, but you don't have to fill your heart with them. Set your heart on that which is heavenly. Fill up your heart with that which is spiritual. For heaven is shamayim, and shamayim has no limitation. And, therefore, a heart filled up with that which is spiritual and that which is heavenly..."

"Becomes unlimited."

The Mission: What are your possessions? Today, let go. Free up your heart of its earthly possessions. And fill it up with the spiritual and heavenly.

Isaiah 55:9; Philippians 4:8–9

The Hebrew Mysteries I–IV

THE SERPENT'S BLOOD

DO YOU SEE it?" asked the teacher.

"Behind the rock," I replied.

It was a snake, brown and black, and slithering in the desert sand.

"What do you know about snakes?" he asked.

"I know to avoid them."

"Nothing more?"

"Not much."

"What you should know is that snakes are cold-blooded."

"Why is that important?"

"You're warm-blooded. And because you're warm-blooded, you can run and keep running. But a snake, being cold-blooded, is limited in its ability to endure, to keep going. Therefore, you can outlast it."

"That's good to know," I replied.

"In the Scriptures, the serpent is a symbol of evil."

"Why is that?"

"Not because snakes are evil in themselves but because they provide a representation of evil. They often move by twisting. And so the nature of evil is to twist. A lie is the twisting of the truth. The impure is the twisting of the pure. And evil, itself, is the twisting of the good."

"So then if snakes are cold-blooded, then, so, in some way, is evil?"

"Yes," said the teacher. "Evil is cold-blooded. What that means is this: Though evil may have its day, its victories, its time to move and strike—it remains cold-blooded. Therefore, it can never endure. No matter how powerful the evil may appear, no matter how triumphant and unstoppable it may seem, it cannot last. Deception is cold-blooded. Hatred is cold-blooded. Slander is cold-blooded. Oppression is cold-blooded. All evil is cold-blooded. And so the power of evil is only for the short-term and the momentary. Its days are always numbered. And in the long run, it always fails."

"But the good is not cold-blooded," I said.

"Yes," he said. "So, in the end, the good will always outlast the evil. Therefore, persevere in the good, keep going in what is true, keep standing for what is right, and you will overcome and prevail in the end."

The Mission: In the face of whatever evil, trouble, attack, or sin you're dealing with, don't give in. Don't give up. But press on in the good.

Isaiah 54:17; Matthew 24:13; John 1:5

THE FACE IN THE WATERS

WE WALKED FOR some time until we came to a pool of water hidden at the foot of one of the desert mountains. We sat down by its edge.

"Smile," said the teacher.

So I did.

"No," he said, "smile into the waters. Lean over the waters and smile."

So I did.

"Now make a face of anger."

So I did.

"Now open your hand and stretch it over the waters as if giving a gift."

So I did.

"Now do the opposite."

"What's the opposite?"

"Stretch your hand to the waters, close it and withdraw it, as if taking something away."

"I'm not seeing the point of this."

"Oh, but there is a point," he said, "and the point is critical for you to learn. When you smiled at the waters, there was a man smiling back at you."

"My reflection."

"And when you glared at it, the face of an angry man glared back at you. And when you stretched your hand out to the waters to give to it, the hand in the waters stretched back to give to you. And when you reached toward the waters to take from it, the hand reached back as if to take from you. This is the law of reflection. As you do, so it will be done to you. If you bless others, you will be blessed. If you withhold blessing, your blessings will be withheld. If you live by taking, it will, in the end, be taken from you. If you live a life of giving, it will, in the end, be given to you. Condemn others, and you will be condemned. Forgive others, and you will be forgiven. Live with a closed hand, and His hand will be closed you. Live with an open hand, and His hand will be opened to you. What you give will be given back. What you take will be taken back. Therefore, live a life of love, of giving, of blessing, of compassion, of an open hand and heart. Whatever you do, remember what you saw here. Live your life in view of the face in the waters."

The Mission: What is it that you seek from life and from others? Today, make it your goal to give to others the very thing you seek.

Proverbs 27:19; Luke 6:37–38; Galatians 6:7–10

The Face in the Waters

THE COSMIC LOVE

DEFINE *LOVE*," SAID the teacher.

"*Love* is to want the best for another," I replied.

"Yes," he said. "And to put it another way, *love* is to put yourself in the place of another, to feel their feelings, walk in their shoes, weep with their tears, rejoice in their joys, take upon yourself their burdens, and give to them your life."

"I like that."

"The Scriptures declare that God is love," he said. "If God is love, He must be the greatest love, the ultimate love. Do you believe God loves us?"

"I do."

"Then what must love do?"

"Love must put itself in the place of another."

"So what would be the greatest possible manifestation of love?"

"That God...would put Himself in the place of another?"

"And how would that actually manifest? What would be the greatest manifestation of love?"

"God would have to put Himself in our place...He would have to walk in our shoes."

"Yes, and feel our feelings."

"And cry our tears."

"And take upon Himself our burdens," he said, "and our judgment...and our death, to save us, to give us life. He would give His life."

"Then if God is love," I said, "that's what He *would* do."

"Then," said the teacher, "the greatest possible manifestation of love has already manifested...on our planet. God putting Himself in our place. And so there is no greater love you could ever know," he said. "When you feel it and when you don't, it doesn't matter—it doesn't change anything. Nothing you do can alter this love. No good work can increase it. And no sin can lessen it. When you feel it and when you don't, it's there nonetheless. We cannot change it—we can only receive it and be changed by it. We can only let it change us. For the greatest possible love has already been manifested. God has come down. It is only for us to receive it and to do likewise."

The Mission: Today, practice the divine and cosmic love. Put yourself in the place of another—your feet in their shoes, your heart in their heart.

John 15:12–13; Romans 5:6–8; Philippians 2:5–9

THE EAST-WEST CONTINUUM

IT WAS DAWN. We were watching the sun rise over the desert landscape.

"*Kedem*," said the teacher. "It's Hebrew for east, a most critical direction."

"Why?" I asked.

"The Temple of Jerusalem was built according to the kedem. It had to face the east. The altar of the sacrifice was at its easternmost end. The holy of holies was at its westernmost end. Everything else was in between. So everything in the Temple existed on an east-west continuum. Everything that took place in the Temple took place on an east-west continuum. Most importantly, on the holiest day of the year, Yom Kippur, the sins of Israel were atoned for, removed from the people, on an east-west continuum. The high priest would offer up the sacrifice in the east, and then sprinkle the blood on the ark of the covenant in the west. He would journey back and forth on an east-west continuum. And the closing act of the day would see the sins of the people symbolically removed from the west to the east."

"But why is that more significant than if it was a north-south continuum?"

"Because," said the teacher, "the earth is a sphere...and it turns on its axis on an east-west continuum. Therefore, the earth has a north pole and a south pole, but no east or west pole."

"I still don't understand."

"How far is the north from the south?" he asked. "Since there are two poles, the distance is limited. All north comes to an end at the North Pole. And all south ends at the South Pole. If the Temple had been built on a north-south continuum, then sin would have been removed a few thousand miles from the sinner. But how far is the east from the west? East and west have no poles. Therefore, they never end. East and west are infinite. They go on forever. In fact, the Hebrew word for the east, *kedem,* also means everlasting."

"But back then no one knew the earth was a sphere."

"God did. And all this is a shadow of the atonement of Messiah, our salvation. So in Messiah, how far does God remove your sins from you? An infinity away...an eternity away. And if you had all eternity, you could never find them again. As it is written, 'So far has He removed our sins away from us...as far as the east is from the west.'"

The Mission: Today, take time to ponder and take in the love of God that removed your sins as far as the east is from the west—and live accordingly.

Leviticus 16:14; Psalm 103:10–12

The Mystery of the Kedem

KISSING GOD

THERE WAS A gathering in the school's open-air tent. It was a time of worship and praise. We were just outside the tent listening.

"What do you think of," asked the teacher, "when you hear the word *worship*?"

"Singing, hymns, prayers, words of praise..."

"That's the outward form of worship," he said. "That's how worship manifests. But what's the heart of worship?"

"I don't know."

"I'll give you one definition, a secret. It's found in the New Covenant Scriptures. It only appears in the Greek. It's the word *proskuneo*. And do you know what it means?"

I had no answer.

"It means to kiss. True worship," said the teacher, "is to kiss. And what does this reveal? What is a kiss? A kiss is the most intimate of acts. Therefore, worship is to be the most intimate thing you can experience."

"To worship God is to kiss God?"

"In the spiritual realm, yes, to kiss from your heart, from your innermost being. And when you kiss, you don't do it because you have to. You do it freely from your heart because you want to."

"So true worship is never done by compulsion, but freely from the overflow of your heart."

"And why does one kiss?" asked the teacher.

"Because of joy."

"Yes," he said, "a kiss is an expression of joy. And kissing brings you joy. So true worship is an expression of joy. You worship out of joy. Your joy becomes worship and your worship becomes joy."

"Teacher," I said, "we didn't say the most obvious."

"Which is...?"

"One kisses because of love," I said. "A kiss is an expression of love."

"It is. So then what is true worship?"

"Worship is an expression of love."

"Yes," said the teacher, "It's as simple as that: It's the most intimate act of love and joy. Worship is as simple as kissing God."

The Mission: Today, draw near to God in worship, in love, in joy, in the deepest of intimacy. Learn the secret of kissing God.

Psalm 42:7–8; Song of Solomon 1:2; John 4:24

Yishkeni: The Divine Kiss

THE NIGHT AND DAY PARADIGM

THERE WAS NO lesson that day. But then in the middle of the night he came to my room and woke me.

"Come," said the teacher. "It's time for the lesson. We're going outside."

I was half asleep and not thrilled at the idea, but, of course, I complied. He led me to a hill where we sat down in the darkness of the night.

"Which comes first," he asked, "the day or the night?"

"The day," I answered. "Night comes when the day is over."

"That's what most people would say. And that's how most people in the world see it. Day leads into night. But it's not how God sees it."

"What do you mean?"

"If the day leads to night, then everything goes from light to darkness. Everything gets darker. Everything is in the process of darkening. And it would appear to be the way of the world. We go from day to night, from youth to aging, from strength to weakness, and ultimately from life to death. Day to night. It's the way of the world, but it's not the way of God. When God created the universe, it was not day and night. It is written, 'There was evening, and then there was morning.' The day began with night. There was night and then there was day. It is the night that comes first."

"So that's why Jewish holidays always begin at sunset."

"Yes, and not only Jewish holidays, but every biblical day. Each day begins at sunset. There is evening and then morning. The world moves from day to night. But in God, it is the opposite. It goes from night to day ... from darkness to light. The children of this world live from day to night. But the children of God live from night to day. They are born again in the darkness and move to the day. And if you belong to God, then that is the order of your life. You are to go from darkness to light, from weakness to strength, from despair to hope, from guilt to innocence, from tears to joy, and from death to life. And every night in your life will lead to the dawn. So live according to God's sacred order of time ... that your entire life be always moving away from the darkness and to the light."

As he said those words, the first light of daybreak appeared and the night began yielding to the day.

The Mission: What darkness is in your life, the darkness of fear, of sin, of problems, of gloom? Today, turn away from it and to the light of day.

Genesis 1:3–5; Psalm 30:5; Ephesians 5:8; 1 Peter 2:9; 2 Peter 1:19

The Night and the Sunrise

THE TALEH

HE TOOK ME through a ravine that opened up into a valley. In the valley, a boy was tending a flock of sheep and lambs. One of the lambs had wandered off in our direction.

"Look," said the teacher, "a lamb, the most defenseless of creatures, so defenseless it needs a boy to protect it. And yet it is of cosmic importance."

"How?" I asked.

"The lamb is the master theme of God's Word. In Genesis, a boy asks his father, 'Where is the lamb...?' That's the question of Scripture. On Passover, it is the lamb that dies to save the firstborn son of each house. The nation of Israel is saved by the blood of the lamb. Then in the Temple of Jerusalem, lambs are offered up in sacrifice every day of every year. And then, in the fifty-third chapter of Isaiah, it prophesied that a man will give His life as a sacrificial lamb, 'as a lamb to the slaughter,' and by His death, we will find healing, forgiveness, and blessing. Do you see the theme?"

"The lamb is the life given to save or bless others."

"Yes, and to cover our sins. In Hebrew, *taleh* means lamb. And from *taleh* also comes the word that means covering. The Lamb will be our covering. So who is the Lamb? In all of world history, is there anyone known above all for giving His life, as an offering, as a sacrifice, that we might be saved?"

"There's only one I know of," I replied. "And wasn't He called 'the Lamb'?"

"Yes," said the teacher, "Messiah, the Lamb of God, the *Taleh Elohim*. It was all about the Lamb from the beginning, the answer was always linked to the Lamb. But why a lamb in the first place?"

"I don't know."

"What the lamb means is this: There will be One who is entirely pure, innocent, without blemish, without evil...and this One will give His life to save those who are not innocent. But what is without blemish, what is entirely pure and good? What is the mystery of the lamb?"

"Tell me."

"The mystery of the lamb is God. The mystery is that God will give His life to save us. For God is love. And the nature of love is to give of itself. The Taleh, the Lamb...is God."

The Mission: Today, live in the spirit of the Lamb. Let everything you do be done in love. And live to make your life a blessing to others.

Genesis 22:1–18; Isaiah 53:7; 1 Peter 1:18–19; Revelation 5:6–13

HOW TO ALTER YOUR PAST

WE WERE SITTING in his study. He was holding a scarlet cord.

"I dyed it myself," said the teacher. "I left it in the solution for several days to make sure the dye soaked into every fiber. Do you think it's possible to *undye* the cord, to make it white again?"

"I doubt it."

"It is written: 'Though your sins are as scarlet, I will make them white as snow.' It would be like undyeing the cord."

"Which would be impossible," I said.

"But it's even more impossible than that. How do you make sins go from scarlet to white? Sins are sins because they're already committed. They're done. They're part of the past, and the past is finished."

"Then the only way to alter a sin would be to change the past."

"Yes, and yet the Scriptures are filled with the promise that God will one day wipe away sin and wash away our guilt. You can't wipe away sin or cleanse guilt without changing the past."

"But it's impossible to change the past."

"The first recorded miracle of Messiah was the changing of water into wine. But wine is only wine if it's aged. But the wine of the miracle had no past to be aged. It had to, in a sense, be given a new past. If God can give a past where there was no past, then He can remove a past where there was one."

"So salvation is the undyeing of the scarlet cord," I said.

"Exactly. God doesn't just forgive the scarlet cord or pretend it isn't scarlet. He changes its past and, by that, changes its reality. He undyes it."

"He can do that?" I asked.

"God brought time into existence. God can bring it out of existence."

"So it's not simply that everything is the same and we're forgiven in spite of it. It's as if we never sinned in the first place."

"And even more amazing than that. It's not just *as if* we never sinned but, in His redemption, it has become that we've never sinned. In salvation, the impossible becomes the reality, the guilty become innocent, the tainted become pure, the rejected become those who were always beloved children, and our sins, which were as scarlet, become . . . as white as snow."

The Mission: Soak in the undyeing. Receive from heaven your changed, innocent, pure, and beloved past, a past as beautiful and as white as snow.

Isaiah 1:18; Luke 7:37–47; 2 Corinthians 5:21; 1 John 1:8–9

As Beloved Children

YESHUA

A MOST IMPORTANT WORD," said the teacher, "the word *yasha*. In Hebrew, it means to rescue, to help, to defend, to preserve, to make free, to attain victory, to bring to safety, to heal, and to save...one word and the answer to everything."

"How is it the answer to everything?" I asked.

"*Yasha* is what we spend our lives seeking for, whether we realize it or not. We all need help, we all need freedom, we all need victory, and we all, in one way or another, seek for salvation. And in Hebrew, salvation comes from *yasha*. From the word *yasha* comes the Hebrew word *yeshua*. *Yeshua* means salvation. So in the Hebrew Scriptures, it is written, 'He has become my salvation.'"

"Who has become salvation?"

"God," he said. "God has become salvation. In other words, God would not only be the Creator of the universe, He would become our salvation. In other words, God would become our help, our defense, our preserving, our freedom, our victory, our salvation. God would become the answer to our greatest and deepest needs. In Hebrew, God would become *yeshua*."

"But if the word *yeshua* means salvation, what's the difference between saying 'God would become salvation' or 'God would become *yeshua*'?"

"From the Hebrew word *yeshua* comes the name Yeshua. And when the name Yeshua was translated into Greek, it became *Iesous*. And when Iesous was translated into English, it became Jesus. Jesus is Yeshua...or Yeshua is Jesus. Yeshua is the real name of the one the world knows as Jesus."

"So then God will become Yeshua. God will become Jesus."

"And that's exactly what the name Yeshua reveals. It means, God is my salvation. The ancient hope was that one day God would become our Yeshua. And so He has. And so what does Yeshua actually mean?"

"It means God has become our rescue, our help, our freedom, our healing, our victory, and our salvation."

"Yes," said the teacher. "God became Yeshua to become the answer to every need. So the key is to take every need in your life and join it to that name, to Yeshua, one word...and the answer to everything."

The Mission: God has become your Yeshua, the specific answer to your deepest needs. Let that get inside your heart and live accordingly.

Exodus 15:2; Psalm 118:14; Isaiah 12:2; Matthew 1:21

ALIYAH

COME," SAID THE teacher.

"Where?" I asked.

"Up," he answered. "Up a mountain."

He then took me on a half-hour journey through the desert to a particularly high mountain.

"Let us go up," he said.

So we did. There was nothing easy about it. I had to rest several times, just to catch my breath. Finally we made it to the top.

"Look at that," he said, pointing to the majestic panorama before us. "It's something you can only see from up here, from the heights. It was worth the climb. Do you know what it's called in Hebrew, what we just did?"

"Torture?"

"No," he said, "it's called *aliyah*. It means the going up, the ascent. When you read in the Scriptures of Messiah going to Jerusalem, you'll find the word *up* used over and over again. Why is that? Jerusalem is a city set on the mountains. So to get there, you have to go up. So the journey to Jerusalem is called *Aliyah*...the ascending. And it was not only because of the physical terrain but because Jerusalem is the Holy City. So to go to Jerusalem is to *make Aliyah*. In the modern age, when the Jewish people began to return to the land of Israel, the return was called Aliyah. Going to the Promised Land was known as 'making Aliyah,' 'the upward journey.' The children of Israel were commanded to make Aliyah. But those who are of Messiah are the spiritual children of Israel. So what would that mean?"

"They also have an Aliyah to make?"

"Yes," said the teacher, "but a spiritual people must make a spiritual journey."

"So what's the journey?" I asked. "What's the Aliyah?"

"Your life," said the teacher. "Your entire life is the Aliyah. Your life is a journey, but in God it is to be an upward journey...an ever higher ascending. How do you do that? The same way you ascended the mountain. Every day you will be given choices. Every choice will give you the chance to go lower, to stay the same, or to go higher. Choose the higher path, even if it's harder, take the higher step...let each of your steps be higher than the step before it, each of your days be higher than the day before it. And you will end up walking on mountain heights...and your life will be an Aliyah."

The Mission: Today, choose the higher step, the higher act, the higher ground, the higher path in every decision. Start making your life an Aliyah.

Psalm 121; Mark 10:32

The Aliyah Mystery

THE FOOTSTOOL WORLD

HE TOOK ME into his study and motioned me to sit down in his chair. In front of the chair was a cushioned stool.

"Relax," he said, "put your feet up."

So I did. He was quiet. Finally I broke the silence.

"And what's today's mystery?" I asked.

"That," he said. "That," he said again, pointing to the stool.

"The footstool?"

"Yes, the footstool. And within it lies a cosmic revelation."

"A cosmic revelation? I never would have thought."

"Cosmic enough to be spoken of by God. 'Heaven is My throne,' He said, 'and the earth is My footstool.' What do you think it means?"

"The earth is the place where God puts His feet?"

"That's exactly right. Heaven is His throne. In other words, heaven is God's dwelling place, the center of His presence, and where He rests His weight. And the word for *weight* in Hebrew is *kavode*. *Kavode* also means glory. Heaven in which rests God's weight and glory."

"And the earth?"

"The earth is *not* His throne. So it can't bear the weight of His glory."

"But it's His footstool."

"Yes. So He rests His feet on it. It bears the imprint of His feet, but never His full weight. And what does this reveal?"

"What?"

"You live in a footstool world. The earth is just a footstool. It means it isn't the place on which you can rest all your weight or your well-being. Its possessions are only footstool possessions. Its issues are only footstool issues. Its problems are only footstool problems. And its glory is only a footstool glory. You don't sit on a footstool; you just place your feet on top of it...on top of its problems, on top of its issues, on top of its glories. You rest your feet on it...lightly. That's the way one must live in a footstool world."

"Then where *do* you rest your weight?"

"In the heavenlies," he said. "But that's another mystery. For now, enjoy the footstool."

The Mission: Today, see the world and everything in it in a new way, as the footstool world, with only footstool issues, and live accordingly.

Isaiah 66:1; Ephesians 2:6; Colossians 3:1–2

THE HEARTBEAT OF THE MIRACLE

WE WERE SITTING on two large stones at the base of a small mountain. The teacher leaned down to the ground, picked up a rock, and handed it to me.

"What do you feel?" he asked.

"Nothing," I replied. "A rock."

Now put your hand on your neck. Do you feel anything?"

"My heartbeat."

"But the rock had no heartbeat," he said.

"Of course not."

The rock exists as a rock with no heartbeat. It retains its shape, its size, its consistency, with no need of a heartbeat. But you have a heartbeat. Every moment of your existence hangs on a heartbeat. The moment it stops, your existence is over. That's the difference between a rock and your life. God ordained it. Rocks just exist. But life never just exists. It must strive to exist, fight to exist. Your heart must keep beating, every moment of your life. Even if you do nothing, your heart beats. Even when you sleep, it keeps beating every moment so that you can remain alive. If you waste your moments on earth, still it beats that you can waste your time. When you sin, when you gossip, when you covet and hate, still it beats while you do so. When you weep, when you give up hope, still it beats so that even in your tears and despair, it still fights for you to live and to be able to cry."

"So the difference between my existence and that of a rock is..."

"Your life doesn't just exist; it *strives* to exist. Your life is a miracle. Your every moment is a miracle. Your joys are a miracle. Even your tears are a miracle. Your life is the gift from God. Every moment is sustained by Him. Every moment is a miracle."

"How does one apply this?"

"You cease taking your life for granted. You stop wasting it, mistreating it, treating it as something less than the miracle it is. You cease to allow your life to be given to sin and what is less than God's will. You treasure the existence with which you were entrusted. You stop throwing away your moments. You treat your life and your time on earth as a treasure. You treat your every moment as if there was a heart beating behind it, striving for that moment to exist. In short... You live a life worthy... of every heartbeat."

The Mission: Live this day in the miracle of your existence. Take account of every heartbeat and make your moments worthy of each one.

Psalm 139:14–17

Forty Million Heartbeats

THE ELOHIM MYSTERY

B'*RESHEET BARA ELOHIM*," said the teacher. "'In the beginning God created...'
The first words of Scripture. The word *Elohim* is God. Do you notice anything about the word?"

"It has the *im* ending that you told me about."

"And what does the *im* signify?"

"That it's a plural word."

"It is...And why is that strange?"

"Because it's the word for *God*?"

"Exactly. It's the word for *God*, and yet it's plural."

"Shouldn't it be translated as 'gods'?"

"It could be translated that way in another context. But the word next to it, *created*, is the Hebrew *bara*. *Bara* is not plural but singular."

"A plural noun and a singular verb. Doesn't that break the rules?"

"It does...and in the very first sentence of Scripture. It's because there's something deeper here...a mystery."

"Which is...?"

"The singularity and plurality of God. And beyond that, in Hebrew, when you
have a plural word that should be singular, it's telling you that there's something
profound about the reality behind the word."

"So it's telling you there's something profound about God."

"What it's saying is that the reality of God is so transcendent, so awesome,
and so beyond, that there's no word in any language that can express it, not even
the word *God*. The word *Elohim* is letting you know that whatever you think
God is, He's more than that. No matter how good you think He is, He's better.
No matter how beautiful, majestic, and amazing, He's more beautiful, He's more
majestic, and He's more amazing. No matter how awesome you think He is, He's
more awesome. And no matter how beyond you think He is, He's even beyond
that. What does *Elohim* reveal? It reveals that no matter how much you think
you know of God, there's always more to know, so much more...and so much
more than so much more. So never stop seeking Him. For His Name is *Elohim*,
and of His awesomeness, there will be no end."

The Mission: Today, seek to know God as one who doesn't know the half of
Him. Seek to know Him more, and afresh, as if for the first time.

Genesis 1:1; 1 Kings 8:26; Job 38

HE WHOSE NAME IS LIKE OIL

THE TEACHER WAS sitting inside one of the school's gardens, surrounded by a variety of plants, bushes, and trees all enclosed by a small stone wall. He had requested I meet him there. As I entered the garden, I noticed a small scroll in his hands that he was studying. As I drew nearer, I could hear him translating its contents.

"'Your name is oil poured forth...'" said the teacher. "It's from the Song of Solomon, the love song of the Scriptures. It's about a bride and a groom. But at its highest level, it's about God and us. God, the Bridegroom and we, the bride. And here, at its very beginning, the bride says of the Bridegroom, 'Your name is oil poured forth...' What do you think that means?"

"The bride is in love. And when you're in love, your beloved's name is beautiful."

"That's right," he said. "And the ancient oils would carry the scent of spices, sweet fragrances. So the bride is saying that her beloved's name is like pouring oil, beautiful, flowing, and filled with sweet fragrance. But if the Song of Solomon, at its highest level, is about God and us, then what does it mean?"

"That the bride should be in love with the Bridegroom. That we should be in love with God, so much so that just hearing His Name would give us joy, that to us His Name would be like pouring oil."

"And could it reveal even more than that? The bride says, 'Your name is oil.' Therefore, the name of the Bridegroom, the Beloved, will be like oil. Is there anyone whose name is oil?"

"I don't know what you mean."

"Is there anyone known in human history whose name is like oil? There is one," he said, "The One who is called 'the Christ.' The word *Christ* comes from *Christos*. *Christos* is a translation of the Hebrew word *Mashiach*, or Messiah. The name *Mashiach* is linked to oil. It means the Anointed One, the One anointed with oil."

"He whose name is like oil...the Bridegroom."

"Therefore, He is the Beloved. And if we're the bride, then we are to be so in love with Him that His Name becomes to us...as pouring oil."

The Mission: Delight today in the name of your Beloved. Let it pour forth from your lips, your mind, and your heart.

Song of Solomon 1:3; John 1:41

Like Pure Oil

THE SECRET PLACE

WE WERE WALKING on the side of a mountain when he found an opening into something of a cave. He went inside and motioned me to follow.

"Do you know," said the teacher, "what the holiest place on earth was?"

"No," I replied.

"It was called the *kodesh hakodashim*. It means the holy of holies."

"I've heard of it."

"It was the holiest place of the holy sanctuary, the innermost chamber of the Temple. It could only be entered on the holiest day of the year, Yom Kippur. It was there that the most important event of the biblical year took place, the act of atonement...the holiest act in the holiest place on the holiest day. And do you know how many people witnessed this most holy of acts?"

"No."

"Only one, the high priest who performed it. No one else saw it. How many people do you think could come into the holy of holies?"

"I don't know."

"One. No more than one. It was made to hold just one person...one person and the glory of God. So no one could see what happened there, even when it was the most important event of the year and that on which everyone's relationship with God depended. It all took place in secret. The most holy event was the most secret of events, the most holy moment, the most secret moment. And the most holy of places is the secret place."

"So what is the holiest place on earth now?"

"The secret place," he replied. "And where is the secret place? It's where you make it. It's where you go to be with Him. It's the place that can contain only one person, just you and the presence of God, and nothing else. So the secret place must be totally separate, totally secret, and totally apart from the rest of your life, from the world, from even the things of God. The most holy place only has room for you and Him. As it is written, 'Oh my dove, in the clefts of the rock, in the secret place of the cliff, let me see your face, let me hear your voice, for your voice is sweet, and your face is lovely.' It's the most important place you can dwell. For it is there that you'll find His presence, hear His voice, and see His glory. For they only reside in the most holy of places...the secret place."

The Mission: Today, go into the secret place, apart from the world and even the *things* of Him, away from everything—but His presence.

Exodus 25:21–22; Song of Solomon 2:14; Matthew 6:6

KING OF THE CURSE

WE SAT DOWN in a desert valley surrounded by mountains. Between us was a little thornbush. The teacher reached for one of its branches, twisted it off, and held it in front of his eyes.

"Thorns," he said. "Did you ever wonder why Messiah wore a crown of thorns?"

"I've always found it a strange thing."

"Think about it, a crown, a symbol of royalty, power, kingship, wealth, and glory...yet made not of gold or jewels, but thorns. Why? When man fell, the consequence of that fall was the curse; the ground would now bear thorns and thistles. The thorns were thus the sign of the curse, the sign of a fallen world, a creation that can no longer bear the fruit it was called to bear, but now brings forth thorns, pain, piercing, blood, tears, and destruction."

He handed me the branch of thorns, then continued, "Now when a crown is placed on a man's head, he becomes king. At that moment, the weight of the kingdom rests upon him. So what is the mystery of the crown of thorns that was placed on the head of Messiah?"

"When the crown was placed on His head, He became..."

"The King of Thorns, the King of the Curse. Thorns speak of pain and tears. So the crown of thorns means He will now bear the pain and tears of man. Thorns speak of piercing. So He will be pierced. And the thorns are linked to the curse and the curse is linked to death. So the crown of thorns ordains that Messiah will die. He will bear the weight of the curse upon His head. He becomes the King of Thorns, the King of the Curse."

"But a crown also signifies authority," I said. "One who reigns."

"Yes, and thus by bearing the weight of the curse, He becomes king over it. He becomes King of the Curse."

"And King of the Cursed."

"King of the Broken, King of the Pierced and Wounded, King of the Rejected, and King of Tears. So all who have fallen can come to Him and find redemption. For the One who wears the crown has authority over these things...to turn sorrow into joy, death into life, and thorns into blossoms. He who wears the crown is Lord of the Fallen, the King of Thorns."

The Mission: Today, bring the thorns, the wounds, the shame, the sorrows of your life to the King of Thorns, and commit them to His authority.

Isaiah 53:3–5; 61:1–3; Matthew 27:29; Galatians 3:13

THE POWER OF EMUNAH

ONE OF THE most important of words," said the teacher, "is *faith*. Without it, you can't be saved. And apart from it, you can't do anything of heavenly worth. You can't overcome and you can't live victoriously. So what is it?" he asked. "What is faith?"

"Faith is to believe," I said.

"To believe what?"

"What you can't see."

"In Hebrew, the word *emun* speaks of that which is sure, solid, and true. Add an *ah* to *emun* and it becomes the word *emunah*. *Emunah* is the Hebrew word for *faith*. What does that tell you?"

"Faith is linked to truth."

"Yes. And so faith is a very solid thing. It isn't a wishful thinking or an unrealistic hoping. Faith is linked to that which is rock solid—the truth. Faith is that by which you join yourself, root yourself, and ground yourself to the truth. And the word *emunah* also means steadfast, established, stable, and steady. The more true faith you have, the more steadfast you become, the more stable, the more steady, and the more established. So faith," said the teacher, "causes you to become strong."

He paused for a moment before continuing. "But there's another Hebrew word that also comes from the same root word as *truth* and *faith*. And you already know it. It's the word *amen*. It even sounds like *emun* and *emunah*. So to say, 'Amen,' is to say, 'It's true, I agree, yes.' So, what is faith? Faith is to give your *amen* to God's *emun*, His truth. Faith is to say amen, yes to God—amen to His reality, amen to His love, and amen to His salvation...not just with your mouth but with your heart, your mind, your emotions, your strength, and your life. 'Truth faith' is to say amen with your entire being. And the greater, the stronger, and the more confident your amen, the greater and more powerful will be your faith. So give the amen of your heart and life, the strongest amen you can give to the word, the truth, and love of God, and your life will become emunah, steadfast, established, and as a solid as a rock."

"Amen!" I added.

The Mission: Take a word from the Word of God today and give it your strongest amen, the total yes of your heart, soul, mind, and will.

Isaiah 7:9; Colossians 2:6–7; Hebrews 11:6

THE IVRIM

I N ANCIENT TIMES," said the teacher, "the people of God were called the Hebrews. Do you know what the word *Hebrew* means?"

"You mean, what does *Hebrew* mean in Hebrew?"

"Yes."

"I have no idea. It's all Greek to me."

"*Hebrew* in Hebrew is the word *Ivri*, the singular of *Ivrim*, the Hebrews. And the word *Ivri* comes from the Hebrew root word *avar*. And *avar* means to cross over."

"What's the connection?"

"The Ivrim, the Hebrews, are those who cross over. In order to leave the land of Egypt, they had to cross over the Red Sea. In order to enter the Promised Land, they had to cross over the Jordan River. They are the cross over people, those who leave one land and enter another, those who end one life and begin a new one. But the Hebrews aren't the only Hebrews."

"And what exactly does *that* mean?"

"The Word of God speaks of another people joined to Israel…the followers of Messiah. They are Hebrews of spirit. So to be saved, you must be a spiritual Hebrew. You must be an Ivri. And in order to be a Hebrew, an Ivri, you have to cross over. You have to pass through a barrier. You have to leave one land and enter another."

"Or one life to enter a new one," I said.

"So who is the Ivri?" he asked.

"The one who has known two lands, two realms, two lives."

"The one," he said, "who is born again. That is the Ivri, the Hebrew, the one who has crossed over, who has left an old life and entered the new, who has passed through the barrier, through Messiah, from darkness to light. As it is written, 'Unless a man is born again, he cannot enter the kingdom of heaven.'"

"So Messiah is the King of the Ivrim, King of the Hebrews."

"He is," said the teacher. "But why?"

"He's the One who broke the ultimate barrier and crossed over from death to life. So He's the ultimate Ivri, the King of the Hebrews."

"Yes, The Ivri of Ivrim, the Hebrew of Hebrews, in whom is the power to cross over any barrier, to leave any darkness, and to enter every promised land."

The Mission: What barriers are hindering you and the will of God in your life? Identify them. Then, by the power of Messiah, begin crossing your Jordan. You are an Ivri. You were born again to cross over.

Joshua 3:14–17; John 3:3; 2 Corinthians 5:17

The Hebrew Mystery

THE MASADA MYSTERY

W E WERE STANDING in the middle of a large valley, harsh and forbidding.

"The prophet Ezekiel was taken in a vision to a valley filled with dry bones, which, by the hand of God, would rise and come to life and become a massive army. It was a prophecy that the nation of Israel, though utterly destroyed, would one day by God's hand be resurrected from the grave."

The teacher began to walk through the valley, unfolding the mystery as he went.

"In the first century the Romans destroyed the nation of Israel. The nation's last stand took place on a desert mountain fortress called Masada. It was there that her last soldiers would meet their end. So Masada became the grave of ancient Israel. But then, after two thousand years, the nation of Israel was resurrected by the hand of God as foretold in the vision of dry bones. The people were resurrected, the cities were resurrected, and the Israeli soldier was resurrected. And then the resurrected nation decided to return to its ancient grave."

"To Masada? Why?"

"To excavate it, to dig it up. The man in charge of the excavation was one of the nation's most famous soldiers and archaeologists. And Israeli soldiers helped in the excavation. So now on the grave of Israel's ancient soldiers walked her resurrected soldiers to see what lay hidden in its ruins."

"And what was hidden in the ruins?"

"A prophetic mystery...a Scripture. It had been buried and hidden there for almost two thousand years."

"And what did it say?"

"It was from the Book of Ezekiel, the section that contained the prophecy of the Valley of Dry Bones: 'Thus says the Lord God: "Behold, O My people, I will open your graves and cause you to come up from your graves, and bring you into the land of Israel."' So the prophecy was hidden right there in Israel's ancient grave, waiting for ages for the day that it would be uncovered, the day when its words would be fulfilled and the nation resurrected from its grave. You see, God is real. And His will is to restore the broken, bring hope from hopelessness, and life from death. Don't ever give up. For with God, nothing is impossible...even restoration of a nation from a valley of dry bones."

The Mission: Bring your most hopeless situations and issues to God. Believe God for the impossible. Live and move in the power of the impossible.

Ezekiel 37:12–14; Luke 1:37

THE DOUBLE

IN ANCIENT TIMES," said the teacher, "on the holiest day of the year, Yom Kippur, the Day of Atonement, a unique ceremony took place. The high priest would stand before the people with two goats at his side. Each goat had to be identical in appearance to the other. The high priest would then reach into an urn and pull out two lots, one in each hand. Each lot had a different Hebrew word inscribed on it. He then placed one lot on the head of the goat to his right, and another on the head of the goat to his left. One stone identified the goat that would die as the sacrifice for the sins of the people. The other identified the goat that would be let go. So before there could be a sacrifice, there had to be the presentation of the two goats before the people and the apportioning of the two destinies. What about Messiah? Before His sacrifice, what took place? He was presented before the people, for the choosing, for the apportioning of destinies."

"And there had to be two presented," I said. "So there had to be two men presented before the people."

"Exactly. And only one could become the sacrifice. So Messiah had to be one of two lives presented before the people in order to be chosen as the sacrifice. And according to the ordinance of Yom Kippur, the other life had to be let go. So what happened to the other life that was presented that day?"

"He was let go."

"And what was his name?"

"Barabbas."

"According to the requirements of the ancient ceremony, the two goats or lives had to be identical. Messiah was the Son of God, the Son of the Father. Do you know what the name Barabbas means?"

"No."

"*Barabbas* comes from two Hebrew words, *bar*, which means son, and *abba*, which means father. *Barabbas* means the Son of the Father...Two lives...Each one bears the name *the Son of the Father*. So the sacrifice and the one set free because of the sacrifice must in some way be identical. So if God were to die in your place..."

"He would have to become like me."

"He would have to become like you, of flesh and blood, in the likeness of sin. He would become...your identical."

The Mission: Live today as one sentenced to judgment, but who has instead been set free and given a second chance of life, because of the love and sacrifice of Him.

Leviticus 16:7–10; Matthew 27:15–24

Azazel

THE DIVINE NONPOSSESSIVE

WHAT DO YOU have in this world?" asked the teacher. "What do you possess?"
"A lot of things," I said. "At this point, most of them are in storage."

"But even when you take them out of storage, you won't have them."

"What do you mean?"

"According to the Scriptures it's impossible to have."

"But there are plenty of Scriptures that talk about having things."

"Not really."

"But you can find the words *have, mine, my, his,* and *theirs* throughout the Bible."

"Those are all translations. And to a degree, they're accurate. But there's more to it. In the Hebrew of Scripture, there's no true verb for 'to have.' There's no real or exact way of saying 'I have.' So in Hebrew you can't possess anything in this world."

"But what about all the things we *do* have?"

"As in the Hebrew, it only seems to be. It's an illusion. If it was really yours, you could keep it. But you can't keep anything of this world. Everything you have is temporary. In the end, you have to let everything go. What you think you have is only entrusted...borrowed. And when you think you have what you don't have, you live in conflict with the truth. And you'll end up fighting to keep what you don't have. It is only when you let go that you can live in the truth. So in order to live in the truth, you have to live in the Hebrew."

"To have 'no have'?"

"Yes, to live with 'no have.' And when you don't have, then you can't have any problems. Or worries. They may be out there, but you don't own them. They're not yours. You can't even be burdened down by the weight of your own life...because you don't have your life...or its burdens."

"But not everything is temporary. So there must be something we can have."

"Yes," said the teacher, "There is one thing you can have."

"What?"

"God...and the blessings of God. That is the only true possession. And it's only when you let go of all that you don't have, that you can be free to have Him."

The Mission: Today, learn the secret of living with "no have." Let go of your possessions, your problems, your burdens, your life—and possess God.

Psalm 16:5; 2 Corinthians 6:10; 1 Timothy 6:6–11

THE PORTAL

W E WALKED THROUGH a dark corridor inside the school's main building. At the end of the corridor was a large wooden door. It had to be at least twice our height, though it was hard to see in the dark. As he pushed it open, the darkness in the hall was broken by the intense light of the desert sun. He stood by the doorway and, gazing into the outer expanse, began to share.

"The portal," said the teacher. "It allows one to enter another realm."

"Sounds mystical," I replied.

"On the night of Passover the Hebrews were told to put the blood of the Passover lamb on the beams of their doorways. They would then enter in through the blood-stained doorway and stay inside their houses. And when they once more passed through that doorway, it would be for the last time. It would be to leave the land of bondage, to leave their old lives, and to enter a new life, a new identity, a new realm, and ultimately a new land. The blood of the lamb transformed the doorways into a portal by which they could leave an old world and enter the new. Centuries later would come another Passover, another Lamb, and another portal."

"The Passover of Messiah."

"And what was the key event of that day?"

"His death."

"Through the cross. And what is a cross made of?"

"Beams of wood."

"Beams of wood marked by the blood of the lamb. And so again on the day of Passover we have beams marked by the blood, and of a sacrificial lamb. So what is the cross? It's not just an execution stake. It's a doorway. It's the set of beams that forms the doorway, the doorway marked by the blood of the Passover Lamb. So the only way it can be truly known is to be entered in."

"But how do you enter in?" I asked. "There's no opening."

"It's not a doorway to another place in this world. It's a doorway to a different realm. It's a portal to a new reality, a new existence. It's the doorway that allows you to leave your old life and enter a new realm and a new life. And the only way to know a doorway is to go through it. And only those who do will know what it is to leave the realm of Egypt and enter the realm of the Promised Land . . . by way of the portal."

The Mission: Today, use the door of God to leave what you could never leave and go where you could never go. Enter through the portal.

Exodus 12:21–27; John 10:9; Hebrews 10:19–20

Heaven's Portal

THE TRIUNITY OF LOVE

WHAT IS THE number of love?" asked the teacher.

"I don't understand."

"How many do you need in order to have love?"

"More than one," I said.

"Love must have a source," he said, "the one from whom it comes, the one who loves. So there has to be at least one."

"But one isn't enough," I said. "You can't have love if there's nothing or no one to love. If you love nothing, then you don't love."

"That's correct," he said. "So what else is needed for love to exist?"

"An object. Loves needs an object. The one loved, the object of love."

"So you have two, the source of love and the object of love. But then you have the love itself, the love between the two, and the love that joins the two together. So if we were to translate love into a sentence, what would we need?"

"A subject," I said.

"The subject is the 'I,'" he replied. "And what else?"

"An object," I said.

"The object is the 'You,'" he answered. "And what else?"

"A verb."

"Love," he said. "Put it together and what does it become?"

"It becomes, 'I love you.'"

"The simplest expression of love . . . and in how many words?"

"Three."

"And yet at the same time, love is one. Love is one and love is three . . . one and three at the same time. Love is triune. In the Scriptures it is written that 'God is love.' If God is love, then God is triune as well, one and three at the same time. Who is the source of love, the 'I'? The Father, the source of all love. Who is the object of His love, the 'You'? The Son, the Messiah, who is called in Scripture, 'the Beloved.' And the love that emanates from the Father to the Son? The Spirit."

"The Lover, the Beloved, and the Love . . . the triunity of love . . . the triunity of God."

"Yes," said the teacher, "as incomprehensible and yet as simple as 'I love you.'"

The Mission: Partake of the triunity of love. As God has made you the object of His love, today, make those who don't deserve it become the object of yours.

Isaiah 48:16–17; Matthew 28:19–20; 1 John 4:16

Shalosh

THE DAY OF THE RESHEET

HE TOOK ME into one of the chambers inside the school's main building. I would learn later that it was called the Chamber of Scrolls. He led me over to what looked like an ornate upright wooden chest called the ark. Inside the ark was long scroll, which he removed, unrolled on a large wooden table, and from which he began to read: "'When you enter the land...and reap its harvest, you will bring in the sheaf of the firstfruits of your harvest to the priest. And he will wave the sheaf before the Lord...on the day after the Sabbath.' This is the Day of the Resheet. The *resheet* is the firstfruits, the beginning of the harvest, the first blossoming, the first grain, of a new harvest. The firstfruits would represent all that would be reaped or gathered in the days that followed, the rest of the harvest. So on the Day of the Resheet, the first sheaf of the spring harvest would be lifted up to God and dedicated to Him. And since it represented all the sheaves that would follow, by its consecration the entire harvest was consecrated. It would all take place 'on the day after the Sabbath' of Passover. It was the day of new life, the day that sealed the ending of winter and the beginning of spring-time...and a day that contains a mystery of cosmic proportions."

"How so?"

"The world is fallen. The curse of winter and the shadow of death hang over it. But God's will is to redeem it. And the promise of redemption is that one day the curse of death and the barrenness of winter will be broken. And the firstfruits break the winter...and bring new life."

He looked up at me. "When did Messiah die?" he asked.

"On Passover," I replied.

"And then He was in the tomb?"

"On the Sabbath."

"The Sabbath of Passover," said the teacher. "So then when did He rise?"

"On the day after the Sabbath of Passover!" I said. "On the Day of the Resheet...as the firstfruits! When the firstfruits are lifted up to the Lord."

"The day of the resurrection is the Day of the Resheet. It had to happen on the day when the firstfruits are raised up from the earth...because He is the Resheet, the Firstfruits, that ends the winter of our lives, that begins spring, and gives us new life. And if the firstfruits stand for all, and if He has overcome death and this world..."

"Then so can I..."

The Mission: If the Resheet has overcome, so then can you. Today, in full confidence of the power given you on the Day of the Resheet, overcome!

Leviticus 23:9–11; 1 Corinthians 15:20–23

The Day of New Beginnings

THE HOUSE OF BREAD

I T WAS A mystery that had the added benefit of a midday snack. We were sitting on the desert sand and the teacher offered me some bread, which I accepted.

"*Lechem,*" he said. "It's Hebrew for *bread*. The word is used in Jewish prayers to represent food and sustenance. Why do you think bread is so important?"

"Because it's 'the staff of life.' It's a basic necessity. It sustains us. It keeps us alive. It's what we need."

"That's correct," he said. "In Hebrew, the word for *place* or *house* is *beit*. When you put the *beit* together with *lechem*, you get *beit lechem*, which would mean..."

"The place of bread or the house of bread."

"And what would you expect to find in the house of bread?"

"Bread...of course."

"You'd expect to find bread, the staff of life in the house of bread. You'd expect to find that which sustains you, what you need above all things."

"I don't understand."

"Only because you don't recognize it yet."

"Recognize what?"

"*Beit lechem,* the house of bread. You already know it. It's Bethlehem."

"Bethlehem!" I said. "The house of bread! And so it's there that we find the bread, that which we most need, that which sustains us, our most basic necessity, the staff of life...in Bethlehem!"

"Yes," said the teacher, "so if what we needed most was money, if money was the bread of our lives, then what we'd find in Bethlehem, the house of bread, would be money. If what we most needed was success, then we'd find success there. Or if it was acceptance or pleasures or substances or careers or possessions or any other thing we desired. If any of these were what we needed most, then that's what we would have found in Bethlehem. But we didn't find any of those things there. What is it that we find in Bethlehem?"

"Him."

"Yes, Him. We find God come down into our lives. So what does that reveal?"

"That more than anything else...we need Him."

"Yes. What we find in the house of bread...is the Bread of Life."

The Mission: Stop filling your needs and desires with that which is not bread. Fill your heart with the love, the presence, and the fullness of your true bread—Him.

Micah 5:2; John 6:32–35

THE ROADS OF ZION

WE WALKED A wilderness path that was at times rocky and winding, and at a few points, treacherous. At the other times it became wider, more even, and easier, as when it traversed valleys and plains. At one point in the journey, the teacher asked me, "How would you name this road?"

"The Rocky Road," I replied.

Then, as the terrain changed, he asked again, "And now what would you call *this* road?"

"The Sandy Road," I replied.

This went on throughout the journey every time there was a dramatic change in scenery. There was no shortage of names I gave it: "the Winding Road," "the Open Road," "the Valley Road," "the Treacherous Road," "the Dark Road," and on and on—until we reached our destination.

"Every time I asked you what you would call the road," said the teacher, "you came up with a name based on what the road looked or how it felt. And many roads are so named. But in the Holy Land, it's different. The most famous roads in Zion are not named for what they look like or feel like, nor on their condition. Instead, they have names like the Road to Bethlehem, the Damascus Road, Emmaus Road, and the Jericho Road."

"So the most famous roads of Zion are named for places."

"Not just places, but their destinations. Their names come not from what they look like but where they take you. This is the secret of the roads of Zion," said the teacher. "So too in the journey of your life, you will find the road to be at times rocky, at times smooth, harder, easier, dangerous, pleasant, unbearable, joyful. But you must never make the mistake of judging your road or your life by what it looks like or feels like. A pleasant road may lead to a cliff. And a hard and rocky road may lead to the Holy City. A pleasant way may lead to hell, and a hard way may lead to blessing and eternal life. Always look to the end of your course, to where it's taking you. And if you're on the right road, don't get discouraged by the terrain. Never give up. Keep pressing forward to your destination. Because it is the end that matters most. And your road, and the journey of your life, will not be known by its terrain, but by the place to which it brought you."

The Mission: Today, take your eyes off your circumstances, and focus only on your destination. Press on to the good, the highest, and the heavenly.

Matthew 7:13–14; Philippians 3:12–14

The Roads of Zion Mystery

THE KHATAN

WE WERE BACK again on the same hill overlooking the city where we had previously seen a bride and her maidens. Again, there was a wedding where the first had taken place. Again, I could see the bride and her maidens.

"Where there is a bride," said the teacher, "there must be a bridegroom. Look," he said, pointing slightly to the left of the bridal party. "What do you see?"

"The bridegroom and his men."

"In the mystery of the bride and groom, who is the Bridegroom?"

"God."

"In the Scriptures, in Hebrew, He is called the *Khatan*."

"Khatan," I repeated.

"*Khatan* means the bridegroom, but it goes deeper than that. It can be translated as he who joins himself."

"Then another name for God," I said, "is He Who Joins Himself."

"Yes. And if you can grasp what this means, it can change your life. Most see God as distant, unapproachable, One we must convince to forgive us. Most religions are based on that...on all we have to do to get God to accept us. But the truth is radically different. God is the Khatan. What it means is this: It is God who wills to join Himself to you. It means it is His nature, His heart, to join His life to yours. It means that you don't have to convince Him to love you. He already does. The Khatan *is* love, and the One who *becomes one with you.* And it not you who must approach Him...but it is He who approaches you. And in the mystery of the Khatan is the mystery of everything...the mystery of salvation. For God is the Khatan. And so He has joined Himself to us. He has joined all that is Him to all that is you. So there's no part of you that He will not join Himself to...no matter how dark it is, no matter how sinful, no matter how ungodly. Because He is the Khatan, He has even joined Himself to your sins. And so what is the death of Messiah on the cross? It is the Khatan, He who joins Himself, joining Himself to everything you are, even and especially to the most ungodly parts of your life. And because of this miracle, there is now nothing that can separate you anymore from His love. For He is the Khatan, the One who has joined Himself...completely, totally, and forever...to you."

The Mission: Bring the most ungodly, dark, and untouched part of your life to the Khatan. Let Him touch it, and every part of your life.

Song of Solomon 5:10–6:2; Isaiah 54:5; 62:5; John 3:29

The Mystery of the Khatan

THE MYSTERY OF THE ZEROAH

WE WERE SITTING around the campfire by night, the teacher and I, and a number of the other students.

"One of the most mysterious objects on the Passover table is called the *Zeroah*."

"What is a Zeroah?" asked one of the students.

"It is written in the Hebrew Scriptures that the Lord made the heavens and the earth by the Zeroah. So it was by the Zeroah that everything you see, the universe itself, came into existence. When God brought the Hebrews out of Egypt on Passover, with miracles and wonders, it is written that He did so by the Zeroah. And concerning salvation, it is written that the Lord will make known His Zeroah and all the earth will see the salvation of God."

"But what is the Zeroah?" I asked.

"The fifty-third chapter of Isaiah contains a prophecy of One who will be wounded and crushed for our sins, who will die for our judgment, and who, by His death, will bring us healing, life, and redemption. The ancient rabbis identified this One as the Messiah. But the opening verse of that chapter, Isaiah 53, is this: 'Who has believed our report? And to whom has the Zeroah of the Lord been revealed?'"

"So then Isaiah 53 itself is the revealing of the Zeroah?" I asked.

"Yes," said the teacher. "So the Zeroah is the One who dies for our sins."

"You said that the Zeroah was also an object on the Passover table. What object?" I asked.

"The Zeroah is the bone of a lamb. It has to do with the death of a lamb."

"The death of the lamb would be the death of Messiah," said another student, "and that would connect it back to Isaiah 53."

"But what was the Zeroah before that," I asked, "if it was there at the creation?"

"The Zeroah is the power of God," he said, "that which accomplishes the will of God, the arm of the Almighty."

"The arm of the Almighty," I said, "weak, broken, and dying on a cross..."

"Yes, the love of God," said the teacher. "There is no greater power than that."

The Mission: Today, take part in the power of the Zeroah. Let go to apprehend, surrender to overcome, and die to yourself that you might find life.

Deuteronomy 5:15; Isaiah 52:10; 53:1–5; 59:16

The Mystery of the Zeroah

THE DOOR OF EVIL

HOW DO YOU deal with temptation?" he asked.

"You resist it."

"Yes," he said. "But how?"

I didn't answer. I didn't know what he was looking for.

"The Book of Proverbs reveals how to deal with the temptation of sexual sin, the seduction of an adulteress. It is written: 'Keep your way far from her. And do not come near to the door of her house.' What does that reveal?"

"Stay away from temptation."

"The best way to deal with temptation is to *not deal with it*."

"I don't understand."

"If you keep yourself away from the temptation, there's less chance of being tempted. But the Scripture goes farther than that. Listen again. It says, 'Keep your way far from her. And do not come near to the door of her house.' This is an even greater key. What it reveals is this: It's not enough to stay away from temptation—you must make it your aim to stay away from the *door of the temptation*. Think about it; which is more alluring, a person trying to seduce you or a door?"

"The person, of course."

"Which is more tempting, a substance that would addict you or a door?"

"The substance."

"And which is more likely to harm you or make you fear, a dangerous situation or a door?"

"The dangerous situation, of course."

"Exactly. So instead of dealing with the person, or the substance, or the situation of danger, deal with the door. Deal with the door and you'll avoid the temptation."

"And the door is what exactly?"

"The door is not the temptation, nor the sin. It's that which would lead you to the temptation and the sin. That's the key. Make it your aim not only to avoid the temptation. Locate the door to the temptation and then stay as far away from it as possible. For it is the wise who, instead of dealing with temptation and sin, deal with doors."

The Mission: Today, make it your aim not just to avoid temptation, but to avoid even the door that leads to it. Focus on the door, and stay far from it.

Proverbs 5:3–8; 1 Corinthians 10:13

Hedges

THE CELESTIAL SEED

HE WAS HOLDING in one hand a cloth bag and in the other a small shovel. He led me to a spot of soil that had been marked out for planting. He reached into the bag and placed in my hand a sample of its contents.

"Seeds," he said. "Potential miracles. Each one is filled with the potential for life, growth, blossoming, and fruitfulness. It's all there in the seed—the plan, everything it will become, the plant, the flower, the tree. It's all there inside the shell. Now what happens if the seed stays in the bag?"

"Nothing. Nothing happens."

"Exactly. All its potential stays unrealized. But if we take the seed and plant it in the soil, everything changes. The seed becomes one with the earth. The shell opens up and the life inside the seed joins itself to the soil around it. It puts out roots and draws in life from the earth. The plan is activated, the promise unlocked, and the potential becomes reality."

"So you're going to plant the seeds?"

"Yes," he said, "but that's not why I brought you here." Reaching into his pocket, he took out a book and handed it to me. It was a Bible.

"What's inside this?" he asked.

"The Word," I answered.

"Seeds," he replied. "The Word of God itself refers to the Word of God as a seed. The Bible is the container of many seeds. And every seed, every word is a potential miracle. And as is a seed, so is the Word of God. Each Word has the potential to produce life, growth, blossoming, fruitfulness, and a miracle. It's all there inside the seed, inside the Word."

"But if the seed stays in the bag..."

"If the Word stays on the pages and is never sown to life, then its life stays unlocked, unrealized. So the Word must be sown."

"Sown to what soil?" I asked.

"Sown to the soil of life," he replied. "To the lives of others. And to the soil of your life. The seed must become one with the soil. The Word must become one with your life. So you need to sow the Word into every situation of your life and let it become one with that soil—the soil of your heart, your thoughts, your emotions, your life. For when the Word becomes one with your life, then its shell will break open, its plan will be activated, its promise unlocked, its life released, and its miracle begun."

The Mission: Today, take a seed from the Word of God and plant it in the soil of your heart. Let its promise be unlocked and bear its fruit in your life.

Matthew 13:3–23; 1 Peter 1:23

Secrets of the Sowers

THE MYSTERY OF THE SECRET ANGELS

HE LED ME up a high desert mountain and into a cave near its summit. Inside the cave, not far from its entrance, was an engraving of a human-like figure with outstretched wings.

"What is it?" I asked.

"An angel," said the teacher.

"What do you know of angels?"

"They're heavenly creatures...sent by God...with wings."

"They don't all have wings," he said. "There are many different kinds of angels...cherubim, seraphim, warring angels, ministering angels, and then...there are the other angels."

"The other angels?"

"The earth angels," he said, "those who walk the earth in flesh and blood, His earthbound division...different from the others but angels nonetheless."

"I thought an angel was a being *not* of flesh and blood."

"The Scriptures say differently. The word for *angel* in the Hebrew Scriptures is *malakh*. And in the New Testament Scriptures, the word is the Greek *angelos*. It is written, 'Then spoke Haggai, the Lord's malakh.' And of the man known as John the Baptizer, the Messiah said, 'This is he of whom it is written, "Behold I will send My angelos."' Haggai and John were both of flesh and blood, and yet they are both called angels—angels of God. What is an angel? It is a being sent by God, a messenger, an emissary on a divine assignment, bringing God's message, especially to those who dwell on earth."

"So who are the earth angels?"

"Those who are born again," he said, "born from above, born from heaven, those who bear the message of heaven to those who dwell on earth."

"And the message?"

"The good news. In Greek it is called the *euangel*, in English, the *evangel*, as in evangelism. Within each of these words is another word. Do so you see?"

"The word *angel*."

"Exactly. It is no accident. For if you will bear the message of heaven to those of earth, your life will become angelic. So take up your angelic assignment and bring good tidings, the divine message, to those of earth. For you are His earth angel."

The Mission: Today, start fulfilling your angelic mission. Bear the heavenly message to those on earth. Live this day as His earth angel.

Haggai 1:13; Malachi 3:1; Mark 16:15; Luke 7:24–27

THE NAZARENE MYSTERY

THE TEACHER HAD given me an assignment based on this Scripture: "And He came and dwelt in a city called Nazareth, that what was spoken by the prophets, 'He shall be called a Nazarene,' might be fulfilled."

"It's from the Book of Matthew," he said. "Your assignment is to search the Scriptures and find the prophecy where it is said that Messiah would be a Nazarene."

Several weeks passed before he brought it up again. But then the day came. "Have you found the prophecy of the Nazarene?" he asked.

"No," I replied. "There's no prophecy calling Messiah a Nazarene."

"Did you notice," he said, "that it doesn't say 'what was spoken by the *prophet*' but 'what was spoken by the *prophets*'? So the answer lies not with one prophet or prophecy but in the collective voice of the prophets. And what do the prophets say of Messiah? They speak of Messiah as the Branch. Why the Branch? For one, He would appear on earth in littleness, in weakness, growing up as a shoot or a sprout. He would be born among us on the genealogy, the tree of humanity. His presence on earth would then grow, becoming greater and greater and bear its fruit to the world. In Hebrew, one of the words for branch is *netzer*. It's the word used by Isaiah in his prophecy of Messiah as the branch that would come forth from the line of David. If you add an ending, the word becomes *netzeret*. *Netzeret* is the Hebrew name for the place you know as Nazareth."

"So *Nazarene* speaks of Messiah the Branch. And *Nazareth* would mean...?"

"*Nazareth* would mean the place of the branch...the place of the branching forth."

"The perfect name," I said, "for the place where Messiah would grow up...as a branch...and from where He would branch out."

"It was considered a nothing place, the most obscure and unlikely of places."

"Then why did God choose it?"

"For that very reason. God loves to choose the unlikely and because it's not about Nazareth—it's about that which comes through Nazareth. In the same way, it's not about who we are. Nor does it matter how likely or unlikely, how imperfect or sinful our life has been...only that we receive. For whoever receives Him, through that life, the life of God will come. And from that life He will branch out to the world. For we are each called to be His Nazareth."

The Mission: Let Messiah's life come through your life. Let His love come through your love and your life become His branching—His Nazareth.

Zechariah 3:8; Isaiah 11:1–2; Matthew 2:23; John 15:1–5

Messiah the Branch

HOW TO MULTIPLY BREAD

IT WAS MIDDAY, just about lunch time. Most of the students had gathered in the common hall for lunch. The teacher and I were sitting outside.

"Messiah was ministering to a multitude of thousands," he said, "when a crisis arose. The people were hungry and had virtually no food, only two fish and five loaves of bread. 'He took the five loaves and the two fish, and looking up to heaven, He gave thanks, broke them and gave them to the disciples to give to the multitudes. And they all ate and were filled, and the disciples collected twelve basketfuls of leftover pieces.' It is called the miracle of multiplication. Starting with just two fish and five loaves of bread they fed thousands of people. But how did He perform that miracle?"

"It doesn't say."

"But it does," he said. "Listen again: 'and looking up to heaven, He gave thanks, broke them and gave them to the disciples...'"

"He gave thanks?"

"Yes. He looked to heaven and gave thanks. He gave thanks and the miracle happened. That's the secret. That's the key to miracles."

"Giving thanks?"

"Giving thanks is crucial to a life of fullness and blessing. On top of that, it also gives you the power to perform the miracle of multiplication."

"How?"

"By doing what He did. You don't look at how little you have or how big your problem is or how impossible the situation is. You don't panic, you don't complain, and you don't get discouraged over not having enough. You take the little you have, whatever good there is, no matter how small or inadequate it is, and you do what Messiah did. You lift it up to the Lord and you give thanks for it. And the blessings you have will multiply, if not in the world, then in your heart. The more you give thanks, the less you will hunger, and the more full and blessed you will be."

"So in order to perform miracles, I need to..."

"Give thanks. Whatever you have, no matter how much or how little. Give thanks even for what is not enough, and it will multiply to become what is enough...and what is more than enough...Practice this key. Then get started multiplying the bread."

The Mission: Stop seeking more and stop living in the realm of "not enough." Today, practice giving thanks for everything. Perform the act of multiplication.

Matthew 14:14–21; 1 Thessalonians 5:18

THE ASHAM

HE LED ME into the Chamber of Scrolls but now behind the wooden ark to the shelves where many more scrolls were kept. He removed one of them from its shelf and placed it on the table.

"This," said the teacher, "is the scroll of Isaiah. And this," he said, pausing until he had unrolled the particular spot, "is the fifty-third chapter, the prophecy of the dying Messiah."

He passed his finger over the Hebrew text and began reading it out loud. "'Yet it was the Lord's will to crush Him and to afflict Him, if He would make His life an offering for sin...' In ancient times," he said, "one of the sacrifices offered in the Temple was called the *Asham*. The Asham was the guilt offering. It removed the guilt of the one who offered it up."

"So *Asham* means the guilt offering?"

"Yes, but it has another meaning as well. *Asham* also means the guilt."

"The guilt offering *and* the guilt? It seems contradictory."

"Yes, but it goes together. The guilt offering could only take away the guilt of the one offering it by first *becoming the guilt*."

"And what you read from the scroll, how does that relate?" I asked.

"Isaiah's prophecy describes the Messiah as wounded, pierced, and crushed for our sins. But in Hebrew it goes further. It says that His life would become an Asham. It's an amazing thing because *Asham* is the same word used in the Book of Leviticus for the animal sacrifices offered up by the priests to redeem the guilty. But here it's used to speak not of a sacrificial animal but of a human life—Messiah. Messiah is the Asham. The Asham is Messiah."

"And that means that He not only dies to take away our guilt, but He becomes the guilt itself."

"Yes," said the teacher. "So when you see Him on the cross, you're seeing the Asham, the sacrifice, but also the guilt itself."

"The guilt being nailed to the cross."

"Yes," he said. "What you're seeing is *your* guilt nailed to the cross. And if Messiah is the Asham and the Asham is the guilt, then if the Asham dies, so too has died all your guilt, all your shame, and all your regrets. They've all died and are gone...completely and forever...It is finished."

The Mission: Take all the regrets, shame, and guilt you've ever carried in your life. Give them to Him who is your Asham, and let them go forever.

Isaiah 53:7–11; 2 Corinthians 5:21

The Asham

THE MYSTERY OF THE RAINS

IT DIDN'T HAPPEN often, but when it did, it was dramatic. It was a desert rain. The teacher came to my chamber just as it began. Together, we watched the downpour through my window.

"The rain brings life," he said. "Without it, life would cease. This is particularly true for the land of Israel, which was especially dependent on the outpourings of heaven. But there was another kind of outpouring in Israel."

"What do you mean?" I asked.

"The Scriptures speak of an outpouring, not of water, but of the Spirit, the rain of the Spirit."

"What's the connection between the two, the Spirit and the rain?"

"The rain pours down from the sky and gives life to the land. The Spirit pours down from heaven and gives life to those who receive it. The outpouring of rain causes barren land to revive and become fruitful. The outpouring of the Spirit causes barren lives to revive and become fruitful."

"And this outpouring...happened..."

"On the Day of Pentecost. The Spirit of God was poured out on Jerusalem, on the disciples. It is the outpouring that causes barren lives to bear fruit. It is the outpouring that produced the Book of Acts and changed the history of the world."

"Has there ever been another outpouring like it?"

"Not quite like it," he said. "But there's a mystery. You see, there wasn't just one rain in Israel. There were two distinct rains, each with its own name. One was called the *moreh*, the former rain, and the other was called the *malkosh,* the latter rain. One came in autumn, and the other in spring...two rains...two outpourings."

"So if there are two outpourings of rain in the land of Israel...then would it not also follow that there would be two such outpourings of the Holy Spirit in the age?"

"It *would* follow," he said. "In the Book of Joel, God promises to send both the former rains and the latter rains, and to pour out His Spirit in the last days. So then there must again be another outpouring. And as the former rains came upon the people of Israel, on Jewish believers and the world, so too will the latter rains. And as it was in the former outpouring, so in the latter, that which was barren will bear its fruit, and that which was dead will come alive again."

The Mission: Seek the outpouring of His Spirit on your life to touch your dry ground and make it fruitful. Prepare and receive your latter rains.

Isaiah 44:3–4; Joel 2:23–29; Acts 2:17–18

THE SWORD OF AMALEK

"THE LORD WILL have war with Amalek...from generation to generation.' Do you know who Amalek is?" asked the teacher.

"Someone at war with God," I replied.

"And at war with God's nation, Israel," he said. "When the Israelites came out of Egypt, they were attacked by the Amalekites, the people of Amalek. The Amalekites were the first to wage war against the children of Israel. They were defeated. But the war would go on. Centuries later there arose a king named Agag, an evil man, whose sword had ended countless lives. God decreed his end, a judgment that would be carried out by the prophet Samuel. Agag was an Amalekite, a descendant of Amalek. It was yet another battle in the war, but not the last. Centuries later, the Jewish people would be scattered throughout the Persian Empire. A Persian official named Haman rose to power...another man of evil. Haman devised a plot to destroy the Jewish people throughout the empire, every man, woman, and child. But he didn't succeed. God used the Jewish queen, Esther, and her relative, Mordecai, to thwart Haman's plan. In the end, Haman was destroyed, and the Jewish people were saved."

"And how does this..."

"In the Book of Esther, Haman is called the Agagite. Thus, the Scriptures connect Haman to Agag. And King Agag was of Amalek. Thus Haman was also of Amalek. So the ancient war continued...in another setting, another language, and another land...and yet the same war. It was Amalek, in Haman, raising again his sword against God and His people, and it was the Lord's hand again warring against Amalek and protecting His people. What does this reveal? God's Word is true. And the darkness will always war against the light. And the light must always war against the darkness. In the end, there is no neutrality. You either let the darkness overcome you, or you overcome the darkness. There is no middle ground. Either the darkness will destroy the light, or the light will destroy the darkness."

"Which will it be...in the end?"

"Until the end, they war. But know and always be assured, that in the end, only one can prevail...the light."

The Mission: Whatever darkness, compromise, or ungodly thing still exists in your life, no matter how small, today, root it out. There is no middle ground.

Exodus 17:8–16; 1 Samuel 15:8–33; Esther 3:1; 2 Corinthians 2:14

The Sword of Amalek

HEAVEN'S MILK

WHEN WE CAME into this world," he said, "we entered it with a longing. We longed for milk. We had no idea what milk was. We had never tasted it. We had never seen it. Nobody ever told us that it existed. And yet the longing for milk was there deep inside our being before we had any assurance that it existed." He paused. "And it turned out that it *did* exist. It turned out that what we longed for, what we knew only from the hunger deep inside our being…was real. There was a mother and a mother's breast to answer our longings. Do you know where the word *mother* comes from?"

"I never thought of it."

"The word was created by babies," he said. "All across the world, in almost every language on earth, you can hear in the word for mother, the cry of a baby: *mamma, mom, amma, ema, mai, mata,* and *ma*. It comes from those first longings, the longing for milk. And all these words bear witness that to our longings there existed an answer."

"But this is not about babies…"

"No. Our longing for milk passes away, but we find another longing within our hearts…another emptiness…another hunger…but deeper…a longing for that which the world never answers. We long for the perfect, for a perfect love, a perfect happiness, a perfect contentment, and a perfect peace. We long for that which doesn't fail, that which never disappoints us, or grows old, or passes away. We long for the eternal and the perfect. But the world can never answer those longings…and still they stay with us all the days of our lives. We long for it though we've never tasted it. And our very longings bear witness that what we had never seen or tasted was real."

"We long for the perfect because the perfect exists…as we once longed for milk?"

"Yes, and we long for a perfect love because there is a Perfect Love. We long for the Eternal because the Eternal exists and the Eternal put that longing into our hearts so we would seek Him…and find Him."

"So in the same way that our longing for milk once bore witness that although we had never yet seen it, milk existed, now the longing that is now in our hearts for the perfect, for the Eternal, for heaven bears witness that, although we have not yet seen it, heaven exists. Heaven is real."

"Yes," he said, "our deepest longings are the witness of the milk of heaven."

The Mission: What are the deepest needs and longings of your heart? Join them to Him. Bring them to Him, and receive from Him their filling.

Ecclesiastes 3:11; Romans 8:22–23; Philippians 4:6–9

Heaven's Womb

THE SIXTH DAY

THE OTHER STUDENTS had gone inside. It was just the teacher and I sitting out-side in one of the gardens that belonged to the school. The sun was just begin-ning to set.

"When was the last day of Messiah's life?" he asked. "When did it begin?"

"Friday," I replied. "Friday morning."

"No," he said. "You forget. When does the Hebrew day begin?"

"The Hebrew day always begins at sundown, the night before."

"So when did His last day begin?"

"At sundown, Thursday night...at the time of the Last Supper, the Passover."

"Yes," said the teacher. "As the sun set over Jerusalem, that's when it all began...His last day...And everything turned toward His suffering and death. It all began at sunset with the Passover and the Lamb. He then went out to the Garden of Gethsemane where they arrested Him and brought Him to the priests. They put Him on trial and condemned Him to death. In the morning they took Him to Pontius Pilate. He was then beaten, mocked, scourged, and led through the streets of Jerusalem to be nailed to the cross. He suffered in agony for hours and then said, 'It is finished,' and died. They took down His body and laid it in a tomb. The sun set over Jerusalem, and the day was finished. It all took place that exact time period, from sunset to sunset. Now what is the day of man?" he asked. "The day when man was created?"

"The sixth day."

"And when is the sixth day?"

"Friday."

"And when does the sixth day begin?"

"On Thursday night at sundown, and it ends on Friday night at sundown...from sundown to sundown, the sixth day."

"So it all had to begin at sunset and last until the following sunset. He accom-plished it all on the sixth day, the day of man. He died for the sins of man, the guilt of man, and the fall of man. He did it all on the day of man to accomplish the man's redemption. And it was on the sixth day as well that man was first given life...So now in Messiah, the children of man can again be given life and again find life, as in the beginning...on the sixth day."

The Mission: The life of man is given on the sixth day. Receive your life, your breath, and your new creation in the sixth day of Messiah.

Genesis 1:26–31; Mark 15:42–43; Ephesians 1:7

The Sixth Day Revelation Mystery

INTO THE DEEP

THE MESSIAH WAS teaching the multitudes from a boat on the Sea of Galilee. He turned to His disciple Simon and said, 'Launch out into the deep, and let your nets out for a catch.' So they did. They caught so many fish that their nets began to break. What do you see in that?" asked the teacher.

"It's wise to listen to the Messiah," I replied.

"Yes, but what did He tell them to do?"

"To launch out into the deep and . . ."

"To launch out into the deep. That's it right there . . . to launch out into the deep."

"What does it mean?" I asked.

"It means that the fish weren't in the shallow waters."

"But what does it mean to us?"

"It means that your blessings aren't in the shallow waters either."

"I still don't get it."

"The blessings of God aren't found in the shallow waters. You won't find them in the shallow waters of faith. They don't swim there."

He paused for a moment as if to think, then continued.

"There are many who call themselves by Messiah's name, but most dwell only in the shallow waters. They stay by the shore. They stay near that which is familiar and comfortable. They never fully leave the old ways, the old life. So they only know the shallow waters of God. Others who are called by His Name never fully launch out. They never enter the deep. They believe, but with a shallow faith. They read the Scriptures, but only get into the shallow of the Word, the surface, the letter. They pray but only in the shallow of prayer. They never allow themselves to enter the deep of prayer. They never allow themselves the time. And they know of God's love, but they never get into the deep of His love. As a result, they never know the deep blessings that God has for them. But if you want the blessings of God, you must leave the shallow and launch out away from the shore, away from its distractions, away from the old and the familiar, and into the deep . . . into the deep waters of faith, the deep waters of His presence, the deep of His Word, the deep of worship, the deep of His joy, the deep of His voice, the deep of His Spirit, and the deep of His heart. That's where your blessings are waiting and will be found."

"And miracles?" I asked.

"Miracles so big that your net will break . . . in the deep waters of God."

The Mission: Launch out into the deep waters of God today. And there let down your net that it might break with His blessings.

Genesis 49:25; Luke 5:4–11; 1 Corinthians 2:10–13

Into the Deep

THE MYSTERY OF THE TAMID

IT WAS MID-AFTERNOON. He took me into a chamber in the middle of which was a large golden stone model of the Temple of Jerusalem. We were viewing it from what would have the Temple's eastern side, the side closest to the altar of sacrifice.

"'Now this is what you shall offer on the altar,'" said the teacher. He was reciting a passage of Scripture. "'Two lambs of the first year, day by day continually. One lamb you shall offer in the morning, and the other lamb you shall offer at twilight.' This," he said, "was the law of the *Tamid*. Tamid was the name given to the sacrifices that were to be offered every day in the Temple. So each day, the offerings would begin with the sacrifice of the morning lamb and finish with the sacrifice of the evening lamb. All the other sacrifices would come in between the two."

"Was there a specific ritual to the offering of the Tamid?"

"The morning lamb would be offered up at the third hour of the day. With its death, the Temple trumpets would sound and the Temple gates would be opened. Then at about the ninth hour, the evening sacrifice would be slain and offered on the altar, at which time all the sacrifices would be finished."

"So the morning lamb was offered up at the third hour. What time is that?"

"Nine o clock," said the teacher. "And when was Messiah crucified? The same hour, nine in the morning. So as the morning lamb was slain on the altar, the Lamb of God was lifted on the altar of the cross, and the trumpets sounded to announce the sacrifice, and the Temple gates were opened."

"And the evening lamb," I said, "at the ninth hour, what time was that?"

"Three in the afternoon," he said.

"Isn't that when Messiah died on the cross?"

"It was. So the sacrifice of Messiah began with the offering up of the morning lamb and ended with the offering of the evening lamb. And it all took place during the six hours of the Temple sacrifices, in between the two lambs, from the first sacrifice to the last. The Lamb of God," said the teacher, "is all in all, covering every moment, every need, every sin, every problem, and every answer. He is the Tamid."

"You never told me; what does *tamid* mean?"

"It means continual, daily, perpetual, always, and forever. And so He will be there for you always...and will be your answer continuously, every day, always, and forever...For Messiah is the Lamb, and not only the Lamb...but your Tamid."

The Mission: Meditate on the fact that Messiah is your Tamid—the covering for every moment of your life—always, and forever. Live accordingly.

Exodus 29:38–39; Mark 15:25–37; Revelation 7:9–17

The Good Friday Sacrifice Mysteries

THE TENT WORLD

HE LED ME to a plateau from which we could see a vast panorama of the wilderness, mountains, valleys, canyons, plains, rocks, and sand.

"It bears a profound mystery," said the teacher.

"What does?" I asked.

"This...the desert. It's the landscape through which God's people journeyed on their way to the Promised Land."

"The Israelites."

"Yes. In order to get to the Promised Land, they had to journey through the desert wilderness, dwelling in tents. In that is the revelation."

"The revelation of what?" I asked.

"This life," he said. "Everything in this world is temporary. It's not the place in which we stay. It's the place through which we journey. We pass through this world. It isn't our home. It's the tent world. And all of us are just campers. Everything in this world changes, every circumstance, every experience, every stage of life...they're all tents. We dwell in one tent for a season, and then move on to another. Your childhood was a tent in which once you dwelt and then you moved on. Your good times, your bad times, your successes and failures, your problems, your joys and sorrows, your adulthood, your old age...they're all just tents. Even your physical being, even that's a tent, temporary and always changing. The very frailty of it all is a reminder that we're only journeying through."

"Journeying through to where?" I asked.

"For the child of God, it's the journey home. It's the home to the Promised Land...to heaven...the place where we give up our tents and exchange that which is temporary for that which is everlasting."

"And how do I apply this?"

"In every way," he said. "No matter what happens in this world or in your life, never forget, you're not home...you're only journeying through. Every problem will pass, and every temptation will fade. So tread lightly. It's not the scenery that will determine your life, it's not the circumstances; it's where you're going. Keep your eyes focused and your heart fixed on your destination—on the Promised Land. And for all the rest, just remember...you're only camping."

The Mission: Live this day as a camper. Don't get caught up in your circumstances. Focus instead on the journeying. And travel lightly.

2 Corinthians 4:16–5:5; Hebrews 11:8–16

The Feast of Camping

HEAVEN'S DESCENT

IT WAS MID-AFTERNOON. We were sitting outside in a desert plain. He was pointing to the sky.

"Look," said the teacher, "the heavens...a shadow of the true and ultimate heaven. How do you get there?" he asked. "How do you get into heaven?"

"Most people would say you get into heaven by doing good deeds."

"Yes," he replied. "Most religions would say that. If you do enough good works, if you avoid enough evil, if you master the discipline, if you end the self, if you attain the enlightenment, then you get into heaven. But is that the way?"

"You would say it's not."

"If it's based on what we do, then the source of our salvation is ourselves. And if we could save ourselves by ourselves, then we wouldn't need salvation in the first place. How can the answer come from the one in need of the answer? It's like telling a drowning man that if he would only swim well enough, he could save himself. If he could swim well enough, he wouldn't be drowning. He'd be the lifeguard."

"So then what's the answer?"

"The answer is that the problem can never answer itself. Only the answer *can answer*. So the earthly can never attain the heavenly. But the heavenly *can* attain the earthly."

"What do you mean?"

"Salvation can never come from earth to heaven...but only from heaven to earth. All these paths are hands reaching up to heaven. But the answer is radically different. It's a hand reaching down to earth. The answer must come from the Answer. So salvation can never just *end* in heaven. It must *begin* there."

"So it's not so much about getting into heaven."

"No," he said, "it's about heaven getting into you."

"Heaven coming down...to us."

"The descent of heaven...the heavenly visiting the earthly...the heavenly One becoming earthly...so that the earthly might become heavenly."

"So it's not about attaining anything."

"No," he said, "it's about receiving everything...starting with heaven."

The Mission: Make it your aim today not to strive for heaven, but let heaven—its love, its blessings, and its joy—get into you."

Isaiah 45:8; 55:10–11; John 6:51

Jehovah of Nazareth

YAMIM NORAIM: THE DAYS OF AWE

THE DAYS THAT open the Hebrew month of Tishri," he said, "from the Feast of Trumpets to Yom Kippur, are seen as the holiest time on the biblical calendar."

"Why?"

"They are the days of repentance. When the shofar sounds on the Feast of Trumpets, it signals that only ten days remain until Yom Kippur. And Yom Kippur is linked to the sealing of one's eternal destiny, as on the Day of Judgment. But it's not just these two days that are considered most holy but all ten. Together they are called the *Yamim Noraim*, the Days of Awe, or the Awesome Days."

"Why awesome?"

"Because their end is linked to the final Day of Judgment. So they declare that one doesn't have forever to repent or to make things right. One only has these set days before it's all sealed."

"So they must be pretty intense."

"They are. During the Days of Awe, observant Jews do everything they can to get right with God, to make things right with others, to forgive and be forgiven, to repent, to seal up loose ends, and to right what was wrong. It all has to be finished before the sun sets on the eve of Yom Kippur."

"But does this apply to us now," I said, "in Messiah?"

"The Days of Awe are a shadow of something much greater. For the days you have on earth are not forever. They have an appointed end. And at their end comes eternity, beginning with the Day of Judgment when your destiny is sealed, either for judgment or redemption. And the only time you have to determine your eternity are the days of this life, the days you now have on earth. Once they end, it's all sealed. So these are the only days you will ever have to get right with God, to make things right with others, and to right what is wrong. So if you would ever get right with God, get right with God now. If you would ever make things right with others, make things right with them now. If you would ever rise to your calling, rise now. And whatever good you would ever do in your life, do it now. For the time you have left on earth is nothing less than the Yamim Noraim, your Days of Awe."

The Mission: Look at the remainder of your days of life in a new way, as the Yamim Noraim. Get right with God and those in your life, for today is a Day of Awe.

Isaiah 55:6–7; Ephesians 5:16

The Awesome Days

GATSHMANIM

I N ONE OF the gardens was a large circular object of stone with a ridge around its top. He motioned for me to sit down next to the object, beside him. At first, he said nothing as to its nature or function.

"On the night before His suffering, Messiah went to the Garden of Gethsemane. There He surrendered His will in the face of His approaching sufferings and death. It was there, in Gethsemane, that the Temple guards came to arrest Him. So Gethsemane is the place where His sufferings begin."

It was then that the teacher turned his attention to the stone-like object.

"This is an oil press," he said. "The olives would be placed here on the top and a large wheel-like stone would roll over them, crushing them. The crushing of the olives would release their oil. In Hebrew, the word for olive oil is *shemen*. And the word for press is *gat*. An oil press is a *gatshemen* or *gatshmanim*. What does gatshmanim sound like?"

"I don't know."

"Think."

"Gethsemane!"

"Yes. Gethsemane is the oil press. And why is it the place where Messiah's sufferings began? The word *Messiah* is linked to oil, olive oil, shemen. But for oil to be released, there must be a crushing. Gethsemane, Gatshmanim, is the olive press, the place where the crushing begins ... first the crushing of His will, then the crushing of His life."

"And what does oil represent?"

"In the Scriptures, oil is linked to healing and joy, and, in its most sacred application, to anointing. Oil would be poured out to anoint kings and prophets. So oil, in its highest symbolism, signifies the outpouring of the Holy Spirit."

"So, then, if the crushing of olives in the olive press releases oil," I said, "then the crushing of Messiah in Gethsemane, the oil press, would be linked to healing, joy, and the outpouring of the Holy Spirit."

"Yes," said the teacher, "It is in the crushing of Messiah in His death that brings healing, joy ... and the outpouring of the Spirit. It all begins in the oil press, Gatshmanim ... Gethsemane."

The Mission: Today, let every desire and ambition that is not of God be surrendered and crushed. And in their crushing, be filled with the oil of the Holy Spirit.

Leviticus 8:10–12; Luke 22:39–44

The God Price

THE MYSTERY NATION

THE TEACHER CAME to me in the late afternoon and shared with me in my room. "God is the Eternal," he said. "Now, what if He placed a witness of His existence, a specific witness, in human history? What if the witness was a kingdom, a nation, a people? What would that people be like?"

"They would be different," I said. "I would think they would stand out."

"And what else would the witnesses of the Eternal be?"

"I guess they would, in some way, be...eternal."

"Exactly. They would bear the marks of eternity, even as the world changed around them. And the very fact of their perpetual existence would defy the laws of history."

"Is there such a people?"

"Yes," he said, "there is such a people...the Jewish people, the nation of Israel. Their very existence on the earth is a witness and a mystery."

"How?"

"Their existence defies the laws of this world. They should, by all reckoning, not exist. In ancient times they lived among the Babylonians, the Hittites, and the Amorites. But the Babylonians have vanished, the Hittites are gone, and the Amorites are no more. If you want to see them, you have to visit the museums of this world, and then you'd only see shadows of what they once were. The peoples of the ancient world have vanished into the dust of history. But the Jewish people have not vanished but endured. You can also find them in the museums of this world, but walking the halls and passing by the stone reliefs of those among whom they once walked. They have witnessed the rise of the great kingdoms of this world and watched them fall. Against all odds, they live. Against all the laws of this world they are as alive as they ever were. They are the eternal nation, the mystery nation."

"And the mystery of their existence is ..."

"The Eternal. The hand of God. Without it, they would have ceased to exist ages ago. Behind the mystery of Israel is the God of Israel. They exist because He exists. They are the eternal nation because they are the witnesses of the Eternal. That which is of God does not pass away, but endures—His Word, His love, His nation, and all who abide in Him...they become, themselves...eternal."

The Mission: Live this day seeking to follow His will and purposes and to bear witness of His existence in everything you do.

Genesis 17:1–8; Jeremiah 31:35–37; Ephesians 2:11–22

The Secret of His Immortality

THE WELLS OF YESHUA

HE LED ME to the school's well. It was built of angular stones, each of a light beige color that matched the desert landscape that surrounded it. We sat down on its perimeter where he began the teaching.

"During Sukkot, the Feast of Tabernacles, a unique ritual took place called the Water Drawing Ceremony. During the ceremony a solemn procession led by a priest would go down to the Pool of Siloam, draw water into a golden pitcher, and then ascend the Temple Mount where he would pour out the water at the altar while a verse from Isaiah would be read: 'And in joy, you shall draw water from the wells of salvation.'"

He paused to lower an empty bucket into the well.

"The Water Drawing Ceremony," he said, "was a central part of the feast, as water, or the lack of it, was a matter of life or death in a Middle Eastern land. So on every day of the Feast of Tabernacles the ceremony was performed."

The teacher then pulled up the bucket, which was now filled with water.

"Messiah spoke of water," he said. "One of the most famous statements He ever made began with the words, 'If anyone is thirsty...'"

"I've heard it."

"Most believers have. But most have little understanding of its context."

"And what is its context?"

"The Feast of Tabernacles," he replied, "and its focus on water, with its drawing water during which these words from Isaiah would be proclaimed: 'And in joy you shall draw water from the wells of salvation.' But in Hebrew, it's not the wells of *salvation*. It's the wells of *yeshua*."

"Which is like saying the name of Yeshua," I said, "which is the name of Jesus. So it's like saying 'you will draw water from the wells of Yeshua' or 'from the wells of Jesus.'"

"Exactly. And it is recorded that He stood up during the feast and cried out, 'If anyone is thirsty, let him come to Me and drink. He who believes in Me, as the Scripture has said, out of his innermost being shall flow rivers of living water.'"

"And we shall draw water," I said, "from the wells of Yeshua."

"And He was speaking of the Spirit. So as much as they needed water to stay alive, we need the waters of the Spirit to stay alive in God. Therefore, you must draw of it every day of your life...and in joy...from the wells of Yeshua."

The Mission: Today, come to the wells of Yeshua, and in joy, draw forth and partake of the rivers of the living waters of the Spirit of God.

Isaiah 12:1–3; John 7:37–39

The Water Pouring

RACHAMIM

DO YOU BELIEVE," said the teacher, "that God has mercy?"

"Yes," I replied. "Of course, you've taught me that."

"No," said the teacher. "God does not have mercy."

"With all respect," I said cautiously, "that's not right." It was the first time I had ever contradicted him in such a direct way.

"Prove your point," he said.

"I was just reading the Book of Daniel. In it, Daniel prays for God's mercy on the people of Israel. He says, 'To the Lord our God belong mercy and forgiveness...'"

"It doesn't say that," he replied, "not in the original language. It says 'to the Lord belong *rachamim*.'"

"What is *rachamim*?"

"Some would translate it as mercy. But *rachamim* is not a singular noun. It's plural. It doesn't mean mercy. It means mercies. It means that God's mercy is more than mercy. God's mercy is so great, so strong, and so deep that it can't be contained in a single word. *Rachamim* means that His mercy has no end."

"What about the word for sin?" I asked.

"What do you mean?"

"Is it by nature singular or plural?"

"The word for sin," said the teacher, "is singular."

"But the word for mercy is plural," I said.

"And what does that tell you?"

"That no matter what my sin is, no matter how great, the mercy of God is always greater. And no matter how much I've sinned, no matter how many sins I have, the mercies of God are more than my sins."

"Yes," said the teacher. "So don't ever make the mistake of thinking that you've exhausted God's mercy. You never have. You never could. And you never will. He will always have more mercies than you have sins, more than enough to cover every sin and to still have enough compassion left over to love you forever. For what the Lord has for you is not mercy...but rachamim."

The Mission: Open your heart today to receive the rachamim God has for you, not only for your sins, but the overflowing rivers of His compassions and love.

Psalm 136; Lamentations 3:22–23; Daniel 9:9; 2 Corinthians 1:3–4

THE MANTLE OF MESSIAH

THE TEACHER LED me into a room I had never before been to. "This is the Chamber of Garments," he said as he lifted up a large brown cloth, which I, at first, took to be a blanket.

"This is a mantle," he said, "as in 'the mantle of the prophet.'"

"And what exactly is a mantle?" I asked.

"A garment, a cloak, and yet more than that. The mantle represents the calling, the charge, the ministry, and the anointing of God. Before Moses ascended Mount Nebo at the finish of his ministry, he laid hands on his disciple, Joshua, and God's Spirit fell upon him along with the mantle, the authority of Moses. When Elijah ascended to God at the end of his ministry, he dropped his mantle on the ground. His disciple Elisha picked it up, and the spirit of Elijah came upon him. Do you see a pattern?"

"Yes," I said. "In each case, the man of God is about to finish his earthly ministry. In each case, he ascends to God. In each case, the ascension and the completion of the ministry are linked to the passing of the mantle."

"Yes," said the teacher. "Now, what happened at the end of Messiah's ministry on earth? As with Moses, He ascended a mountain, and as with Elijah, He ascended to heaven. As with both of them, His disciples were present at the departure. But where's the mantle? Every other element of the pattern is there. But where's the mantle of the Messiah? Upon whom did it fall?"

"I never thought of it. Messiah's mantle appears to be missing."

"The answer," said the teacher, "is this: The mantle of Messiah is too big to fall on any one person. It can never fall on one disciple. It can only fall on all. When the mantles of Moses and Elijah fell, the Spirit of God came upon their disciples. So what happened after Messiah ascended to God?"

"The Spirit of God fell on His disciples...the Day of Pentecost."

"And what was it that was given that day with the giving of the Spirit? The mantle of Messiah. And to whom is it given? His disciples. All of them. You see, we are all given a part of Messiah's mantle. And it is in His mantle that our calling and ministry are found. And if we have a part in His mantle, then we also have a part in His anointing. For with every calling, God gives the anointing to fulfill it. So find your place and ministry in that mantle. For your calling can only be fulfilled in the mantle of Messiah."

The Mission: Today, fully take up your mantle in Messiah. And by the power and the authority of the Spirit, step out to fulfill your high calling.

Deuteronomy 31:7–8; 34:9; 1 Kings 19:9; Acts 2:1–4

The Mantle

THE DAVAR AND THE OLAM

WE WERE SITTING in an open desert plain under the night skies. He had started a small fire. I think it was only so he could read the words on the parchment he was holding in his hand. It was a clear night. The sky was filled with stars.

"What you see," he said, "is the *olam*...Everything you see is the olam, the universe, the creation. And this," he said, lifting up the parchment, "is the *Davar*, the Word. The Davar and the olam, the Word and the world. Which seems greater, the Davar or the olam?"

"It would seem that the universe is greater," I said, "the olam."

"Yes, it seems so much bigger. And which seems more real and solid?"

"The olam," I said again.

"Yes, it would seem to be so," he said. "But it's not." Then, holding the parchment to the light, he began translating its words.

"It is written in the Psalms, 'For He spoke, and it came into existence. He commanded, and it was established.' And in the Book of Hebrews it is written, 'The universe was formed at God's command...' So which came first, the olam or the Davar, the world or the Word?"

"The Word came first," I said, "then came the world."

"Then which is greater, the world or the Word?"

"The Word would be greater."

"Then which is more real and more solid?"

"The Word is more real."

"Yes," said the teacher. "The Word came first; the world came second. The Word was spoken, and the world followed. So the Word doesn't follow the world. It is the world that follows the Word. And what does that mean for our lives?"

"We must not be led by the world, but by the Word."

"Yes," he said. "It means you are never to be led by the circumstances and events of your life. All that is part of the olam, and so is secondary. The olam, the world, changes and passes away. But the Davar, the Word, never changes or passes away. Be, therefore, led by the Word, even when it goes against everything you see around you—especially then. Stand on the Word, despite the world. For what He has spoken shall come to be in the universe and in your life—the Davar and then the olam. The Word is first...and only then, the world."

The Mission: Choose the Word over the world, over your circumstances, your problems, and everything else. Let the Davar rule your olam.

Psalm 33:6–9; John 1:1–4; Hebrews 11:3

The Word

THE EXODUS FACTOR

WE WERE WALKING through a vast desert plain, spotted with small plants and shrubs and surrounded by mountains in every direction, far into the distance.

"I told you of the *Ivrim*," said the teacher.

"The Hebrews," I replied.

"Yes. Do you remember what *Ivrim* means, what *Hebrew* means in Hebrew?"

"The one who crosses over."

"Yes, and what did the Hebrews cross over to get to the Promised Land?"

"The Red Sea and the Jordan River."

"They crossed the Jordan River to enter into the land of Israel. But they crossed the Red Sea to get out of the land of Egypt. So before they could enter the new land, they had to leave the old land. As important as is the act of entering is the act of exiting. So you have an entire book of the Bible named after it, the Book of *Exodus*, which means the leaving or the exiting. Exiting is as holy as entering. You can't have the one without the other."

"You can't enter unless you leave."

"It's a law of physical existence. It's simple, but profound. Abraham is the first Hebrew, the first of the Ivrim. And what was the first thing he had to do?"

"Leave?"

"Yes. The first call of Abraham was 'Get out of your country…and to a land I will show you.' The first command was 'Get out.' The rest, all the blessings, all the promises of the Promised Land, and the future, all rested on the words 'Get out.' You see, getting out is a holy act. Messiah called His disciples to come with Him. But in order to do that, they had to first leave, drop their nets, get out of their boats, and leave their old way of life. If they didn't leave, they couldn't come. God calls us to come, to move, to follow, to pilgrim, and to enter into blessing. But we can't know any of these things without first being willing to leave. There are many who long for change, for something better, something new. But few are willing to leave. But the law is not only of the physical realm, but of the spiritual. If you want to get to the place where you aren't, you must first leave the place where you are. Leave the old, and you will enter the new. Cross the Red Sea out of your Egypt, and you will also cross the Jordan River into your promised land."

The Mission: Where do you need to go? What promised land has God called you to enter? What must you first leave? Begin your exodus today.

Genesis 12:1–3; Exodus 12:51; 2 Corinthians 5:17; Ephesians 4:22–24

The Secrets of Change & Breakthrough

THE SECRET OF YOMA

HE TOOK ME into what was known as the Chamber of Books, a massive room of towering bookcases filled with volumes of mostly old or ancient-looking books. Retrieving one of these from the shelves, a large reddish volume, he laid it on a wooden table, opened it up, and began to share.

"There were in the Temple of Jerusalem two major barriers separating God from man, the holy from the unholy. One was formed by two massive doors of gold—the doors of the *hekhal*, the holy place. These separated the holy place from the Temple courts. The other, deeper inside, was called the *parochet*, the colossal veil that separated the holy place from the holy of holies and through which only the high priest could enter on the Day of Atonement. They were the representations of the barrier separating each of us from God, the chasm between the sinful and the most holy. But it is recorded in the New Testament that at the time of Messiah's death, the parochet, the veil of the holy of holies, was torn in two. What would that have signified?"

"That the barrier between man and God was removed?"

"Exactly. But there was still a second barrier, the golden doors of the hekhal. Should not that barrier have been opened as well? Could there have been a second sign, a second witness? There was, and of the most powerful kind...an opposing witness. This is in Tractate Yoma 39," he said, pointing to the open book, "from the writings of the rabbis, the Talmud. It contains a most amazing thing. The rabbis record that before the destruction of Jerusalem in AD 70, a strange thing began to take place in the Temple. The second barrier, the golden doors of the hekhal, began to open *by itself.*"

"When?" I asked. "When did they start doing that?"

"The rabbis record that it began to happen about forty years before AD 70."

"Then it comes to about the year AD 30!"

"Yes, and which just happens to be the same time that something else took place in Jerusalem, the Rabbi Yeshua, Jesus, died as the final atonement, to remove the barrier from man to God."

"Has that ever happened in the history of faith where a hostile witness..."

"So powerfully testifies to such a fact? Never. And the fact remains that rabbis themselves bear witness concerning the removal of the second barrier, and, thus, that at the time of Messiah's death, that which was separating God from man...God from us...was removed...and that the way to His presence has been opened."

The Mission: Even the rabbis bear witness, around AD 30 the way was opened. Use the power of Messiah today to open the doors that are closed.

Psalm 24:7–10; Matthew 27:50–51; Hebrews 6:19–20; 10:19–20

The Mystery of the Temple Doors

THE REVELATION LAND

JERUSALEM," SAID THE teacher, "is built on Mount Moriah. Surrounding Jerusalem is the land of Moriah. It's the land of the Holy City. So what exactly is the land of Moriah? What does it mean? Moriah comes from two Hebrew words. The first, *ra'ah,* means the seen, the visible, the shown, or the revealed. The other is *Yah*, the Name of God."

"So Moriah," I said, "means the revealed of God."

"Moriah is the land of revelation, the place where God will reveal Himself. There are many who see God as a distant king, an impersonal cosmic force, a capricious puppet master, or an angry judge wanting to bring judgment. But Moriah is the land where God is to be revealed, the invisible made visible. Therefore, that which appears in Moriah will be the true revelation of the true God. So what was it that was revealed in the land of Moriah? What was the revelation of God that was made visible in that land?"

"In the Temple?" I asked. "The Temple was in Jerusalem."

"It was," said the teacher, "but there was another manifestation, a revelation of God even more graphic and amazing than the Temple."

"What was it?"

"It was in the land of Moriah that God appeared taking our sins and our judgment upon Himself. It was in the land of Moriah that God willingly gave His life, wearing a crown of thorns, being beaten mercilessly, scourged and bloodied because of us...It was in Moriah that God was mocked, ridiculed, beaten, stripped naked, pierced through, impaled, and raised up on a wooden execution stake. It was in Moriah that God hung on a cross, bleeding, suffocating, dying, agonizing, and breathing His last breath...and doing it all to save us from judgment...doing it all because of love. It was all in Moriah, the land of God revealed...God willingly hanging naked on an execution stake, bleeding and dying because of us. Who is God? God is love. God is total, unconditional, extreme, incomprehensible, self-sacrificing cosmic love for us...the greatest love we can or will ever know. That is the absolute and ultimate revelation of God that was manifested once and for all in Moriah, the land of the revelation of God."

The Mission: Take in the revelation of Moriah personally—that if you were the only person in the world, He still would have given His life for you.

Psalm 122; Matthew 27:29–50; Romans 5:8

The Moriah Miracle

THE JONAH PARADOX

WE WERE OUTSIDE looking up at one of the buildings when we noticed a dove perched on one of the stones just under the roof.

"The word for *dove* in Hebrew is *yonah*," he said, "as in the prophet Jonah…who did everything he could to reject God's calling and yet unwillingly ended up fulfilling it, leading an entire godless city to salvation…and then ended up completely miserable over his success."

"Why miserable?"

"Because Nineveh was filled with his enemies, and he knew that if he gave them God's Word, they would repent, and God would have mercy on them. The word he gave them was this: 'Forty days and Nineveh shall be overthrown.' Not a very encouraging message. In fact, there's no hope in it. It's a paradox. If Jonah refuses to give them the prophecy of judgment, then the judgment and the prophecy come true. But if he delivers the prophecy of judgment, then Nineveh could repent and the judgment and the prophecy fail to come true."

"The opposite of a self-fulfilling prophecy."

"A self-nullifying prophecy. And therein lies the other paradox. God told Jonah to tell the people, 'Forty days and Nineveh shall be overthrown.' But in forty days there was no judgment. Because the people of Nineveh believed the prophecy to be true, the prophecy became as if untrue. People have used the fact that the prophecy didn't come true against God and His Word. What does it tell you?" he asked. "It tells you that man is more concerned over the fact that the warning didn't come true than the fact that 120,000 people were saved because it didn't. It tells you that it is not God who lacks mercy, but man. God would rather save the lost even if by doing so it would appear to void His Word…even if by doing so it would void His own life…as in His death. It is His love, His mercy, and His grace that bring about the impossible."

"So in this case, the love of God caused the Word of God to not come true."

"Or did it?" said the teacher. The prophecy was 'Nineveh shall be overthrown.' But the word *overthrown* is the Hebrew *hafak*. And *hafak* also means to be overturned, changed, and converted. And that's how they were saved from judgment."

"So the same word that signified judgment also signified repentance and salvation from judgment…a paradox of paradoxes."

"A wonderful paradox," said the teacher, "the paradox by which we are saved."

The Mission: Today, let His mercy triumph over all judgment and condemnation. Let logic of judgment yield to the paradox of His love.

Jonah 3; 2 Peter 3:9

The Book of Jonah I–VII

IN HIS DEATHS

WE WERE IN the Chamber of Scrolls, examining again the scroll of Isaiah, the fifty-third chapter. He began reciting one of its passages.

"'He made His grave with the wicked...and with a rich man in His death...' It's describing the Suffering Servant, the Messiah who dies for our sins. His death will be linked to wicked men and to a rich man."

"'He made His grave with the wicked.' So Messiah was crucified in the midst of criminals, among wicked men, and He was buried in the tomb of a rich man."

"Yes," said the teacher, "and there's even more...a mystery that you can only find in the original language. If you read almost any translation of Isaiah 53, it will say 'in His death.' But it doesn't really say that. What it does say, in the original language, is so big, and so cosmic, it's hard for any translator to do it justice."

"And what does it say?"

"In the original Hebrew it says 'in His *deaths*.'"

"What does that mean?"

"Remember, in Hebrew, when a word should be singular, but is rendered plural, it is often a sign that the reality behind the word is so unique, so intense, so extreme, or so colossal that the word alone cannot contain it."

"So in other words, His death..."

"In other words, the death of Messiah is such a unique reality, such an extreme reality, such an intense reality, and such a colossal reality that the word *death* cannot even begin to approach it. What happened in His death goes beyond anything we can express with our words or comprehend with our thoughts."

"But plural can actually mean plural."

"Yes. But it's a singular combined with a plural. 'In His death' would make sense as would 'in their deaths.' But it doesn't say either. It says 'in His deaths.' That breaks the rules. What is it revealing?"

"That Messiah would die not just His death, one death, but many deaths. He wouldn't die for Himself but for all. His would be the one life that dies the death of all."

"Yes," said the teacher, "including yours. Your death, and the death of all who read the words of the prophecy...Every death is contained inside that plural word. It is the witness in black and white that your old life and the judgment thereof is finished...in His deaths."

The Mission: One of the deaths *in His deaths* is the death of your old life. Give that which is old a eulogy and a burial. Be finished with it and be free.

Isaiah 53:9; Romans 5:18; 2 Corinthians 5:14–15

In His Deaths

THE TALMIDIM

IT WAS NIGHT. The teacher and I and several other students were sitting around the campfire.

"Messiah had twelve disciples," he said. "They were with Him wherever He went and in everything He did. They assisted Him with ministry, traveled with Him, ate with Him, rested with Him at night, rose up with Him in the morning, and lived their lives with Him. Who were they?"

"People from all walks of life," said one of the students.

"Yes, but who *were* the disciples?"

No one answered.

"You must remember," he said. "Messiah was a rabbi. Every great rabbi had disciples. The twelve were not just disciples, but the disciples of a rabbi. They weren't called *the disciples*. They were called the *talmidim*."

"What does *talmidim* mean?" asked another student.

"It comes from the Hebrew root word *lamad*. *Lamad* is linked to teaching or learning. So the disciples were the taught ones, the learners."

"Like us," said another.

"Yes," said the teacher. "But you must be *His* disciples. It must be *Him* who teaches you. And if you are a disciple, then what is your purpose?"

"To be a *learner*," I said.

"Yes, your first calling is to be a learner. And you're not learning on your own. No disciple learns on his own. You have a Rabbi. You have *the* Rabbi of rabbis. That means you have One who teaches you every day, every hour, and every moment. It means your life is not just a life, but a course. And it means you're not to waste your time here."

"Our time in the school?" asked another.

"Your time on earth," said the teacher. "This life is your school. And Messiah is your teacher. And as it was for the disciples, so it will be for you ... Every day He will teach you. Every day there will be lessons given you. Every circumstance will be a class. Every event will be a teaching tool, an illustration for the lesson. Do not fail to recognize them. Don't miss your classes. Seek them. Let every day be a journey. Make it your joy to learn from the Master. For the world is your classroom ... and Messiah is your Rabbi."

The Mission: Start living today as a true disciple, a learner. Seek the Rabbi's teaching. Listen to His voice and follow His instruction.

Matthew 4:18–22; Matthew 9:9; John 1:36–40

The Cosmic Rabbi

THE BIRTH TOMB

WE WALKED THROUGH a dry riverbed that wound around two mountains until we emerged in a small hidden valley. "Look," said the teacher, as he pointed to the top of one of the mountains. "Do you see that?"

"What is it?" I asked.

"It's a tomb."

"As in someone's buried there?"

"Yes," he answered, "that kind of a tomb."

"Are we going there?"

"No. It's a place of death. But that's what makes it so amazing."

"Makes what so amazing?"

"What place in this world is more hopeless, more depressing, more sorrowful, more despairing, and more forbidding than a tomb? And yet of all places on earth, it all begins in a tomb."

"What all begins?"

"Redemption begins. The faith begins. The good news begins. The word of Messiah begins. The message of salvation begins. The Gospel begins. Think about it. It all begins in a tomb. Did you ever consider how radical and completely upside down it is?"

"I never did."

"What is a tomb? It's the place where hope ends, where dreams end, where life ends, where everything ends. The tomb is the place of the end. But in God, the tomb, the place of the end, becomes the place of the beginning."

"Why?"

"It's the radical way of the kingdom. In God, the journey goes not from life to death, but from death to life. The end is the beginning. So to find life, you must come to the tomb."

"You must come to a place of death to find life."

"Only those who come to the place of the end can enter the new beginning. For in Messiah, it is in the place of ending that we find the beginning, and in the place of hopelessness that we find true hope, and in the place of sorrow that we find true joy, and in the place of death that we are born again. In God, it is in a tomb, that we find our birth."

The Mission: What is it in your life that must end? Bring it into Messiah's tomb. And wait there. For after you've come to the end, you'll find the beginning.

Matthew 28:1–6; 1 Corinthians 15:55–57; 1 Peter 1:23

Yom Rishon: The Beginning of Days

THE MYSTERY PRIEST

HE LED ME back into the Chamber of Garments. He disappeared for a few moments, then returned holding a white linen tunic around the middle of which was a sash of blue, purple, and scarlet.

"What is that?" I asked.

"It's the garment of the *cohanim*," said the teacher.

"And who was the cohanim?"

"Who *were* the cohanim," he said. "They were the priests of Israel, the sons of Aaron. It was the cohanim who ministered in the Temple and who were given charge by God over the offerings and sacrifices by which the people of Israel were reconciled to God."

At that, he laid down the garment.

"Messiah came as the final and ultimate sacrifice, by which those who received Him would be reconciled to God. He came at a time when the Temple was still standing, when the priesthood of Israel was still in effect, and when the sons of Aaron had charge over the sacrifices. Shouldn't there have been some connection, some recognition given by the priests, those in charge of the sacrifices, of the final and ultimate sacrifice?"

"It makes sense," I said. "But I've never seen anything like it in the Gospels."

"You have," said the teacher. "You just didn't realize it. There was, born to the cohanim, to the house of Aaron, a child who was not only a priest, but one descended from Aaron on both his father's and mother's line, a pure-blooded priest. The child was given the name *Yochanan*."

"I've never heard of him."

"You have," said the teacher. "You know him as John the Baptist."

"John the Baptist! Of the house of Aaron...of the cohanim...I didn't..."

"And what did the cohanim do? They presented the lambs for sacrifice. So it was John who presented the Lamb, Messiah, the final sacrifice, to Israel. It was the cohanim who identified the sacrifice and certified that it was acceptable to be sacrificed. So it was Yochanan, John, who first identified Messiah as the acceptable sacrifice. He was the first to identify Messiah as the sacrificial Lamb. It was he who said, 'Behold the Lamb of God who takes away the sin of the world.' You see, God made sure to have a priest of Aaron to certify the Lamb. That means your sins are completely and certifiably taken away forever by the Lamb who comes with priestly certification."

The Mission: The cohanim have spoken. The Lamb has been slain. And every one of your sins has been taken away. Rejoice in it. Live accordingly.

Luke 1:5–25, 57–80; 3:1–4; John 1:29

The Mystery of the Hikriv

THE HAFTORAH MYSTERY

HE TOOK ME into the Chamber of Scrolls and led me over to a scroll unique from the others in that it rested permanently on its own wooden platform.

"Every week," he said, "on the Sabbath, in synagogues throughout the world, a word from the Prophets is read along with a word from the Torah. The word from the Prophets is called the *haftorah* reading. It comes from this scroll, and is often just a few verses long."

"How long has this been going on?" I asked.

"From ancient times," he said.

He then rolled the scroll forward to find the passage he was looking for.

"For two thousand years," he said, "the Jewish people wandered the earth in exile from their land. But the Word of God prophesied that in the latter days God would bring them back to their homeland and the nation of Israel would come back into the world. The prophecy came true on May 15, 1948, when the nation of Israel was resurrected. The exile of two thousand years was over. May 15, 1948, happened to be a Sabbath. That means there was a word appointed from ancient times to be read in every synagogue throughout the world on the day that Israel came back into the world."

"What was it?"

"It was from the Book of Amos. It was this." Placing his finger on the Hebrew words in the scroll, he began to read: "'I will restore David's fallen tabernacle. I will repair its broken walls and restore its ruins. I will rebuild it as it used to be...And I will bring my people Israel back from exile. They will rebuild the ruined cities and live in them. They will plant vineyards and drink their wine. They will make gardens and eat their fruit. I will plant Israel in their own land, never again to be uprooted from the land I have given them.' It was the ancient prophecy foretelling the future restoration of Israel...And it just happened to be appointed from ancient times to be read throughout the world on the very day that Israel's restoration was fulfilled. What does it tell you?"

"The Word of God is true, truer than circumstance, and stronger than history."

"Yes," said the teacher. "And so fully trust in it. And when God gives a promise, He will fulfill it. It will come to fruition at the time ordained for it...at the appointed and exact moment."

The Mission: Take a Word from Scripture you can walk in this day. Seek for the exact and appointed moments for the Word to come to fruition.

Psalm 18:30; Amos 9:11–15; 2 Timothy 3:16

THE SUNSET MYSTERY

IT WAS EARLY evening. We were sitting on the side of a mountain watching an orange sun descend into the landscape.

"In the biblical calendar," said the teacher, "the moment the sun goes down, the day is over. Whatever happened during that day now belongs to the past, to yesterday. The day's problems become yesterday's problems; its concern, yesterday's concerns; its mistakes, yesterday's mistakes; and its sorrows, yesterday's sorrows. When the sun sets, it's all past."

"Why is that significant?" I asked.

"When Messiah was in the world, He said, 'I am the Light of the World.' But He came into the world to die."

"I'm not seeing a connection."

"When He died, it was the Light of the World dying. It was the Light of the World growing dark and disappearing. It was the Light of the World descending to the earth...It was the sunset. In fact, as He died, the sun was descending in the sky. And when they placed Him in the tomb, the sun was descending into the earth. That's why they were rushing to put Him there. It was because the sun was setting. And when they had closed the tomb, and sealed Him in the earth, the light of the world, the sun, was, likewise, disappearing into the earth."

"So, the Light of the World disappeared into the earth as the other light of the world disappeared into the earth."

"Yes," he said. "And what does that mean?"

"If the Light of the World has descended into the earth, that means it's sunset."

"It means it's the sunset of this world, the sunset of the old life. The moment the sun goes down, the day is over, the old day, the old world, our old life is over. Whatever happened in that life now belongs to the past. The events of our old lives now belong to yesterday. The mistakes of our lives, the problems, the sins, the fears, the shame, the guilt, they belong to that which is no more. The sun has set on the old. The sun has set on your past, on your sins, on your shame, on the person you once were. And so it all belongs to yesterday. And for all who will let the sun set on their old life, for all who will die to the old, in the sunset of Messiah, the old has passed away, and they're free to rise with the dawn of the new day."

The Mission: Let the sun set on all in your life that is old. Let all that has been...become yesterday, forever, in the sunset of Messiah.

John 8:12; 9:5; 19:30–41

The Sunset of Messiah

THE HOUSE OF SPIRITS

WHAT'S THAT?" I asked.

"A house," he replied, "the ruins of a house. And that's where we're going."

It was a simple rectangular dwelling made up of irregular stones and set on a plateau overlooking a small valley. It looked ancient, though whether it was decades old or thousands of years, I had no idea. We went inside and sat down. The wind was blowing through the doorway and through the many cracks and openings in its walls.

"Messiah spoke of an unclean spirit," said the teacher, "coming out of a man and finding no other place to inhabit. The spirit says, 'I will return to the house I left.' And when it returns, it finds the 'house' uninhabited, swept clean, and having been set in order. The spirit then brings along seven other spirits more evil than itself. The man is now inhabited by eight spirits instead of one."

"So if someone turns away from evil but then returns to it, the person will end up worse off than at the start."

"Yes, but the principle applies to more than that. It applies to a generation, and to a civilization...even to Western civilization," he replied. "In ancient times Western civilization was a house inhabited by gods and idols—pagan and indwelt by unclean spirits."

"A house of spirits."

"Yes, but into that house came the Word of God. And it was cleansed, purified, and exorcised of its unclean spirits, idols, and gods. But then what is the principle and the warning? If that civilization should then turn from God and away from His Word and back to the darkness, it will end up far worse than before."

"Than its ancient and pagan state?"

"Yes," said the teacher. "It will be inhabited by greater evils. Thus a pre-Christian civilization is far less dangerous than a post-Christian civilization. The pre-Christian may produce a Caligula or a Nero, but it is the post-Christian that produces a Hitler and a Stalin. And so the warning is this: Once you've come to the truth, never turn away, even to the slightest degree. Rather, make it your aim to draw continually closer."

"And the warning concerning civilization..."

"If it turns from the light it has once known...it will end up a house of spirits."

The Mission: Move all the more away from the darkness you left. And pray all the more for the civilization in which you dwell.

Matthew 12:43–45; Luke 8:26–36; Philippians 2:15; 1 Peter 2:11–12

THE BOOK OF THE UNMENTIONED GOD

THE TEACHER TOOK me to the Chamber of Scrolls. We sat down at a small wooden table upon which he placed a small and ornate scroll.

"This," he said, "is unique of all books of the Bible. Do you know what makes it different from the rest? The Name of God."

"The Name of God makes it different?"

"The *absence* of the Name of God makes it different. The Book of Esther is the only book of Scripture that contains absolutely no mention of God."

"That seems very strange."

"It would seem to be a godless book. In fact, it's filled with godlessness...evil people and evil plans to annihilate the people of God. And it's not just the Name of God that's missing but also, it seems, His presence. Darkness reigns, and God is nowhere to be found."

"So is the Book of Esther less holy than the other books in the Bible?"

"No," he replied. "Not at all. It's as holy as all the other books that mention His Name. That's the point. Even though the Name of God isn't mentioned, the hand of God lies behind every event. He is there, unseen, unmentioned, yet working all things together and turning every event around to fulfill His purposes. Esther is the Book of the Unmentioned God. And the Book of the Unmentioned God is a most holy book. It's the book that speaks of all the times you don't feel the presence of God, when you don't hear His voice, when you don't see His hand, when there's no sign of His love or purpose, and when He seems far away or not there at all. So when all you see is darkness, that is the time of the Book of the Unmentioned God. And it's telling you this: Even though you don't feel His presence, it is there still. Even though you don't see His hand, it is still moving. Even when you don't hear His voice, He is still speaking, even in the silence. Even when you feel abandoned and alone, still His love is there. And even when He seems hopelessly far away from you, He is still right there beside you, working every detail in your life for His purposes and your redemption. And in the end, the light will break the darkness, the good will prevail, and you will know that you were never alone. He was with you all along. And it was holy. It was the time of your Book of the Unmentioned God."

The Mission: Whenever you can't see or feel the presence of God in your life, know that He's fully there. It's just your Book of the Unmentioned God.

Psalm 139:7–12; Matthew 28:18–20; Hebrews 13:5

THE OMEGA JOY

THE GREATEST CELEBRATION," said the teacher, "in the days of the Bible was Sukkot, the Feast of Tabernacles. During the festival the people of Israel would go up to Jerusalem to give thanks to God for His blessings, for the fruit of their harvests, the produce of their fields, for His provisions, His faithfulness, and for the gift of the Promised Land itself. And so the Feast of Tabernacles was filled with celebration, praises, thanksgiving, dancing, and joy. In fact, the very command that ordained the feast states, 'You shall be altogether joyful.' So great was this celebration that it was simply known as the festival. Tabernacles was the feast of joy. It came in the autumn. What part of the sacred year is autumn?"

"The end," I said.

"Yes, and Tabernacles is the last feast of the sacred year. It's the greatest celebration and it comes at the end. What does that reveal?"

I had no answer.

"In the world," he said, "the greatest things come at the beginning. Everything starts out young, and then gets older and older. In the world, the celebration comes at the beginning. Then it fades away, ultimately ending in death. But the Feast of Tabernacles reveals that in the kingdom of God, it's the opposite. The greatest celebration comes at the end. So if you live in God's power, you don't move from life to death, but from death to life."

"Then we grow younger," I said.

"In the Spirit," he said, "we *are* to grow younger."

"And what about joy?" I asked. "Wouldn't Tabernacles also reveal that the greatest joy comes at the end?"

"Yes," said the teacher. "The joys of the world come at the beginning. They're fleeting. They grow old and pass away. The joys of sin lead to sorrow. The laughter of youth leads to tears of mourning. But in God, the greatest joy comes at the end. In other words, the ways of God all lead in the end to joy. Even that which seems hard for the moment, the way of sacrifice, self-control, and righteousness ... in the long run it all leads to joy. God's calendar ends with the Feast of Tabernacles, and those who walk in His ways end up altogether joyful. For the ways of God all lead to joy. And the best is saved for last."

The Mission: Today, look to the joy at the end of your path. And so live all the more confidently in what is good and right—to the Omega joy.

Leviticus 23:33–44; Psalm 16:11; Isaiah 51:11

The Last Joy

THE OTHER TREE

WE WALKED THROUGH a garden of trees.

"Today," said the teacher, "we open up the mystery of two trees. In Genesis it is written that inside the Garden of Eden grew the tree of the knowledge of good and evil. It was the one tree, the fruit of which man was not to partake."

"But man did partake," I replied.

"Yes, and through that partaking came sin and death. Through that one tree came the fall of man. Now why did the Messiah die?" he asked.

"To bring salvation."

"And to end what?"

"Sin...death..."

"And to undo what?"

"The fall."

"And on what did He die?"

"A cross."

"And of what was it made?"

"Wood."

"And what is wood?"

I paused for a moment before answering.

"A tree...The cross is a tree."

"There's a reason for that," he said. "The cross is the second tree. Through the first tree, sin begins. Through the second tree, sin ends. Through the first tree man fell."

"And through the second tree," I said, "man rises."

"Through a living tree came death."

"And through a dead tree," I said, "comes life."

"In the partaking of the first tree, we die."

"And in the partaking of the second tree, we come alive."

"And as God placed the first tree in the center of the garden, so He has placed the second tree in the center of history, the center of this world, so that all can partake of it and find life. And the more you partake of this tree...the more alive you will become."

The Mission: The second tree must be the center. Make it the center of your life and center everything else around it. Partake and live of its fruit.

Genesis 2:16–17; Galatians 3:13

The Tree

THE TWO WATERS

THE PROMISED LAND has two seas," said the teacher. "One is called the Kinneret, or the Sea of Galilee. The Sea of Galilee receives its water on its northern end from the inflow of the Jordan River. On its other end is its outflow. There it becomes again the Jordan River flowing southward."

"And the other sea?"

"The other is called the Sea of Salt, or the Sea of Death."

"The Dead Sea."

"Yes," he said. "It's called the Dead Sea because virtually nothing can live there. There's no fish and no vegetation. Its salt and minerals prevent life from growing."

"And where does the Dead Sea get its water from?" I asked.

"From the Jordan River and the Sea of Galilee."

"So it's the same water."

"Yes," he said.

"Then why is it dead?" I asked.

"The difference is that the Dead Sea only has one opening to the north where it receives water from Jordan. But it has no outlet. The water only pours in . . . and becomes dead. But the water of the Galilee is alive, freshwater filled with fish. And yet the very same water flows between the two. So how can the same water produce life in one place and death in the other?"

"Because of the outlets," I answered.

"That's right," said the teacher. "But why?"

"I don't know. I was only guessing."

"The Sea of Galilee is always giving what it receives. It's always flowing. But the Dead Sea only receives and never gives. So the life that gives of what it receives, the life that always blesses others, that life is the Sea of Galilee. Its waters are always fresh. It's always filled with life. But the life that only takes and doesn't give, that life becomes dead and barren . . . and all with the same waters. You see," said the teacher, "it's not what you have in this life, how much or how little, that, in the end, will matter. It's what you do with what you have. If you only take, the waters become dead and your life becomes the Dead Sea. But if you give, then the waters become alive and your life becomes . . . the Sea of Galilee."

The Mission: Live this day after the pattern of the Sea of Galilee, always receiving and always giving. Live to be a blessing in the flowing of His love.

Proverbs 11:24; Matthew 10:8; Luke 6:38; 2 Corinthians 9:6–11

The Waters of Zion

THE POEM OF GOD

THE TEACHER WAS sitting on a rock by the campfire. I was sitting on another to his right. He was reciting the words of a poem in a language I didn't recognize. The words didn't rhyme, but I could tell it was a poem by its structure, its rhythm and flow, and by the way he was reciting it.

"You know it's a poem," he said.

"Yes."

"What is a poem?" he asked. "How would you define it?"

"I would say it's a piece of writing that has a rhythm to it, that flows like a song without music."

"Have you ever heard of the Poem of God?"

"No," I replied. "I've never heard of it. I didn't know He wrote poetry."

"Not exactly," he said, "but there is a Poem of God."

"What is it?"

"It is written in the Scriptures, 'We are His workmanship...'"

"I don't see it."

"You wouldn't in English," he said. "But in the original Greek it says we are His *poiema*, which means that which is made, something fashioned, crafted together, someone's workmanship, as in a masterpiece."

"And the connection to poetry?"

"From *poiema* comes the word *poem*."

"Then the Poem of God is..."

"You."

"Me?"

"If you become His work. You see, you can either live trying to make your life your own work, or you can let your life become His workmanship. A poem can't write itself or lead itself. It must be written and led by its author. It must flow from its author's heart. So to become the Poem of God, you let your life emanate from the Author of your life. You let it flow out of the heart of God. You follow His will above your own, and His plan above your own. You let His Spirit move you and His love become the impulse of all you do. Then your life will flow as it was meant to flow, with rhyme and beauty, and you'll become His masterwork...the Poem of God."

The Mission: Let your life this day be led and written by God. Move at the impulse of the Author and in His flow. Live as the Poem of God.

Isaiah 43:1; Jeremiah 29:11; Ephesians 2:10

The Poem of God

EEM-ANU-EL

I'M GOING TO teach you how to speak Hebrew," said the teacher, "or at least one sentence."

"I'm ready."

"The Hebrew word for *with* is *eem*. And the word for *us* is *anu*."

"Eem...anu," I said.

"And the word for *God* is *El*."

"El."

"So how would you say 'With us is God'?" he asked.

"Eem...anu...El."

"Say it again."

"Eem...anu...El. Eem anu El...Immanuel!"

"Yes, Immanuel. So Isaiah prophesied of Messiah, 'A virgin shall conceive and give birth to a child and shall call Him Immanuel.'"

"The Name of Messiah."

"And more than a name. In Hebrew, it's a sentence. It's a declaration, a reality. It's the reality of Messiah. His very life on earth was this Hebrew sentence, a declaration in Hebrew—eem anu El."

"How was His life a sentence?" I asked.

"When He was sorrowful. Who was it who was sorrowful?"

"Immanuel."

"It was Immanuel in sorrow," said the teacher, "Eem anu El in sorrow. It forms a sentence: 'God is with us in sorrow.' And when He was in the boat on the Sea of Galilee in the midst of the storm, it was Immanuel in the storm. Eem anu El in the storm. It forms another sentence: 'God is with us in the storm.' And when He was despised and rejected of men, it was eem anu El in rejection."

"God is with us in rejection," I replied.

"When He hung on the cross in judgment, it was eem anu El in judgment."

"God is with us in judgment."

"And when He ascended to heaven, where He is, it is eem anu El forever."

"God is with us forever."

"Immanuel came into the world and to every circumstance of life, so that we could say, 'At all times, in all places, in every circumstance...eem anu El, God is with us...always.'"

The Mission: Today, practice the Hebrew of His name. In every circumstance speak and fathom the reality of eem anu El—God is with you, always.

Isaiah 7:14; Matthew 1:21–25; Luke 8:22–25

Immanuel I-II

BEYOND THE SPEED OF LIGHT

IT WAS NIGHT. The moon was full. The teacher had led me to the edge of a great desert canyon, in the middle of which was a dried-up riverbed. One could see what was in the canyon by the light of the moon.

"Shout," he said. "Shout into the canyon. Shout anything you want."

So I turned to the canyon and at the top of my lungs shouted, "I'm shouting into a canyon!"

The words echoed against the distant rocks.

"Notice the delay," said the teacher. "Why is there a delay?"

"Because it's echoing against the walls of the canyon."

"Because," he said, "it takes time. It takes time for the sound of your voice to travel to the walls of the canyon. And not just what you hear with your ears, but what you see with your eyes."

"What do you mean?"

"Look up into the sky. Can you see the stars?"

"Of course."

"Not really," he replied. "It takes years and years for the light to reach your eyes. You're not seeing what is, but what was. You're seeing what was years ago. You're seeing the past."

"But when I look at things on earth, I see the present."

"No," he said, "you don't. Look at the canyon. What you're seeing is its light. The light takes time to reach your eyes. Even if an instant, it takes time. So you never see what is, only what was. The moment you see it, it's already past. You only see the past, what was, never what is."

"But then you can never see the Truth?"

"Not with your eyes," he said. "It's beyond sound and light."

"Then how?"

"The only way to see the Truth, then, is to see without sight...to see by faith...to perceive that which is beyond perception, to know beyond sensing. For that which is seen is passing away, but that which is unseen is forever...Live by faith and, by faith alone, you will see the Real."

The Mission: Live today not by what you see, but beyond your seeing, beyond your hearing, and beyond your sensing. Live by the unseen—by faith.

Habakkuk 2:2–4; 2 Corinthians 4:18; 5:7

THE PRIESTS OF THE OFFERING

TEACHER," I SAID, "I have a question. If the death of Messiah was ordained by God, an event of the highest holiness, why did it happen through such unholy means?"

"How do you know that the means weren't holy?" he asked.

"It happened through evil men, through bribery, treachery, brutality, and murder...evil."

"In ancient Israel, who were the ones ordained by God to offer up the sacrifices?" he asked.

"The priesthood," I said, "the sons of Aaron."

"And who were the key people involved in delivering Messiah to his death?"

"The Sanhedrin."

"Led by the high priest and including chief priests of the Temple, the sons of Aaron, the same ones ordained by God to offer up the sacrifices. Why were they so obsessed with Messiah? They were the priests and He was the Lamb, the sacrifice. So they were the ones to initiate His death. That was their ministry and calling. Only they could deliver the Lamb of God to His death. That's why they conspired and arrested Him and handed Him over to the Romans to be crucified. It was *their ministry* to offer up the sacrifice."

"So they killed him because they were the priests and He was the sacrifice?"

"Not because they knew it, but nevertheless, because they were the ones ordained to do so. And beyond the Sanhedrin, it was the high priest who, alone, was ordained to offer up the most holy sacrifice, the atonement by which the nation's sins were forgiven. And who was it that presided over the Sanhedrin and was more than anyone else responsible for delivering Messiah to his death? The high priest. His intention was murder. Yet he was the one appointed in the Law to offer up the sacrifice. Messiah was the sacrifice. So it was the high priest who had to offer Him up."

"But they were evil," I said, "and their motives and actions were corrupt."

"And yet through their actions came salvation," he said. "The world is filled with evil, with the imperfect, and the wrong. But God causes all of these things, the wrong, the imperfect, and the evil, to work together for the good, the holy, and the perfect...in this world and in your life. The tears, the crises, the heartbreaks, the evil, and all the wrong will, in the end, become the priests of the offering, to fulfill the sacred purposes and blessings God has ordained for your life."

The Mission: What or who in this world is against you or working for evil? Commit it to God. And give thanks beforehand that He will turn it for good.

Leviticus 16; Matthew 20:18; Romans 8:28

The Good Friday Sacrifice Mysteries

SHEPHERDLESSNESS

WE WERE SITTING on a hill, watching a shepherd tend his flock.

"The shepherd is their provider," said the teacher, "their leader and their protection from predators. But what if the shepherd was struck down? Or what if the sheep departed from the shepherd? What would happen?"

"The flock would be scattered. They would wander the wilderness with no protection. They would be attacked, devoured."

"What people's history, more than any other, is the manifestation of that phenomenon, that very picture—a flock that was once together, then scattered throughout the world as sheep without their shepherd, wandering the earth with no one to protect them, attacked by their predators, wounded, and ravaged? What people more than any other have dwelt on this planet as a shepherdless flock?"

"The children of Israel...the Jewish people...more than any other."

"And do you know which people of all peoples are called in Scripture the flock of God? The Jewish people. And yet for two thousand years they've borne all the signs of a scattered flock, separated from its shepherd. So if they are the shepherdless, then who is the missing shepherd of whom their wanderings and shepherdlessness bear witness?"

"The Messiah, the protector of Israel, Yeshua...Jesus."

"And who is it that said to them, 'I am the Good Shepherd'? And who is it that happens to be the same One who was struck down in their midst, and from whom they have been separated? And how long have they been separated from Him? Two thousand years. And how long has it been that they've wandered the earth and borne the signs of shepherdlessness? The same two thousand years. And so it is written in the Hebrew Prophets: 'Strike the shepherd and the sheep will be scattered.' It is because He is the true Shepherd, their protection, their defense, their provider, and their keeper, the Messiah. And so it is for all of us; if we live without Him we end up wandering this life, lost, unprotected, and without hope, and bear the signs of shepherdlessness. But it is foretold that in the end the people of Israel will return to their Shepherd, and He will bind up their brokenness, heal their wounds, and keep them as a shepherd keeps his flock. And so it will be for each of us, for each wandering sheep that returns. It will be gathered in the Shepherd's arms."

The Mission: Cease from all straying. Draw near to your Shepherd. Be fed from His hands. Rest in the protection and the tender love of His arms.

Isaiah 40:11; Ezekiel 34:5–16; Zechariah 13:7; John 10:11–16

Strike the Shepherd

THE AKEDAH MYSTERY

"**H**AVE YOU EVER heard of the *akedah*?" asked the teacher. "It's the offering up of Isaac by his father, Abraham."

"I've heard of it," I said, "but I never understood why it happened."

"It was a test," he said, "but also a mystery. At the end of the test God sealed His covenant with Abraham. In such a covenant, each party had to be willing to do what the other was willing to do. Now let's open up the mystery. Abraham was willing to offer up his son as a sacrifice. Therefore..."

"Therefore, God," I replied, "would have to be willing to offer up His Son as a sacrifice."

"The father brings his son on a donkey," said the teacher, "to the land of the sacrifice."

"So then God would bring His Son on a donkey to the land of the sacrifice...Palm Sunday...Messiah is brought on a donkey to the place of the sacrifice."

"The father places the wood of the sacrifice on his son's shoulder..."

"God would place the wood of the sacrifice, the cross, on Messiah's shoulders."

"The son carries the wood up the mountain to the place of the sacrifice..."

"Messiah carries the wood to the place of the sacrifice."

"The father lays his son upon the wood and binds him to it."

"The Messiah is laid on the wood of the cross and bound to it."

"The father lifts up the knife of sacrifice but is stopped..."

"And so the knife, the judgment of God is lifted up...but is not stopped. Messiah is killed on the wood of the sacrifice."

"Do you know what appears in this account for the first time in all of Scripture?"

"No."

"The word *love*. The first *love* in the Bible is from this account, the love of the father for the son...just as the first love in existence was that of the Father for the Son. And yet the Father was willing to offer up the Son of His love, to save us. And what does that reveal? If God offered up the Son of His love to save you, then He must love you with the same love with which He loved the Son. As it is written, 'God so loved the world that He gave His only begotten Son, that whoever believes in Him should not perish but have everlasting life.' So you don't ever have to wonder how much God loves you. The sign is already there on the wood of the sacrifice...As much as He loves His only begotten Son...the greatest love in all existence...that's how much He loves you."

The Mission: Today, ponder the price of love that was paid for you, and live your life likewise as a sacrifice of love to Him.

Genesis 22; John 3:16

The Moriah Miracle

THE BRIDEGROOM'S VISITATION

"COME," SAID THE teacher. "We're going to see the beginning of a wedding."
We journeyed through the desert until we arrived at the tent village of the bridegroom where we watched the events unfold as uninvited and mostly unnoticed guests. It all focused on a young man and the entourage that surrounded and followed him.

"That's the bridegroom," said the teacher, "with his relatives and friends."

The procession made its way to the end of the camp where the bridegroom got on a camel and continued, while the others followed behind on foot. We joined in. No one seemed to mind. We walked for about half an hour until we arrived at our destination, another tent village where a small crowd was waiting. The bridegroom dismounted the camel, was welcomed by the group, and then led to one of the tents.

"What you just witnessed," said the teacher, "was the journey of the bridegroom. It goes back to the Hebrew wedding of ancient times. In order for there to be a marriage, the bridegroom had to first make a journey from his house to the house of the bride. It didn't matter where she lived, across the camp or across the desert; wherever she was, he had to journey to her."

"And there's a mystery in it?" I asked.

"The bridegroom is a shadow of God. And we are each born to be the bride. But in order for there to be a marriage, the joining of the two, the bridegroom must always journey from his house to the house of the bride. So according to the mystery, two thousand years ago the Bridegroom, God, undertook the journey of the bridegroom. He traveled not across a city or desert, but across time and space...from heaven, the house of the Bridegroom, to earth, the house of the bride."

"Does the bride ever journey to the bridegroom?" I asked.

"Never," he replied. "And so in the same way, you can never reach God or heaven on your own. But you don't have to. It is the Bridegroom who journeys to the bride. It is God who journeys to you. He comes to your tent, to your life...no matter where you are, no matter what your life is like, no matter how far away you are from Him. He still comes to your house, to wherever you are. And no matter where you find yourself, He will be the One who comes to you...and who knocks on the door of your heart."

"And what does the bride do?" I asked. "What are we supposed to do?"

"Open up," said the teacher. "You open up...and you let Him in."

The Mission: Today, encounter the Bridegroom. But instead of trying to reach Him, let Him reach you, just where you are, just as you are.

Matthew 25:1–13; John 3:29; 16:28

The Visit of the Bridegroom

THE CELESTIAL CURRENCY EXCHANGE

WE WERE SITTING in his study when the teacher got up from his desk, went over to one of his cabinets, opened the drawer, pulled out a container the size of a shoebox, placed it on his desk, and asked me to open it.

"Go ahead," said the teacher. "Take them out. Look at them."

So I did. The box was filled with the paper currency of many nations.

"Souvenirs," he said, "of my travels in the nations. It probably surprises you, but I haven't always been here."

He paused for a moment while I put the paper bill I was examining back in the box.

"If you travel to different nations," he said, "you have to convert the currency of the place you're leaving into the currency of your destination. Now what if you were going to a place from which you would never return? And what if in that place your native currency was of no value? And what if it was impossible to transport anything from your native land to that place? What would you do?"

"Convert everything I had into the currency of my destination because anything not converted would be lost."

"And where would you do all the converting?"

"I'd have to do it my native land, before I left on the journey."

"Yes," said the teacher. "And this is why currency conversion is critical for the children of the kingdom. You see, we're all going on a journey. We're all leaving the land of our origins for another realm. And the currency of the earth, of all we possess on earth, is of no value there. And we can't bring any of it with us. And so whatever earthly currency we hold on to, we lose. But who are the wise? They are the ones who in the days before the journey make the exchange. They convert their earthly currency into heavenly currency."

"How?" I asked. "How do you make the exchange?"

"You give your earthly currency, what you possess in this world, to the purposes of heaven, to the kingdom. And you do so without getting any earthly return. And since no one knows the exact time of their departure, you make the most of your time and convert as much as you can into the heavenly currency. For it is only wisdom," said the teacher, "to exchange that which you can never keep to obtain that which you can never lose."

The Mission: Today, start your heavenly currency exchange. Give of your time, your energy, your wealth, and your love to the purposes of heaven.

Proverbs 10:2; 19:17; Matthew 6:19–21

Tithes to Jerusalem

THE WAY OF THE YASHAR

WE WERE STANDING on a ridge overlooking a vast desert expanse. The teacher began reciting the words of the prophet: "'The voice of one crying out in the wilderness, "Prepare the way of the Lord, make straight in the desert a highway for our God."' How does the prophet describe the way of God?"

"The way of God is straight," I replied.

"That's right," he said. "And in physics, in geometry, in space, what is the shortest distance between two points?"

"A straight line."

"And not just in the physical realm, but in the spiritual realm as well. The way to walk the path of God is to walk straight."

"How do you walk straight in the spiritual realm?"

"A straight line is a consistent line. It has only one direction. The opposite of a straight line is a crooked or wavering line, a line that's inconsistent and follows more than one direction. But the more the line wavers, the longer it takes to get to the same point. So the more you waver on your path in God, the more you veer back and forth, the more time it takes, the more effort you must put in, and the more energy you must expend to get to the same place. And the less you will go forward. And in the end, the wavering and crooked road is the much harder path, and the straight path, the much easier. For it is the straight path that takes less time, with less effort and less energy spent. And it's the straight path that allows you to go farther."

"How exactly do you apply that in the spiritual realm?"

"You walk with a single aim, a single motive, a single goal, and a single heart. You eliminate any wavering to the right or the left of that goal. And whatever doesn't line up with your calling, with your faith, with your convictions, and your purpose, you eliminate it from your life. You eliminate it from your actions, your words, your thoughts. When you walk straight, everything lines up—your words with your actions, your actions with your faith, your life with your heart. And one more thing," he said, "In the prophecy, the word *straight* is the Hebrew *yashar*. And *yashar* also means good, upright, pleasant, and prosperous. And those are the blessings that are given to those who 'make straight' their path and walk in the way of the yashar."

The Mission: Today, make it your aim to eliminate all wavering in your life and whatever is not in line with God's will. Walk and live in a straight line.

Isaiah 40:3–5; Hebrews 12:13

Making Straight the Crook

THE IMPOSSIBILITY OF EXISTENCE

IT WAS NIGHT. We were outside under a clear, star-filled sky.

"The law of cause and effect," he said. "It lies at the foundation of science, logic, and reason: For every effect, there must be a cause. For every phenomenon, there must be a reason. Nothing can exist without a cause behind it. It would go against reason, science, and logic. You cannot have something from nothing. Everything has to have a cause."

"That sounds logical enough," I said.

"But if everything has a cause, then what is the cause for everything? What is the cause for the universe? The universe exists. So, what is the cause behind its existence? What caused the universe itself? What caused everything to exist?"

"The big bang?" I said.

"And what caused the big bang? If it's the beginning, then it came from nothing. But if it came from nothing, it has no cause. And if it has no cause, then it can't exist. Then it's magic."

"But what if the universe always was?"

"If it always was, then it had no beginning. And if it has no beginning, then it never started. And if it never started, it can't exist. Again...magic. Either the universe began from nothing and thus cannot exist, or it has no beginning and never began, in which case it can't exist."

"So we can't exist...but we do exist. Then what's the answer?"

"The answer can only be that which cannot be explained yet explains all things...that which you cannot make sense of, yet which makes sense of all things...Only an uncaused cause could cause the universe to exist. And only that which exists beyond the laws of the universe could cause the laws of the universe to exist."

"Which is..."

"God," said the teacher. "By definition, it is God, I Am, the One you can't explain but who explains all things. It is His unfathomability that causes our impossibility to exist. The universe can never make sense of itself by itself. Nor can you ever make sense of your life by your life...or by your life give your life meaning. The only way to find the meaning and purpose of your life is to find it in a mystery...the mystery of Him...and to make that mystery the cause of everything you do and the reason for everything you are."

The Mission: Today, ponder the miracle of every moment you have. Treasure each moment and make the most of it. And make Him the cause of all you do.

Genesis 1:1–2; John 1:1 3; Hebrews 11:3

The Unknowable Love

THE KNEELING GOD

IT WAS A time of worship. Everyone was gathered under the large open-air tent, praying, worshipping, singing, being silent, as each was led. In the midst of it all, I noticed the teacher dropping to his knees and staying on his knees for some time in silence. It struck me. Later that day, when I saw him outside with no one around, I approached him.

"I noticed you were kneeling during worship," I said. "I never understood the purpose of it. Why does one kneel?"

"To kneel," he said, "is to lower yourself, to humble yourself. Kneeling is an act of submission. You're submitting to another. I was led to kneel down, to humble myself before the Almighty, to submit myself to His will."

"I've never heard it explained that way before."

"Do you know what the word for *bless* is in the Hebrew Scriptures?"

"I have no idea."

"*Barach*. It means *to bless* but it also means *to kneel*. And who is it that blesses more than anyone else? Whose nature is it to bless?"

"God."

"And what is the greatest blessing He gave?"

"Salvation...redemption...eternal life."

"So God's nature is to bless, and the greatest blessing He could give is the blessing of salvation. But to bless is to barach, and to barach is to kneel, and to kneel is to lower yourself."

"So for God to give us the blessing of salvation, He has to lower Himself..."

"Yes. And to give us the greatest blessing," said the teacher, "would require the greatest lowering of Himself, the greatest descending."

"So He descended to this world and humbled Himself in the form of man."

"Yes, and to kneel is also to submit. And so He submitted Himself to man's mockery, abuse, and condemnation. He submitted Himself to judgment, to crucifixion, and to death—the ultimate lowering... the cosmic kneeling...the kneeling of God. And yet in the kneeling of God, comes the barach, the blessing, salvation. To bless is to kneel. And He who kneels is He who blesses. And by His kneeling...we are blessed. And in light of such blessing we can do nothing less than kneel before Him and bow down our lives."

The Mission: Whom do you need to bless? Be a blessing to them today. As God humbled Himself to bless you, humble yourself likewise, to become a blessing to others.

Psalm 95:6–8; Philippians 2:4–10; James 4:6–10

The Purple Crimson King I–II

THE MYSTERY OF EPHRATAH

WE SAT AROUND a low wooden table on which rested an oil lamp, a metal goblet, and a plate with two pieces of matzah, unleavened bread.

"Every Passover Seder," said the teacher, "has these two elements, the bread and the wine...so too at the Last Supper, Messiah's last Passover on earth."

He then lifted up the plate with the unleavened bread.

"In Hebrew, the word for *bread* is *lechem*. Messiah took the bread, and then said an ancient Hebrew blessing that gives thanks for lechem." The teacher then recited the Hebrew blessing, and we partook of the bread together. "Then," said the teacher, "Messiah took the cup and gave thanks. He said the ancient Hebrew blessing over the *peree hagafen*, the fruit of the vine, then gave the cup to His disciples as a symbol of His blood." The teacher then recited the Hebrew blessing over the cup, and we partook.

"The two elements," said the teacher, "the bread and the fruit of the vine, the lechem and the peree, the lechem, representing His body, and the peree, representing His blood. And now a question: When was His body and blood first revealed? When did He first appear in flesh and blood?"

"At the nativity," I said, "in Bethlehem."

"And what is Bethlehem? *Bethlehem* means the Place of Lechem, the House of Bread. So the place of His birth, where He first appeared in bodily form, contains the same word He spoke over the bread that represented His body, *lechem,* Bethlehem. But Bethlehem had another name," said the teacher. "It was also called *Ephratah*, 'Bethlehem Ephratah.' Do you know where *Ephratah* comes from? It comes from the same word from which we get *peree*, the same word He spoke over the cup that represented His blood. So the place of His birth, where He first appeared in flesh and blood, contains the same word He spoke over the wine that represented His blood, *peree*."

"So the place where Messiah first appeared in flesh and blood bears the name of the symbols of His flesh and blood, Bethlehem Ephratah, the bread and the fruit of the vine. It was all there from the beginning."

"Yes," said the teacher, "as His death was there from His birth. For the sacrifice comes to be sacrificed. So He lived His life as a gift, to be given, a sacrifice of love...Let us do likewise."

The Mission: What gifts, resources, and abilities do you possess? Turn each one into a gift to be given and seek today every chance to give of them.

Micah 5:2; Luke 22:14–20

Ephratah: The Mystery

NISAN

WE WERE WALKING along a barren plain when he stopped to pick up a desert flower that had just blossomed.

"Even in the desert," said the teacher, "you can find blossoms."

"It's beautiful," I replied.

"The word for *winter* in the Scriptures is the Hebrew *setav. Setav* means *the season of hiding* or *the time of darkness*. The winter is the season of darkness, barrenness, and death. But each year, the winter ends with the coming of the Hebrew month of Nisan."

"In the spring."

"Yes," said the teacher. "Nisan is the month that ends the season of darkness, that breaks the death of winter. Nisan is the month when the earth again bears its fruit, and its flowers again begin to blossom. Nisan is the month of new life. In fact, the word *nisan* means the beginning. Nisan is the month when the sacred Hebrew year begins anew."

"Why is that significant?"

"Because Nisan is the month of redemption, the month of Messiah. It's the month Messiah chose to enter Jerusalem, to die on the cross, and to rise from death to life. Why do you think it all happened in Nisan?"

"Because Nisan is the time of new beginning. So when Messiah comes, it must be a new beginning. So it must be Nisan. And Nisan is the season of new life. So Messiah's coming brings new life...a new birth."

"Yes," said the teacher. "And what else does Nisan do?"

"It ends the winter."

"What winter would be ended?" he asked.

"Our winter," I said. "The winter of our lives. The season of our darkness...the time of our hiding...the days of living in the shadows...the season of our barrenness...when our life can't bear the fruit it was meant to bear."

"Yes," said the teacher, "Messiah's coming is our Nisan, that which ends the winter of our lives and begins the spring of our lives. That's the power of Messiah, the power of Nisan. And for those in Messiah...it is always Nisan. And that's where we must always stay, in the season of new life, of new beginnings, of blossoming, and the end of winter."

The Mission: Break out of the winter and out of every darkness, and bear the fruit your life was to bear. Live in the power of Nisan.

Song of Solomon 2:8–13; 2 Corinthians 5:17

Nisan

THE SIMILITUDE

THERE HAD BEEN a storm that night. The teacher met with me in the morning. We sat outside the main building. We noticed a rainbow in the sky.

"Did you know that the rainbow surrounds the throne of God?" he asked.

"No," I replied. "Where does it say that?"

"In the Book of Ezekiel: 'Like the appearance of a rainbow in the clouds on a rainy day, so was the radiance around Him.'"

"Why didn't Ezekiel just say 'rainbow' instead of 'like the appearance of a rainbow'?"

"He didn't say 'throne' either but 'the likeness' or 'similitude' of a throne. 'And upon the likeness of the throne,' he writes, 'was the similitude as the appearance of a man.' Now listen to how he sums it all up: 'This was the appearance of the similitude of the glory of the Lord.' It wasn't the glory of the Lord. It was the *similitude* of the glory of the Lord...and not quite that. It was the *appearance* of the similitude of the glory of the Lord."

"What does it all mean?" I asked.

"Here is the prophet Ezekiel being given a vision of the glory of God. And yet he can only speak of likenesses and appearances and similitudes and resemblances. What does that reveal? It reveals that no matter how hard he tried, he couldn't describe it. He could only speak of what it appeared to be like. So it is with God. No matter what we use to describe Him, He's still beyond it. No word can contain Him...not the highest praise, not the deepest thought, not the most sophisticated theology. They can't even begin to grasp at His similitude. If even the prophet Ezekiel, to whom God showed visions of His glory, could not even describe, much less comprehend, what he was seeing, how can we?"

"How do I apply this?"

"Since God is always more than you think He is, then there's always more for you to find. Therefore, you must seek Him every day and every moment. Never stop seeking, never stop learning, never stop drawing nearer and nearer. Draw near to Him with an open heart, and He will meet you...beyond the appearance of the likeness of the similitude."

The Mission: Whatever you know of God, He's more and beyond it. So seek today to find the more and beyond of God than you have yet known.

Ezekiel 1:26–28; Philippians 3:10

The Stranger

THE PORTABLE MOUNTAINTOP

HE LED ME to the top of a mountain, a stark, jagged mountain. When we reached the summit, we looked out. The view was breathtaking. The mountain was surrounded by a landscape of desert plains and more mountains, similarly stark, jagged, and dramatic, as far as one could see.

"It was on a mountain like this," said the teacher, "that the glory of God descended in front of the nation of Israel...on Mount Sinai, one of the great high points of Israel's history, literally a mountaintop experience. And then the moment passed. But before they moved on from Sinai, God told them to build the tent that would be called the Tabernacle. And He would dwell within it and be continually in their midst. So they built it. And God's presence and glory that appeared on the mountaintop now descended to the plain. The glory would now be with them in the wilderness, in their everyday life, and in their journeying. Everywhere they went, God's presence and glory was with them. What does this reveal?"

"God's will is to come down to earth to dwell with us."

"And so He did. In the opening of the Gospel of John, His coming down is recorded this way: 'And the Word became flesh and dwelt among us.' But in the original language it says that the Word *tabernacled* with us. In other words, He 'pitched His tent among us' just as He did at Mount Sinai. What does this mean?"

"It means that every day of our lives, we can dwell in His presence."

"Yes," he said. "It means you can dwell in the glory of God every day of your life. In the natural, life is a series of ups and downs, the ups and downs of circumstances, and the ups and downs of emotion. But in God, the up has come down. Heaven has come to earth. The mountaintop has come down to the valley. What that means is that even in the lowest places of your life, you can still dwell on the heights. And no matter where you are, even in the darkest valley, you can still dwell in the glory of the mountaintop."

"How?" I asked.

"By entering into the Tabernacle, by entering into communion with Him, in prayer, in worship, in just dwelling with Him, every day, deep in His presence. Do that, and no matter where you are, you will dwell in the glory of the heights. Think about it. He's given you a most amazing thing to have in every moment of your life...He's given you a portable mountaintop."

The Mission: Today, even in the most unlikely or lowest of circumstances, set up your portable mountaintop and dwell with God on the heights.

Exodus 25:8; John 1:14

THE MYSTERY OF THE EIGHTH DAY

HE TOOK ME back into the Chambers of Scrolls, approached the ark, removed the scroll, unrolled it on the table to the passage he was looking for, then began translating it aloud: "'You will celebrate the feast of the Lord for seven days, with a complete rest on the first day and a complete rest on the eighth day.' It's speaking of the Feast of Tabernacles," he said. "But there's something strange about it. It says you will celebrate the feast for seven days, with a rest on the Eighth Day. How do you get an Eighth Day from a seven-day feast? Seven is the number of the days in the feast and the days of creation. Every week there are seven days. So then what is the Eighth Day?"

"There is no Eighth Day."

"No," said the teacher. "And yet there is. If the seventh day speaks of the end, then of what does the Eighth Day speak?"

"The day after the end?"

"Yes," said the teacher. "Eight speaks of that which comes after the end."

"But nothing can come after the end...or it wouldn't be the end."

"Exactly," he replied. "That's the point. It contradicts everything else. Seven is the number of the days of the creation. But eight is the number that transcends the creation, that breaks out of time...the number beyond numbers, of time beyond time."

"And so what exactly happens on the Eighth Day of the feast?"

"It's a mystery," he said. "It's called *Shemini Atzeret*. It means the Gathering of the Eighth Day. The Feast of Tabernacles is the last of the holy days appointed by God, the final feast. So it speaks of the end, the end of days."

"The end of time," I said, "and then comes the Eighth Day."

"It's the very last day appointed by God...the mystery day. And those who belong to God belong to the Eighth Day. And when the creation ends, they will enter it...the day beyond days, when the finite yields to the infinite...and its limitations are no more...the age beyond ages...eternity."

He paused for a moment before continuing, "And one more secret."

"What?"

"Those who live in the Spirit can partake of the Eighth Day...even now."

"How?"

"Go beyond the end...beyond the end of yourself...and you'll find out."

The Mission: Seek today to live beyond your circumstances, beyond the world, beyond the finite, in the day beyond days, in the Eighth Day.

Leviticus 23:39; Romans 6:11; 2 Corinthians 5:1–6; Revelation 20:11

The Mystery of the Eighth Day I–III

THE LAND OF GEZARAH

WE WERE SITTING on the ridge of a mountain we had often visited and gazing out into the distance. The teacher was holding a parchment.

"This is the command concerning the scapegoat, how it was to be led out into the wilderness."

He began reading it.

"'He shall send away the goat by the hand of a man who stands in readiness into the wilderness. And the goat will bear upon himself all the iniquities to a land not inhabited . . . '

"So where did the goat go?" asked the teacher.

"Into the wilderness," I replied.

"To a 'land not inhabited.' It's this," he said, as he pointed to one of the words on the parchment. "It's the word *gezarah*. The scapegoat had to be led to the land of gezarah."

"What's the land of gezarah?"

"Gezarah comes from the root word *gazar*. *Gazar* means cut off, excluded, or destroyed. So the land of gezarah means a place that is cut off, excluded, uninhabited, a place where no one can dwell."

"No one except the scapegoat."

"Yes," he replied. "And when Isaiah prophesied of Messiah's death, he used the same word. He said, 'He was cut off out of the land of the living for the transgression of My people to whom the stroke was due.' The words *cut off* are a translation of *gazar*, as in the land of gezarah."

"So then, in some way, the Messiah goes to a land cut off, excluded, destroyed, uninhabited, and where no one can dwell."

"As the scapegoat carries the sins of the people to the land of gezarah."

"So then, Messiah carries our sins to the land of gezarah."

"And what does that mean," asked the teacher, "that He carried your sins to the land of gezarah?"

"It means . . . my sins are cut off. And no one can go to where they are."

"Yes," said the teacher, "they are where no one can dwell. No one can visit them . . . not even you. So *you* can never go there, to visit them or to dwell with them. They're gone, taken away, excluded, and cut off . . . forever . . . in the land of gezarah."

The Mission: Say good-bye to your sins, to your guilt, to your past, and to all that has been removed. Let it go and cut it off forever—in the land of gezarah.

Leviticus 16:21–22; Psalm 103:12; Isaiah 44:22; 53:8

Azazel

THE SHADOW

IT WAS A dark night. There was no moon. And only a few stars could be seen in the desert sky...just darkness and the howling of the cold night winds.

"Are you afraid of the dark?" asked the teacher.

"Sometimes," I replied.

"In the Scriptures, darkness is a symbol of evil. Darkness is an absence, the absence of light. So too is evil..."

"Evil is an absence?"

"Evil is not so much a reality as the absence of a reality. It is not of the creation, but a denial of creation, a negation of what is, the negation of God. And so it can't exist on its own, but only in opposition to existence."

"What does that mean?"

"Truth exists on its own. It just is. But a lie cannot exist without truth. A lie is a twisting of the truth and so it can only exist by the truth, and in the denial of it. So too life exists without death. But death cannot exist without life. Death only exists as the negation of life. And good can exist without evil. But evil cannot exist without good. Evil is the denial of the good."

"It's the force of opposition," I said.

"Yes," he replied, "and in Hebrew that which opposes, that which goes against, is called the *sahtan*."

"Sahtan," I repeated, and paused until it hit me. "Satan! You can have God without Satan, but you can't have Satan without God."

"Yes," he said. "So we can only discern darkness, because light exists, and what is false because the true exists, and what is wrong because the right exists. So then evil is actually..."

"A witness," I said, "a hostile witness, that, despite itself, testifies of the truth."

"Yes. The witness of a shadow. The darkness of falsehood bears witness that the Truth exists. The darkness of hatred bears witness that Love exists. And the darkness of evil bears witness that God exists. So never let your heart lose its focus by dwelling on evil. But seek always to see the Good, which is always there, beyond it and above it, on the throne, to which even evil must bear witness and bow its knee."

The Mission: Today, practice seeing through the darkness of every problem or evil that confronts you—to the good that lies beyond it.

John 3:20–21; 8:24; 18:37

The Strategies of Warfare I–IV

THE SECRET ISRAEL

WE WERE WATCHING a shepherd leading his flock through a long canyon when we noticed a second flock and shepherd descending the bordering hills to join them. The two flocks became one.

"Two peoples of God," said the teacher, "have dwelt on the earth for the last two thousand years: the children of Israel, the Jewish people, and the followers of Messiah, the Christians, the church. For most of that time they have been at enmity with each other, each seeing the other as an alien presence. But the two are joined together in a mystery. Messiah is the Shepherd of Israel. But He is also the Shepherd of those who follow Him from all nations, the church. So He told His Jewish disciples: 'I have other sheep that are not of this pen...'"

"The church and Israel are two flocks with one Shepherd, the Messiah."

"But the mystery goes deeper," said the teacher. "In the Book of Ephesians it is written that the one who follows Messiah, the true Christian, has become a fellow citizen in the commonwealth of Israel. Thus the two are joined together. The church, in reality, is a Jewish entity. The church doesn't replace Israel, but complements it. The church is, *in spirit*, Jewish. It is the Israel of Spirit. What the Jewish people are in flesh and blood and in the realm of the physical, the church is in the realm of spirit. To the one people belongs a Promised Land of earth; to the other a Promised Land of heaven. To the one belongs a Jerusalem of mountains and stone; to the other, the heavenly Jerusalem. The one is a people physically gathered out from the nations; the other, a people spiritually gathered. The one is born of the promise through flesh and blood; the other, born by the Spirit. The one comprises Messiah's family of flesh and blood; the other, His family by spirit. The one reaps a harvest of fruit and grain; the other a harvest of new life. And as the spirit is joined to the body, so the two are by nature intrinsically bound."

"But the two have been separated," I said.

"Yes," said the teacher, "to the detriment of each. But the consummation of the one will not come without the other, nor the fulfillment of the other without the one. For when the spirit and the body are separated, it is death. But when the spirit and the body are again united, what is it?"

"Life," I said. "It means life from death."

The Mission: Today, seek to find the riches of the Jewish roots of your faith and your secret identity as a spiritual Hebrew, an Israelite of God.

Genesis 12:3; John 10:16; Ephesians 2:11–22

THE BRIDE IN THE TENT

BEHOLD THE *CALAH*," said the teacher, as he drew my attention to a young woman in the tent village. "It's how you say *the bride* in Hebrew. Do you remember when the bridegroom made his visit? It was for her."

"And yet she's still here," I said. "She's the bride but not yet married."

"In the Hebrew wedding, the bridegroom journeys to the house of the bride. There in that house, or tent, the covenant is made. They are from that moment on considered bride and groom, husband and wife. But the bridegroom must then leave the bride and her house and journey back to where he came from. The two are joined in the covenant of marriage. But they don't see each other until the day of the wedding. They spend their time preparing for that day."

"But for the bride, it seems as if nothing's changed. She still lives with her family in that tent. She's still doing her daily chores. Her surroundings are the same. Her life is the same. She's married, but what's changed?"

"*She's* changed," he said. "She is now the calah!"

"I don't understand."

"Two thousand years ago the Bridegroom journeyed to the house of the bride, God journeyed to this world, to our house, to our lives. And, likewise, it was to make a covenant. According to the mystery, the bridegroom must leave the bride's house and return home. So Messiah then left this world to return to heaven. So these now are the days of the separation. The Groom is in His house, heaven. And we, as the bride, are in our house, this world. And if you've said yes to the Bridegroom's covenant, you are as she is. You're still in the same tent, this present world. Things around you may look the same and feel the same. Your life, your circumstances may look unchanged. But something very big *has* changed...you. It is not the tent that has changed, or your world, but you. And so you are no longer of the world. You're *in* the world, but no longer *of* it. You no longer belong to your circumstances, nor to your past, nor to your sins and limitation. No longer are you bound to these things. You don't belong to the world. You belong to the Bridegroom. You're free. You're the calah!"

The Mission: Live this day as the bride in the tent—as one no longer bound by your circumstances, but belonging to the Bridegroom—free of this world.

John 17:9–18; 2 Corinthians 11:12; 1 Peter 2:11–12

The Great Preparation

THE LAW OF THE FALLOW GROUND

WE WERE ON our way back from the city, having finished a number of errands, when we arrived at one of the agricultural settlements. We walked by several fields of grain until we came to an open area that appeared neglected.

"Do you know what this is?" he asked. "It's called the 'fallow ground.' It's the ground purposely left unsown, unreaped, and unharvested. You see, if one works the same land the same way over and over again, the soil becomes depleted and the land grows less and less productive. Therefore, farmers would, every so often, allow a field to rest, to lie fallow, unsown and unreaped. So if we planted on ground that had been allowed to lie fallow, what might we expect to happen?"

"It would become fruitful, more fruitful than other ground?"

"Yes," said the teacher. "And this is the law of the fallow ground, a law that contains one of the most important secrets of living a fruitful life. What is the fallow ground? It's the ground that hasn't been touched, worked, or cultivated. And what is the fallow ground in God? It's the ground that hasn't been touched by God. It's every life, every heart, and every soul, that hasn't allowed God to touch it, that hasn't allowed God's life to enter in. It is, therefore, crucial that you sow the Word and love of God to the fallow, to the lost, the unsaved, the unknowing, to the farthest and the most ungodly—to the fallow ground. And if they receive, they will bear much fruit."

"Does the law of the fallow ground also apply to those who know God?"

"So much so," he said, "that applying it can transform your life. Even for those who know and love the Lord there is fallow ground. Whatever part of your life has not been touched by God's love and truth—that is your fallow ground. Whatever area of your life remains unchanged, unredeemed, ungodly, and dark, whether of actions, thoughts, habits, emotions, or ways—that is your fallow ground. And the law of the fallow ground says that it is that very thing, that very soil, that very area you haven't allowed God to touch and change—that will bear the most fruit. It is that part you must plow, and sow, and water. For it is that ground that is waiting to bear a harvest. As it is written in the Prophets, 'Break up your fallow ground; for it is time to seek the Lord.'"

The Mission: Identify the fallow ground in your life. Open it up to this day, to the touch of God, His Word, and His will. Let it bear its harvest.

Hosea 10:12; Matthew 13:23

Neru Lachem

THE LAMBS OF NISAN

HE TOOK ME back to the Chamber of Scrolls, removed the scroll from the ark, laid it on the table, unrolled it to the passage he was looking for, then began reading or translating it aloud.

"'On the tenth day of this month, each one shall take for himself a lamb...a lamb for a house.' It is one of the most important biblical holy days," he said, "and yet most people have never heard of it."

"What holy day?"

"The tenth day of the Hebrew month of Nisan. The day of the Passover took place on the fifteenth day of Nisan; the tenth of Nisan was the day that the lamb was chosen and taken to the house that would, on Passover, offer it up."

He lifted his eyes from the scroll and turned to me.

"So the Tenth of Nisan is the Day of the Lamb," he said, "the day of its choosing, of its being taken, and of its being identified with the house that would sacrifice it. You know of Palm Sunday?" he asked.

"Of course. It's the day Messiah was led on a donkey into the streets of Jerusalem...greeted by the people with celebration and palm branches."

"Yes, but it's also a day of mystery. If Messiah is the Passover Lamb, then He must also be linked to the Tenth of Nisan."

"So the mystery is..."

"What we call Palm Sunday is, in reality, the Tenth of Nisan, the Day of the Lamb. As the people of Jerusalem were leading the Passover lambs to their homes, Messiah was being led from the Mount of Olives into the city gates. The bringing in of Messiah to the city with palms and hosannas was actually the fulfillment of what had been commanded from ancient times, the bringing in of the lamb. So on the day when the Passover lamb was to be brought to the house, God brought the Lamb of God to His house, to Jerusalem, and to the Temple. And just as the lambs of the Tenth of Nisan had to be sacrificed on Passover by those who dwelt in the house, so too the Lamb of God would be sacrificed on Passover by those who dwelt in Jerusalem. The Lamb of God had to come to the House of God that the blessings of salvation could come. So, it is only when you bring the Lamb home, when you bring Him into the place where you actually live your life, when you bring Him into every room, every closet, and crevice, only then can the fullness of the blessings of salvation begin."

The Mission: Bring home the Lamb to the place you really live your life, and let Him come into every room, closet, dark space, and crevice in your life.

Exodus 12:3; Matthew 21:1–11

The Nisan Lamb

THE CAPERNAUM MYSTERY

DO YOU KNOW where Messiah lived?" asked the teacher.

"Tell me," I replied.

"In Capernaum. Capernaum was the place Messiah dwelt and ministered from. It was to Capernaum that people came from all over Galilee, the sick, the crippled, the blind, the lame, the paralyzed, the fallen, the unholy, the condemned, and the outcast. And it was in Capernaum that He received them and showed them mercy and forgiveness. It was there that He showed them compassion and restored their lives. Capernaum was the center of His ministry. Do you know why it's called Capernaum?"

"No."

"Capernaum was a translation of its real name. The first part, *Caper*, stands for the Hebrew *kaphar* and can be translated as village. The second part, *naum*, stands for the Hebrew name *Nachum*, the same name as the prophet Nahum. So Capernaum could be called 'the village of Nahum.'"

"Why would Messiah choose 'the village of Nahum' as the center of His ministry?"

"It's a mystery. There's no record of any connection between Capernaum and the prophet Nahum. And if there was another Nahum, we have no record of his existence. But there are no accidents. If we go deeper, we find something beautiful. *Nachum* is not just a name; it's a Hebrew word filled with meaning. It means to comfort, to console, and to repent. So *Capernaum* could be translated as 'the village of comfort,' 'the village of repentance,' and 'the village of consolation.' So the center of Messiah's ministry was 'the village of comfort.' That's where the sick were healed, where the sinful were forgiven, where the broken were made whole, and where the outcasts were received."

"And it's where they turned to God," I said. "Capernaum is also the village of repentance."

"Yes," he said. "And it is as we turn to God that we become whole and are comforted. And that's where you will always find Him still."

"In Capernaum?"

"In the village of mercy, repentance, comfort, healing, restoration, and tender love...in Kaphar Nachum."

The Mission: Come to Kaphar Nachum today. Repent of anything not in His will. Then dwell in the comfort of His presence where your miracle awaits.

Isaiah 61:1–3; Matthew 4:13–16, 24

The Hands of Messiah

WHERE YOU GO

WE STOOD IN front of a sandy plain.

"You may not thank me for this," said the teacher.

"For what?" I asked.

"For what you're about to do...which is to walk across this plain...backward."

I complied. Trying my best not to fall, I began walking backward across the plain. But it wasn't long into it that I found myself lying on my back, having tripped over one of the many small bushes that dotted the landscape. After several such falls, the teacher came over to me to help me up.

"OK," he said. "I think it will be enough. Now why did I make you do that?"

"You have the same question as I do."

"We were all created with eyes to face the direction in which we walk. So we walk in the direction in which we look. And where we look, we walk."

"I could have told you that and saved us both the trouble."

"The reason I asked you to do this was not so you would learn that fact, but that you would never forget this truth. The principle is so basic we never think about it. But where you look is where you go. Go against that principle, and it will never end up well. But apply that principle on a larger scale, on the scale of life, and it can change your life...Your life is a journey. Throughout that journey it's critical that you look in the direction that you're going and that you don't look in the direction you're not going. If you focus on that which is ungodly, impure, negative, evil, dark, sinful...you'll end up going there, away from God...to a dark place. In the end, you won't go where you say you'll go. You'll go where you looked. That which you dwell *on*, you will end up dwelling *in*. It is written that Messiah fixed His eyes on Jerusalem. That was His goal. So that's where He looked, long before He ended up there. Focus on those things that are consistent with your calling. You have a heavenly calling and a heavenly destination. Therefore, look to that which is heavenly. Dwell on what is pure, high, and of God. Focus on what is good. Stop dwelling on what is not...and on that which has nothing to do with your heavenly calling. You'll end up where you are to go, when you look...where you're going."

The Mission: What is the direction of the calling of your life? Today, dwell only on that which leads to that destination, and on nothing that doesn't.

Proverbs 4:25–27; Philippians 3:13–14; 4:8; Ephesians 4:1

The Look Where You're Going Principle

THE FOOD OF THE PRIESTS

WHAT IF THERE existed a food with special powers?" asked the teacher. "And whoever ate of this food became holy and was given the ability to perform works for God they could never have done before?"

"It would save a lot of time and effort," I replied.

"The priests of Israel didn't just offer up the sacrifices," he said. "They partook of them. The priests lived on the sacrifices. It was their food and sustenance. A holy priesthood had to partake of a holy food. And what is food? It's that which you live on and that which becomes you."

"You are what you eat," I said.

"Yes. And you *do* what you eat," he said. "It is food that gives you the energy to move, to work, to act, to do, and to accomplish. So it is with spiritual food."

"What is spiritual food?"

"It's that which you live on, what you partake of in your heart and spirit. And what you partake of in the spiritual realm is what you will become in the spiritual realm. If you partake in that which is spiritually unclean, if you eat the food of bitterness, of impurity, of lust, of gossip, of darkness, then you will become unclean, impure, and of darkness. But if you partake of that which is spiritually pure and holy, then you will become spiritually pure and holy. And physical food gives you physical energy; spiritual food gives you spiritual energy. So if you partake of spiritual food that is holy and of God, it will give you spiritual power and energy to do what is holy and good and to accomplish the works of God. So what exactly was the food of the priests?"

"The sacrifice."

"And what is the sacrifice? Messiah. And the Scriptures say that if you're born again, you are now part of a holy priesthood. So if you're a priest, you must now live on the food of the priests, the sacrifice. In other words, you must make Messiah the food you live on, every day. His love, His goodness, His mercy, His presence must become your daily sustenance. And if you partake of Messiah, then His nature will become your nature, and His essence your essence. His energy, His spirit, and His power will be given you that you might accomplish the works of God and do what you never could have done before. So from now on live on the food of the priests. Partake of the holy. For you are what you eat, and that which you partake of becomes you."

The Mission: Partake today only of what is good and holy, the food of the priests. Dwell on the good and nothing else. And you will become so.

Leviticus 6:29; Psalm 34:8; John 6:51

Food of the Priests

SONG OF THE STONE

WE SAT ON the floor of a dark room, illuminated only by the light of a solitary oil lamp. In the teacher's hand was a small parchment.

"In the New Covenant Scriptures it's recorded that at the end of the Passover Seder, the Last Supper, Messiah and His disciples sang a song. What song would they have sung?"

"How could we possibly know?"

"The word used to describe the song is the Greek *humnos. Humnos* was used to speak of the Psalms of Israel. And from ancient times it was ordained that the Passover Seder would always end with the singing of songs, specifically, the Psalms, and a specific set of Psalms called the Hallels. The Passover would end with the singing of the last of these, Psalm 118."

"And is Psalm 118 significant?"

"Extremely so," said the teacher as he opened up the scroll to read. "It is Psalm 118 that contains the words, 'The stone which the builders rejected has become the chief cornerstone.' The Hebrew word for *rejected* means as well despised and abhorred. Who is the rejected stone?"

"Messiah," I answered, "'He was despised and rejected of men...'"

"Two thousand years ago that song was sung all over Jerusalem, the song of the rejected stone. And it would be fulfilled on that very Passover. It was right after Messiah and His disciples finished singing the song that they went to the Mount of Olives where He would be arrested, despised, and abhorred—and finally cast away at the crucifixion, the epitome of rejection. But what also does it say? 'The stone which the builders *rejected has become the chief cornerstone.*' So the despised and rejected man on the cross would end up becoming the cornerstone of faith, of civilization, of history, and of the world. Think about it...kings and queens, general and emperors, bow down to a man nailed to a cross. The most pivotal, world-changing life on this planet is that of a crucified Jewish Rabbi...the stone of rejection. And that crucified Rabbi becomes the cornerstone of history. In God, the object of man's hatred becomes the center of His love, and the object of man's despising becomes the vessel of His glory. How amazing is that? And it was all there, that night, at the Seder...in the song of the stone."

The Mission: Make Him who is the Cornerstone, the cornerstone of all you do today. Build everything else from that foundation.

Psalm 118:22–23; Isaiah 53:3; Hebrews 13:12–13; 1 Peter 2:4–8

The Rosh Pinah

THE MYSTERY OF THE TRIANGLES

WE SAT FACING each other on the desert sand. The teacher was holding a stick, which he would use in the revealing of the mystery. "On the night of Passover," he said, "the Israelites marked their doorposts with the blood of the lamb. Do you know how they did it?"

"No."

"They put the blood on three places, on the right beam, on the left beam, and on the top beam."

Using the stick, he made three dots in the sand: one on the top, and two below it to the right and the left.

"Now let's connect the dots," he said as he began drawing a line from dot to dot. "What does it form?"

"A triangle."

"A triangle pointing upward to heaven. The act was performed by man looking toward God, from earth to heaven, from man to God."

"In the first Passover the blood of the lamb appeared on the beams of their doorposts. But over a thousand years later, in the Passover of the Messiah, the blood appeared on the beams of the cross. In how many places did that blood appear?"

I thought for a moment before answering. "Three," I replied.

"Where?"

"At His right hand, at His left hand, and at His feet."

At that, he put the stick back in the sand and drew three dots, one on the bottom, and two above it. Then he again connected the dots. It formed another triangle alongside the first. But this one pointed down.

"Again, three marks of blood...Again it forms a triangle. But this triangle points downward, just as this Passover sacrifice comes not from man to God, but from God to man. And now what happens if we join the two Passover triangles?"

He then drew the two triangles, the one overlapping the other.

"The Star of David!" I said. "It forms the Star of David, the sign of Israel."

"Two Passovers, two lambs, two triangular patterns of blood, separated by over a thousand years and yet forming the sign of God's nation. A sign formed in the blood of the Passover Lamb...a sign that the Passover Lamb has come...to set free all who take refuge in His blood."

The Mission: The blood of the Lamb breaks every chain and bondage. Walk today in the power of the Lamb and break free.

Exodus 12:3–7; 1 Corinthians 5:7

The Lamb and the Doorway

THE CHALDEAN MYSTERY

HE WAS TURNING the pages of a large black book filled with old maps and lithographs. "Assyria, Babylon, Persia, Rome...Even the greatest of kingdoms," he said, "cannot escape the laws of history, or the laws of God. And one of those laws is four thousand years old. God speaks to a Middle Eastern man named Abram, from the land of Chaldea, and tells him, 'I will bless those who bless you. And I will curse those who curse you.' In other words, those people, nations, and powers that bless the Jewish people, the children of Abraham, will be blessed, and those who curse them will be cursed. Could a four-thousand-year-old promise lie behind world history and the rise and fall of nations? The answer is yes."

"Can you give an example?" I asked.

"In the second millennium BC, the world's preeminent empire is Egypt. But Egypt oppresses the children of Abraham. So, according to the ancient mystery somewhere around the time of the Exodus and at the peak of its oppression, the Egyptian Empire suddenly collapses, never to rise again. In the modern age, Great Britain becomes for the Jewish people a refuge from persecution and one in which they would prosper. And so according to the ancient mystery Britain is exalted to the point that its empire becomes the most expansive in world history. But when the British Empire reverses its position and turns against the Jewish refugees fleeing the Holocaust, this greatest of empires suddenly collapses to virtually nothing. Starting in the late nineteenth century and into the twentieth America becomes the greatest refuge and defender of the Jewish people. And thus according to the ancient mystery, in the same period of time, becomes the most blessed, prosperous, and powerful nation on earth. From ancient Egypt to modern America the ancient biblical mystery has determined the rise and fall of kingdoms and empires. What does that tell you?"

"It is wisdom to bless Israel and the Jewish people."

"Yes," said the teacher. "And it also tells you that God is real, faithful, and more powerful than history. When He gives His Word, believe it. And know that His love for His people is so great that He will even move empires for their sake."

The Mission: Take a promise from His Word. Believe the promise with all your heart. Step out and live your life in light of it.

Genesis 12:1–3

The Chaldean Secret of World History I–III

THE MIRYAM MYSTERY

THE MOST FAMOUS woman in all of human history...loved, cherished, and adored more than any other woman on earth...Mary."

"The Virgin Mary?"

"But the real Mary was very different from the way most have imagined her. She was Jewish. And she was never called Mary."

"What was she called then?"

"Miryam. She was named after the Miryam of Egypt, the sister of Moses, the one whose most critical act was to keep watch over her baby brother as he drifted down the Nile River. Her mission was to protect his life. Moses would grow up to become the deliverer to set his people free from bondage. But it was Miryam who ensured that he would survive as a baby in order do that. Her calling was to usher the life of the redeemer into the land of Egypt where he would bring salvation. Over a thousand years later, another Hebrew child would be given the same name, *Miryam*...and the same calling."

"The same calling?"

"What was Mary's calling? It was to usher in the life of the Deliverer, the Messiah, Yeshua, Jesus, into a fallen world. And remember what *Yeshua* means— salvation. So it is Miryam who ushers in salvation."

"And what does the name *Miryam* mean?"

"In Egyptian," he said, "the name can mean love."

"So Yeshua is born of Miryam, born of God's love."

"Yes, but in Hebrew, *Miryam* means something very different. It means bitterness and rebellion."

"That doesn't sound good."

"But it *is* good," he said. "God causes Miryam to give birth to Yeshua. So too God causes a world of bitterness and rebellion to give birth to salvation. He causes Yeshua to be born in us...the other miracle. He even takes lives of rebellion and causes them to bring forth blessing and new life. And when does that life come? When does that miracle happen? Mostly it comes in times of trouble, crisis, fear, or sorrow...in bitterness. So through Miryam is born Yeshua."

"And so 'through bitterness is born salvation'...even through us."

"And if salvation, Yeshua, is born of us," he said, "then we are all Miryam."

The Mission: Take up the mystery of Miryam. Make it your aim this day, to bear His life, His presence, and His joy into the world.

Exodus 2:1–9; Luke 1:26–38

Miryam

YOM RISHON: THE COSMIC BEGINNING

H E CAME TO my room early in the morning to invite me for a walk. So we walked outside.

"Why do you think the resurrection took place on Sunday?" he asked.

"I don't know," I replied.

"Because Sunday," said the teacher, "was the day everything began...Sunday is the day the universe began, the day of creation."

"But there were no Sundays back then."

"It wasn't called Sunday. But it was Sunday nevertheless. Every Sunday is a commemoration of the beginning, the creation of the universe."

"So the resurrection took place on Sunday because..."

"Sunday is the day of the beginning. And all who receive it are given a new beginning for their lives. And why else on Sunday?" he asked. "Because Sunday comes after the Sabbath. And the Sabbath is the last day, the day of the end. So the resurrection happens on Sunday because it's the power of what happens *after the end*. It's what happens after Messiah's end on the cross. And it's what happens after the end of the old life. So for all who reach their end, for all who let their old lives end in Messiah's end, the resurrection is the beginning that comes after that end. Why Sunday? Because Sunday is the commemoration of the cosmic beginning and the resurrection is the cosmic new beginning. Sunday is the day that begins the creation, and the resurrection is the beginning of the new creation, the firstfruits. And all who enter it become, themselves, new creations. And to them all things become new...And lastly, why Sunday?" he asked. "Because in the Scriptures Sunday is not called Sunday but *Yom Rishon*. And *Yom Rishon* means Day One. Messiah rose on Yom Rishon, Day One. Why? Because before Day One there is no other day. So all who receive the resurrection are receiving Day One. And in the power of Day One the old is wiped away. For before Day One...there is nothing, no sins, no guilt, no failures, no shame. And so all things become new. Learn the secret of living in the power of Yom Rishon, and all things will become new, and every day will become the first day...the beginning...Day One."

The Mission: Live today as if it was Day One, as if everything that should never have been, never was, and all is new. For in redemption, it is so.

Genesis 1:1; Mark 16:2–6

Yom Rishon

THE SHADOW MAN

WE WERE SITTING on a hill in the midst of a valley on a warm windy day.

"Do you see that?" asked the teacher. He was pointing to the patches of darkness moving across the valley, the shadows of the rapidly moving clouds above us.

"You see their shadows," he said, "before they come. In the same way, before Messiah came, there were shadows of His coming. One of the shadows was Yosef or Joseph, the son of Jacob. The rabbis have long seen in the story of Joseph a shadow of the coming Messiah. Joseph was the beloved son of his father. Of what could that foreshadow concerning Messiah?"

"Messiah was the beloved son of *the* Father," I replied.

"Joseph's father, Jacob, sent him on a mission to his brothers."

"So God would send Messiah," I said, "on a mission to *His* brothers, the nation of Israel."

"Joseph's brothers," said the teacher, "despised him, rejected him, and conspired to kill him."

"So Messiah would be despised and rejected, and His enemies would conspire to kill Him."

"Joseph was taken to a foreign land, Egypt, and separated from his family."

"So Messiah would become separated from *His* own people and family, the Jewish people."

"Joseph was falsely accused and, though innocent, was arrested and taken to prison, suffering for the sins of others."

"So Messiah would be falsely accused and, though innocent, would be arrested and taken away to suffer for the sins of others."

"Joseph," said the teacher, "was then raised up from the dungeon and placed on the throne."

"So Messiah," I said, "would be raised up from the depths of death and seated on a throne of glory."

"Joseph became the redeemer of Egypt and was responsible for saving an entire nation from death."

"And Messiah would become the Redeemer of all, the Savior of the world."

I thought about it all for a moment. "How great He must be," I said, "for the history of nations to be just a part of the shadow of His coming!"

"The history of nations," said the teacher, "and the history of our lives. He's the reality that fulfills every hope...even of our lives... and of all the shadows that lie waiting until He comes."

The Mission: Joseph means he shall increase, a shadow of Messiah who, like Joseph, triumphs through all things. In Messiah, you have that same power. Use it this day.

Genesis 50:19–21; Isaiah 53; John 1:9–13

The Shadow Man I–VI

THE MAN BORN TO PAUSE AND ASK

I N THE ANCIENT world," said the teacher, "there was born a Jewish child to an affluent family. His parents gave him two names. The one name could be translated as 'small' but which came from a root word meaning to pause, to desist, or to stop. His other name came from a root word that meant to ask, to seek, or to inquire. The child grew up and rarely paused or desisted from anything. Nor was he one to question his course. He was headstrong. But one day all that would change. He finally paused...in the form of a blinding light that caused him to fall to the ground."

"The apostle Paul?"

"Yes. The name *Paul* or *Paulus* comes from the root word *pauo*, which means to pause, to stop, to desist, to cease from one's course, or to come to an end. So the man whose name was linked to pausing and stopping finally pauses and stops. God caused him to finally stop, to desist, and come to an end. So his whole life, from the moment he received his name, was leading up to that moment."

"And what about his other name?"

"In Hebrew," said the teacher, "the word for *ask* is *shoel*, from which we get the name *Shaul* or *Saul*."

"Paul and Saul," I said, "he who pauses and asks."

"And what happened," asked the teacher, "right after he paused? God said to him, 'Saul! Saul!' In Hebrew that's like saying, 'Ask! Ask!' And what did Paul do? He finally asked the question: 'Who are You, Lord?' Finally, he who was born to ask, asked. For the first time in his life, he realized that he didn't even know who God was. And only when he asked was he able for the first time to know. His whole life was waiting for that moment. And his question was answered with the words, 'I am Yeshua, Jesus.' And so the life of the man who paused and asked would be changed forever. He would become what he was born to become. You see," said the teacher, "if you can't stop, if you can't pause enough to seek, you'll never find anything more than what you already have. And if you can't ask, then you'll never know anything more than you already do. Pause that you might find. And ask that you might know. For we were all born to pause and ask."

The Mission: Today, pause, stop what you're doing, cease from your routine and your course, and with no preconceptions, seek Him.

Jeremiah 29:11–13; Acts 9:1–8; Romans 1:1

The Name of Paul

THE AUDIBLE SAPPHIRE

THE TEACHER OPENED one of the drawers in his desk and took out what appeared to be a precious stone of deep blue. He placed it in my hand.

"It's a biblical sapphire."

"It's very nice," I replied, not knowing what else to say.

"I didn't give it to you because of its appearance, but because of what it signifies...because of its origin."

"Its origin?"

"The origin of its name," he said.

"Sapphire?"

"Yes," said the teacher. "*Sapphire* comes from a French word, which comes from a Latin word, which comes from a Greek word...which comes from an ancient biblical Hebrew word...*sappir.*"

"So sapphire comes from biblical Hebrew," I said. "What's the significance of the name?"

"The Hebrew word for sapphire comes from the Hebrew root *saphar*. And *saphar* means to speak, to tell, or to declare."

"So the word *sapphire* ultimately means to speak? What's the connection?"

"The connection is this," said the teacher. "More precious than any treasured jewel is the Word. Every Word of God is a sapphire, a spoken sapphire, and yet much more precious. If one has no treasures in this world, but has the Word of God, then one is rich. Every Word of God is a treasure of priceless value. So when you read or hear a Word from God, receive it as if you were receiving a priceless jewel. And give it the same way."

"How?"

"Your words are to be as sapphires. You don't need to possess precious jewels—you just have to speak them. Every time you open your mouth to speak, let what comes out be a sapphire, a gift to be given to those who need to receive a precious jewel. So let every word that comes out of your mouth be a precious jewel. Give jewels to those in need, jewels of blessing, jewels of encouragement, jewels of strength, jewels of mercy, jewels of love, jewels of forgiveness, jewels of joy, and jewels of hope. Let your every word bring life to those who hear it...an audible jewel...a spoken sapphire."

The Mission: Today, make every word that comes out of your mouth a precious jewel, a gift of life, the spoken sapphire.

Ephesians 4:29; 5:19; Colossians 4:6; 1 Peter 4:11

Not a Rotten Word

THE OTHER ELOHIM

W HEN MOSES WAS on Mount Sinai receiving God's Law," said the teacher, "at the bottom of the mountain the Israelites decided to build a golden calf and worship it. When the calf was finished, they said, 'These are your gods, O Israel, that brought you out of the land of Egypt.' But in other translations and in another part of Scripture, the words come out differently: Instead of "These are your gods, O Israel,' it reads, 'This is your God, O Israel.' How can the same declaration be translated so differently? Think back to what I told you about the Hebrew word for *God*. What was strange about it?"

"Elohim," I said, "is a plural word, but it speaks of a singular reality—God. That's it!" I said. "The word they used in their pronouncement had to be *Elohim*. So it could be translated either as 'your God' or 'your gods.'"

"Exactly. It's the same word. Elohim refers to the majesty of the one true God, but it also can speak of the many false gods of the nations. It's interchangeable. And this interchangeability reveals a profound thing: If you turn away from Elohim, the one true God, you will end up serving the elohim, the gods. So when the people of Israel turned away from God, they always ended up turning to the gods of the nations. They turned from one Elohim to another elohim. For in the end, it all comes down to a choice between Elohim or elohim. If you turn away from the one Elohim, you will end up with the other."

"And what exactly is the other elohim you end up with?"

"The same elohim they ended up with at Mount Sinai, the gods, but in different guises—the gods of money and pleasure, the elohim of success, possessions, comfort, vanity, self. There's no end to the elohim. And as it is for an individual, so for peoples, nations, and civilizations. Any civilization that turns away from the Elohim of God will end up serving the elohim of the gods. And that which serves the elohim ultimately loses its unity. It becomes as divided, fractured, and scattered as the elohim themselves. That which worships the elohim ends up devaluing, degrading, and debasing itself, just as in the day of the golden calf."

"So what do you do if you find that the elohim are present in your life?"

"The same thing they did with the golden calf—you get rid of it. Only then can things be right...when you turn away from the elohim and back to Elohim."

The Mission: Get rid of the elohim in your life, the idols you seek after, the gods that drive you. Get rid of your elohim and return to your Elohim.

Exodus 32:7–8; Romans 1:23; 1 Thessalonians 1:9–10; 1 John 5:21

The Golden Calf Revelation I–IV

THE MAGIAN JOURNEY

HE LED ME into a room known as the Chamber of Vessels. There he retrieved a small wooden box from which he removed an intricately adorned metal container. Inside the container was a white powder.

"Frankincense," said the teacher, "one of the gifts of the Magi."

"Who exactly were the Magi?" I asked.

"Priests of an ancient Persian religion called Zoroastrianism, one of many pagan religions. Star gazers who followed one particular star in their search to find the newborn King of the Jews."

"But how did they know for sure that Messiah was born?"

"No one knows for certain," he said. "It's a mystery. They only had shadows to go on, glimpses, hints, traces, longings, and the star. But they were seeking for the truth as best they could. They had no idea where it would all take them. They just followed the star, step by step, knowing only the next step and nothing else. Yet they ended up finding Him. And they had no idea what was written in an ancient prophecy."

"About Messiah."

"About *them*. Seven centuries before they arrived in Bethlehem, the prophet Isaiah prophesied of Messiah's coming to Israel: 'Arise and shine, for your light has come, and the glory of the Lord has risen upon you...and the Gentiles will come to your light...and a multitude of camels will cover your land...*and they will bring gold and frankincense...*'"

"Gold and frankincense, those were the gifts of the Magi."

"A prophecy of Gentiles coming to Israel in light of Messiah's coming and bearing gifts as they came...a prophecy that waited over seven hundred years to be fulfilled. And the Magi had no idea. They were only seeking to follow God's will, as if walking in the dark, step by step. And yet they ended up fulfilling their appointed destiny, ordained and foretold for hundreds of years. Learn their secret," said the teacher. "You don't have to know all that lies ahead of you...you never will. But set your heart on seeking His presence and His will, doing what you know is right, taking the next step, and the next, and you'll end up in the place appointed for your life, even from ancient times, even from the beginning...the glory at the end of the Magian journey."

The Mission: Today, set out on a Magian journey. Journey away from the familiar to the new as you seek more of Him, His will, and His presence.

Isaiah 60:1–6; Matthew 2:1–11

The Journey of the Magi

THE MAGNITUDE OF THE SUN

IT WAS EARLY morning. The teacher took me on a journey to the city through the desert riding on camels. The purpose was to pick up supplies for the school. But, of course, he had more than one purpose in mind.

"One thing I want you to do," he said, "keep watch over the sun."

It was a strange directive. I did my best, noting from time to time its position in the sky. At the journey's end, upon our return, he questioned me.

"What did you see?" he asked.

"Nothing," I answered. "Nothing of note. The sun was just the sun."

"I imagine," he said, "that at times it was obscured by the mountains, the trees, and the buildings of the city. But otherwise, I imagine it stayed the same, certainly the same size. I would also imagine that the landscape was continually changing, everything was changing except for the sun."

"That's true," I said. "But isn't that the way the sun works?"

"Yes, but why is that the way the sun works?" he asked. "It's because . . . although a mountain or a house or even a hand can appear bigger than the sun and can, for a time, obscure it, the reality is that the sun's true magnitude, its actual size, is so enormous, so colossal, that the highest mountain on earth is as nothing in comparison. It doesn't appear so in the short run, but it becomes clear over the long run. Even in our little journey, everything we saw completely changed, the hills, the mountains, everything but the sun. And if we had traveled thousands of miles, it wouldn't have made a difference. The sun's colossal magnitude is manifested by its changelessness."

"And what does it reveal?" I asked.

"Two thousand years ago, Messiah said, 'I am the Light of the World.' Since that time, ages have begun and ended, continents and civilizations have been discovered, kingdoms and empires have risen and fallen. And some of these things have, for a time, seemed larger. For a time they obscured the figure of the Nazarene. But in the long run, over the course of the long journey, they've all passed away. Everything has changed . . . except Him. All the rest lies in ruins and rubble or in the pages of history . . . but He remains unchanged, undiminished . . . as central, as pivotal, and as colossal as He has ever been. Everything changes but Him. He is the sun. And His colossal magnitude is manifested by His changelessness."

The Mission: Today, see all things in view of the big picture. Whatever problems or issues you have are small in comparison to Him and will pass away in the magnitude of the Son.

John 8:12; Ephesians 3:16–19; Hebrews 13:8

Two Thousand Years Ago

THE TWO THREE THOUSANDS

HE TOOK ME back to the Chamber of Scrolls, and to the scroll in the ark, which he removed and read out loud: "'You shall count fifty days to the day after the seventh Sabbath; then you shall offer a new grain offering to the Lord.' This," said the teacher, "is the ordinance of the Feast of *Shavuot,* which takes place seven weeks, or fifty days, after the Passover. When the rabbis realized that this was the same time that Moses ascended Mount Sinai to receive the Law, Shavuot became the day that commemorated the giving of the Law. Over a thousand years after the giving of the Law, Messiah's disciples were together in Jerusalem and the Spirit of God came upon them. It was the day that the new covenant was empowered by God's Spirit. It all happened on the Hebrew feast of Shavuot. When the rabbis of the Greek world had to give a Greek name to this Hebrew holy day, they called it The Feast of the Fiftieth Day or in Greek, *Pentecoste.*"

"Pentecost!" I said. "So Pentecost is the Hebrew Feast of Shavuot."

"And do you know what this means? It means that the Spirit of God was given to the believers on the same day that the Law of God was given to Israel. The old covenant and the new covenant are joined together. They were both inaugurated on the same day. And do you know what happened when the Law was given? There was judgment. People perished. And the number of those who perished, the ancient Hebrew records, was 'about three thousand.' And do you know what happened on that second Shavuot and Pentecost, when the Spirit was given?"

"No."

"There was salvation, eternal life. And the number of those who came to new life, the ancient Greek records, was 'about three thousand.' Two different languages, ages apart, yet the same exact expression."

"So three thousand died and, centuries later, three thousand came to life on the same exact holy day."

"And so the apostle Paul writes, 'The letter kills, but the Spirit gives life.' The Spirit was given on the same day as the Law. Why? Because the Law can tell us the will of God, but only the Spirit can give us the power to live it. Therefore, live by the Spirit of God and you fulfill the will of God for your life just as precisely as the coming of the Spirit on Shavuot, Pentecost, the Day of the Law."

The Mission: Instead of struggling to accomplish the will of God, live, move, and be moved by the Spirit of God—and you will fulfill His will.

Exodus 32:20; Leviticus 23:15–21; Acts 2:41; 2 Corinthians 3:4–6

Tablets of the Spirit

CHAYIM

FROM A MOUNTAIN in the distance we watched an event I had never before witnessed in my days in the desert—a funeral among the tent dwellers. It was a simple event, a burial in the sand, with a single stone and a palm leaf to mark the grave. We were silent for some time. Then he spoke.

"Death," said the teacher, "the shadow that hangs over all who live in this world, the destroyer of creation, the ender of our time on earth. As we see it from this world, life is for a limited time, and then comes death, and death is permanent, forever. But the sacred tongue of Scripture holds a revelation, a revelation of life and death. The word for *death* in Hebrew is *mavet*. The word for *life* is *chayim*. *Mavet* and *chayim*...Do you notice anything about the two words?"

"The word *chayim* sounds like some of the other words you've shared."

"It does," he said. "It's because of the *im* at its end."

"That makes it plural."

"It's one of the mystery words of Hebrew with the strange property that it can only be spoken in the plural form and never in the singular."

"And what does it signify?"

"*Mavet* is singular. But *chayim* is plural. It's the exact opposite of what we think. It is death that is singular and life that is plural. In God, it is death that is limited, and death that is finite. In God, it is death that is *not* forever, but which has an end."

"The ending of ending...would be endlessness."

"All endings will be ended," said the teacher. "For in God, it is not life that is limited, but death, and not death that goes on forever, but life. For the word *chayim* is plural. And so it speaks of life beyond life. And Messiah said He is the Life. But in Hebrew, He is the Chayim. He is the Life that cannot be ended. So death could not overcome Him. For chayim is greater than mavet. Life is greater than death. And we, who are born of God, are of chayim. Thus we are the people of life. Therefore, take no part in that which is of death. Have no part in sin or darkness. For you are of chayim, of life with no end. And you are of that which cannot be overcome but overcomes all things, even death itself."

The Mission: Remove from your life today any action or thought that which leads to death, starting with sin. Replace them with that which leads to life.

Isaiah 25:5–9; John 11:25; Acts 3:15

The Hebrew Mysteries I–IV

THE MYSTERY OF THE CHERUBIM

HE LED ME through a winding ravine that opened up into a hidden enclave hedged in by steep mountain walls. In one of the walls was an entranceway. We went inside. There were several chambers. On the walls of one of those chambers was the remnant of an ancient painting of two winged creatures and a glowing sword.

"So He drove out the man," said the teacher, "and He placed cherubim at the east of the Garden of Eden, and a flaming sword, which turned in every direction, to guard the way to the tree of life. The fall of man...the loss of paradise...the separation of man from God, the unholy from the holy. And the sign of that separation was the cherubim with the flaming sword. The cherubim formed the barrier to prevent evil, sin, fallen man, from entering the presence of God. So the sign of the cherubim represents everything that separates us from God, everything that separates us from peace, purpose, meaning, and love."

"As every separation began with the first separation in Eden," I replied, "it would seem impossible for such a barrier ever to be removed."

"It would," he replied. "Do you remember the supernatural event that took place in the Temple when Messiah died?"

"The veil in front of the holy of holies was torn in two."

"Yes, the parochet, the colossal barrier that separated man from God, torn apart from top to bottom. But the parochet was not simply a cloth, but the vessel of a mystery. Embroidered on its fabric were images of the cherubim...the guardians of Eden, still guarding the way back to God, and the barrier separating man from God. But when Messiah died, the sign of the cherubim separating man from God was pulled apart. As the veil was pulled apart, so too were the cherubim. For Messiah was passing through...as through the cherubim...the return to paradise."

"And through the flaming sword?"

"Yes. And to pass through a flaming sword would means one death. And by passing through, He crossed the uncrossable barrier. The sign of the cherubim is broken. The barrier between God and man is gone."

"So does that mean that all barriers are nullified, and all separations removed?"

"For those who are in Messiah, there are no more separations, no more judgment, no more rejection, no more shame, no more guilt, no more curse. It means that whatever was separating us from our purpose, our blessing, and our redemption is gone. It means that every barrier separating us from God is removed. The way is open...We can come home."

The Mission: In Messiah all barriers are gone. Move forward this day in that power, through every veil, wall, separation, hindrance, and cherubim.

Genesis 3:24; Exodus 26:31; Mark 15:38; Romans 8:31–37

The Day of the Cherubim

THE MIND BINDERS

THE TEACHER TOOK me into the Chamber of Vessels where he opened a small wooden box and removed a black leather container attached to a black leather band.

"This is called a *tefillin*. And this is how it's worn by Orthodox Jews." He placed the black leather box just above his forehead, then wrapped the leather band around his head, fastening the box in place.

"I don't understand the purpose of binding a box to your head."

"It's not the box. It's what's *inside* the box. Inside the box are scrolls of parchment. And on the scrolls is the Word of God. It's their way of applying a command from the Law concerning the words of God's commandments: 'You shall bind them...as a sign upon your forehead.' They do it as an outward observance. But there is in this a spiritual key that can change your life...and your mind."

He removed the tefillin from his forehead and continued. "What goes on inside your mind, the world of your thoughts, is the most private part of your life. You may do what is right on the outside, but what happens on the inside is often very different...wandering thoughts, restless and straying thoughts, dark thoughts, sinful thoughts. But what this leather box is telling you is that it doesn't have to be that way. When God speaks of binding the Word to your head, it's about more than this box. It's revealing that even your thought life can become holy. The secret is to take the Word of God and bind it to your mind, to your thoughts, to your emotions, and to your will.

"And the Hebrew word here for *bind* is *kashar*," he said. "It speaks of knitting together. So you are to knit the Word of God to your thoughts. How? By dwelling on the Word, by meditating on it, agreeing with it, and affirming it from the center of your being. You let the Word lead your emotions, and your thoughts flow out of the Word. The mystery contained in this leather box is that the Word can be bound to your thoughts, knit so closely together that you actually think the thoughts of God. And since the head is what rules your life, if your thoughts are one with God's Word, then so too will be your life. If you let the Word of God change your thoughts...it will also change your life."

The Mission: Take a word from Scripture. Dwell on it, agree with it, and bind it to your thoughts, your emotions, your heart, and your mind.

Deuteronomy 11:18; 2 Corinthians 10:4–5; 1 Peter 1:13

THE FOURTH CREATURE

IT WAS NIGHT. We were sitting by the fire. The teacher had a small scroll in his hand from which he was reading by the light of the flames: "'I saw in my vision by night, the four winds of heaven were stirring up the great sea. And four great beasts came up from the sea...' This," said the teacher, "is the vision given to the prophet Daniel of the four creatures, the great world kingdoms of ancient times, and one last kingdom of the end times."

"What were they, the creatures?" I asked.

"The first was like a lion with eagles' wings, that was Babylon. The second was like a bear, Persia. The third was like a leopard with four heads and wings, Greece. And the fourth represented both the Roman Empire of ancient times and a global civilization yet to come."

"And what did the fourth creature look like?"

"It's hard to say," he replied. "Even Daniel was mystified by it. He described it as exceedingly powerful, destructive, and terrifying. But he used another Hebrew word over and over again to describe it. The word is *shainah*. *Shainah* can be translated to mean different. The fourth creature is especially different from all the creatures that went before it. Thus, the civilization of the last days will be different from every civilization that preceded it. The word *shainah* also means changed or altered. Thus the state of the last days will be a changed state...an altered civilization. The first three creatures were based on the forms of nature. But the fourth creature has no clear grounding in nature. Its teeth and claws are of iron and bronze. It's different...altered...changed."

"Sounds more like a machine," I said.

"The revelation of the fourth creature is this: End-time civilization will be based not on the natural, but on the unnatural. It will exist against nature. It will be of an altered or transmuted nature...a civilization at war with creation, with nature, and with the order of God."

"Sounds like...now."

"And thus," said the teacher, "those who live in the end times must resist a civilization that wars against the order of creation and uphold the Word of the Eternal. They must stand firm against the power, the nature, and the terror of the altered creature."

The Mission: Separate your heart, your mind, your actions, and your way of life from any defilement of the present culture and anything that goes against the Word and ways of God.

Leviticus 20:26; Daniel 7:1–7; 1 Peter 2:9–12

The Iron Creature

THE SCROLL OF DAYS

TEACHER," I SAID, "How does one know the plan of God for one's life?"

"Come," he said. He led me into the Chamber of Scrolls, opened the ark, removed the scroll, and laid it on the table. But he didn't unroll it.

"In the Psalms it is written, 'And in Your book, they all were written, the days fashioned for me, when as yet there were none of them.' So all our days are written in God's book before they come to pass. But in the Hebrew Scriptures, the word for *book* is *sefer*. And in the Greek of the New Testament Scriptures, the word is *biblion*, from which we get the word *Bible*."

"And what exactly do *sefer* and *biblion* mean?"

"They refer to a scroll, a rolled parchment. God's book is a scroll. His Book of Days is the Scroll of Days. The scroll holds the Word of God, the will of God, and the plans of God. So how does the scroll reveal His Word, His will, and His plan?"

He placed his hands on the knobs at the bottom of each roll. "You can only see what's inside the scroll," he said, "as it unrolls." At that, he began unrolling it. "So you can only see the fullness of God's plans for your life as they unfold...as the scroll unrolls. And unlike the books you've been used to reading, with a scroll, you can't skip ahead to a future section. Everything has to unroll in its order. So with your life, you can never be shown all that lies ahead of you. You wouldn't understand it, and you wouldn't be able to deal with it. Everything must unfold in its order, in its place and time."

"But what lies ahead in the scroll is already written, finished."

"So too God's plans for your life are already written and finished. And so it is written that He has prepared for us good works beforehand that we should walk in them. It's already there beforehand, but only unfolds in its time. And notice," he said, pointing to the words on the scroll, "everything in the scroll is connected. You don't see the words that haven't yet been unrolled, but the words you do see lead directly to them and foreshadow them. So with God's plan for your life; you don't see all that lies ahead, what hasn't yet been revealed, but the part you do see in the present foreshadows what lies ahead and leads directly to what is yet to be revealed. The key, therefore, is to live in the present. To live the present day and every present moment of your life in the fullness of God's will. And the words you see, living in the course of His Word, will lead you to the perfect will and the appointed destiny waiting in your unrolled scroll of days."

The Mission: Make the Word of God the plan for your day. Focus on fulfilling His Word over anything else, and you will be led to His perfect will.

Psalm 139:16; Jeremiah 29:11; Ephesians 2:10

The Book of Days

THE OHEL MOED

WE WERE STANDING on a low mountain range that enclosed a vast open expanse.

"Imagine," said the teacher, "this plain completely filled up with tents. If you can imagine it, that's what it would have looked like when the Hebrews journeyed through the wilderness. But there was one tent that stood apart from the rest. It was called the *Ohel Moed*, the Tent of the Appointed Time, or the Tent of Meeting."

"What exactly was it?" I asked.

"It was the tent of God's presence, where God and man met together. Now imagine you were in the camp. How would you find that tent?"

"I don't know."

"You would simply walk to the center. The Tent of Meeting was always set up in the center of the camp. The rest of the camp was built around it. This one tent set the position of every other tent. The entire order of the camp itself was determined by its location. What does that reveal?"

"I don't know, I'm not a camper."

"Nevertheless, you need to build a tent of meeting."

"And what does *that* mean?"

"Every child of God must dwell with God in prayer, worship, and communion. And to dwell with God, you must build a tent of meeting."

"How so?"

"By setting apart an appointed time every day and establishing its parameters for one set and sacred purpose: to meet with God. That is your tent of meeting, your tent of the appointed time. But where do you set it up?"

"In a quiet place?"

"More than that. The tent of meeting must always be set up in the center of the camp. It must be the center of your day, the center of your schedule, the center of everything you do, the center of your life. That's the key. If it's not the center, then every other thing will crowd it out of existence. You don't fit your time with God around your day or around your activities; you fit your day and activities around your time with God, your tent of meeting. Your relationship with God and the sacred meetings of that relationship can only occupy one place in your life—the center. Center your life and everything of your life around God and your time with God. When you do that, everything else will fall into its place."

The Mission: Today, build and place your tent of meeting in the center of your day and life, and place the rest of your day and life around it.

Exodus 25:8–9; Matthew 6:6, 33

The Mishkan Kit I–II

THE HUPOGRAMMOS

H E TOOK ME into the Chamber of Books and to a wooden table on which was something of a tablet, a very shallow wooden box filled with soft wax. He had in his hand a small pointed rod, what I would imagine a stylus would look like. He placed the rod into the wax of the tablet and began to write. The letters were foreign to me.

"It's ancient Greek," he said. "And the word is *hupogrammos.*"

"What does it mean?"

"*Grammos* means writing, and *hupo* means under. *Hupogrammos* means the underwriting."

"So you're an underwriter," I said.

 He didn't respond.

"In ancient times, the hupogrammos was used to teach students how to write. It was the model or master writing. In one form it would appear as a word or collection of words to be copied by the student. In another, the teacher would write the hupogrammos on a wax tablet. The student would then place his stylus in the grooves of the letters and trace out the word for himself."

"But this is about more than writing," I said.

"Of course it is," said the teacher. "In the First Book of Peter it says this: 'Messiah suffered for us, leaving us an example, that you might walk in His steps.'"

"And that has to do with this?"

"In the original Greek, it doesn't say 'example.' It says 'hupogrammos.'"

"So Messiah left us a hupogrammos?" I said. "An underwriting?"

"Messiah *is the hupogrammos*," he said. "He is the hupogrammos by which you are to trace everything else. His life is the hupogrammos life by which you are to trace your life. The actions of His life are the hupogrammos actions by which you are to trace the actions of your life. The thoughts of Messiah are the hupogrammos thoughts, the manner of Messiah is the hupogrammos manner, His love, the hupogrammos love, His heart, the hupogrammos heart...And by that you are to trace your thoughts, your manner, your heart, your everything, from the grooves of His life and the imprint of His footsteps. Messiah is the hupogrammos of your life."

The Mission: Don't just go through this day, but seek first the hupogrammos of your day. Receive your actions and steps from Him—and then trace them.

Ephesians 5:1–2; 1 Peter 2:21

THE COSMIC BRIDAL CHAMBER

IT WAS EARLY evening. We were gazing down at the tent camp in which we had first seen the bride. We didn't see her that night, nor did we expect to.

"I wonder what she's thinking," I said. "And what she's doing."

"The bride?" asked the teacher.

"Yes."

"She's preparing for the day of her wedding."

"How exactly is she preparing?"

"She no longer focuses on her home as she once did...not on how comfortable it is or how uncomfortable."

"Because she's leaving it."

"Exactly. And the more she focuses on her present circumstances, on what she'll be leaving, the less she'll be able to focus on where she's going. She knows that her time in her present home is now temporary and limited. It's not for her to grow more attached to it, but less attached. It's for her to tread lightly. It's her time to let go, to begin to say good-bye. Everything she once knew as her home is no longer so. It's now her bridal chamber. She must now use everything she has to prepare herself for the wedding and the life that lies ahead of her."

"So she prepares herself by letting go," I said, "by saying good-bye?"

"Yes, and by whatever she can do to ready herself for her future life...not by beautifying her tent, but by beautifying herself. She prepares herself."

"But there's a spiritual realm to all this...yes?"

"Yes. If you belong to God, you're His bride. And the world is your tent, your present home. And as the bride, your focus can no longer be on this, nor on your circumstances, nor on how comfortable or uncomfortable you are in this world. This is the place you're leaving. And the more you focus on what you're leaving, the less you'll be able to focus on where you're going. Your days in the world are temporary. You're not in the world to grow more attached to it, but less attached. It's your time for letting go, of treading lightly, of saying good-bye. So use every part of this life to prepare yourself for the life yet to come. Use the time you have in this world to prepare yourself for the days of eternity. You're here to become beautiful. And from now on when you look at this world, no longer see it as your home, but see it for what it has now become...your bridal chamber."

The Mission: Live today as one preparing for the wedding. Use every moment as a chance to become more beautiful and heavenly.

Isaiah 52:1–2; Ephesians 5:26–27; Revelation 21:2

THE COVENANT OF THE BROKEN

I WAS IN THE common hall at lunchtime. I accidentally bumped into a clay jar that was set on one of the tables. It fell to the ground and shattered into a multitude of pieces. For a brief moment everyone's attention was fixed on me. I noticed someone kneeling down at my side. It was the teacher.

"I'm sorry," I said.

"I didn't come over to correct you," he said, "but to help you." He then joined me in gathering up the fragments. "But I thought we'd make the most of the opportunity. This will be our next class," he said as he continued to gather together the pieces.

"Where," he asked, "is the new covenant first spoken of?"

"I don't know."

"In the Hebrew Scriptures, God spoke to the prophet Jeremiah saying, 'The days are coming when I will make a new covenant with the people of Israel and with the people of Judah, not like the covenant I made with their fathers when I took them by the hand to take them out of Egypt, the covenant that they broke...'

"'The covenant that they broke,'" he repeated. "So the new covenant is born of brokenness. It exists because of brokenness. It was first spoken of in the days when the land of Israel lay in ruins in the wake of judgment. It's the covenant God made for those who had fallen from grace, a covenant for the broken."

"But the new covenant is given to everyone, not just to the Jewish people."

"Yes," said the teacher, "but its nature is the same for all. All have sinned, all have broken His precepts, all have failed, all have fallen and have become in some way broken. So the new covenant is the covenant God gives to all who have sinned, all who have failed, all who have fallen, and all who should have no hope of any covenant with God, all who don't deserve it. It is the covenant He makes with them regardless. So what is the power of the new covenant?" he asked. "It's the power to put together that which is broken, the power of restoration and healing."

"It's the power," I said, "to pick up and bring together all the broken pieces of our lives."

"It's the covenant of the broken."

The Mission: As much as you've failed, get up. As much as you've fallen, get up. He redeems that which is broken. Go and do likewise.

Jeremiah 31:31–34; Hosea 14:4–7; John 8:9–11

The Brit Haddashah

THE MYSTERY OF THE SEMIKHAH

TODAY," SAID THE teacher, "we open up the mystery of the *Semikhah*."
"What's a *Semikhah*?" I asked.

"It was a sacred act that had to take place before a sacrifice could be offered up for the sins of the one offering it, or before the scapegoat on Yom Kippur could take away the sins of the nation."

"And what did it involve?"

"Physical contact. The priest or the one offering the sacrifice had to make physical contact with the sacrifice. He had to touch it. Specifically, he had to place the palms of his hands on the head of the sacrifice. As it is written, 'Aaron shall lay both his hands on the head of the live goat and confess upon it all the iniquities of the children of Israel...' Only after the Semikhah was performed could the scapegoat take away the nation's sins, or the sacrifice be offered up as an atonement...And here is the mystery. Messiah is the sacrifice, the atonement. But before the sacrifice can die for sin, the Semikhah must be performed. So who was it that offered Him up, that delivered Him to His death?"

"The priests."

"Therefore, according to the mystery, the priest had to make physical contact with the sacrifice...with their hands. So it is recorded that after condemning Messiah to death, the priests began to strike Him repeatedly with their hands. For the Semikhah to be accomplished, they had to touch the head of the sacrifice with their hands. So it is recorded that priests specifically struck His face...His head. In the Semikhah, the one offering the sacrifice had to touch it with his palms. So the account records that they struck His head with their palms. There is even a rabbinical writing that states that when more than one person offers a sacrifice, they must all perform the Semikhah, taking turns touching the head of the sacrifice. So in accordance with the ancient mystery, it was only after hands were laid on its head, that the sacrifice, Messiah, was led away to be slain. And what happened in earthly realms is a symbol of what took place in heavenly realms...It was ultimately God who performed the Semikhah. He placed your sins upon Messiah. He placed the sins of you specifically upon Messiah specifically. And in His death those sins are gone and can never come back...For the act of the Semikhah has been performed."

The Mission: The Semikhah has been performed. Therefore, live this day as one whose sins have been absolutely, for certain, and for real, taken away forever.

Leviticus 16:21; Mark 14:65

THE SHERESH

TEACHER," I SAID, "what is key to being fruitful in God? What causes some to become great in the kingdom and not others?"

He got up from the rock, walked over to a small plant that was growing just a few yards away. Grabbing the bottom of its stem, he slowly and carefully pulled it out of the soil.

"This," he said, "this is the secret...the part of the plant you don't see. The hidden part. Look at it. It's hidden, yet it's the most important part. When you look at a tree, you never see the whole tree. You just see what grows above the earth. The most important part is unseen, growing downward into the earth. From the roots come the tree's water, its minerals, and its nourishment. Without the roots, the tree ceases to exist. And if its roots are shallow or weak, the tree and its fruits will wither away. A tree's fruitfulness can never exceed its *rootfulness*."

"So to apply this to our lives..."

"In God, your life is like a tree. There are two parts to your existence, the part that's visible to the world and the hidden part that no one can see. It's the visible of your life in God that manifests the fruit...all your good works, your acts of love and righteousness. But the hidden part...these are your roots."

"And what exactly are the roots?"

"Your inner life with God, your faith, your devotion, your love, communion, your time with Him in prayer, that which is in your heart. No one can see it, but it's the most critical part...the part by which you receive spiritual life and nourishment. It is this which causes the rest of your life to grow and bear fruit. If your roots are shallow or weak, the fruits of your life in God will wither away. Your fruitfulness in God will always be directly proportionate to your rootfulness in God."

"What's the Hebrew word for *root*?" I asked. "And does it reveal anything?"

"The word is *sheresh*. And it's linked to deepness, depth. And so if you would become great in God, you must become deep in God. Focus on strengthening your roots. Make it your aim to grow deeper in the hidden and secret places...and your life will bear much fruit. And so it is written, 'The root of the righteous will bear fruit.'"

The Mission: Focus today on strengthening your roots, going deeper in God's presence, deeper in receiving. And from those roots, bear your fruit.

Psalm 1:3; Proverbs 12:12; Colossians 2:6–7

Radically Rooted

THE ANTI-WITNESS

H E TOOK ME to a ruin not far from the school, but one I had never before seen or noticed. There wasn't much to see, only the barest remnants of ancient buildings and artifacts and largely obscured by the desert sand.

"These are the ruins of an ancient fortress," said the teacher. "It was destroyed not by age but war. They bear witness of two opposing sides and the conflict between them. The Scriptures speak of two opposing realities and a war in the spiritual realm, the kingdom of darkness against the kingdom of light. If we were visitors from another world, what evidence might we see on the earth that such a war exists?"

"The conflict over evil," I replied.

"Yes, but even more specific than that. What if God were to use a people to accomplish His purposes, to advance the kingdom? What would happen in the conflict?"

"They would become the target of the enemy's attacks. They would become the most attacked people on earth...the focus of a satanic hatred, the war of darkness."

"Who are the most attacked people on earth?" he asked. "And what people have been the most hated, vilified, and persecuted in human history?"

"The Jews."

"And what is the natural explanation for this fury, a fury with no rationale or natural explanation, a supernatural war that was there in the ancient world and is just as much there in the modern? And the greater the fury, the more overtly satanic the manifestation. Why is it that those most obsessed with destroying the Jewish people happen to be most evil and satanic, from the Third Reich to the masters of terrorism? It's because evil is obsessed with destroying this people, the same people who just happen to have brought into the world the Word of God, the salvation of God, and the One called the Messiah."

"It's the proof of the war," I said, "and of the existence of God and the enemy, and of a kingdom of darkness to which Jewish existence is a threat and against which it wars."

"It is the witness of the dark," said the teacher, "the anti-witness. And yet despite itself it bears witness that the Word of God is true and that the light, the good, and the answer are all linked to this people and to that which they brought into the world. The fact that, after all this, the Jewish people still exist bears witness that greater than all darkness is the light, stronger than all evil is the good, and, in the end, the fury of hell is nothing against the power of heaven."

The Mission: Today, believe, take courage, and live confidently in the truth that the good will, in the end, prevail over all evil—in the world and in your life.

Ezekiel 34:5–8; 1 Peter 5:8–9; Revelation 12:9–17

The Dragon's Secret and the Plans of Heaven I–II

THE MYSTERY OF SPRING

THE TEACHER LED me into the Chamber of Vessels and to a room within it in which several platforms had been built into the walls. On one of the platforms were the elements of Passover, on another, sheaves of grain, and on another, a basket with more grain, several fruits, and two loaves of bread.

"Tell me the theme," he said, "that binds all these things together."

I wasn't sure what the basket represented, but the overall theme soon came to me.

"Spring," I said, "all these are linked to the spring, to the spring holy days."

"Yes. In the Hebrew calendar, it's known as the spring cycle, the cluster of holy days joined together in timing and theme. The Hebrew year has two such cycles, the spring cycle that opens the sacred year, and the autumn cycle that closes it. So God has set up the age according to the sacred Hebrew year. What then do you think is revealed by the spring and autumn cycle?"

"That the age has two cycles, one at the beginning and one at the end...The two comings of Messiah...a spring coming and an autumn coming."

"Yes," he said. "And at another time I will share with you of the autumn cycle. But tell me now, what are the themes of the spring cycle?"

"The end of winter, new life, the Passover, the lamb, the sacrifice, leaving the old life, firstfruits, new beginnings, new birth, new harvests...springtime."

"And so it is the spring cycle that holds the mystery of Messiah's first coming. Messiah's first coming is all about Passover and the sacrifice, the ending of winter, the leaving of the old, the beginning of new life, birth, new harvests, salvation...rebirth...and all beginning with the Lamb. And not only is this the mystery of the age, but the mystery of our lives."

"What do you mean?"

"When you receive Messiah, it is then that the spring cycle begins. He comes into your life and makes everything become spring. He ends the winter of your life. He gives you a new beginning, salvation. He brings you out of the old life. He gives you a new birth, a new harvest...springtime. And He never ceases to be the Passover Lamb. Therefore, the spring cycle never ends. Therefore, you must never stop living in it. Never move away from the newness of your salvation. Never leave the springtime. For in the Passover Lamb, it is always springtime. And all that lives within it...is forever new."

The Mission: Live this day in the springtime of salvation. Leave the old. Come back to the new. For in the Passover Lamb it is always springtime.

Song of Solomon 2:10–13; Romans 6:4; Revelation 21:5

Nisan

THE SEVENTH DAY

WE WERE HALFWAY up a mountain, sitting on a ledge. The teacher had set two candles in two candleholders on the rock. And the sun was setting.

"When the sun sets," he said, "the Sabbath begins...the *Shabbat*, the seventh day, the day of rest, still kept to this day by the observant of His ancient people. Do you know why the Sabbath comes on the seventh day?"

"Because of the creation?"

"Yes," he replied. "God labored for six days, bringing creation into existence. He finished His labor at the end of the sixth day, then rested on the seventh day. But the creation is fallen and without rest or peace. So the work of God is now to bring forth a new creation, a redemption. And redemption comes through..."

"Messiah."

"Through His death on the cross. And what is that? It is the laboring of God to again bring forth life, to bring into existence a new creation. God finished His labors on the sixth day. The sixth day is for finishing one's labors. What about the redemption? So when did Messiah finish His labors?"

"On Friday."

"And what is Friday?"

"The sixth day."

"Yes. So Messiah finished His labors on the sixth day as well. And after God finished His labors, the Sabbath came, the seventh day. And what happened after Messiah finished His labor over the new creation?"

"The Sabbath came."

"The Sabbath came, and that's why they rushed to take Him down and place His body in the tomb...because the sun was setting and the seventh day was nearing...As in the beginning, it was time again to rest. On the seventh day of creation, God rested. So now in the new creation, the seventh day came and God rested...in the tomb."

"So He had to finish His labors because the Sabbath was coming."

"Or," said the teacher, "He finished his labor so that the Sabbath could come...the sign that His work was done...that His labors over the new creation were finished. And so the Seventh Day has come...a new rest, a new peace, a new blessing, a new completion, for all who enter the new creation through the Sabbath of Messiah."

The Mission: Leave the sixth day. Leave your struggling, your laboring, and your works. And come to the Sabbath of Messiah. Enter the seventh day.

Genesis 2:2–3; Matthew 11:28; Hebrews 4:4–11

Adon Ha Shabbat

THE TEMPLE LAMBS

IT WAS A moonlit night, bright enough to light up the tent camp in the valley below us. But our attention wasn't on the camp but on the other side of the valley where a shepherd was tending his flock at night.

"The sacrificial lambs offered up in the Temple, from where did they come?" asked the teacher.

"I would think they were raised in Israel for that purpose," I replied.

"They were," he said. "In the writings of the ancient rabbis it is recorded that In the days of the second Temple, the only place where one could shepherd a flock was in the wilderness. But there was one exception—the flocks or lambs that were specifically appointed and destined for the Temple sacrifices, the sacrificial lambs. These needed to be kept in close proximity to the Holy City. There was, in the days of the second Temple, one particular region of Israel, not of the wilderness, but of hills and valleys conducive for sheep and known for its flocks and shepherds. The Scriptures specifically cite it as a place where flocks of sheep were kept in the days of Messiah. And it happened to be in close proximity to Jerusalem where the sacrifices were offered. Thus, it is undoubtedly where the lambs for the Temple sacrifices were raised."

"What was it called?"

"It was called *Bethlehem*."

"Bethlehem!" I repeated. "So that's why..."

"That's why Messiah was born in Bethlehem. The Lamb of God was born in the place where the lambs were born. 'While shepherds watched their flocks by night...' And not just in the place of the lambs, but in the place of the sacrificial lambs, where the lambs destined to be offered up in the Temple of Jerusalem as sacrifices to God were born."

"And that's why the first ones to see Him in this world were the shepherds," I said, "because when a lamb is born, the shepherds attend its birth."

"And not just by shepherds," said the teacher, "but by the shepherds of Bethlehem, the shepherds who attended the birth of the sacrificial lambs. So the Lamb of God was born among the sacrificial lambs for the same reason, to be sacrificed in Jerusalem. The mystery was there from the beginning, from His birth. The entire purpose of His life was to give Himself, to give His life as a gift of sacrificial love for us. His entire life...even from the moment of His birth...was love."

The Mission: Messiah's entire life was a living sacrifice, every moment a gift given, the incarnation of love. Be and do likewise.

Micah 5:2; Luke 2:8–20

The Bethlehem Mysteries

THE MYSTERY HARVESTS

WE WENT TO the city to purchase some goods. On the way we came to an enclave, an agricultural settlement in the desert filled with harvesters.

"It's their harvest," said the teacher. "And when they finish, they'll celebrate. People have been celebrating harvests from the beginning of history." He paused. "But then there are the mystery harvests. And the celebrations of the mystery harvests."

"The mystery harvests?"

"Imagine a people celebrating a harvest that never took place, a harvest they never reaped or sowed, the celebration of a nonexistent harvest. And imagine a people persisting in celebrating these nonexistent harvests year after year for centuries."

"I can't imagine it," I said.

"But it actually happened. It's one of the strangest phenomena of history."

"Who would do that?"

"The Jewish people," he said. "God commanded them to celebrate the harvests of the Promised Land. But in AD 70 the land of Israel was destroyed, and the Jewish people were scattered to the ends of the earth. There were no more harvests, no more grain or fruits to be gathered. But even though they had no more harvests, they kept celebrating them anyway. They celebrated nonexistent barley harvests, gave thanks for nonexistent fruit harvests, and rejoiced over nonexistent vines overflowing with nonexistent grapes. And then something just as strange happened. After two thousand years of celebrating the nonexistent harvests, the nonexistent harvests reappeared on the earth." He paused a moment before continuing.

"It is crucial," he said, "that you learn this secret of the kingdom. The children of this world rejoice after seeing their blessings. But the children of the kingdom do the opposite. They celebrate *before* the blessings. Don't wait to see your blessings in order to rejoice. Rejoice, and you will see your blessings. Don't wait for the gift to come in order to give thanks. Give thanks, and the gift will come. Don't wait until your circumstances are right in order to celebrate. Celebrate anyway, and it will be right. Don't wait for the victory to be won in order to become victorious. Become victorious, and the victory will be won. Learn the secret of Israel's mystery harvests. Celebrate the blessings you don't yet see. Celebrate the harvest you don't have...and you will have a harvest to celebrate."

The Mission: Live today in the way of the kingdom. Before you see the blessing, rejoice and give thanks for it. Celebrate your mystery harvest.

Deuteronomy 16:15; Jeremiah 31:3–6; Mark 11:24

The Mystery Harvests

THE DAYS OF FUTURE PAST

TIMELESS," SAID THE teacher. "The sacred tongue is timeless."

"You mean timeless in that it doesn't change?" I asked. "Or timeless in that it's eternal?"

"I mean timeless in that it knows no time."

"What do you mean?"

"In the original Hebrew of Scripture, that which happens knows no time."

"But the Bible speaks of time all the time, of days and years."

"Yes, but the Hebrew language has no absolute tense concerning time."

"How can a language have no past, present, or future?"

"It has other tenses," he said, "tenses that are used and understood or taken to mean the past, present, and future. But the truth is these other tenses have no absolute relation to when they occur. In fact, at times, the Scriptures speak of future events as if they've already taken place...the future past."

"So what are the tenses?"

"The perfect and the imperfect. The perfect tense speaks of an action that's finished, thus complete, perfect. The imperfect tense speaks of an action that's unfinished and thus, incomplete, imperfect. So in Hebrew you only have two choices: to live in the perfect or in the imperfect. If you live always striving to finish that which is unfinished, to complete that which is incomplete, if you live trying to be saved, trying to be loved, to be good enough, worthy, complete...then you're living in the imperfect tense...and you're living in the imperfect. And living in the imperfect tense never works, because that which comes out of incompletion can never be anything other than incomplete."

"Then how do you live in the perfect tense?"

"To live in the perfect tense you must learn the secret of living from that which is already completed, to do from that which is already done, to triumph from a victory already won."

"But what is it that is already accomplished, complete, finished, and perfect?"

"The work of God," he said, "salvation. The completed work of Messiah."

"'It is finished,'" I said.

"Yes. For that which is perfect is that which is finished. And salvation is a perfect work...in the days of future past."

The Mission: Live this day in the Hebrew perfect. Do all things from His finished work. Triumph from the victory already won. Live from the completion.

Matthew 5:48; Ephesians 2:10; Philippians 3:13–15

DUNAMAHEE: THE POWER OF I CAN

WE WERE ALL sitting down. The teacher was on a large rock, and several of the students were gathered in a semicircle at his feet.

"In the world are many powers," he said, "the power of the sun, the power of the wind, the power of rivers, the power of fire, the power of atoms, the power of kings, the power of armies, and the power of man. Each of these powers has conditions and limitations. But what if there was a power beyond all these powers…a power with no limitations, the power to do anything?"

No one answered.

"Messiah gave His disciples, and all the disciples who would come after them, including all of you, the Great Commission to proclaim the message of salvation to the world, to teach His Word, to do His will, and to make disciples of all nations. But what did He tell them to do first?"

"To wait in Jerusalem," said one of the students, "to receive power."

"Yes," said the teacher. "And what power was that?"

"The power of the Spirit," said another.

"That's correct. And do you know what lies behind the word for the power they were to receive? The word used in the Scriptures is the Greek *dunamis*. It comes from the root word *dunamahee*. *Dunamahee* means to be able. And Messiah gave no condition, no qualifier, no modifier, and no limitation concerning the power to be given. What power is given to you in the Spirit? The power to become able to do that which you could never do before…the power to do that which is above your ability to do. *Dunamahee* means to make possible. So if you live by the Spirit, you will have the power to make possible that which was not possible. And one more thing," he said. "*Dunamahee* also means can, as in I can. The power of the Spirit is *the power of I can*."

"I can do what?" asked a student.

"It doesn't say. Again, there's no qualification on it. You've been given *the power of I can* to do anything, the power to do all things, and the power to do whatever you need to do to fulfill the will and calling of God. There's no limitation. It's the power of powers, the power to do whatever it is that you need to do. It's the power to nullify and overcome every I can't in your life…with the power of the I can of the Almighty."

The Mission: Live this day in the dunamahee of God. Whatever you have to do in the will of God, claim the power of I can. And in that power, *do it*.

Zechariah 4:6–9; Luke 24:49; Philippians 4:13

Dunamahee: The Power of I Can

THE PROMISE

HE REMOVED A scroll from one of the shelves in the Chamber of Scrolls, placed it on the wooden table, and unrolled it.

"Thousands of years ago," said the teacher, "God gave a prophecy to the Jewish people. They would be taken captive from their homeland, scattered to the nations, and driven from one land to the next, to the ends of the earth. And it all came true. For the last two thousand years the Jewish people have been wandering the earth, from nation to nation. But He gave them a promise: At the end of the age He would gather them from the nations and bring them back to the land of Israel. So it is written in the Book of Jeremiah, 'I will bring them from the land of the north and gather them from the ends of the earth, among them the blind and the lame, the woman with child, and the one who is in labor together.' It was an impossibility. In all of human history nothing like this had ever happened before. And few believed it ever could."

"Even those who read the Bible?"

"Most had convinced themselves that God was finished with the Jewish people. And most Jewish people didn't think they would ever live to see the prophecies come true. For two thousand years the land of Israel was in the hands of their enemies or in the hands of those who had no intention of giving it back. And the Jewish people were overwhelmingly powerless. But God said it would happen. The promise was inscribed in His Word. And despite all the powers and all the odds against it, after two thousand years of impossibility, in the midst of a secular and cynical age, God fulfilled the prophecy and His promise. He gathered His ancient people back from the ends of the earth and brought them back to their ancient homeland, the blind and the lame, the woman with child, a great multitude...as a shepherd gathers his flock."

He closed the scroll.

"You see," said the teacher, "between the Word and the world, it was again the Word that was the more real and the more true. And between the promise and the hell that came against it, it was the promise that was the stronger. Never forget that. His Word is true, truer than the world, and His promise is sure, and stronger than all that come against it. And if after two thousand years God remembered His promise to fulfill it, He will also remember His promises to you."

The Mission: Today, find a promise in the Word of God that applies to you and stand on it, believe it, and live this day in light of it.

Jeremiah 30 31; 2 Corinthians 1:20

The Ingathering

KINGDOM OF THE LAMB

THE TEACHER HAD in his hand a small parchment from which he began to read. "'I looked and behold in the midst of the throne and of the four living creatures, and in the midst of the elders, stood a Lamb'...In the midst of the throne stood a Lamb. This is the vision given to Yochanan, John, in the Book of Revelation. Do you see anything strange about it?" he asked.

"Everything," I said. "The four living creatures, the elders, the lamb..."

"How about a lamb on a throne?"

"Why is that stranger than the rest?"

"Think about it, a lamb, the most defenseless of creatures, so weak it must be protected not only by its mother but by a shepherd...That's what's so strange about the vision. The Lamb is on the throne. The Lamb is king. The Lamb reigns over all. A lion would make sense, but not a lamb...the most powerless of creatures reigning on the throne with all power and over all."

"It's a symbol of Him? Correct? Messiah, the Lamb of God."

"Yes," said the teacher. "And He will reign over God's kingdom. So the kingdom of God will be the kingdom of the Lamb. How radical is that...a Lamb upon a throne? It goes against the way of the animal kingdom and that of man's kingdoms. But the kingdom of God doesn't work according to the laws of this world, but by its own. And to prosper in God you must learn the secrets of that kingdom. In the world, it is the strong and fierce who rule. But in the kingdom of God, it is the Lamb that rules. So in the kingdom of the Lamb, the weak are strong, and the strong are weak. In this kingdom, if you would have, you must let go. If you would receive, you must give. If you lower yourself, you will be lifted up. If you become little, you will become great. If you lose yourself, you will find yourself. If you surrender, you will prevail. And if you die to yourself, you will find life."

"As He died and found life," I said, "and as He surrendered all and has prevailed over all and overcome the world."

"And if you walk in the footsteps of the Lamb, you too will prevail and overcome the world. For we are of the most radical of kingdoms...the kingdom of the Lamb."

The Mission: Live this day in the way of the Lamb. Let go that you might have. Die that you might live. And surrender that you might overcome.

Matthew 5:30–45; 20:25–28; 2 Corinthians 6:3–10; 12:9–10; Revelation 5:6–14

The Lamb Mysteries I–VI

THE UNSCRIPTURES

HE TOOK ME into the Chamber of Scrolls and to the ark. He removed the scroll, placed it on the wooden table.

"I want you to look carefully to see what's on the scroll."

He began unrolling it.

"These are the Holy Scriptures," he said, "the Word of God in its original form. Tell me what you see."

"Writing, words, letters."

"Is that all?" he asked.

"What else is there?"

"You haven't even described the half of it."

"What do you mean?" I asked.

"You've only described to me the black...and not all the rest."

"The white?"

"Yes, the white background. The black is holy; so too is the white. Without it, you wouldn't see the black of the ink, there would be nothing with which to contrast it, nothing to delineate it. Without the white, you wouldn't see the Word of God. The white is the sacred *unscripture* of God."

"The unscripture?"

"Yes, the unscripture. When the Word is sent into the world, it must have a context, it must have a parchment, a paper, a voice, some medium to bear and manifest it to the world. This is the sacred white of the unscripture. And do you know what the holiest unscripture is?"

"No."

"Your life," he said. "Your life is the sacred white upon which His Word appears, the holy parchment that bears and manifests the eternal script. Therefore, the key is to join your life, your heart, your emotions, your soul, and your will to the Word of God...to join the black with the white, the ink with the scroll, to receive the holy oracles, to carry it and manifest it to the world. Let every part of your life become the white of God's Word...the sacred unscripture.

The Mission: Today, join the Word to the parchment of your heart, your will, your emotions, and your ways. Let your life become the sacred white of God's Word.

Psalm 119:11; Matthew 7:24; Colossians 3:16

The Invisible Scriptures

THE BISORAH

I T WAS A particularly windy day and even more where we stood on the top of a desert mountain.

"What does the word *Gospel* mean?" he asked.

"An account of Messiah's life," I replied.

"It means good news. It's the good news of Messiah's redemption, the forgiveness of our sins on the cross, the overcoming of death in the resurrection, salvation, eternal life. Now where in the Bible does the word *Gospel* first appear?

"In the New Testament."

"No. It appears first in the Hebrew Scriptures."

"How? As what?"

"As the word *Bisorah*. *Bisorah* is the word from which the *Gospel* of the New Testament comes. In fact, Messiah began His ministry by quoting a Hebrew verse in which that word appears: 'The Spirit of the Lord God is upon Me, for the Lord has anointed Me to proclaim the Bisorah, the Gospel, the good news.' And there's more to it. *Bisorah* comes from the root word *basar*. *Basar* means cheerful or joyful. So the effect of the Bisorah, the Gospel, has to be joy. Its nature is to make one's life joyful. To know that you're saved from judgment and been given heaven as well is more than enough to give you joy every day of your life."

"But there have to be believers who don't live with joy."

"Then they're not receiving the Bisorah, not as it is. Do you know what else *Bisorah* means? It's a word that describes you right now."

"What do you mean?"

"The wind has caused your cheeks to become rosy. The word *Bisorah*, the *Gospel*, means rosy."

"Rosy?"

"Yes, for the effect of the Gospel is to make the one who receives it rosy, as in filled with life. And do you know what else *Bisorah* means? Fresh. For the Gospel, the good news of salvation, is always new, always fresh. It never gets old. And if one is not living in the freshness of life, then one is not receiving the Bisorah, or has stopped receiving it. Since the Bisorah is always fresh, it must always be freshly received…as if for the first time. And those who receive it in this way, their lives become new, revived, and refreshed. For the Gospel is the Bisorah, and the Bisorah never ages, never gets old, and can never be anything else…but new, fresh, and enough to make your life rosy-cheeked."

The Mission: Receive today the Bisorah, the good news, as if for the first time. And by that power walk afresh in the newness of life.

Proverbs 25:25; Isaiah 52:7; 61:1

The Nisan Gospel Mystery

THE PRIVATE AND THE GENERAL

WE WERE SITTING by where the campfire would have been if it had been lit, but it was morning. There was no fire and we were alone.

"In an army," said the teacher, "who has the most authority?"

"The general," I answered.

"Correct," he said. "He submits to no other rank but exercises authority over every other rank. Now who in an army has the least authority?"

"The private."

"That's correct. The private is the opposite. He submits to all other ranks and exercises no authority over any other."

He paused for a few moments, then spoke again.

"A riddle...When does the private have the same authority as the general?"

"Never," I said. "Or he wouldn't be a private."

"But there is a time when the private exercises the same authority as a general. It's when the private is carrying out an assignment given to him by the general. When a private carries out a directive, an errand, a mission, or an order given to him by the general, then, with regard to that directive, he carries the general's authority. Every other soldier, every rank, every captain and colonel, must yield to him in the fulfilling of his assignment. Before him, every gate must open and every door must be unlocked. Now," said the teacher, "let's take it to the ultimate. In the universe, who has all authority?"

"God."

"Yes. He is the General. And who has the least authority?"

"Us...man?"

"Yes. So when does the private, you, bear the authority of the General, God?"

"When...we carry out the assignment given to us by God, when we carry out His mission."

"Exactly," he replied. "If you live outside the will of God, if you act against it, then you will live and act with the authority of a private, which is to have no authority. But if you live inside the will of God, if you follow the directives of God, if you carry out His assignment, if you set your course on fulfilling His mission, then you will live in the authority of God. Then every rank in this universe must yield to your steps, every door must unlock, and every gate must open. So make it your aim to live your life wholly in the will of God. Find your mission and fulfill it. And you will walk in the power and the authority of the Almighty."

The Mission: Today, aim to walk fully in the will of God. Carry out a mission from the General. And as you walk in His will, walk also in His authority.

Matthew 28:18–20; John 20:21–23; 2 Corinthians 10:3–5

The Private and the General

THE SKELETON PROPHECY

DO YOU REMEMBER this place?" he asked.

In front of us was a large and forbidding valley.

"This," he said, "is where I shared with you of the Valley of Dry Bones."

We began walking in its midst as we had done the first time.

"Imagine you're the prophet Ezekiel. God places you in the midst of a valley like this, and it's filled with bones. He tells you, 'Prophesy to these bones.' So you do. Suddenly you see the bones coming together, one by one, and forming skeletons. Then on the skeletons appears flesh, and then skin. Then they come alive. Do you remember what it was all about?"

"Israel would come alive again as a nation in the land."

"Yes," said the teacher, "but how? Israel was not to appear on the earth as other nations. It would happen as in the Valley of Dry Bones. First would be the bones, the broken, scattered remnants of the ancient nation, the dispersed bones of its culture, of its national memory, the people themselves scattered throughout the earth. So God began to gather the bones together from the nations. And what do you then have?"

"A skeleton?"

"A skeleton. And so Israel first appears in the world as a skeletal entity, the skeleton of a nation. Its language, Hebrew, comes to life first as a skeletal language, the skeleton of a once living ancient language. The government appears first as a skeletal government, the culture as a skeletal culture, a skeletal army, a skeletal land...a skeleton nation. And then, over time, the flesh appears, exactly as in the vision. And on the day when Israel was raised from the dead, do you know what appeared on its proclamation of existence?"

"What?"

"The words 'Prophesy to these bones!' The words from the Valley of Dry Bones. How impossible is it to raise up bones and skeletons and cause them to come alive?"

"Totally impossible."

"And for two thousand years it was totally impossible to raise Israel from the dead. But God said it and God did it. Never forget that: He's the God of the impossible...the God who touches what is completely hopeless and dead and causes it to come alive again. With God, nothing is impossible. For He is the God of the impossible and of the Valley of Dry Bones."

The Mission: Even modern history bears it witness: God is the God of the impossible. Seeing the reality, believe God today for the impossible.

Ezekiel 37:1–14; Luke 1:37

The Valley of Dry Bones Revelation

THE PREEMPTOR

WE WERE WALKING through a large plain flanked by low-lying mountains when something caught the teacher's attention. In the sand between the rocks at the base of the mountain was a snake. Its mouth was stretched around an egg much larger than its body.

"This," said the teacher, "is a *dasypeltis scabra*, the egg-eating snake. You don't have to remember the name, but take note of what it does."

"It swallows eggs," I said.

"Yes," he said, "and it reveals a critical principle in the spiritual realm. The serpent is a symbol of evil and of the enemy. And serpents of this kind are known for swallowing eggs. What are eggs? That from which life emerges. Moses was called to free the Hebrew slaves from Pharaoh. But in the days of Moses's birth the pharaoh decreed that all male babies born of the Hebrews were to be killed. Only by a miracle did the baby Moses survive. So too it was in the days of Messiah's infancy that King Herod tried to end His life. What does this reveal?"

"The enemy attacks the young."

"More than that," he said. "The enemy would again attempt to destroy Messiah's ministry in the wilderness just before it began."

"So the enemy especially attacks at the beginning of God's purposes."

"Yes, and *before* the beginning. God had promised to gather the Jewish people from the nations and resurrect the nation of Israel. But just before the words of the prophets were to be fulfilled, a satanic fury broke forth on the earth in the form of Nazism, to wipe out the Jewish people just before the prophecies could be fulfilled, before Israel could be reborn. The pattern repeats again and again. What is the enemy? He is a preemptor. He attacks the purposes of God not only after they begin, but *before they begin*, to preempt them."

"Just as the serpent seeks to swallow the egg."

"So when you're in the will of God and all hell comes against you, don't be discouraged. Be encouraged. It's a good sign. The enemy doesn't waste his time. He's doing everything he can to keep God's purpose from being accomplished. So keep going all the more strongly. The attack is a sign of how great is the calling, the blessing, the purpose, and the victory God has just ahead of you. Just don't give up, but press on all the more...until you see those purposes break through their shell."

The Mission: Today, respond to any problem, setback, hindrance, or attack by pressing on all the more to apprehend the victory that lies just beyond it.

2 Corinthians 2:11, 14; Hebrews 10:36

THE HEAVEN-TO-EARTH LIFE

IT WAS A beautiful day with clouds slowly drifting through a deep blue sky.

"Heaven and earth," said the teacher. "We think of the one in contrast to the other. But the secret is the opposite."

"What do you mean?"

"Messiah told us to pray 'Your will be done on earth as it is in heaven.' Thus the two, heaven and earth, are to be in union. Messiah's redemption is the joining of heaven to earth, and earth to heaven. Therefore, to live in redemption you must live in the joining of heaven and earth."

"So we're to live looking to heaven."

"Yes," said the teacher, "but that's not the secret. It's much deeper than that. 'On earth as it is in heaven' means it is to be on earth as it *first* is in heaven. Heaven is first, and then earth. 'In the beginning God created the heavens and the earth,' not the earth and the heavens. Heaven is always first. Life and blessing proceed not from earth to heaven, but from heaven to earth. And yet most live the other way, even those who seek God."

"From earth to heaven."

"Yes. They seek to ascend, to become holier, more spiritual and godly, more pure, righteous, loving, more heavenly. They seek to rise higher. But the answer never comes from earth to heaven."

"So the secret is to live not from earth to heaven...but from heaven to earth?"

"Yes, the exact opposite of everything we've known and how we're used to living and thinking. The answer is to live a heaven-to-earth life."

"So we shouldn't seek to be holy?"

"We should, but not from ourselves. It must start with heaven. The only way you can become holy is to live *from* the Holy. The only way to become pure is to live *from* the Pure. The only way to become good is to live *from* the Good. The only way to become loving is to live *from* Love. The only way to become truly giving is to live *from* the Gift. And the only way to become godly is to live *from* God. You don't attain heaven. You let heaven attain you. You start living a heaven-to-earth-life, where everything you do begins from heaven and proceeds to earth. You let heaven, through your life, touch the earth, touch every part of your world...on earth as it is in heaven."

The Mission: Learn the secret today of living a heaven-to-earth life. Live each moment *from* above, *from* the good, *from* the glorious, *from* heaven.

Isaiah 55:10–11; Matthew 6:10; Colossians 3:2

As It Is in Heaven

SHALOM ALEICHEM

IT WAS ON the first day of the week, morning. All the students were gathered together in the open-air tent waiting for the teacher to speak.

"Peace be to you," he said. "That is what Messiah said to His disciples when He greeted them. As is written, 'As they said these things, Yeshua, Jesus, Himself stood in the midst of them, and said to them, "Peace be to you!"' It's the only record of Messiah saying those words. It was the first thing He said when He appeared to them after the resurrection. He could have said anything, but He chose to say, 'Peace be to you!' In fact, He said it twice in the same encounter. There must be something about those words. Why do you think He said it, and that it's only recorded after the resurrection, not before?"

The students were silent.

"When Isaiah prophesied of Messiah's atoning death, he wrote this: 'He was wounded for our transgressions. He was bruised for our iniquities. The punishment for our *peace* was upon Him...' Peace only comes after the atonement is made. So it was only *after* Messiah died on the cross and rose that peace could be given. But Isaiah's prophecy doesn't say 'our peace.' It says 'our *shalom*.' And when Messiah spoke the blessing to His disciples, He didn't say 'peace' either. He said, '*Shalom aleichem*.' '*Shalom be upon you*.'"

"But if *shalom* means peace," said one of the students, "then what's the difference?"

"The difference is everything," he said. "For *shalom* means much more than peace. *Shalom* means safety, rest, prosperity, wholeness, welfare, completion, fullness, soundness, and even well-being. So what blessing did Messiah speak to His disciples? His blessing can be taken this way: 'May you be blessed with safety, with rest, with prosperity, with wholeness, with completion, with fullness, with soundness, with well-being...and with peace.'"

"All that in that one blessing?" asked one of the students.

"All that in His shalom. All that in His sacrifice. And all that is the blessing that Messiah gives to His disciples...and what He gives to you. Their part, and your part, is to learn what that exactly means...and to receive it."

The Mission: Today, make it your aim to receive the shalom of Messiah—His peace, fullness, rest, completion, well-being, and wholeness. Shalom Aleichem.

Isaiah 53:5; John 20:19–21; Colossians 3:15

The Shalom I Give

THE LEPER KING

THE TEACHER LED me into the Chamber of Books where he removed from one of the shelves a large reddish book and placed it on the wooden table.

"The Sanhedrin," he said, "was the council that put Messiah on trial. They accused Him of being a false Messiah, judged Him guilty of blasphemy, and delivered Him over to the Romans to be executed. What you're looking at is the writing of the rabbis from the Talmud. It's called 'Tractate Sanhedrin.'"

"As in the same Sanhedrin that judged Messiah guilty?"

"Yes," said the teacher. "And that's what makes what you're about to hear amazing. The writers of Sanhedrin said that the Messiah of Israel would be called the Leper."

"Leper?" I replied. "A strange name to call your Messiah. Why?"

"The words of Sanhedrin explain why as they say this of the Messiah: 'Surely he has borne our griefs, and carried our sorrows: yet we did esteem him a leper; smitten of God, and afflicted.'"

"So Tractate Sanhedrin is describing the Messiah as the One who bears our sufferings."

"Yes. They're quoting Isaiah's prophecy of the redeemer who dies for our sins. And they're identifying the one who dies for our sins as the Messiah of Israel. And they named Him 'the Leper' to speak of Him as a man of afflictions, stricken, and plagued, despised and outcast. And the prophecy goes on to say: 'He was wounded for our transgressions, He was bruised for our iniquities; the punishment that brought us peace fell upon Him. And by His stripes, we are healed...The Lord laid upon Him the iniquity of us all. He was oppressed and He was afflicted, yet He did not open His mouth; He is brought as a lamb to the slaughter...He was cut off from the land of the living; for the transgression of My people to whom the stroke was due.'"

"There's only One who fits that description, only One who could be that Messiah—the very same One that the Sanhedrin condemned to death for not being the Messiah. And yet the words of Sanhedrin describe the Messiah as Him."

"Yes," said the teacher, "think about it. By condemning Him to death on the charge of not being the Messiah, they caused Him to be despised and rejected, wounded, afflicted, bruised, punished, and killed."

"To become the very One they describe as their Messiah."

"So if even they who deny Him...bear witness of Him, how much more must we bear witness of Him...and fully partake of the atonement that bring us healing and shalom. The Sanhedrin's Leper King is Messiah."

The Mission: Even the rabbis bear witness: Messiah has taken your sins, your infirmities, your sorrows, and your condemnation. Today, let Him have them.

Isaiah 53:4–8; Matthew 8:16–17; 1 Peter 2:22–24

The Leper King

THE APOKALUPSIS

WE WERE ALL sitting around the campfire, the teacher and I, along with several other students. But because I was sitting next to him, only I could hear his words as he read from the scroll in his hand.

"'The dragon stood on the shore of the sea. And I saw a beast coming out of the sea. It had ten horns and seven heads, with ten crowns on its horns, and on each head a blasphemous name.' It's from the Book of Revelation," he said, "the apocalypse."

"It definitely sounds apocalyptic."

"Many fear the apocalypse. Do you?"

"I guess."

"But do you know what the most apocalyptic of things is?...A wedding."

"How could a wedding be apocalyptic?"

"The word *apocalypse* comes from the Greek *apokalupsis*, which, in turn, comes from two root words: *apo*, which means away or to remove, and *kalupsis*, which means a veil or covering. So the *apocalypse* is the removing of the veil. It speaks of the revealing, the opening of the vision concerning the end. But there's another connection. When you get to the end of the Bible and to the end of the apocalypse, you find there a bride and a Bridegroom. You find a wedding. In the ancient Hebrew marriage, on the day of the wedding, when the bride and groom, after their long separation, now stand face-to-face, the bride lifts the veil from her face—the removing of the veil, the apokalupsis, the apocalypse. So the two stand there, with no veils and no more separations, face-to-unveiled-face. In the same way, there will come a day, a wedding day, when all veils will be removed and we will see Him as He is, and He will see us as we are, unveiled, face-to-face. You see," said the teacher, "we are all heading to one apocalypse or another, the apocalypse of judgment or, in salvation, the apocalypse of the wedding. And if you are of the wedding, then you must even now come before Him and remove your veil and your coverings, with no more separations and nothing hidden. For only if you come as you are, can you know Him as He is. And only then will He be able to touch you as you must be touched and changed. Learn the secret of living as on the day of the wedding...even now...with no coverings...in the apokalupsis of the bride and groom...face-to-face...and beyond the veil."

The Mission: Come to God today in the apokalupsis of the bride, unveiled, nothing hidden, and nothing covered. Let Him touch what must be touched.

1 Corinthians 13:12; Ephesians 5:27; Revelation 13:1; 19:7–9

The Person Behind the Veil

THE SECRET OF COLORS

HE LED ME into a garden filled with small fruit trees and flowers. It had to be one of the most beautiful places in the entire school.

"So many colors," said the teacher. "What do you see?"

"Red, blue, and purple flowers, yellow and green fruits, white lilies..."

"Why is the red flower red?" he asked.

"Because...that's its color?" I replied. "I don't understand."

"The red flower is bathed in the light of all colors. It absorbs all colors except one—red. Red is the color of the one light it doesn't receive or absorb. So red is the one color it reflects or gives back. Now what if a flower took in and kept all the colors of the light? What color would it be?"

"No color," I said. "It would be dark. It would be a black flower."

"Correct," he said, "and not only with flowers but with all things. That which you take and keep to yourself is not that which you *are*...but that which you *are not*. It is that of which you are empty. It is those who take from this world and don't give...who are the empty. It is those who seek to acquire love from this world, but not to give love...who are the loveless. And it is those who take blessing but don't give blessing...who are the unblessed...the black flowers."

"So that which you give is that which you are."

"Or what you become," said the teacher. "It is those who give love who are the loved. It is those who give of their possessions who are the rich. And it is those who bless who are the blessed. So that which you would have your life to become is the very thing you must give. Therefore, live a life of giving love, and you will have love. Live a life of giving of your possessions, and you will be rich. Live a life of blessing others, and your life will always be blessed. For the light shines on every flower. But each flower becomes the light it gives back. So His love shines on all. But only that which you give back is what you will be and become."

He paused to pick up a white lily, which he held up to the sunlight.

"And what happens to those who keep nothing but give everything back?"

"They become white," I answered.

"More than that," he said. "They become light."

The Mission: Commit to become a vessel of giving, to fully give of every blessing. Start today. And your life will become the reflection of God.

Proverbs 11:25–26; Matthew 5:16; 2 Corinthians 3:18

THE SECRET OF THE AXE

WHILE ON ONE of our walks, we came across a groundskeeper. He was cutting down a small tree with an axe.

"'If the axe is dull,'" said the teacher, "'and one does not sharpen its edge, then more strength must be exerted.' It's from the Book of Ecclesiastes. In other words, if you use an axe with a dull edge, the energy you expend and the power you apply will be spread out and dissipated over a dull edge. The axe becomes inefficient and ineffective. You need to put in more time, energy, or force to accomplish the same amount of work. On the other hand, if the axe's edge is sharp, it will focus and concentrate your energy and power. Therefore it will take less time, energy, and force to accomplish more."

"I'll remember that," I said, "when I cut down my next tree."

"You won't cut down trees," he said. "But you'll still need to remember it."

"Why?"

"Because it can change the way you live."

"How?"

"Replace the word *axe* with the words *your life*. If your life is dull, and you don't sharpen its edge, then more strength must be exerted. A dull edge is one that is less focused. It doesn't converge to a single point. The same with your life. If your life isn't focused, if your life doesn't have a single focus, if it's spread out in many directions or with unclear purpose, then it will have a dull edge. But if you apply to your life the secret of the axe, if you sharpen your life..."

"How?"

"First, you need to have a clear focus and aim. Then you need to bring everything in your life into harmony with that focus and aim, so that everything you do is consistent with that aim and converges to that focus. Then your life will have a sharp edge. Then your life will become powerful. Such were the lives of the giants of Scripture from Elijah to Paul to Messiah. Live life with a sharp axe, a focused edge, and your energy, your strength, and your efforts will be multiplied. Make God the point of everything you do. Make His will the aim of your life, and His purpose the focus of your life. Sharpen the axe and the tree will fall."

The Mission: Today, sharpen your axe. Focus your life. Make God and His purposes the point, the aim, and the goal of everything you do.

Ecclesiastes 10:10; 1 Corinthians 9:24–27; Colossians 3:17

Sharp

RECHEM AND RACHAM

WE WERE OVERLOOKING a village of tent dwellers, one with which the teacher was well acquainted. There was a single person in sight, a young woman sitting by the door of a tent.

"She's with child," he said. "Within her womb is the most delicate of beings . . . a new life. The only real protection it has is the womb. In Hebrew, the word for *womb* is *rechem*. It comes from the word *racham*."

"And what does *racham* mean?"

"*Racham* speaks of tender love, deep compassion, and mercy. In fact, *racham* means both mercy and womb."

"How are the two connected?"

"The womb is a place of tenderness, nurturing, and protection. If not for that tender love we never would have been born. And yet the word *racham*, which can mean both mercy and womb, is used in Scripture for the love and mercy of God."

"So the word used for God's love is linked to the womb."

"And that's the mystery."

"What's the mystery?"

"The love and mercy of God is as a womb."

"How?"

"It is God's racham, His tender love and deep compassion, that causes us to be born . . . again. In the Book of John, Messiah tells the Jewish leader Nicodemus that to enter heaven, one must be born again. Nicodemus responds with a question, 'Can a man enter his mother's womb to be born when he is old?' The answer is, 'No.' But there *is* a womb that we can enter, the rechem, the womb of God's tender mercy. And it is that mercy, that rechem, the womb of His love, that tenderly keeps us throughout our lives, that keeps us, holds us, nurtures us, and protects us from harm. And it is by living in that love and mercy that we grow and are formed into the child of heaven we were called to become. The racham of God is the rechem of our new birth. For every birth must have a womb. And the womb of our new birth is His love."

The Mission: Take time today to dwell in the racham, the deep compassions and tender mercies of the Lord. Let it change you into His image.

Isaiah 44:24; John 3:3–8

Rachamim

TZEMACH: THE BRANCH MAN

IT WAS EARLY afternoon. The teacher and I were sitting outside in the shade of one of the school buildings. He pointed downward.

"Do you see this?" He directed my attention to a little green plant sprouting up from the soil. "This could be called a *tzemach*," he said. "It comes from a Hebrew root word that means to sprout, to blossom, to bear, to prosper, to branch out, and to spring forth. So a tzemach is that which sprouts up, that grows, branches out, springs forth, and blossoms. In the Book of Zechariah it is prophesied of Messiah that He will be the One who, in the days of the kingdom, will build God's Temple. But the prophecy gives Him a name: 'Behold the man *whose name is the Branch.*' So the Name of Messiah is the Branch. But what it actually says is, 'Behold the man whose name is the Tzemach.' Messiah is the Tzemach."

"And what's the significance?"

"Messiah's life is the sprout, the branch, the blossom, that which springs up from the earth. The prophecy goes on, '…for He shall grow up out of His place…' In other words, His Name will be the Tzemach, because He will branch out from His place. His life will start out as a small shoot coming up from the earth, like this plant. But the effect of His life on the world will grow. It will grow so much that it will transcend the place of His origins. His life will branch out beyond Galilee, beyond Jerusalem, beyond Israel. It will branch out to cover the entire world. And His life will blossom. And the blossoming of His life will fill the world with its fruit…Think about it," said the teacher. "In the natural, a peasant carpenter dying on an execution stake has little effect on the world. But this crucified peasant is the Tzemach. Therefore, the impact of His life grows and grows and grows until it covers the world. And so the Tzemach changes the course of the world."

"And would that also be true for His presence in our lives?"

"Exactly," he said. "So it is also for all who receive Him, for all who truly know Him…He is the Tzemach of their lives. So He must continually grow. His life and the effect of His life must always be increasing. Therefore, if you truly know Him, then He is always becoming greater and greater in your heart and in your love. It must be that way…for His Name is Tzemach."

The Mission: Is He greater in your life than before? Today, make Him greater in your heart, your mind, your ways, and your love.

Zechariah 6:12; Philippians 2:9

The Tzemach

THE SUNRISE COMMANDMENT

L OOK ALL AROUND you," said the teacher. "What do you see?"

"Mountains, plains, buildings, rocks, plants, gardens...Why?"

"Why do you see them?"

"Because I'm looking."

"But if you were looking at night, you wouldn't see anything. You only see them by the light of the sun. Everything is illuminated by the sun...the beautiful and the ugly, the good and the bad, the holy and the unholy. All across the world everything is illuminated by the sun, lands, oceans, cities, deserts, cathedrals and prisons, hills of grass and mounds of garbage, saints and criminals, the good and the evil, all of it is lit up by the same sun."

"How could it be otherwise?" I said.

"That's the question. Messiah told His disciples, 'Bless those who curse you, do good to those who hate you, and pray for those who spitefully use you and persecute you, that you may be children of your Father in heaven. For He causes His sun to rise on the evil and on the good...' He causes His sun to rise on the evil and on the good. What would happen if it was otherwise...if the sun only shone on the beautiful of this world and not on the ugly? And what would happen if the sun only gave its light to the good and the righteous but not to sinners and evildoers? What if the sun only gave its light to those who deserved its light? What if the sun only gave its light to those who blessed the sun and withheld its light to those who cursed it?"

"I guess it would alter the world."

"It would do more than alter the world," he said. "It would alter the sun. If the sun shone only on the good, the beautiful, and the worthy, then it would, to that degree, cease to be a light. In the same way, if you love only those who love you, then it alters *you*; then you cease to be a light. The sun must shine regardless of the world, and a child of God must love regardless of circumstances and bless regardless of the world. You must never let your circumstance define who you are or the darkness around you determine your shining. Love the good, the bad, and the unworthy. Love those who hate you...not because of who *they* are, but because of who *you* are. Shine regardless and shine no matter what...For you are the light of the world. And the necessity of the light...is to shine."

The Mission: Live like the sun today, as the light. Shine God's love on all, regardless of people and circumstances. Shine rather because you're the light.

Isaiah 60:1–3; Matthew 5:14–16, 44–45

THE SILENCE OF THE TRUTH

WHAT IS TRUTH?" I asked.

"Ah," said the teacher, "a question asked by philosophers for ages. Do you know what the word *philosophy* means? It comes from two Greek words: *sophia*, which means knowledge, and *philo*, which means love. So *philosophy* can be taken to mean the love of knowledge or wisdom. Man has been pondering and seeking after the truth for thousands of years. And after all those years, do you know what the conclusion of philosophy is?"

"No."

"No conclusion," he said. "They all came up with different answers...no answer. And yet in the midst of all this, the question was once posed, in a very unique context and not by a philosopher, but by a man of bloodshed. He asked the question to one of his prisoners. The man was Pontius Pilate, the Roman governor of Judea, and the prisoner was the Messiah. So Pilate posed the question, 'What is truth?' Then he went outside to the multitude and said, 'I find no basis for a charge against Him.' So what was the answer to the question?"

"He didn't give an answer," I said. "There was no answer."

"But there *was* an answer. In the absence of the answer *was* the answer. It came in the silence of the truth. It was in His *not* saying anything, that He said everything, in His *not* answering, that the question was answered. Truth is deeper than words. The truth wasn't the truth about something, or even the truth about Him—it *was* Him, standing there right in front of Pilate's eyes, in flesh-and-blood reality. You see, the *idea* of truth, the *talk* of truth, and the *study* of truth...is *not* the truth. Philosophies and religions may be *about* the truth, but that which is about the truth can blind you from seeing the truth itself. Never let yourself end up in the realm of the about and lose that which the about is all about. The truth is that which is...as God is. The truth is Him. And so the only way to know the truth...is to know Him...directly, personally, in His presence, face-to-face, heart to heart...What is truth?" asked the teacher, "*He* is the truth. And what is the answer to all philosophy, the love of knowledge? It is to know Him. It is to love the truth. Therefore, the answer...is to love Him."

The Mission: Today, leave the "realm of the about" and go beyond the talk and words to the bare truth of His presence. Be still and know that He is God.

Psalm 46:10; John 18:38

Him

THE WINGS OF MESSIAH

HE LED ME into the Chamber of Garments. There he found a prayer shawl, white with blue stripes, and draped it over his head.

"Do you know what this is?" he asked.

"A prayer shawl," I replied.

"It's called a *tallit*. The most important part of the tallit is its corners and the fringes of its corners. Look," he said as he pointed to the cloth. "In the law of Sinai, it was commanded that the children of Israel were to wear fringes on the corners of their garments. The corner itself is called the *kanaf*. And the fringes on the corners are called the *tzitzit*. In the New Covenant accounts there are no physical descriptions of Messiah. We don't know what He looked like. But we do know what He wore. He wore on His garments the kanaf and the tzitzit. In one of the most famous of the Gospel accounts, a woman touches the hem of Messiah's garment and is instantly healed of her infirmity. This was not a one-time miracle. In fact, it's recorded that everyone who touched the hem of His garment was healed. But they didn't just touch the hem of His garment. The word in Greek for what they touched is *kraspedon*. *Kraspedon* is a translation of the Hebrew words *kanaf* and *tzitzit*."

"So they weren't just touching the hem of His garment; they were touching the sacred corner and fringe of His garments as ordained in the Law."

"Exactly. And at the very end of the Hebrew Scriptures is an amazing verse. It is written, 'The sun of righteousness shall arise with healing in His wings.' But in Hebrew, it doesn't say wings. It says, 'The sun of righteousness shall arise with healing in His *kanaf*'—the very word that also means the corner and fringe of His garment. So they touched the *kanaf,* the corner, the fringe, of the sun of righteousness, Messiah, and they found 'healing in His wings.' Therefore, never be afraid to touch God. If God puts fringes on His garment, it means He is touchable. He is not afraid to be touched. So touch God with your infirmities, your wounds, your uncleanness, your sins, with the darkest part of your life, and you will be changed. For the Sun of Righteous will arise with healing in His wings...with healing in His *kanaf*."

The Mission: Touch God today with the darkest, most painful, most ungodly part of your life—that you might find healing in His wings.

Numbers 15:38–40; Malachi 4:2; Matthew 9:20–22; 14:35–36

THE MYSTERY OF THE YEHUDIM

DID YOU EVER wonder," asked the teacher, "what the word *Jew* means or where it comes from? In Hebrew, the word for the Jewish people is the *Yehudim*. It comes from the Hebrew word for praise, thanksgiving, and worship. A Jew is one whose identity is based on praising God, giving thanks, and worshipping the Almighty. A Jew is one whose very existence is a praise and witness to the existence of God."

"It's strange," I said, "that a name linked to praise should become a word of vilification, that a word linked to worship should be used as a profanity, and that a word linked to thanksgiving could be used for cursing."

"It's a strange world," he said, "where those born to praise and give thanks should be so hated, cursed, and warred against. When Messiah died, what was written over His head?"

"*King of the Jews*," I replied.

"'King of the Yehudim,' said the teacher. "His life was the epitome of the word *Jew*. His life itself was praise to God. Everything He did was to bless, to worship, to glorify God."

"And the world crucified Him whose life was a praise to God."

"A strange world," said the teacher again. "It was the forces of darkness that crucified Him. And yet even in the crucifixion, He didn't stop being the King of the Jews, or the epitome of the Yehudim. Even the act of dying was an act of praise, a glorifying of God. He never succumbed to the evil but overcame the evil with good. He blessed those who cursed Him and even gave His life to save His enemies."

"And those who follow Him," I said, "those who are His, must do likewise."

"Yes. You must never be overcome by the darkness or let it stop you from giving praise, nor let evil stop you from blessing. You must give thanks in all things and give praise at all times. You must bless in the face of cursing. You must make your life a praise no matter what. For if He who is King of the Yehudim is your King, then you too must, in some way, be of the Yehudim."

"Jewish?"

"One whose very existence is a praise to God."

The Mission: Today, praise God, give thanks, and bless. No matter what the circumstance, no matter what goes on around you or against you, praise God.

Psalm 34:1–3; Romans 2:29; Philippians 4:11–13

The Yehudim

THE AVANIM: WEIGHTS OF THE BALANCE

THE TEACHER LED me into a chamber he had never shown me before. It was illuminated by the light of oil lamps and filled with round stones of varying sizes. We sat down by a small table. He opened up a cloth bag filled with small stones and poured them out onto the tabletop. They were round and light in color, and each was engraved with what appeared to be ancient letters.

"What are they?" I asked.

"They are the *avanim*," he said, "the weights of the balance. And this is the Chamber of Measures. These were the measures and standards used in ancient times to determine values, weights, and quantities." He then took out a second bag and emptied its contents on the table. "These look the same as the others, but they're not. These are false measures, altered weights. The inscriptions have been changed so that they no longer match the weight of the stone. This one says shekel, but it weighs less than a shekel. It would be used by a corrupt merchant to make an item appear to be heavier or greater than it was. The merchant had redefined the measure to conform it to his will and want."

He picked up one of the stones, then continued. "Altered weights not only concern corrupt merchants . . . but corrupt civilizations. When a civilization redefines its values, when it changes the meanings and definitions of reality away from God and away from the created order, when it alters the measures of morality, of right and wrong, to conform them to its will and desires, it is dealing in altered weights, false measures, deceptive balances. It is turning the objective into the subjective, and man into God."

At that he emptied another bag of weights onto the table and began reading their inscriptions. "This one says Good, and on the other side Evil. This one says Life, and on the other side Death . . . Idol, and on the other side God. Male and Female . . . Sacred and Profane. This one says Marriage. And this one says Child in the Womb. They've all become altered weights, false measures, changed values, signs of corruption."

"So how do you escape the corruption of altered weights?"

"Never bend the truth to fit your will. Bend your will to fit the truth. Never alter the Word of God or conform God to your image; alter your ways to the Word of God and conform your life to the image of God. Beware of false standards . . . and stay far from altered weights."

The Mission: Conform today your will to the truth, your ways to the Word, and your life to the image of God. Uphold the weights of the balance.

Proverbs 11:1; 16:11; Isaiah 5:20

The Weights of the Bag

THE SUMMER FRUITS

WE STOOD AT the edge of the school grounds in a dry summer wind. The teacher was holding a sheaf of wheat bound in the middle by a cord of straw.

"The firstfruits," he said. "In ancient Israel this was cause for great celebration. During the Feast of Shavuot, the people of Israel would come from all over the land bringing the firstfruits of the summer harvest to Jerusalem. They would place them in baskets, load them onto oxen, and lead the oxen in a great procession to the Temple to be presented by the priests before the Lord. The presentation of the firstfruits would stand for all the rest of the harvest yet to be reaped. By dedicating the firstfruits to God, the rest of the harvest fruits were deemed holy."

He paused to look at the sheaf, then continued.

"Two thousand years ago God's Spirit was poured out on one hundred twenty disciples in Jerusalem on the Day of Pentecost."

"Some consider it the birth of the church."

"And what is Pentecost?"

"The Greek name for the Feast of Shavuot."

"Yes. And Shavuot...is the day when the firstfruits of the summer harvest are presented to the Lord. So who were the one hundred twenty on which the Spirit fell that day?"

"The firstfruits," I said, "the firstfruits...of the summer harvest!"

"They were the firstfruits of new life, and they were gathered together on the same day when the firstfruits of the summer harvest were gathered together before the Lord. It was now God presenting *His firstfruits* to the world...the firstfruits of the age...and in the city of Jerusalem where the firstfruits must be presented and consecrated as holy."

"So the pouring of the Spirit on the one hundred twenty, that was the consecration."

"Yes, and the consecration of all the other fruits."

"The other fruits?"

"The people of all nations and ages who would yet come to new life."

"And that's why they spoke in the tongues of foreign nations...because as the firstfruits, they represented everyone else, from every tongue and nation."

"Exactly," he said, "a sign that all who come after them would likewise be consecrated as holy to God...and would be given the same anointing and the same power, just as it was given to the firstfruits, the first believers...that they...that we too could live in the power of the Spirit and overcome the world."

The Mission: The apostles were the firstfruits. Live this day in their anointing and power, to spread the light, to touch the earth, and overcome the world.

Leviticus 23:16–17; Acts 2:2–4, 39; Galatians 5:16, 22–25

The Passover-Shavuot Resurrection Power

MOVING THE UNIVERSE

WE WERE OBSERVING one of the desert tent camps from a nearby hill. It was late afternoon, and the women were coming to draw water from the well.

"It was a similar scene," said the teacher, "nearly four thousand years ago. When Abraham sent his servant to the city of Nahor to find a wife for his son Isaac. His servant stood by the well and prayed that God would show him the right woman by having her come to draw water at the well and offer to draw water as well for his camels. Before finishing the prayer, a young woman named Rivkah, or Rebekah, came out to the well and did exactly as he had just prayed. So when did God answer the servant's prayer?"

"When Rebekah came to the well."

"But in order to come to the well, Rebekah had to have already been on the way to the well before the servant saw her, and before he prayed."

"Then when she left her house."

"But before she left her house, she had to plan her day to go out to the well exactly as she did in order to arrive exactly when she arrived. And for that to happen, every event of that day had to take place exactly as it did. The slightest delay or lack of delay and it wouldn't have happened. You see, behind every event are countless previous events in an incalculable chain of time leading up to and causing the event to happen just as it does. And it is not only a chain of time, but of space. Surrounding every event are countless other contributing events, countless interactions and confluences—a gust of wind, a drop of rain, a random thought, the movement of the sun and stars, and the gravity of a galaxy. They must all work together with absolute precision for any specific event to happen as it does. So for God to answer the servant's prayer and bring Rebekah to the well that day, He had to make those things work perfectly together in time and space. To answer that prayer, He had to move the universe...And so it is for you, and for all His children. For God to answer even one of your prayers, even the smallest of your prayers, He must direct all things and move and coordinate all events of time and space to make it happen. He must move the universe. And for you He *will* move the universe...For that is how much He loves you...with a love greater than time and space...greater than the universe."

The Mission: Think of your answered prayers. God worked everything together to make it happen. Ponder that love, that He would move the world to bless you.

Genesis 24:1–28; Romans 8:28, 32

The Isaac Rebekah Wedding Mystery I–III

THE MYSTERY WRESTLER

IT WAS EVENING. The school was having an outdoor tournament, lit up by torch-light. The teacher and I were watching a wrestling match involving two of the students.

"Why is wrestling included in the curriculum?" I asked.

"It's a part of life," he said, "even in God."

We continued watching for a time. Then he broke the silence.

"Israel is the name of God's people," he said. "Do you know where it came from?"

"No."

"From a wrestling match...in the night. It is recorded that Jacob was alone and a man wrestled with him until the breaking of dawn. Finally the man said to Jacob, 'What is your name?' He answered, 'Jacob.' The man then replied, 'Your name shall no longer be called Jacob, but Israel. For you have struggled with God and with men, and have prevailed.' That's how the name Israel came about and the name of God's people and nation. It all came from a wrestling match. But the man who wrestled with Jacob wasn't just any man. Jacob would call the ground on which it all took place *Peniel,* which means the face of God. For he had 'seen *God* face-to-face.' What happened there that night was a prophecy. No nation has ever wrestled with God and man in this world as has the nation of Israel. And in that wrestling match is contained the mystery of the Jewish people. They are called Israel because they wrestled with a man who turned out to be God. That is their prophecy. And so they have wrestled for ages with one particular man, whose name means Messiah and who, in the end, turns out to be God. But they aren't the only wrestlers. The Scripture say that everyone who is born again becomes a citizen of Israel."

"Israel...the wrestling nation," I said. "Then we are all wrestlers."

"It is not a bad thing to wrestle, even with God, as long as you come to the point that Jacob came to...to the end of your strength...where you can do nothing else but cling to Him and ask Him to bless you. In fact, that's how most come to the kingdom...at the end of a wrestling match."

"And what about His people Israel?"

"They will come so as well...at the end of the night, at the breaking of dawn."

The Mission: Is there something you're wrestling with God about, or resisting? Surrender today to His will. And in that surrender, ask for His blessing.

Genesis 32:24–30; Ephesians 2:12, 19

Messiah in the Torah

SECRET OF THE LILIES

ONE OF THE school's gardens was more of a small field than a garden, yet enclosed inside a stone wall and filled with grass and what appeared to be wild flowers of every color. As we were walking through it, the teacher bent down and picked up a purple lily.

"You know," he said, "Messiah spoke of these. He said, 'Consider the lilies of the field, how they grow: they neither toil nor spin; and yet I say to you that even Solomon in all his glory was not arrayed like one of these.' He was speaking of the care and provision God gives to His children, comparing King Solomon in all his riches and glory to a wildflower. And King Solomon in all his glory could not equal the beauty of a lily of the field. What does it reveal?"

"If God cares enough to adorn a wild lily, how much more does He care for His children."

"Yes. And yet there's more. Solomon's clothing was the work of man. The lily of the field is the work of God. And between the two, there's no comparison. It is the lily that is the more beautiful, the more perfect, and the more majestic. You see, the works of man are never perfect. But the works of God are always perfect. And so perfection is not based on one's striving to produce good works. Perfection is found in the way of the lilies. Learn their secret. Lilies neither toil nor spin. They don't strive to produce works. Their secret is…they *are* the works of God. And in this, lilies are much wiser than men. A life spent trying to produce works of righteousness and holiness will not produce them…and will be focused on the source of those works—the self. But a life focused on the works of God will be focused on the source of those works—God. So the secret is to *not* focus on your work for God. The secret is to *become* the work of God. Cease striving to do the work of God…and start letting your life *become* the work of God. Let your doing become the doing of God. Stop struggling to produce good works for God and let God produce His good work in you. Let His goodness cause your life to *become His good work*. Let everything you do and are begin with Him. Let your righteousness be the outflowing of His righteousness. Your love, the outflowing of His love, and your life, the outflowing of His life. And your life will become as beautiful as a lily of the field."

The Mission: Today, don't focus on your works. But learn instead the secret of becoming His work. Become today the work of God.

Psalm 139:14; 149:41; Luke 12:27–31

THE PRIESTS IN THE WATERS

THE TEACHER LED me into the Chamber of Garments to show me the most intricate of clothing, a linen tunic, a breastplate of precious stones, finely woven colored fabrics, and a crown of gold. They were the garments of the high priest. Later on that day I approached him with a question.

"When the covenant changes," I said, "there must also be a change of priesthood. So a new covenant must mean a new priesthood. But if there's a changing of the priesthood, shouldn't there have been some sort of changing of the guard, a passing of the torch between the old and the new, a recognition...a transference...a blessing from the priesthood of Aaron to the priesthood of Messiah?"

"How could that have happened?" he asked. "The priesthood and the high priest at the time were corrupt and plotting His murder...But...what if there was someone...someone more of a high priest than Caiaphas, someone who represented the priesthood more than any other?"

"Who?"

"The one called *Yochanan* and known to the world as John the Baptist. He was the only priest in the history of the priesthood whose birth was announced by an angel in the sanctuary of the priests, the Temple, in the holy place during the priestly ministry. And what was the high priest's highest ministry? To cleanse the people of their sins. And what was John doing in the waters of the Jordan? Baptizing them for the cleansing of their sins. It was he who was the highest priest of Israel, the true representative of the Aaronic priesthood. So Messiah's ministry, His priesthood, must begin with John...the two priests, standing in the waters of the Jordan, the place of endings and beginnings, the two priesthoods, the priesthood of the old covenant and the priesthood of the new."

"That's it," I said. "That's the changing of the guard...the transference of the priesthood."

"And as the two high priests stand face-to-face, the old priesthood bears witness of the new. In the waters of the Jordan, Yochanan, John, bears witness of Messiah's ministry and declares it greater than his own. The blessing is spoken. The torch is passed. The cosmic changing of the guard is complete. And thus begins the priesthood of Messiah."

The Mission: The priesthood has been given to Messiah and to those who are His. Live this day as a priest of God. Minister His will and purposes.

Jeremiah 31:31–33; Matthew 3:13–16; Hebrews 7:11–17

THE CHILDREN OF EVE

L ISTEN," SAID THE teacher.

The sound was coming from one of the tents in the camp, a tent that appeared to be the center of commotion and excitement. The sound was distant but distinct. It was the cry of a woman in childbirth.

"It goes back to the garden," he said, "to the fall of man, the curse. For Adam, it would involve toil, thorns, and death. But for Eve, it would involve the pain of childbirth. And yet that very pain would be part of bringing forth new life. You see, the curse did not stop life from coming. Life would come, but it would now come through tears. God's purposes would still be fulfilled, but through the pains of labor. In fact, the Scriptures declare that all creation is undergoing the pains of childbirth."

"What does that mean?"

"It means that the creation was meant to bear fruit, to bring forth the life and purposes of God. But the creation is fallen. And yet even in its fallenness, it will still bring forth God's purposes and life, but now with birth pangs."

"How does that happen?"

"Through the creation comes the new birth, a fallen world brings forth the children of God. Even in the darkness and brokenness of this creation, God's children are born, but now through the pains of childbirth. They're born again through the birth pangs of emptiness, of disillusionment, of frustration, of disappointment, of broken dreams, of unanswered longings, of wounding, and of tears. The creation groans and brings forth God's life."

"Listen," I said. At that moment there was an eruption of shouting and joy from the tent. The child was born.

"And now," said the teacher, "she will forget her pain in the joy of her new life. So too it is for the child of God, whatever pains and tears they knew in this life become the birth pangs of new life. So don't despise the tears, but know that in God, every tear will bring forth birth, and every sorrow, new life... And the pains of this world will be forgotten in the joy of new life and the miracle of birth."

The Mission: Remember how God used emptiness, pain, and brokenness to bring you to life. So let every pain of this life become the pangs of birth.

Genesis 3:16; Romans 8:22–23

The Children of Eden Mysteries I–IV

THE HOUSE OF THE BRIDEGROOM

WE WERE OBSERVING the same tent encampment from which the bridegroom's journey to the bride had begun.

"You asked me what the bride does in the time of her separation," said the teacher, "but you never asked me what the bridegroom does."

"What does the bridegroom do in the time of their separation?"

"This is his camp, his home. This is where he returned to after entering into the covenant with his bride. The time of their separation is for the purpose of preparing. Do you remember what the bride does to prepare?"

"She readies herself for her future life with the bridegroom. She prepares to leave her home and everything else behind. She prepares herself."

"That's right," he said, "and the bridegroom prepares as well. But his preparation is different. He prepares a place, a place for the bride, their future home, a place to spend their lives together...And this is the mystery...The Bridegroom is God. The visit of the Bridegroom is the visitation of God to this world. But then the Bridegroom must depart from the house of the bride. So the Bridegroom departs from this world. The mystery decrees that the Bridegroom must then prepare a place for the bride. And so it is recorded that before He left this world, He said, 'I go to prepare a place for you.'"

"So then now is the time of the separation."

"Yes," said the teacher, "and now is time of the preparation. While we prepare ourselves for Him, He prepares a place for us. Think about it...the bride is born into the first house. But the second house is built for the bride, built of the Bridegroom's love for her. In the same way, we were born into the first house, this world. But the second house, the new creation, is being made especially for us, out of the Bridegroom's love, out of God's love...for you. So Messiah said, 'If I go to prepare a place for you, I will come again, and receive you to Myself, that where I am, you may be also.'"

"What is it like, the second house, the place He's preparing?"

"It's beyond our fathoming. Whatever you think it is, it's better than that."

"It's heaven," I said. "The house built in His love for the bride...for us...is heaven."

The Mission: Dwell on the blessings of the place being prepared for you. Meditate on the house of the Bridegroom. Dwell in the heavenlies.

John 14:2–3; 1 Corinthians 2:9

BARUCH ATAH

THE JEWISH PEOPLE have blessings for almost everything, a blessing for food, for the lighting of candles, for special days, and for every day. And the most typical beginning for a Hebrew blessing are the words *Baruch Atah*."

"*Baruch Atah*," I repeated. "What does it mean?"

"Much," said the teacher. "*Atah* means You. The blessings are focused on the word *You*. So the first revelation is this: You can't relate to God only as a He. You must first relate to Him as Atah, You. You must first relate to Him directly, personally, one on one, and heart to heart, not simply by speaking *about* Him, but speaking from your heart directly *to* Him."

"All that from one word?"

"And more," he said. "The blessing must *start* with God. God is first, everything else is second. This is crucial. When you pray, don't let your problems or even your requests become your focus. The focus and the beginning of the Hebrew blessing is the word *Atah*, You. The blessing is not me-centered, but Atah-centered. So a life of blessing is an Atah-centered life. If you want to live a blessed life, you must follow the pattern of the Hebrew blessing. Live an Atah-centered life. Make your heart an Atah-centered heart. Let go of yourself. Put Him first, His will first, His desires first, and His glory first. And to live an Atah-centered life, you must focus on the other atahs, on every other you in your life, putting them above yourself as well...It is a life of love that is the life of blessing. 'Love the Lord your God...and love your neighbor as yourself.'"

"And what about the *Baruch* in Baruch Atah?"

"*Baruch* means to bless. Therefore, you must not only live a *You-centered life* but make it your specific aim to bless the You of your life. Make it the purpose of your life, above everything else, every other aim and purpose, to bless God. And then make it your purpose to bless every other you in your life. Two simple words: *baruch* and *atah*. Yet they are the words that begin the blessing...of every kind. Make it simple. Make it your life's purpose to *baruch* the *Atah*. Bless the You. Live a Baruch Atah life...and your life will be a blessing."

The Mission: Set your heart today on two words: *baruch* and *atah*. Purpose to be a blessing. Live not for the self but for the Atah, the "You."

Psalm 103; Matthew 22:36–40

A Guide to the Baruchas

THE DOER

HE REMOVED THE scroll from the ark in the Chamber of Scrolls, laid it on the table, and unrolled it.

"We've spoken of Joseph," said the teacher, "in the Book of Genesis, how he was a shadow of the Messiah, and how even the rabbis saw this."

"Yes," I said, "the redeemer who is despised and rejected of men."

"And imprisoned," he said, "Some translations say that Joseph was put in charge over the prisoners and their work. And the rendering is accurate. But the original Hebrew says something a bit different. And every word is crucial. It says this: 'And the ruler of the dungeon gave into Joseph's hand all the prisoners who were in the dungeon. And all that they did there, *he was the doer of it.*' One could interpret that to mean that he was in charge of their labors or responsible for their work. But what it literally says is that whatever they did, Joseph was the one who did it."

"So what would that mean as a shadow of the Messiah?"

"Messiah would likewise be numbered with the sinful, with those under judgment. He became as one under judgment. And all the acts of the sinful, all that they did...all that *we* did, He, Messiah, became the doer of it. He was counted as the doer of our sins, the One who made our mistakes, the One who failed in our failures, the One who transgressed in our transgressions. So if He becomes the doer of our sins, then we become no longer the doer...of our own sins.... no longer the ones who sinned, who failed, who transgressed, and fell. In the grace of God, we are released from being the doers of our deeds...that we might become the doer of His deeds."

"The doer of His deeds? What exactly does that mean?"

"Just as He was joined to our works, we are joined to His good works. We are reckoned as being the doers of it. We become the doers of His works, the works of perfect righteousness. And in all that we now do, all that is good, He is the One who does it in us. That's the secret. Live in such a way that whatever we do...He is the doer of it."

The Mission: Let God become the doer of your works, and you become the doer of His works. Whatever you do, let Him do it in you.

Genesis 39:22; Isaiah 53:12; Philippians 2:13–14; 4:13

The Shadow Man I–VI

THE AFIKOMEN MYSTERY

ALL OVER THE world," said the teacher, "believers have partaken in the bread of the Lord's Supper. But most have no idea that it all comes from Passover. And at the same time, the Jewish people partake in the Passover, but most have no idea how deeply joined it is to the Lord's Supper. Nor do most realize the ramifications of its mystery. During the Passover meal a plate of unleavened bread is lifted up, three pieces of matzah, one on top of the other."

"Why three?" I asked.

"No one knows," he said. "It's a mystery. But it's always three...a trinity of bread. And then the middle of the three pieces...is removed from the rest."

"The second of the trinity."

"It is then broken in two."

"As Messiah broke the bread and said, 'This is My body.'"

"The second of the trinity is broken. And it's given a name. It's called the *afikomen*. The broken matzah is then wrapped in a cloth."

"As the broken body of the second of the Trinity was wrapped inside a cloth, a burial cloth."

"And then," he said, "the broken matzah is hidden away."

"As His shrouded body was hidden away in a tomb."

"Yes...and as Messiah Himself has been hidden from His people for millennia. But without the afikomen, the Passover Seder cannot be completed."

"And without the Messiah, the nation of Israel cannot find its completion."

"So a search is made for the missing bread. And when it's found, the cloth is removed, the afikomen is revealed...and partaken of. Only then can the Passover come to its conclusion."

"So," I said, "in the end, the Jewish people will search for their missing Messiah, and He will be revealed to them, and received, and their destiny fulfilled."

"And do you know what *afikomen* means? It's a Greek word that means that which comes after. Messiah is the Afikomen. He is not now among His people. But He will be. He is the One who comes after, who is yet to come to His people. And so He is still yet to come to His people. And as it is with Passover, so it is with all to whom He comes...only in His coming, can you find your completion. He is the Afikomen of your life."

The Mission: What in your life is still incomplete? Instead of trying to fill it, find your completion in Him, and let His fullness fill what is empty.

Zechariah 12:10; Luke 22:19; Romans 11:25–26

The Bread and the Wine

YERUSHALAYIM

OVER THERE," SAID the teacher, "beyond those mountains, far beyond them, is the city of Jerusalem. That's the direction in which Jewish people have prayed for ages...to the Holy City."

"I've never been there," I said. "I've heard it's like no other place."

"It's a city of rocks on the edge of a desert...And yet there's something about it, a beauty, a glory, an awesomeness one can't quite put into words...as in no other place. The mystery is in the name."

"The name Jerusalem?"

"In its real name...*Yerushaluylm.* Notice what it ends with?"

"The *im*. So the word is plural."

"Yes. So *Yerushalayim* doesn't really mean Jerusalem, but *the Jerusalems.* And the mystery goes deeper. It's not just an *im* at the end, but an *ayim,* a unique ending that speaks specifically of duality, as in two. In other words, *Yerushalayim* means the two Jerusalems."

"What are the two Jerusalems?"

"They are the Jerusalem you see and the Jerusalem you don't...the Jerusalem that is and the Jerusalem that it is yet to become...Jerusalem, the earthly, and Jerusalem, the heavenly...Jerusalem of time and space, and Jerusalem, the Eternal...Jerusalem, the flawed and imperfect, and Jerusalem, the perfect, the beautiful, and the glorious. And the mystery of Jerusalem has everything to do with you. For if you belong to God, you are a child of Jerusalem...a child of Yerushalayim. Therefore, you share in her nature."

"How?"

"As it is with Jerusalem, so with your life. To your life is an *ayim*. It means there's always more to it than you see with your eyes. There are two realms, two lives...the life you see and the life you don't see...the person you are and the person you are yet to be...you, the earthly, and you, the heavenly; you, the imperfect and flawed, and you, the perfect, the beautiful, and the glorious. So no matter what you think of your life, in God, the truth is always more and better. And even in your lowest places, there's a glory beyond anything you see or feel or understand...an ayim, a duality...and therefore a choice. Choose, therefore, to live not by the earthly, but the heavenly. Believe not what is, but what is yet to be. Dwell not in the flawed, but the perfect. For you are the Jerusalem of God...His Yerushalayim."

The Mission: You are a child of Yerushalayim. Therefore, choose to live this day not as you are, but as you will yet be, the perfect and the heavenly.

Psalms 122; 147:2–3; Revelation 21:1–2

Yerushalayim: The Mystery

THE COHANIM CONFESSION

I WAS WONDERING," I said. "When the priests performed the Semikhah, placing the sins of the people onto the sacrifice, they had to lay their hands on the sacrifice, but they also had to confess their sins over it. They had to do both. Otherwise the sacrifice couldn't die for those sins. But when Messiah was taken by the priests the night before His death, the priests laid hands on Him, but there was no confession of sin."

"Come," said the teacher. "Let's see what we find."

He led me into the Chamber of Scrolls where he retrieved from a high shelf a scroll of medium size, laid it on the wooden table, unrolled it to the place he was looking for, and began translating it out loud: "At that Caiaphas tore his clothes and said, 'He has spoken blasphemy...' to which those in the council agreed that He was guilty and deserving of death."

"They condemned Him to death on false charges."

"In the Semikhah, the priest confessed the sins upon the sacrifice. Was the sacrifice guilty of those sins?

"No. The sacrifice could only die for those sins if it *wasn't* guilty of them."

"Correct. Therefore, for the Semikhah to be performed on the sacrifice, on Messiah, the high priest had to speak over Him sins He was *not guilty of*. So what sin was it that they spoke upon Him? The sin of blasphemy. But the sin that's spoken upon the sacrifice is *not* the sin of the sacrifice, but the sin of *those who speak it*. So the blasphemy was not the sin of Messiah—it was the sin of the high priest and of the priesthood. They judged God of blasphemy against God. To judge God of blasphemy...is itself a blasphemy. The priests were confessing their own sin. But it wasn't their sin alone. The priests represented Israel and Israel represented the world. So the priests were confessing the sin of man...the sin of the world...in the Semikhah of the sacrifice for man...the first sin, and the beginning of all sins, 'You shall be as God'...blasphemy."

"So the sin was confessed over the sacrifice by the high priest, and the priests touched His head with their hands. And so the Semikhah for the sins of man was performed."

"And by God," said the teacher. "He confessed your sins upon Him. As it is written, 'He made Him who knew no sin to become sin for us...that we...that you...might become the righteousness of God.'"

The Mission: He became sin—your sin, that you would become righteousness— His righteousness. Live today as the righteousness of God.

Genesis 3:5; Leviticus 16:21; Mark 14:63–64; 2 Corinthians 5:21

Footsteps on the Altar

THE MYSTERY OF THE SECOND SCROLL

I⁣T WAS A warm and windy afternoon. We were sitting outside on the ground. The teacher was reading from a small scroll.

"This is one of the *hamesh megillot*, the five scrolls. Each one is read publicly during the year. And this, the second scroll, is the Book of Ruth."

"What's it about?"

"It's the story of the love between a Jew and a Gentile. But behind the story is a prophetic revelation that involves the entire world, the mystery of Israel, the church, and the age itself.

"The Book of Ruth begins with a Jewish woman named Naomi. She will represent the nation of Israel. Naomi is married to a man named Elimelech. *Elimelech* means My God is King. So Israel is joined in a covenant of marriage to God, her King. In the course of the story Naomi finds herself with no husband and living in exile from her homeland, a stranger in a foreign land, an existence of pain and sorrow. So too the Jewish people, for the last two thousand years, have found themselves living in exile from their homeland, strangers in foreign lands, in an existence of pain and sorrow. But in the days of Naomi's exile, a Gentile woman named Ruth becomes, through Naomi, part of the nation of Israel and is brought to the knowledge of God. So in the days of Israel's exile in the nations, those who are not of Israel, Gentiles, are, through the Jewish people, brought to the God of Israel and are spiritually joined to His nation."

"The church," I said, "those who are born again. They are Ruth."

"Ruth becomes Naomi's adopted daughter."

"So those of the new covenant are the adopted children of Israel. Israel is their mother. And the church is Israel's daughter."

"At the end of the story Ruth bears a child who becomes the blessing of Naomi's life. So through Naomi came Ruth's redemption, and through Ruth comes Naomi's blessing."

"So it is through the Jewish people," I said, "that blessing has come to the Gentiles...and it will be through the Gentiles that blessings will come to Israel."

"Yes," said the teacher. "And so those who are blessed with salvation are blessed through Israel and to Israel they are joined. They are Ruth, and Israel is their Naomi. And only when Ruth blesses Naomi and Naomi blesses Ruth will the circle and the story be complete."

The Mission: Be a Ruth today. Pray for and bless your Naomi. Pray and bless Israel and the Jewish people. Help bring their story to completion.

Ruth 1:16–17; 4:13–17; Isaiah 40:1–2; Romans 11:11; 15:26–27

The Bethlehem Allegory

THE GIFT OF THE LAHMED

YOU TOLD ME that in Hebrew, the verb *have* doesn't really exist," I said, "that you can't really *have* anything in this world. But then there has to be a way around it. There has to be a way of speaking about one's possessions. The Bible uses the word *have*."

"In its translations, yes. But in the original, not really."

"So then what does it say in the original that we translated as 'to have'?"

Instead of answering the question, he picked up a stick and began drawing a symbol in the sand.

"What is it?" I asked.

"It's a *lahmed*," he replied. "The twelfth letter in the Hebrew alphabet. It is from the lahmed that comes the letter *L*. This is how you would communicate what we understand as 'to have' by using the lahmed. So to say 'I have' or 'mine,' you would use the Hebrew word *li*. To say 'he has' or 'his,' you would use the word *lo*. And to say 'you have' or 'yours,' you would use the word *l'cha*. So you can't really have in Hebrew. But what you end up 'having' is better than having. The *lahmed* means to. So instead of saying 'I have,' you say, 'It is *to* me.' And instead of saying 'he has' or 'his,' you're actually saying, 'It is *to* him.' In God you must live in accordance with the sacred tongue. That means giving up the idea that you 'have' in this world. But when you do that, when you give up the idea of having, then something miraculous will happen."

"What?"

"Everything will become *to you*. When you 'have,' then that which you have cannot be given to you. But when you don't 'have,' when you cease to 'have,' then that which you don't have is freed up to be given. When you give up the 'I have,' it becomes 'to you.' And when you take no good thing for granted, then every good thing becomes a gift given *to you,* your means, your belongings, your friends, your loved ones, your talents, your time, every day, every moment, every breath, your life itself, your salvation, they all become gifts of grace, blessing, and love. Give up your having 'to have,' and everything in this world will become *l'cha,* a blessing from God to you...the gift of the lahmed."

The Mission: Give up 'having.' Take no good thing today for granted, every blessing, even our life. And receive everything as a gift from God.

2 Corinthians 6:10; Ephesians 5:20; James 1:17

THE APPOINTED

WE WERE SITTING outside, not far from the well. The teacher was reading a passage out of one of the scrolls: "'Some of them also were appointed over the vessels and over all the instruments of the sanctuary ...' It's speaking of the Levites, those appointed by God as His ministers in the Temple of Jerusalem, ordained for the fulfilling of sacred purposes. Now Jonah was a prophet called by God to give a message to Nineveh. But he ran away from his calling. God caused a large fish to swallow him and carry him back to the shore. Then He caused a leafy plant to grow and give Jonah shade, then a worm to eat the plant, and then a desert wind to blow from the east. Only after all these things took place was Jonah able to know the heart of God."

"I'm not getting it," I said. "First you spoke of the Levites as the ministers of God, and now you're speaking of worms and fish. I don't get the connection."

"In the Book of Jonah," he said, "in the original language, it doesn't say God caused a fish to swallow Jonah. It says that God *appointed* the fish to swallow Jonah. It's the same Hebrew word used of God appointing the Levites to minister in His sanctuary."

"And the plant?"

"The same word. God *appointed* the plant. And God *appointed* the worm. And God *appointed* the east wind. The same word used of God's appointing the Levites, His holy ministers, is used of the fish, the plant, the worm, and the wind. You see, they too were holy ministers, equally appointed to accomplish the purposes of God and bring His prophet to the appointed place."

"I just never thought of a worm as a ..."

"No," said the teacher, "and you probably never thought of your problems as appointed ministers either. But for the child of God, everything, the good, the bad, the joys, the sorrows, the problems, the victories and defeats, the wounds, the rejections, the losses, the past, the worms and the winds, all things are appointed. In fact, each is an appointed minister ordained to bring about God's purposes, God's blessings, God's calling and destiny in your life. So be blessed. For in the end, what you thought were your problems were actually holy ministers, appointed to bring you to the appointed fulfillment of God's calling on your life."

The Mission: Today, see your problems and challenges in a new way, as God's appointed ministers to bring you to the place of His will and destiny.

1 Chronicles 9:28; Jonah 1:17; 4:6–8; Psalm 139:16; 2 Thessalonians 1:11

The Book of Jonah I–VII

THE ZICHARYAH MAN

BY THE WATERS of Babylon, the children of Israel wept in exile as they remembered Zion, their homeland, which now lay in ruins. They had turned away from God, broken the covenant, rejected His ways, persecuted His prophets, did and celebrated what was evil, and lifted up their children as sacrifices on the altars of foreign gods. They had every reason to believe that their days as a nation were over and that they would be a people forgotten by God. But after many years a small remnant of the exiles returned to the land of Israel to find it a desolate wasteland and their Holy City a heap of ruins. They tried to rebuild but at every point were hindered. They had to have been haunted by the continual question, Has God forgotten us?"

The teacher paused as if in thought, then continued. "And then a prophet appeared in their midst named Zechariah. He came with a message: They were to rebuild Jerusalem, and it would be to the rebuilt Jerusalem that Messiah would come. But who was Zechariah?"

"A prophet sent by God," I answered.

"Zechariah is just another way of saying his real Hebrew name: *Zicharyah*. And what does *Zicharyah* mean? The *Yah* of Zicharyah means God—the *zichar* means has remembered. So in the days of their judgment and exile, when they thought God was finished with them, that God had forgotten them, a baby was born and given the name 'God has remembered.' And the baby would grow up to be the prophet God sent to them in the days of their discouragement, the prophet named 'God has remembered.'"

"So it was not only what Zicharyah said to them, but what he was."

"Yes. In the midst of the people was Zicharyah, 'God has remembered.' Every word of encouragement came from that. He was the sign in flesh and blood that even in their greatest fall and their darkest sins, even when they should have been cast away and forgotten forever, God had not forgotten them. Even when they had forgotten God, God would not forget them. He remembered His promise, His love, and His tender mercies. And so He did not give up on them, and they would be restored. And so," said the teacher, "for all who have fallen, for all who have failed, all who have sinned, all who have lost, and all who have wondered, 'Has God forgotten me?,' remember this one, and his name, Zicharyah. It means that God will never forget you, and His faithfulness to you will always be greater than your sins."

The Mission: Remember the times when you've fallen—and yet when God didn't give up on you. In view of that dedicate your life to blessing Him all the more.

Psalm 98:3; Isaiah 49:14–16; Zechariah 8:3–9

Zechariah: God Remembers

THE LULAV

WE SAT IN the midst of a desert plain surrounded by mountains. The teacher was holding in one hand a fruit and, in the other, a cluster of three branches.

"This," he said, holding up the branches, "is called the lulav. It comes from the biblical command to worship God on the Feast of Tabernacles with branches. During that feast the people of Israel would remember how God led them through the wilderness through the waving of these branches."

"How so?" I asked.

"This, the largest of the three branches, is the palm. The palm tree grows in the valleys. So the palm branch reminded the Israelites of their journeys through the valleys, that God was with them. And this," he said, pointing to a smaller branch with dark green leaves, "is the myrtle. It grows in the mountains. So the myrtle reminded them of their journeys through mountains, and that God was with them there as well. And this," he said, pointing to a drooping branch of light green, "is the willow. The willow grows by the water brooks. It reminded them of their journeys through the dry places that God was with them to give them water in the desert. Now, what is the mystery of the lulav?" he asked.

"I have no idea."

"The wilderness is the world. The journey is this life. And this is the message of the lulav to the child of God: The palm tells you that no matter what valley you go through in your life, no matter how deep or dark, you will never be alone, He will be with you. The myrtle tells you that when you go through the rockiest of times, He will go through it with you and will keep you from falling. And the willow tells you that in the dry and empty places of your life, He will never leave you, but will stay close, and will even give you rivers in your desert."

"And what about the fruit?" I asked.

"The fruit speaks of the Promised Land, and its message is this: No matter what you go through in this life, it's not the end, only the journey to your destination. And when you get there, you'll give thanks that your journey was blessed, that you were never alone, and that He was with you every moment, making sure that you made it to the Promised Land."

The Mission: Today, gather your lulav. Remember and give thanks that in all your valleys, mountains, and deserts He was there—and always will be.

Psalm 23; Isaiah 43:1–2; Jude 1:24–25

The Lulav

THE SECRET OF THE BLESSED LIFE

WHAT IS A blessed life?" asked the teacher. "And how do you live it?"

"A blessed life is a life that's been endowed with God's favor and blessing."

"But if God blesses, why are some blessed and others not? Why do some of His children live lives that are especially blessed and others do not?"

The teacher led me to the well in the middle of the open square where the students would often gather together. On the well's circular stone ridge he placed two cups, one upside down and the other right side up. He then lifted up a bucket of water drawn from the well and held it over the two cups. "The blessing," he said. He then poured the water over the two cups. Then he lifted the upside-down cup and turned it right side up. It was, of course, empty.

"The blessing was poured out on both cups," he said, "but only one is filled with the blessing. The other is empty. Both were blessed...and yet only one is blessed. You see, there are *two parts* to being blessed and living a blessed life." We began walking away from the well as he continued talking.

"Isaac was preparing to give a blessing to his firstborn son, Esau. But it was his other son, Jacob, who ended up receiving the blessing. He received the blessing because, more than his brother, he set his heart on receiving it."

"But Jacob went about it the wrong way," I said.

"He did," said the teacher. "But his desire to receive the blessing, and his willingness to go to any length to receive it, was not wrong. You see, it is not just the giving of the blessing that was crucial, but the receiving. And so, there are two parts to a blessed life. Most people focus only on the one; they want the blessings to be given to them. But they miss the other part. You see, the blessing has already been given. It's here. It's pouring out from the wells of salvation, the wells of Messiah's redemption. But who is the one who is blessed? The one who receives the blessing. And who is the one whose life is *especially* blessed? The one who *especially* receives the blessing, the one who values it so much that they go to any length to receive it. So if you want to live an especially blessed life, then make it your aim to become especially great at receiving the blessings of God, and doing whatever you have to do to receive it. For a blessed life is not simply the life that has been blessed...but the life that has received it."

The Mission: The blessings of God are pouring down. Open your heart and life to receive them. Focus on receiving that which is already given.

Genesis 27:15–29; Ephesians 1:3–12, 18–20

The Blessing

THE TEMPLES OF DESECRATION

IT WAS EVENING. I and several others of the students were sitting around the campfire listening to the teacher.

"Who was the most famous person," asked the teacher, "ever to celebrate The Festival of Chanukah?"

He waited for a response, but no one said anything.

"Jesus," he said, "Yeshua. Most people have no idea that He did or that Chanukah is found in the New Testament. But it is written: 'It was the Feast of Dedication in Jerusalem. It was wintertime, and Yeshua was walking in the temple...' Do you know what the word for dedication is in Hebrew?"

Again there was no response.

"It's *Chanukah*. The Feast of Dedication is Chanukah. Do you know why it's called that?" There was no response. The teacher continued. "In ancient times, the Temple of Jerusalem was desecrated by pagan invaders. Idols were set up in its courts. It became, in effect, a pagan temple filled with degradation. In the end, the Jewish people drove out the invaders. They found their Temple defiled and desolate. They removed the idols, cleansed its courts, repaired its chambers, restored its vessels, rekindled its holy lampstand, and rededicated it to God. The Temple's rededication was called 'Chanukah.'"

"But God has another temple," he said, "another holy dwelling place created for His presence."

"But God's Temple could only be built in Jerusalem," said one of the students.

"There is another," said the teacher, "many others. The temple is you. Each of you were created to be the dwelling place of God's presence, the holy temple of His glory. It's man. Man was created to be God's temple. But now the world is filled with the temples of desecration."

"What does that mean?" asked another of the students.

"Every life is made to be a temple filled with God's presence. But without God's presence we become a temple desecrated, defiled, darkened, filled with idols...a temple created to be holy but fallen from its purpose."

"So, what do you do," I asked, "if that's you?"

"You open the doors of your life and you let God come in. You let Him take out your idols, cleanse your impurities, restore your purpose, light up your heart, and fill your life with His presence. For when you rededicate the temple to God, God will fill it with His glory...In other words, you become the temple of God and your life becomes...Chanukah."

The Mission: Today, celebrate your own Chanukah. Remove the idols. Cleanse your chambers. Rededicate and reconsecrate your temple to God.

Ezekiel 36:25–27; John 10:22–23; 1 Corinthians 3:16; 2 Corinthians 6:16–7:1

Rededicating the Temple

THE LAW OF COSMIC MOTION

I T WAS THE warm afternoon of a sunny day. The teacher and I were sitting under the shade of a nearby tree.

"Newton's First Law of Motion," he said. "An object in motion stays in motion with the same speed and in the same direction unless acted upon by another force."

At that he threw a small rock up into the air, then caught it as it came down.

"When I threw up the rock, it was an object in motion. But then it stopped rising. It was acted upon by another force, the force of gravity. Newton's law applies to forces within the natural world. What if we take it to its ultimate level? What about the motion of the world itself?"

"What do you mean?"

"The world is fallen. Its motion is that of a fall, the motion of sin, of evil. So how do you stop that motion, the motion of the fall? How can you end sin and evil?"

"Many religions and ideologies would say you just turn away from evil and turn to good."

"How?" asked the teacher. "An object in motion remains in that motion . . ."

"Unless acted upon by another force," I said.

"Yes, so it could only happen through another force. So what is the other force? It can't be of the world, but must be other than the world, beyond the world. What is other than and beyond the universe?"

"God."

"Yes. So the answer can only come from God. But how?"

"'Unless acted upon . . .' The other force must act upon the object."

"So the force must come into contact with the object in motion. Therefore, the presence of God must come into contact with the fallen world to act upon it. And what is the cross? It is God taking all the motion of sin and evil and bringing it to an end. And what is the resurrection? It is God giving the world a new motion, the motion of life. It is God giving the fallen the motion of rising. And that's why the only way to truly change the motion of your life is by the motion of God, by the motion of *His* life. And the only way to change your heart is by the motion of *His* heart. But unlike this rock, it's your choice to let it happen. So the key is to let Him act upon you . . . to receive the presence of God and let the force of His life and the power of His love act upon and change the course of your life . . . For an object in motion will stay in that motion . . . unless it comes into contact with the motion of God."

The Mission: Today, seek to receive the cosmic motion of God's love, God's life, and God's salvation. And let it change the motion and course of your life.

Ephesians 2:1–9; 1 Peter 2:9–10; 1 John 3:16

Apprehending the Momentum of Heaven I–II

THE MOON BRIDE

E TOOK ME out in the early evening. It was a full moon, and its light illuminated us to the point where I could have taken notes right there had I chosen to do so.

"Do you remember what the Song of Solomon is about?" he asked.

"It's a love song between a bride and groom."

"And in its deepest realms?"

"An allegory of God and His people, the Lord and Israel, Messiah and His bride, God and us."

"And we are the bride," he said. "In one of the verses of the Song of Solomon the bride is described as one as beautiful 'as the moon.' Do you find the moon to be beautiful?"

"I guess if you look at its surface, it's not very beautiful."

"No, it's filled with imperfections, markings, irregularities, patches of darkness, and craters. And yet it's called *beautiful* and connected to the beauty of the bride. And it's fitting. For as the moon is filled with imperfections, irregularities, and darkness, so too is the bride. And as the moon is filled with the scars of past wounds, so too are we."

"Then how can the bride be called *beautiful*?"

"Her beauty is the beauty of the moon. The moon isn't beautiful in itself. Neither are we. The moon's beauty is in something other than itself. Its beauty is in its light. And its light is not its own, but of the sun. The moon is beautiful inasmuch as it reflects the light of the sun. If it were able to look at itself in a mirror, it would only see imperfection, scars, and darkness. But if it forgets about itself, and looks into the face of the sun, then it shines with the radiance of the sun. And that is the secret of the bride's beauty."

"That we aren't beautiful in ourselves, but that our beauty is in that which is other than ourselves."

"We are as the moon and He as the sun. And as the moon's light and beauty come from the sun, so our light and beauty come from God. If we focus on ourselves, we only see imperfections, scars, and darkness. But if we forget about ourselves and focus on Him, and see the beauty of His light, then we ourselves will shine with His brightness. And His light will overcome our imperfections. And we become beautiful. Never make the mistake of living a life focused on yourself. Forget yourself. Turn to Him. Dwell in the beauty of His presence. Then your life will become a reflection of His, and you'll shine with the light of His radiance."

The Mission: Today, turn your focus away from yourself and to Him. Let your imperfections be lost in His radiance. And let your life shine with the light of His beauty.

Exodus 34:29; Song of Solomon 6:10; John 3:2; 2 Corinthians 3:18

She Like the Moon

THE SERPENT AND THE HEDGE

WE WALKED ALONGSIDE a garden lined with a hedge-like fence. It was a low fence and made up of intertwined sticks and thorn branches. The teacher picked up a stick and struck one of its corners. I watched as a snake emerged from the branches and slithered away.

"You know," he said, "there's a Scripture that relates to this, to hedges and serpents. It's in the Book of Ecclesiastes: 'Whoever breaks a hedge shall be bitten by a serpent.' In the natural it makes sense. Snakes dwell in hidden spaces, like hedges. So if you break down a hedge, you risk being bitten by a serpent."

"I'll keep that in mind."

"You don't think it applies to you, do you?"

"Not very much."

"But it does very much, and it's a crucial key for you to know. It could end up saving your life. Hedges are what you put around gardens and anything else that needs to be protected. You put hedges around that which is alive and that which is precious to you. So you must build hedges around that which is alive and precious in your life, around your family, your marriage, your children, your relationship and walk with God, your integrity, your purity, and your calling...to protect them."

"How and with what hedges?"

"Hedges not of sticks and thorns, but of godly parameters, godly boundaries...hedges built of safeguards, decisions, guidelines, principles, and standards...parameters concerning what you will and will not allow...lines you will not allow to be crossed...whatever is needed to protect such things from harm."

"And what about serpents?"

"In the spiritual realm, the serpent represents evil, the enemy, and the satanic. 'Whoever breaks a hedge, a serpent will bite him.' The darkness, the sin, the evil, the temptation, the danger, and the enemy are waiting for a broken hedge. So build the hedges you must build to protect that which is precious in your life. Build them strong and firm. And once you build them, never break them. And you'll be kept far from serpents...And your garden will be fruitful."

The Mission: What is it that is precious in your life and that you need to protect? Build strong hedges around it and, having done so, don't break the hedge.

Proverbs 22:5; Ecclesiastes 10:8; 1 Peter 2:11; 5:8–9

THE SEPARATION OF THE PRIEST

THAT WHICH IS holy," said the teacher, "is that which is separate, set apart for the purposes of God. Israel was called to be a holy nation. In order to be a holy nation, it had to be a separate nation. Within Israel were the Levites. As God's ministers, theirs was a more holy calling. So they had to be separated from the rest of Israel. And from the Levites, God called the cohanim, the priests, with a holier calling. So the cohanim had to be separated from the Levites. And from the priests, God called the high priest with an even holier calling. So the high priest had to be separated from the priests. Every degree of holiness was matched by an equal degree of separation. That which is holy must be separated...And this has everything to do with you."

"How?" I asked.

"Because it is written, 'You are a chosen people, a royal priesthood, a holy nation, a people for His own possession...' So if you belong to God, you're a priest, one of His cohanim. And every priest and holy vessel must be separated from everything else, set apart to God."

"But the days when people were separated like that are gone."

"Yes, so now He separates His priests by other means...by whatever it takes to separate them from everything else and bring them to Himself. He will use everything to bring you to Himself, to separate you from the rest of this world, the rejection of men, disappointment, heartbreak, crisis, hurt, sorrow, disillusionment, unfulfillment, discontentment, trouble, abandonment, failure, whatever it takes to separate His priest from the world and to Himself."

"So then all things are used for holy and sacred purposes."

"And more than that," he said. "All these things were, in the end and from the beginning, holy and sacred...no matter how they came or how they felt, or what they involved. They were, by reason of their purpose, holy. They were the vessels in the holy separation of the priest. And He will continue to use them, as much as they are needed, to bring His priest back to Himself, and closer to Himself and to greater realms of the holy. For that which is separated to God...is holy."

The Mission: Today, give thanks for all those things that brought you to God—even the heartaches—as the holy separation of the priest.

Exodus 28:1–2; Ezekiel 44:16; 2 Timothy 1:9; 1 Peter 2:9

The Priest's Separation

THE PROPHECY NAME

THE TEACHER LED me into one of the rooms used by the students to study the scrolls. There was no one there, but one scroll was left out on a wooden platform and opened to its beginning. He began to read from its text.

"'*Va yomair Elohim y'he or, va y'he or.*' 'And God said, "Let there be light!" And there was light.' Notice what God did. In the world, we speak of that which is. But God speaks of that which is not. He spoke the light when it was not, and then it was. This is the way of God…not only with light, but with people."

"What do you mean?"

"There was an old man whose wife was past the age of bearing children. But God gave him the name *Avraham* or *Abraham*, which in Hebrew means father of the multitudes. He gave him a name of that which was not…and then it was. Abraham became the father of nations. His name was a prophecy. Then there was the man who was rejected by his family, falsely accused, and thrown into prison. But God had caused him at birth to be given the name *Yosef. Yosef* means he shall increase. And so he would. He would increase even to become the ruler of Egypt."

"Joseph," I said.

"And then there was the man who lived in fear of his enemies. But God had caused his name to be *Giddone*. The name means he who strikes down. He would end up a hero who against overwhelming odds struck down the enemies of Israel."

"Gideon."

"He too was given a name of that which was not…and then it was. And then there was a man of great passion but little stability. But God had given him the name *Kayfah. Kayfah* means the rock. By the end of his life, that's exactly what he would become, a rock of strength." He rolled up the scroll. "We see ourselves as we are. But God sees us not as we are, but as He called us to be. He gives you an identity not based on your past but based on your future, what you are to become. The secret is to receive that identity and believe it before you see it. Live it as if it is. So your name is no longer *Rejected*, but *Beloved*; no longer *Weak*, but *Mighty*; no longer *Defeated*, but *Victorious*. He has given you a name of that which is not. Receive it and it will be. Live by your prophecy name. It is as simple as, 'Let there be light.'"

The Mission: What is your prophecy name? Live by it today. Start with what the Word declares you to be: Beloved, Royal, Holy, and Victorious.

Genesis 1:3; 17:5; Matthew 6:18; Revelation 2:17

The Kayfah Principle & Your New Name

THE PERUSHIM

WE WERE SITTING in one of the gardens. He picked up a branch and drew my attention to it. It had leaves and was still somewhat green.

"It looks like the other branches," said the teacher, "but with one difference; it's no longer connected to the tree. It still has the appearance of life on the outside, but the inside is dry, and it will soon wither away."

He laid down the branch in the same place where he had found it.

"There was once a people who sought to be holy. They wanted to separate from sin, worldliness, compromise, and impurity. So they separated themselves And they called themselves the *Perushim. Perushim* means the Separated Ones. But as they focused on their own holiness, they grew self-righteous and proud. Their godliness became one of outward appearances, a substitute for what was no longer in their hearts."

"So the Separated Ones ended up separating themselves from God," I said, "as a branch, cut off from the life of the tree."

"Exactly," said the teacher. "They still had the outward form, the leaves, blossoms from the past, and the remnants of what had been when they were joined to God. But the inside was dead. And then the God whom they had once sought came to them. And what did they do?"

"I don't know."

"They killed Him."

"Who were the Perushim?"

"*Perushim* is the original name of those we know as the Pharisees, the Separated Ones. Never forget the warning of the Perushim. It is easy to go from righteousness to self-righteousness, from the inner reality to outward appearance, and from godliness to godhood."

"How do you guard against it?"

"Always dwell on the heart and not appearance. No matter how much you know, stay always childlike in spirit, as having nothing but having everything to receive. Never rest on what you have known or done, but come to Him newly, each day, as for the first time. And most of all, stay always close to God, heart to heart, connected, as a fruitful branch that always receives from the tree. And you will never be of the separated ones...but of the joined."

The Mission: Come to Him this day as a little child, as knowing nothing, and having all to know, as having nothing, and having everything to receive.

Isaiah 57:15; Mathew 16:6; 23:2–3; Luke 7:37–48

Fasting for Nothing

THE GOSPEL-ACTS CONTINUUM

HE LED ME into a small room within the Chamber of Scrolls with just under thirty scrolls, mostly small. But one was larger, by far, than the rest. It was this one that he took down and unrolled on the wooden stand that stood by the shelves.

"What do you see?" asked the teacher.

"Two columns of writing," I said. "And the column on the right has what looks like a title above it."

"The column on the left is the closing of the Gospel of John and the end of the Gospels, the accounts of Messiah's work of salvation. And the column on the right is the opening of the Book of Acts, the Acts of the Apostles. Therein is the revelation."

"The revelation? You didn't even read anything out of it."

"The revelation is the end of the Gospels and the beginning of Acts."

"What does that mean?"

"The placement of the two," he said. "That is the revelation. You see, the Gospel could have been the end. But it's not. It's the beginning. The Gospel leads to Acts. The Gospel must *always* lead to Acts. It's not enough to hear the Gospel message. It must produce change. You must act on it. The good news leads to action. Every time you hear the good news, every time it enters your heart, you must let it turn into acts. Otherwise it's not complete. The Gospel leads to Acts. That's one side of the revelation."

"And the other?"

"The Book of Acts begins with the Gospels. It can never exist on its own. Acts must *always* begin with the Gospel. You can never produce the acts of God or the acts of godliness on your own. Your acts must always begin with the good news. They must be birthed out of it as its natural outflowing. The Gospel of love must produce the acts of love. The Gospel brings forth Acts. That's the order and the flow. And it will flow if you let it. The Gospel of mercy will produce acts of mercy. The Gospel of resurrection will produce the acts of resurrection. So let the Gospel produce its acts in your life and let the acts of your life be birthed in the Gospel...For the Gospel must always lead to Acts."

The Mission: Today, let the Gospel produce the acts of God in your life. And let all your acts proceed from the good news. Get wholly into the Gospel and you will enter the Book of Acts.

Isaiah 61:1; John 21:25–Acts 2; James 2:17–26

The Sequel

THE MYSTERY OF SUMMER

THE DAY WAS hot and marked by the gusts of scorching desert wind. We were sitting on a hill overlooking a field that belonged to one of the agricultural settlements. It was now filled with laborers harvesting the grain.

"The age has unfolded," said the teacher, "according to the mystery of the Hebrew calendar, with each prophetic event foreshadowed by a Hebrew holy day. But where in the age are we now?"

"Where did we leave off?" I asked.

"What was the last of the Hebrew holy days to have already been fulfilled?"

"Shavuot, the Feast of Pentecost."

"So then, if we want to know where we are in the age, we have to look at what took place in the Hebrew year after Shavuot, Pentecost. At the end of Shavuot, the Hebrews went out from Jerusalem to their fields and vineyards to reap the long summer harvest. They would labor throughout the summer months until the return of the holy days in autumn. They would then finish the harvest and return again to gather together before the Lord in Jerusalem."

"So if Pentecost, Shavuot, was the last holy day to be fulfilled, then..."

"Then it is now the summer of the age, the time of the summer harvest," he said. "Just as Shavuot was the time of going forth from Jerusalem out to the fields of harvest, so it was on Shavuot, on Pentecost, two thousand years ago, that the apostles went forth from Jerusalem to bring salvation to the ends of the earth. The field is the world, the season is the age, and the harvest is salvation, the gathering in of new life. What was it that Messiah said of the present age?"

"He said that now was the time of the harvest...the time to go out and reap."

"And did you know that in Hebrew the word for *harvest*, *kayitz*, also means the summer? And so the mystery of where we are in this present age is hidden in Israel's summer harvest. It means that your primary goal must be to reap eternal life, to spread the word of salvation, to go out into world and save the lost. Make that your aim. For the days of the harvest are numbered. And the time to reap new life and save the lost comes only once. Therefore, go out and reap all you can in the time you have...until we all appear in Jerusalem...at summer's end."

The Mission: It is the summer of the age. Make it your aim this day to reap the harvest all around you. Bring forth salvation and bring in eternal life.

Proverbs 10:5; John 4:35–36; Matthew 9:37–38

The Joy of the Harvest

HA MAKOM: THE PLACE

THERE IS ONE place on earth," said the teacher, "that has borne the Name of God and a prophecy for almost four thousand years, long before most of the world's great cities or nations bore any name at all."

"What place?" I asked.

"At first it's referred to as *Ha Makom*, The Place. But then it's given a specific name: *YHVH Yireh*. *YHVH* is the sacred Name of God. And *Yireh* means to make appear, to make visible, to present, to provide, to reveal. So *YHVH Yireh* means the Lord will make appear, make visible present, provide, and reveal. It was Abraham who gave that name to the place. And it was Moses who recorded its naming and added the words: 'In the mount of the Lord it shall be revealed, or it will be provided, it will be presented, it will be made visible.'"

"What would be revealed and made visible?"

"The answer is found in what happened in that place. It was there that Abraham offered up Isaac as a sacrifice. And when Isaac asked his father, 'Where is the lamb...?' Abraham answered, 'God will *provide* for Himself the lamb...' But in Hebrew it says 'God will *yireh* the lamb. *Yireh* is the same word by which the place would be named. So YHVH Yireh identifies the place where God will *yireh* the lamb, provide the lamb, present the lamb, reveal the lamb. The lamb will be made visible in that specific place. And The Place, YHVH Yireh, is Mount Moriah."

"Does Mount Moriah have any connection to the revealing of a lamb?"

"I would say so," he replied. "It was there on Mount Moriah that the central event of human history place—the crucifixion. It was there that Messiah was crucified as the Lamb."

"So Messiah was revealed as the Lamb...in the place called 'God will reveal the lamb'!

"Revealed," he said, "presented, and made to become visible in the place of the revealing, the presenting, and the making visible."

"And of the providing," I said.

"Yes, in the place of God's provision. That which appears on that mountain is God's provision for the needs of all, for every need, every emptiness, and every longing of our hearts."

"Messiah is the Lamb...and the Lamb is the provision...Messiah is the provision of all."

"Yes," said the teacher. "And in the mountain of the Lord it has been revealed."

The Mission: Bring every unanswered question, every unmet need, and every unfulfilled longing to Calvary, Mount Moriah, the place of God's providing.

Genesis 22:7–8, 14; Luke 23:33; John 1:29

The Moriah Miracle

THE ALPHA OMEGA MAN

WE WERE SITTING on the sandy plain just beyond the school grounds. Using a wooden stick, the teacher began drawing symbols in the sand. The first appeared to be the capital letter *A*. The second looked something like a horseshoe.

"In Isaiah 44," he said, "it is written, 'I am the First and the Last. Apart from me there is no God.' God is the First of existence and the Last. And this," he said, pointing to the first symbol, "is the *Alpha*, the first letter of the Greek alphabet. And this," he said, pointing to the second, "is the last letter of the Greek alphabet, the *Omega*. These are symbols of God. God is the Alpha, the Beginning of all things, and the Omega, the End of all things...the Alpha and the Omega, the source of all existence...and its object. So, in the very last chapter of the very last book of the Bible, the Book of Revelation, it is written, 'I am the Alpha and the Omega, the Beginning and the End, the First and the Last.'"

"As in Isaiah," I said.

"Yes, but in the Book of Revelation the words are about Messiah. He is the Beginning and the End, the First and the Last, the Alpha and Omega."

"I guess He'd have to be."

"So what would happen if the Alpha and Omega came into the world?"

"He would become the Alpha and the Omega of the world?"

"He would become the Alpha and Omega of time and history. His presence would cause time to divide and history to split in two. He would become the End, the Omega, of one age, and the Beginning, the Alpha, of the other...BC and AD, the Omega of BC and the Alpha of AD. He becomes the Alpha and Omega of history...and not only that, but the Alpha and Omega of all who find Him. He divides our history into two ages as well...our old life, our BC to which He is the Omega and End, and our new life, our AD to which He is the Alpha, the Beginning, a new beginning...a new birth."

The teacher then drew a line in the sand joining the Alpha and the Omega. "All time proceeds from the Alpha to the Omega. So the secret is to receive each moment of your life from Him the Alpha...and live each moment to Him the Omega. For He is the Alpha and Omega of existence...and the Alpha and the Omega of your life."

The Mission: This day make Him your Alpha. Receive every moment from Him. And live every moment to Him as your Omega.

Isaiah 44:6; Revelation 22:13

The Alpha Stone

THE ALTAR OUTSIDE THE HOLY PLACE

A QUESTION," SAID THE teacher. "Salvation is the reconciliation of God and man, heaven and earth. So why couldn't it have taken place in heaven instead of on earth?"

"A good question," I said. "But I have no idea."

"The Tabernacle, the Tent of Meeting, represented that reconciliation in the realm of symbols. Its most sacred part was the holy of holies, inside of which rested the ark of the covenant and where the glory of God resided. Outside the tent was the court. In the midst of the court was the brazen altar. It was on that altar that the sacrifice was slain. So which part of the Tabernacle represents God's dwelling, heaven?"

"The holy of holies."

"Yes," said the teacher. "The holy of holies represents God's throne in heaven. And which part of the Tabernacle represents man's dwelling, earth?"

"The court?"

"Yes. The court was the place farthest away from the holy of holies, just as earth is far removed from heaven. The court was the place where sin was dealt with…the place of blood and death…where the sacrifice would be led to the altar and slain. Sin could never exist in the holy of holies. It had to be dealt with outside the tent."

"That's the answer," I said. "Salvation could never have taken place in heaven, because heaven is the holy place, the holy of holies—sin can never dwell there. And heaven is the place of eternal life, so death could never dwell there. So the sacrifice could only take place outside of heaven. Sin had to be dealt with outside heaven, in heaven's outer court…earth. Earth is the place of sin and the place of death. And only in a place of sin and death could the sin be borne and the sacrifice be killed. That's why the altar must be outside the holy of holies. That's why the sacrifice must die outside. And that's why He had to come into this world…because it was only here that He could bear our sins…and only here that He could die for them. The altar could only be set up on earth. So He came to the world to be slain on the altar of the outer court…outside the holy place and the gates of heaven…that we might leave the place of sin and death and enter in."

The Mission: You dwell in heaven's outer court, the place of sacrifice. Therefore, the life you live here must be one of sacrifice, a life of love. Begin today.

2 Chronicles 7:7; Romans 12:1; Hebrews 13:10–13

THE BAALIM

HE LED ME up a small mountain. When we reached its summit, we came across what looked like the remains of some sort of ancient gathering place. One could discern that by the arrangement of the stones, which had clearly not been produced by nature.

"When Israel turned away from God," he said, "they turned to Baal. Baal was the god of their turning away, the god of their apostasy ... or gods. You see, there wasn't just one Baal, but many, many manifestations of the one. And the many were called the *Baalim* or the *Baals*. There was a Baal for everything, a Baal for every desire, every indulgence, and every sin. When you turn away from God, you end up worshipping the Baalim."

"But who worships Baal anymore?" I asked.

"Whatever you give the highest place in your life to, whatever you live for, if it's something other than God, that's your Baal and you're worshipping it. And whenever one turns away from God, one turns, in one form or another, to Baal. And there's a mystery to Baal. It's in his name. Do you know what *Baal* means?"

"I have no idea."

"*Baal* means master. The Hebrews thought the Baals were there to serve them, but it was the other way around. Because of the Baalim, the people of Israel would end up losing everything they valued most. You see, whatever your Baal is, it will always end up mastering you ... it will always end up becoming your master. Some are mastered by the Baal of success, others by the Baals of power, others by the Baals of pleasure, others by the Baals of money and increase, others by the Baals of self. But they are all Baals, cruel and merciless masters."

He looked away from the gathering place and into the distant mountains.

"And do you know what else *Baal* means?" he asked.

"No."

"*Baal* means owner. And what does that reveal?"

"You become owned by the Baal you worship."

"Yes, possessed by your possession, by the idol you serve."

"How different from God," I said.

"Yes," he said. "God is the true Master, the true Owner ... and yet the One who gives Himself to you to become *your possession*, so that by giving yourself freely to Him you will no longer be mastered or owned by anything but His love."

The Mission: Identify your Baal, that which has mastered you. Submit to the will of the Master and you'll have the power to break free from that Baal.

Judges 2:11–13; 1 Kings 18:20–39; Hosea 2:16–23; 1 John 5:21

The Mask of the Gods

THE MYSTERY BREAD

WE WENT FOR a walk through the wilderness. He shared as we walked.

"Imagine what it was like," said the teacher, "wandering through the wilderness and having your food come down from the sky."

"You mean the manna from heaven?" I asked.

"Yes," he said, "a miracle with a spiritual revelation: The true bread of our lives comes not from earth but heaven. It is not the earthly but only the heavenly that can fill us. And as bread is to our bodies, so is the Word of God to our souls."

"An amazing picture," I said. "Manna from heaven."

"It is," he said. "But there's something even deeper. Do you know the meaning of *manna*?

"No, what is it?"

"Exactly," said the teacher.

"Exactly what?" I asked.

"Exactly what," he answered. "That's what it is."

"Exactly what is what it is?"

"Right again. What is it *is* what it is."

"At this point, I have no idea what you're saying or what I'm saying."

"*Manna* is really two Hebrew words: *mah* and *nah*. It literally means, What is it?"

"So *manna* is a question that means, What is it?"

"Yes," he replied. "They called it manna because they had no idea what it was. It didn't fit into any of their preconceptions. So they named it *mahnah,* What is it? So the Bread of God, the Word of God, and the blessings of God that come down from heaven are called mahnah, What is it? That means if you are to receive the blessings of God, you cannot receive them as something you're familiar with, something to be expected, or something you already know. You must receive them as *mahnah,* as 'What is it?'—as one receiving it for the first time…as a little child, continually surprised by His love, in awe of His wonders, and overwhelmed by His grace. Receive it as something totally new—and it will become totally new, and bread from heaven. Open your heart to the mahnah of His Word, the mahnah of His grace, the mahnah of His love. And never stop living in newness and wonder of so great a love that it must leave you saying, mahnah, What is it?"

The Mission: Today, partake of the bread of heaven. Seek the mahnah of His Word, the mahnah of His love, and the "What is it?" of your salvation.

Exodus 16:14–18, 30–31; John 6:32–35

Mannah

THE MAZMERAH

WE WERE WATCHING one of the gardeners at work trimming the branches of a fruit tree.

"Do you see what he's using?" asked the teacher. "In the Hebrew Scriptures it's called the *mazmerah*, the pruning hook. He's pruning the branch. Do you know why?"

"Tell me."

"A tree," he said, "has a limited amount of resources and energy to distribute to its branches. If a branch becomes unfruitful, it will hinder the tree's overall health and its ability to bear fruit. It will drain the tree's resources. So the purpose of pruning is to remove the unfruitful branch or that which is hindering the tree from fruitfulness. Pruning allows the tree to redirect its resources to the healthy and fruitful branches and thus to become even more fruitful."

"And if one is not a gardener," I said, "how does this apply?"

"Your life in God is a branch, a branch of His life, a conduit of His blessings. And just as any gardener must prune that which is unfruitful, so it is written that God must also prune His branches to allow them to bear the fruit they were meant to bear."

"How does that translate into life?"

"To a tree being pruned, the process of pruning takes on the appearance of loss. So every child of God in this life will experience what appears to be loss. Some things will pass from your life; others will be taken. They will appear to you as losses. But they will not be. The purpose of pruning is not to harm the tree, but just the opposite. It is to allow the tree to bear the fruit it was meant to bear. So too in your life with God. When you experience losses, they will not be for your harm. Every loss will be redeemed. Each will be used to cause you to become what you were made to be. So don't dwell on what was and is no more. Dwell on that which is yet to come, the purposes of God, and the fruit that is yet to be brought forth. For the mazmerah, the pruning hook of God, only touches the branch of His caring, and then only for one purpose, that it might allow, cause you, and enable you to bear the fruit for which your life from the beginning was created to bring forth."

The Mission: What losses have you known in your life? God has used and will use them to bring good and new life. Do likewise. Use them for good.

Psalm 92:13–14; John 15:1–5

The Secrets of Pruning I–III

THE MYSTERY OF THE KEHILAH

WE WERE OVERLOOKING a barren valley through which one of the nomadic desert communities was moving. With the help of a few camels and donkeys, they were carrying all their worldly goods, black tent curtains, multicolored clothes, and the utensils of daily life.

"What is the name given to Messiah's people," asked the teacher, "as a whole?"

I was surprised by the question as it didn't seem to have anything to do with what we were seeing.

"The church," I replied.

"That's a translation. The actual word that appears in Scripture is *ekklesia*. *Ekklesia* means the gathering, the congregation, or the convocation. So the church is not a physical organization, location, or building. It is the gathering of God's people, the congregation of Messiah, no matter where they are in the earth. But there's more to it. The biblical roots of the word *ekklesia* go back much further."

"The church goes back before the New Testament?"

"The word does," he replied. "The word *ekklesia* appears in the Greek translation of the Hebrew Scriptures, over and over again."

"To speak of what...if there was no church then?"

"Overwhelmingly the word refers the nation of Israel."

"So Israel was called the ekklesia...the church?"

"In a sense, yes. The word *ekklesia* is a translation of the Hebrew *kahal* or *kehilah*, words especially used to speak of the congregation of Israel as it journeyed through the wilderness and dwelt in tents on its way to the Promised Land. In fact, the Book of Acts speaks of Israel at Mount Sinai as the ekklesia or church in the wilderness."

"So Israel is an ekklesia," I said, "and the church is an Israel?"

"Yes, an Israel journeying through the wilderness. And that's the mystery. The church is the kehilah, a caravan, an Israel of spirit, not yet home, but journeying, caravanning, tenting, pilgrimming, camping out in the world, always moving, always farther from Egypt, and always closer to the Promised Land. The church is the kehilah, Messiah's caravan."

The Mission: Live today as on a spiritual caravan. Your goal is to move continually forward, away from Egypt and closer to the Promised Land.

Exodus 16:10; Acts 7:38; 1 Peter 2:9–10

The Two Kehilahs

THE CHIASMA

E WERE SITTING on opposite sides of a small wooden table in one of the school's courtyards. The teacher reached into a cloth bag, pulled out a few pieces from a chess set, and set them on the table in this order: the white king, the white bishop, the white knight, the black knight, the black bishop, and the black king.

"What pattern do you see here?" he asked.

"The white side is the inverse of the black side and the black of the white."

"It's called a *chiasma*. It's a pattern that appears in Scriptures· 'Whoever exalts himself with be humbled, and he who humbles himself will be exalted.' 'The last will be first, and the first will be last.'"

"So God used the pattern of the chiasma in the Word."

"Yes, and not only in His Word," he said, "but in the age."

"How so?"

"He ordained the end to be as the beginning, and the beginning as the end."

"I still don't understand.

"In the beginning of the age, Israel disappeared from the world. But it was prophesied in the Scriptures that at the end of the age, Israel would reappear into the world. In the beginning of the age, the Jewish people were scattered from Israel to the ends of the earth. But it was prophesied that at the end of the age they would be gathered from the ends of the earth back to Israel. In the beginning of the age, the Jewish people were driven from Jerusalem. But at the end of the age, they must dwell in Jerusalem once again. In the beginning of the age, believers in Messiah were persecuted by an anti-Christian world civilization. So at the end of the age, it is prophesied there will again be an anti-Christian world civilization and persecution against believers in Messiah. At the beginning of the age, Messiah left this world from Jerusalem. So at the end of the age, He will return to this world and to Jerusalem. And, lastly, it was at the beginning of the age that the believers of the Book of Acts walked the earth. So at the end of the age . . ."

"They are to walk the earth again," I said. "And we are to be that people."

"Yes," he said. "Therefore, live as if you were one of them. Stand as they stood. Go forth as they went forth. And overcome as they overcame. It is our role, our part, and our calling . . . on the other side of the chiasma."

The Mission: Live today as if you were one of the believer at the very beginning. As they overcame their world, overcome yours.

Matthew 20:16; 23:12; 24:12–13; Acts 2:17

The Nisan-Tishri Revelation

THE IDUMEAN MYSTERY

WE WERE LOOKING at an old volume in the Chamber of Books and, specifically, at an image, a lithograph of the Magi standing before King Herod.

"Most people have heard of King Herod," said the teacher, "and how he slaughtered the children of Bethlehem in his attempt to kill the Messiah. But there's more to the story...a mystery that begins ages before."

At that, he turned his gaze away from the image in the book and paused.

"When Isaac blessed his son Jacob, he told him that he would have dominion over his brothers, and men would bow down before him. But when Isaac blessed Esau, he told him that he would live by the sword and under the dominion of his brother Jacob. Esau was so filled with rage that he plotted Jacob's death. But what happened to Jacob? Who were his descendants?"

"The Jewish people, Israel. And what about Esau?"

"Esau also had descendants. They were called the *Edomites* and became the nation of Edom. Isaac's prophecy would come true. Esau's children, the Edomites, would live under the dominion of Israel, under the children of Jacob. In the days of the Roman Empire, they would be called the *Idumeans*. But it was then that something strange happened. An Idumean became the king of Israel; a child of Esau ruled over the children of Jacob."

"And the child of Esau was...?"

"Herod," said the teacher. "King Herod was the child of Esau. It was the ancient battle, Esau warring over the birthright and the blessing, and seeking to have dominion over Jacob. But then another extraordinary thing happened...Messiah was born. Messiah was a child of Jacob, with the true birthright and the true blessing of dominion and lordship. So we have two kings, the true and the false, Esau and Jacob, Herod and Messiah. And just as Esau plotted to kill Jacob, so Herod, the son of Esau, plotted to kill Messiah, the son of Jacob. Behind it all was the ancient mystery. What does the Idumean mystery tell you? It is crucial that we receive the blessing. Without it, we will spend our whole lives reacting to and trying to compensate for its absence. Whatever you didn't receive in this world no longer matters. Receive now from your heavenly Father your blessing and your birthright. For if Messiah is your King, you are of the kingdom of Jacob...the kingdom of those who have received the blessing, the kingdom of the blessed."

The Mission: Have you lived trying to compensate for the lack of a blessing? Stop striving. Focus today on fully receiving your blessing from God.

Genesis 27:27–14; Matthew 2:1–18; Ephesians 5:1

The Idumean Mystery

THE IMAGE OF THEIR KING

WHAT IS A king?" he asked. "A king is the leader and ruler of his people. He leads his people. And the people, in one way or another, follow him. In one way or another they walk in his path and reflect his image. The two are joined together. Messiah is the Sovereign of Israel, King of the Jews."

"But that would seem to go against what you've said before. A people follow their king. But the Jewish people, for the last two thousand years, have not been following their King."

"But if He's their King, then they must, in some way, still follow Him or be joined to Him. That's the mystery," he said. "They still follow Him. You just don't see it. Two thousand years ago Messiah became an outcast, a pariah, a man of suffering. Since that time, what has happened to the Jewish people? They became an outcast nation, a pariah nation, and a people of suffering. Messiah was falsely accused, mocked, vilified, abused, and dehumanized. In the same way, for two thousand years, the Jewish people have been falsely accused, mocked, vilified, abused, and dehumanized. Messiah was forcibly apprehended, robbed of his dignity, wounded, and condemned to death. So too the Jewish people have over and over again been forcibly apprehended, robbed of their dignity, wounded, and condemned to death. Messiah was led as a lamb to His death, stripped naked, and executed. So too His people have, through the ages, been led as lambs to their deaths, stripped naked, and executed. You see, Messiah remains the King of Israel…and, in one way or another, a people will follow their king. And so for two thousand years, the Jewish people have followed in the footsteps of their King and, in that time, have borne His image."

"But after his death," I said, "He was resurrected."

"And so the children of Israel were also crucified in the Holocaust. But after it was over, the nation of Israel was resurrected, the only nation on earth to have undergone such a resurrection from life to death. It is no accident that it was resurrected. For so too was its King. And if His nation, without intending to, still follows Him and still bears His image, how much more must we. How much more must you walk in His footsteps and follow in His ways. How much more must you be conformed to and bear His image to this world. They have done so without knowing. How much more must you in your knowing…For a nation must follow its king."

The Mission: Today, make it your first priority and aim to be conformed to the image of your King. Walk, act, think, and become in the likeness of Messiah.

Isaiah 53:3; Romans 8:29; 1 Peter 2:21

The Isaiah 53 Rabbinical Mystery I–II

THE AGENT

WE CAME TO a tent camp I had never seen before and sat down in a nearby stretch of sand. I noticed a man making his way through the camp to one of the tents. He entered it and stayed inside for some time before emerging with two others, a middle-aged man and woman, who I presumed to be husband and wife. There, by the tent, they spoke into the nightfall.

"That," said the teacher, "is an agent. He represents a man and woman from one of the other camps. His mission is to see if a marriage can be arranged between the son of those who sent him and the daughter of those to whom he was sent. It happened the same way in ancient times. Abraham sent his servant to a foreign land to find a bride for his wife Isaac. So the servant embarked on the journey, bringing with him Abraham's treasures, gifts for the bride. He ended up meeting a young woman named Rebekah. After saying yes to the proposal of marriage, Rebekah embarked with the man on a journey back to the tents of Abraham where she would, for the first time, see Isaac face-to-face."

"There's a mystery there," I said.

"Yes," said the teacher. "Let us open it. Abraham offered up Isaac as a sacrifice. Not long after that comes the account of Isaac's bride. To what would that correspond?"

"The offering of Isaac foreshadows the sacrifice of Messiah. So after Messiah's sacrifice...comes the search for the bride...the bride is the church...each of us."

"And whose mission then begins?" he asked. "Who is sent to the bride?"

"The Spirit of God," I said. "And the Spirit's mission is especially to the bride."

"Yes. The Spirit is the Agent, the Agent of the Father, the Agent of God. And the Spirit comes to the bride and shares with her of the Father and the Son...and draws her to them. And it is the Spirit that comes bearing gifts from the Father to the bride, the gifts of the Spirit. And it is the Spirit that leads the bride on a journey to the Son and the Father. And do you know what the name of Abraham's servant was? It was *Eliezer*. And do you know what *Eliezer* means? It means my God is the helper. And what is the Spirit called? The Helper. So as real and as present as the servant was to Rebekah in her journey, just as real and present is the Servant of the Father, the Spirit, in your journey. So you're never alone, not one moment of your life. You have one beside you, who is...the Agent of God...God, your Helper."

The Mission: Live today in the awareness that you are not alone. God Himself dwells with you in the Spirit. Live as one with whom He is present.

Genesis 24:2–4; John 14:14, 26; 15:26; 16:13

The Isaac Rebekah Wedding Mystery I–III

THE NIGHT OF ADAM

YOU SAID THAT Messiah died on the sixth day," I said, "as the sixth day was the day of man, the day of his creation. And the sixth day began at sunset on Thursday night before the crucifixion. But in Hebrew, the word for *man* is *adam*. So could it be said that he had to die on the 'day of Adam'?"

"Yes," said the teacher, "it could be said."

"And were there any signs linked to Adam the night before the crucifixion when the sixth day began?"

"On the day of Adam's fall, it was said, 'You shall eat bread until you return to the ground.' Adam would toil to eat bread and then die. In the curse, bread is linked to death. How did the sixth day begin, the night before Messiah's death?"

"It began at sundown with the start of the Last Supper."

"And what was the Last Supper?" he asked. "It was the Feast of Bread, Unleavened Bread. 'You shall eat bread.' So as the night of Adam began, Messiah ate bread. And He ate the bread in the face of death. When He lifted up the bread at the Last Supper, He did so to join it to His death. As in the curse of Adam, the bread was joined to death."

"And after the meal, they went out to Gethsemane. Was there anything there linked to Adam?"

"It was in Gethsemane that Messiah toiled in prayer and sweated what appeared to be drops of blood falling to the ground. Toil, sweat, and ground, all three appear in the curse of Adam. And where did that curse begin? In a garden. And where was Messiah on the night of Adam? In Gethsemane. And what is Gethsemane? A garden. And what happened to Adam because of the fall? He was removed from the garden."

"To the place outside the garden," I said. "The place of the curse, and ultimately to his death. So too on that night Messiah was removed from a garden...and taken to the place where the curse of Adam would fall upon Him...where He would be judged, cursed, and taken to His death. And it began on the night of Adam."

"Yes," said the teacher, "so that the children of Adam could be redeemed from the toil of their lives...and leave the curse...and come back to the blessing in the presence of God."

The Mission: Messiah took upon Himself the curse of man. By the power of His redemption, live now against and beyond all curses, and in the blessing.

Genesis 3:19; Luke 22:19, 39–46; 1 Corinthians 15:21–22

Lord of Eden

THE POWER TO CAST A FOREST

I HAD TO WALK a bit to see what he wanted to show me. It was a forest, not far from the city, man-made and carefully tended. As we walked through the forest he began to share.

"A question," said the teacher. "Could you uproot this entire forest and then throw all the trees at once into the distance?"

"Of course not," I replied.

"But what if you could?"

"But it's impossible."

"No," said the teacher. "It *is* possible, but you need to learn the secret. It's all a matter of timing. If you tried to uproot this particular forest and throw it, in its present condition, it would, of course, be impossible. But if you tried at an earlier stage..."

"What earlier stage?"

"The seed stage," he said. "If I gave you a bag of seeds, seeds which, if given root, would grow into this forest, and told you to throw the bag, you'd be able to do it. You would, in effect, be throwing an entire forest, the same forest, just at a different stage. But if you let the seeds become the forest, then you could never do it. It would take heavy earth-moving machines, countless days of hard labor to clear even a small portion of it. Or you could toss the bag of seeds. Thus, by doing so, you possess the equivalent power of all those earth-moving machines combined, and more. You would be, in effect, stronger than Samson. It would be as if you were living with superpowers."

"Assuming I'm not going to move a forest," I said, "how do I apply this secret, this power, to my life?"

"In every way," he said. "The way to deal with sin, every temptation, every evil thought, anger, gossip, lust, worry, bitterness, anything, is not to deal with it after you've let it take root and grow to become a tree or a forest. The more you allow the seed to take root, the harder it becomes to remove it, and the more energy, time, and effort it takes to get rid of it. But rather deal with these things when they're only seeds, the moment they rear their heads. Practice this secret and you'll save yourself countless heartaches, problems, and hours. And you'll live with the equivalent of superpowers...the power of one who is able to throw a forest."

The Mission: Today, practice dealing with every sin and temptation in its seed form and moment. Throw it out, and be glad. You just cast a forest!

Deuteronomy 29:18; Hebrews 12:14–15; James 1:14–15

The Sledgehammer Principle

THE COSMIC DICE

WE WERE SITTING in the circle of stones around the campfire, but there was no fire as it was midday. The teacher was holding a clay jar. He began to shake it, then thrust it downward to release onto the ground its contents, what appeared to be small white stones.

"One of the most famous physicists in the world asserted that God does not play dice with the universe. What do you think he meant?"

"That what happens in the world doesn't happen by chance?"

"Yes, and the question is bigger than physics. It's something that most people ponder at least once in their lives: Do things in life just happen to happen, as if by chance, by the random rolling of the dice? Or is there a reason, a plan, and a destiny? Does God play dice with the universe?"

"And what's the answer?"

"Do you see the white stones? These are the lots. In ancient times they were cast to make decisions, the ancient equivalent of the rolling of the dice. The Book of Esther focuses on this very thing, the casting of the lots. It's what Haman used to determine the day he would destroy the Jewish people. The lots were called the *purim*. It is from that act and this word that comes the Jewish holiday of Purim. It could be called The Feast of Dice. It's the dice or lots that sum up everything else that happens in that book. Evil reigns. And everything seems out of control, random, without purpose, the casting of lots, the roll of the dice. But by the end of the story, every out-of-control event, every evil, is turned around to accomplish the purposes of God and the salvation of His people. Every random event is turned to redemption. The very fact that there exists a holy day called Purim, Lots, Dice, is itself a revelation and the answer to the mystery. They both exist. As long as free will exists and evil exists, there will exist in the world the principle of randomness, that which seems to be without purpose or meaning, the rolling of the dice. Yet above and beyond the dice is the will and hand of God. And in the end, that hand causes every lot and die, every out-of-control detail, to fall into His will. And so it is written, 'God causes all things to work together for good for those who love Him...' So the dice may roll, and the lots will fall, but in the end, He will cause it to roll into the good, and to fall into the purposes of God, into destiny, into redemption...into the celebration of the purim."

The Mission: Ponder those events of your life over which you've never had peace. Be at peace and give thanks that He will work all these things for your good.

Esther 9:26–28; Romans 8:28

The Purim

NIGLATAH: THE BARING

I HAD ASKED THE teacher to show me more of Isaiah's prophecy of the suffering Messiah. So he took me back into the Chamber of Scrolls and over to the scroll that he began to read: "'Who has believed our report and to whom has the arm of the Lord been revealed?'"

"I remember the verse," I said. "You shared it with me when you spoke of God's arm."

"Good," said the teacher. "Then you remember that the arm of God is the power by which He accomplishes His purposes...by which He created the universe, by which He delivered His people from Egypt, and by which He will bring salvation to the world. But now I want to show you something that's hidden in the translation and that can only be seen in the original language. It's in that question: 'to whom has the arm of the Lord been revealed?'"

"What's the answer?"

"The arm of the Lord is revealed to those open to seeing it...even right here."

"What do you mean 'right here'?"

"The arm of the Lord is being revealed in this very question. It's in the word *revealed*. *Revealed* is a translation of the Hebrew word *niglatah*. But *niglatah* means much more than revealed. *Niglatah* means to be taken captive. So the arm of the Lord, the power of God, will be taken captive."

"The Messiah was taken into captivity, arrested. He became a prisoner."

"And *niglatah* also means put to shame, disgraced. So the arm of the Lord will be put to shame and disgraced."

"So Messiah was put to shame, mocked, degraded, and condemned as a blasphemer."

"And *niglatah* also means stripped naked, exposed, and laid bare. So the arm of the Lord will be stripped naked and exposed."

"So Messiah was stripped of His garments and exposed, naked on the cross."

"It is the most famous image in this world of one who has been taken captive, laid bare, disgraced, put to shame, and stripped naked. It is the arm of the Lord revealed, the power of the Almighty. But how could the strongest power in existence be revealed in the death of a naked man on a cross? That is the revelation of the arm of God...the strongest force in the universe...the power of the Almighty...the power of love."

The Mission: Today, fight your battles, overcome, and win your victories—not by your strength, but by God's naked arm, the power of His love.

Isaiah 53:1; John 19:23–24; 1 John 3:16

The Isaiah 53 Witness I–11

SEEING THE COLORS OF HEAVEN

IT WAS A sunny afternoon. The teacher led me into one of the school's most beautiful of gardens, a garden filled with flowers of all varieties and colors. Then he handed me a piece of colored glass.

"Now look at the garden through the glass. How many colors do you see?"

"Just one," I replied. "Everything's red."

"Yes. The glass filtered out every ray of light except for the red. Even though the garden is filled with colors, all you can see through the glass is the red. The world, like this garden, is a mix of colors. What God created is good. But the creation is fallen and is now a mix of good and evil. It will be your glass that will determine what you see and what you receive of the world...The things you take for granted will become the filter of your glass. If you live expecting and requiring of this world heaven and perfection, if you live as one who deserves to be blessed, and thus taking the blessings for granted, you'll become blinded from seeing your blessings."

"I would have thought it to be the opposite."

"No," said the teacher. "What you take for granted is that what you blind yourself from seeing and what you end up losing. If you take the good for granted, you'll filter out the good. And the only thing you'll see is all that is wrong and not good—the imperfect and the dark. So requiring heaven of this life ends up removing heaven from this life, and makes life hellish."

At that, he handed me a second glass. When I lifted it to my eyes, I saw all the other colors, everything except the red.

"This is the secret," he said, "and it's linked to hell. If instead of taking heaven for granted, you take hell for granted...in other words, that you deserve judgment but have been given grace instead...and thus that no blessing is deserved or warranted...and no good thing is taken for granted...what then will happen? The opposite. Your heart will see only the good and every blessing. Everything will become a gift from God, and every moment, His grace. You see, compared to hell, this life is heaven. Learn to see through the second glass, and you'll filter out hell. And what will remain? Heaven...and a heavenly life....and you will see everything in heavenly colors."

The Mission: Take judgment and hell for granted and the fact that you're saved from it, and every other blessing in your life as total undeserved grace. And, by this, live a heavenly life.

Romans 5:8; 1 Timothy 1:15–17; James 1:17; 1 John 3:1

The Third Practice

THE SECRET OF THE MAKHZOR

A PARADOX," SAID THE teacher. "What is *Yom Kippur* with no *kippur*? What is a Day of Atonement with no atonement of the day?"

"Just a day," I said.

"That's the mystery. The holiest day of Judaism, the center of the biblical calendar, is Yom Kippur, the Day of Atonement. And yet for two thousand years the Jewish people have kept a Yom Kippur with no kippur, the Day of Atonement with no atonement. The center of the center is missing. And what is the atonement of Yom Kippur? It's a sacrifice. So we have a missing sacrifice. Two thousand years ago Messiah came as the Kippur, the Sacrifice, the Atonement at the center of the Jewish faith. Right after He came, the Temple of Jerusalem was destroyed, so no more sacrifices could be offered up. Since then, Yom Kippur has had no kippur."

"So a Day of Atonement without the atonement is a witness that the center is missing."

"Not completely missing. Come." He continued speaking while we walked. "You've heard it said that the Jewish people cannot believe in a Messiah who dies as a sacrifice for sin, or a salvation that comes from a man bearing their iniquities." He led me into the Chamber of Books. There, from one of the highest shelves, he retrieved a small black book and leafed through its pages until finding the place he was looking for. "This is a Jewish prayer book. It's called the *Makhzor*. It's used in synagogues throughout the world, specifically for the Yom Kippur service. Listen to the mystery it contains, the words appointed to be read on the day when the Jewish people seek atonement for their sins: 'Our righteous Messiah has departed from us ... we have no one to justify us. He has carried the yoke of our iniquities and our transgression. And He is wounded because of our transgression. He bears our sins upon His shoulders, so that we might find forgiveness for our iniquities.'"

"Amazing," I said. "The missing Kippur of Yom Kippur, right there in the Yom Kippur prayer book. How can they not see it? How can they miss it?"

"The same way we miss it," he said, "and our lives become as a Yom Kippur without the Kippur. The same way we miss the reason for our being and the center of our existence ... even when it's right there in our midst."

The Mission: God is present even when you don't realize it or sense that He is. Take time today to dwell in stillness that you might know and behold the presence of the Lord.

Isaiah 53:4–5; Romans 5:11; 1 Corinthians 3:11

The Rabbinic Mysteries I–VI

THE IMMANUEL SOLUTION

I T WAS EARLY evening, just after dinner. The teacher and I were sitting by the campfire along with others. He was holding an empty cup.

"An empty cup," he said. "How do we get rid of its emptiness? There's only one way...by filling it."

So the teacher went over to the fountain and filled the cup with water.

"So we have successfully removed the emptiness," he said with a slight smile, "not by focusing on the emptiness or by concentrating on removing it. We removed the emptiness by simply filling the cup with water. A simple solution—yet profound, even revolutionary when applied to life. How did God accomplish salvation? By removing evil from the world? No. Salvation came through His presence, by His coming into the world, by becoming God with us, Immanuel."

"By pouring water into the cup," I replied.

"Exactly. He didn't take away our problems or remove them from the world. He did something better—He gave us the answer. He poured the answer into the world. Salvation is not the absence of sin. It's the presence of God. Salvation is not the removing of the world's darkness. It's the shining of God's light into the darkness. And by the light, the darkness is driven away. Salvation is the incarnation of God. It's His presence. It's Yeshua. It's the Immanuel Solution. What does it reveal?"

"You don't overcome the darkness by focusing on the darkness. You overcome the darkness by focusing on the light."

"Yes. And you don't overcome sin by dwelling on sin. You overcome sin, not by dwelling on sin, but by dwelling on God. You overcome emptiness by dwelling on His presence. You solve your problem, not by dwelling on your problem, but by dwelling on the Answer...by being filled with the Answer. You overcome sorrow by the presence of joy, and hate by the presence of love, and evil by the presence of good. Apply this secret, and it will change your life. Overcome the absence by the presence of its opposite. It's as simple and as deep...as pouring water into a cup...the Immanuel Solution."

The Mission: Apply this day the Immanuel Solution. Overcome the problem with the Answer, the bitterness with forgiveness, hate with love, and evil with the good.

Isaiah 7:14; Luke 6:26–36; Romans 12:9–21

THE SHEVAT: THE CEASING OF GOD

IT WAS THE end of the week and the sun was about to set. The teacher and I were sitting on a hill overlooking the school. Many of the students were finishing up their work and their week to get ready for the weekend.

"As the Sabbath approaches," said the teacher, "the observant among the children of Israel must finish up all their work. Do you know why?"

"Because it's the Sabbath," I replied.

"But why is it the Sabbath?" he asked. "The Sabbath is only called the *Sabbath* because of an event, an act of God. As it is written, 'God ended His work which He had done, and He rested on the seventh day from all His work which He had done.' What is translated as 'rested' is the Hebrew word *shevat*. *Shevat* means to cease. On the seventh day God ceased. And from that act, from the ceasing of God, His shevat, comes the word *Shabbat*, from which we get the word *Sabbath*. So the Sabbath is the Sabbath because of the ceasing of God. All its blessings come from God's act of ceasing."

"But with the fall, the peace of the Sabbath and all its blessings were gone from the creation and from our lives."

"So then a new Sabbath is required," he said. "But only God can bring the Sabbath. And the Sabbath can only come in the ceasing of God. So for God to bring a new Sabbath, He would have to cease. And the timing of that ceasing would have to be linked to the timing of the Sabbath. It was Friday afternoon, the end of the sixth day, not of creation, but now of redemption. And as in the beginning, the sixth day was the day of the completion of God's labors. So the labors of God were completed on the cross...And then on the cross...He ceased. He ceased from His labors and His life...the ceasing of God...God's shevat. As in the beginning, God ceased and then came the Sabbath, a new Sabbath, not of this world, and a new peace, greater than the world...for all who will enter it. How? By ceasing...in the shevat...the ceasing of God."

The Mission: Learn the secret of shevat. Cease with God from laboring, struggling, and from yourself. Enter the Shabbat, the Second Sabbath.

Genesis 2:2–3; John 19:30–31; Hebrews 4:4, 9–10

The Sabbath Entrance

KHANANYAH

"HE WAS A blasphemer," said the teacher, "a violent man, and a murderer...Saul of Tarsus. He hunted down the followers of Messiah and delivered them to judgment. And then with a flash of light, on the road to Damascus, he was blinded. The Lord then spoke to a believer in the city named Ananias. He told him to go to Saul. So Ananias approached the blind persecutor, and with the touch of his hand, Saul regained his sight. Now a question: What was the first thing that Saul ever saw as a believer?"

"Ananias?"

"Yes," said the teacher, "but what was it that he saw?"

"I don't know what you mean."

"In God there are no accidents. He chose the man Ananias as the first thing Saul's eyes would see in his new life. What is Ananias? It's a translation of his real name, his Hebrew name, Khananyah. And what does it mean? *Yah* is the Name of God, and *khanan* means grace. *Khananyah* means the grace of God. So what was the first thing that Saul saw in his salvation?"

"Khananyah."

"The grace of God," said the teacher. "The first thing he saw was the grace of God. And it was Khananyah who touched him and caused his blindness to be removed and allowed him to see."

"So it was the grace of God," I said, "that touched Saul's life and the grace of God that allowed him to see."

"Yes, and so it is for all of us. It is the grace of God that touches our lives, that removes our blindness, and allows us to see. Only by the grace of God can we see. And the first thing we see in salvation is khananyah, the grace of God."

"And it was khananyah," I said, "that gave Saul the ability to rise up and walk and then to live as a disciple, to minister, and to fulfill his calling."

"And so it is only the grace of God that gives you the ability to rise and walk in Messiah, and only His grace that enables you to be His disciple, to live in righteousness and holiness, to minister and to fulfill your calling. And that's why Khananyah was the first thing Saul, in his new life, was able to see, because it's all the grace of God...It is that which saves those who have no reason or right to be saved. It all begins by seeing khananyah. Thus, you must never move away from that grace, or from seeing it. For without khananyah, we become blind. And every good thing we do comes from it. It all begins...and is all fulfilled...in khananyah...the grace of God."

The Mission: In all things today look to see khananyah, the grace of God. Follow it, dwell in it, act in it, and let everything flow out of it.

Psalm 84:11; Acts 9:8–18; 20:24; 1 Corinthians 15:10

The Power of Being Wrong

NEKHUSHTAN: THE DOUBLE NEGATIVE REDEMPTION

THE *NEKHUSHTAN*," SAID the teacher, as he pointed to a lithograph on his wall. "The brazen serpent. When the Israelites were dying in the wilderness from the bite of venomous snakes, God told Moses to make a serpent of brass and suspend it on a pole. And when the dying looked at that brass serpent, they were healed."

"Strange," I replied, "healed of the serpent's venom by an image of a serpent."

"The negative of a negative nullifies the negative and produces its opposite—a positive. So the power of the serpent is nullified by the power of the serpent—a double negative. And what is the serpent a symbol of in Scripture?"

"Evil," I said. "The enemy...darkness...Satan...sin."

"So what does the Nekhushtan reveal?" he asked. "It reveals that the power of sin and evil will be nullified...by a double negative redemption. So Messiah said this to Nicodemus: 'As Moses lifted up the serpent in the wilderness, even so must the Son of Man be lifted up, that whoever believes in Him should not perish but have eternal life.' What does that mean?"

"The Nekhushtan...is the cross," I said. "He made Him to become sin for us. He came in the image of sin, of evil, as in the image of the serpent...as the brazen serpent lifted up on the pole...so that all who were infected by the serpent's poison...by sin...would, by looking to the image of sin...by believing in Him who died on the cross...be healed of sin and its power."

"Yes," said the teacher. "The cross is the Nekhushtan. It is the double negative redemption...the binding of all bondage...the taking captive of captivity...the rejection of rejection...the abandonment of all abandonment...the turning away from turning away...the crippling of all crippling...the limiting of all limitations...the separation of all separations...the barring of all barriers...the banishing of all banishment...the cursing of all curses...the defeating of defeat...the destruction of all destruction...the death of all death...and the end of all endings. And the double negative of judgment equals salvation, and of separation equals reconciliation, and of condemnation equals love, and of death equals eternal life. That is the power that you have in Messiah. Live in that power and, from the negative of the negative, bring forth redemption."

The Mission: Live today in the power of the double negative redemption. Doubt the doubt, defy the defiance, bind the bondage, reject the rejection, defeat the defeat, and turn death into life.

Numbers 21:8–9; John 3:14–15; Romans 8–3; 1 Corinthians 15:26;
2 Corinthians 5:21; Ephesians 4:8

The Double Negative Redemption

THE ARCH OF TITUS

HE LED ME into a room opposite the Chamber of Scrolls. It was dimly illuminated by the light of an oil lamp. He picked up the lamp and lit the first light of a giant seven-branch lampstand, the menorah. He proceeded to light each lamp until it was fully ablaze.

"In the year AD 70," he said, "the armies of Rome, under the command of the general Titus, destroyed the land of Israel and the ancient nation of Judea. To commemorate the end of Israel along with other Roman victories, a monument was built and called *the Arch of Titus*. Inside the arch was carved an image of Israel's destruction, the carrying away of the sacred vessels from the Temple of Jerusalem. Two thousand years later, the Roman Empire lay in ruins. But the nation of Israel was miraculously raised from the dead. The new nation needed a symbol. And do you know where they found it, Israel's national seal? On the Arch of Titus. By building a monument to seal in stone the destruction of Israel, the Romans ended up doing the very opposite. They preserved in stone the image of Israel's sacred golden seven-branch menorah for two thousand years. And that very image from that arch became the symbol of Israel's resurrection, the national seal of the newborn nation...the menorah, the symbol of God's light overcoming the darkness. What does the Arch of Titus reveal?"

"That in the end," I said, "you can't stop the purpose of God."

"Yes," said the teacher, "and more than that. God not only causes His purposes to come to pass, but He will even use that which is against His purposes to cause those purposes to come to pass. He not only overcomes evil, but causes evil to be used for good. And so He will turn death into life, destruction into rebirth, darkness into light, the curses set against His people into blessings, and the tears of His children into rejoicing. And He will turn everything in your life that was meant for evil around for good and that which was meant to harm you to save and bless you instead. It's all there in the menorah of God's light kept safe for the ages on the Arch of Titus."

The Mission: Identify the "Arches of Titus" in your life—all the bad that God redeemed for your good. Take part in turning the present bad into blessing.

Genesis 50:19–20; Psalm 30:11–12; Romans 8:28

The Arch of Titus

THE INFINITY SOLUTION

WE WERE SITTING in the desert sand when I asked him a question.

"God is one. And God is three. Mathematically speaking," I said, "I don't see how it can work. One can never equal three and three can never equal one."

At that, it was I who picked up a stick and began writing numbers in the sand.

"One plus one plus one equals three, not one."

"And if it was one divided by three?" asked the teacher.

Again I wrote it out on the sand.

"One divided by three equals one-third, not one."

"You're right," he said. "It doesn't work. How could it?"

"I guess it can't. So I should forget about trying to use equations."

I lifted the stick to erase the numbers when his hand took hold of the stick.

"I didn't say that. You just used the wrong equation. God is infinite. You can't use that which is finite to comprehend the infinite."

The teacher then took the stick and pointed it to the first equation. Next to every number he inscribed the symbol of infinity.

"Now let's try it again. One infinity plus one infinity plus one infinity equals three infinities. How big is three infinities?

"It's infinite. It's infinity. Three infinities equal one infinity…So three equals one."

Then he pointed the stick to the second equation and did likewise, inserting again the symbol of infinity.

"One infinity divided by three equals one-third of infinity. And what is one-third of infinity? One-third of infinity is…infinity. When you speak of God, you speak of the infinite. And one infinity and three infinities are equal. One-third of infinity and one infinity are likewise equal. So in the realm of God, the realm of the infinite, one does equal three and three equals one. You can never fit the infinite inside the finite, and you can never fit God inside of your understanding. If you could, then He wouldn't be God. Then your understanding would be God. But God, by definition, must be greater than your understanding. And this will set you free. You don't have to figure out God. But there is a way that the finite can understand the infinite."

"How?"

"Believe!"

The Mission: Seek this day to live not limited by the limitations of your circumstances, problems, thoughts, and ways. Live by faith beyond them.

1 Kings 8:27; Isaiah 40:28; Romans 11:33

THE EUCHARISTIA

WE WERE SITTING by the fire at night. The teacher had in his hand a piece of matzah, unleavened bread. He broke off a piece and handed the rest to me. We partook.

"The bread of the Passover, as Messiah gave to His disciples at the Last Supper."

"Communion," I said.

"Which is from the Passover," he said. "And do you know what some call that bread?"

"The Eucharist," I replied.

"Yes. And do you know where that word comes from? It comes from the Greek word, *eucharistia*. It appears in the Scriptures. But it has nothing at all to do with bread."

"What then?"

"*Eucharistia* means to give thanks or to say a blessing.

"So why do people think it's the bread?"

"It was what Messiah said *over* the bread. It's what the Jewish people have said over the bread for ages. It was the Hebrew blessing known as the *Motzi*. He said, '*Baruch atah Adonai, Elohaynu Melekh Ha Olam, ha motzi lechem min ha aretz*,' which means, 'Blessed are You, Lord our God, King of the Universe, who brings forth bread from the earth.'"

"So it's not the bread but the blessing of thanks He gave over the bread."

"Yes," said the teacher. "And what does that tell you?"

"That life is not about things."

"Yes. It tells you that your life does not consist of objects, but of the blessings you say over them...the thanks you say over them. You see, it doesn't matter how much or little you have on earth. What matters is how much thanks you give for what you have. The one who is rich in possessions but poor in thankfulness is, in the end, poor. But the one who is poor in possessions but rich in giving thanks is, in the end, rich. And what was the bread over which Messiah gave thanks? It was the symbol of His suffering and death. Yet He spoke a blessing over it and gave thanks for it. For those who give thanks in all things have the power to turn curses into blessings and sorrows into joy...the power of the eucharistia."

The Mission: Seek today not to increase what you have, but to increase your thanks for what you have. Give thanks in all things. The greater your thanksgiving, the greater will be your life.

Psalm 136; Luke 22:14–23; 1 Timothy 6:6–8

The Eucharistia

YOVEL

THE TEACHER LED me up a hill in the middle of a plain. Only when we reached the top did I understand why we had come there. He took out a ram's horn, a shofar, and, from the top of the hill, began to sound it in every direction.

"'And you shall consecrate the fiftieth year,'" said the teacher, "'and proclaim liberty throughout all the land to all its inhabitants.' It was called the *Yovel*, a name based on the shofar that was sounded to proclaim its coming. In the year of Yovel, slaves and prisoners were set free. And God had decreed, 'Each of you shall return to his possession, and each of you shall return to his family.' So the Yovel was also the year of restoration. If you had lost your land, your inheritance, your ancestral possession, then in the year of the Yovel you would go home, you would return to your land, you would receive back your inheritance and your ancestral possession, all that you had lost. But the Yovel is known by another name."

"What name?"

"The Jubilee. Most people know the word, but few people realize its key. You see, the Jubilee can only begin on one specific day. That day was Yom Kippur, the Day of Atonement. The blessings could only come after being reconciled to God. And the only way to be reconciled to God was through the atonement. So apart from Yom Kippur, there can be no Jubilee, no release, no freedom, and no restoration. And what is the atonement?"

"The sacrifice of Messiah."

"And here's the key. Yom Kippur brings the Yovel. The atonement brings the Jubilee. Therefore if Messiah is the atonement, He must also bring the Jubilee. And the more you dwell in the atonement, the more you will live in the Jubilee. So go deeper in Messiah. And go deeper in His atonement. And you'll have the power of Jubilee, the power to walk in freedom, the power of returning home, the power of reconciliation, the power of liberty, and the power to be restored to your God-given inheritance. For from Yom Kippur comes the Yovel...and from Messiah comes your Jubilee."

The Mission: Make today your Yovel. Walk in the power of freedom, restoration, reconciliation, and release. Live the power of Jubilee.

Leviticus 25:10–11; Luke 4:18–19; Galatians 5:1

THE ADERET

IT WAS THE middle of the afternoon. We went up a high mountain and to the same cave in which we had seen the engraving of the cherub with the outstretched wings. The teacher went inside without me and soon emerged holding a large garment, a robe of sorts, made of a rough light brown material.

"A mantle," he said, "but unlike the one I showed you earlier, it's made of camel's hair, as in the mantle of Elijah, the one he cast onto the shoulders of Elisha, signifying that Elisha would follow in his footsteps as a prophet of the Lord. Can you imagine being Elisha and feeling Elijah's mantle coming over you?"

"It must have been overwhelming. He must have felt totally inadequate."

"Undoubtedly," said the teacher, "but so did all the others who received their mantles. From Moses, to Isaiah, to Jeremiah, to Peter, they all felt unworthy of the mantle given them, and with good reason...the mantle was too big. It didn't fit. But that's the nature of the mantle. In Hebrew the mantle is called the *aderet*. *Aderet* means large, big, great, wide, powerful, excellent, noble, mighty, and glorious. You see, the mantle is bigger and greater than the one it's given to. And so too it is with you."

"With me?"

"With all His children. Each one is given a mantle, a calling. And you will be given yours. But remember, your mantle is your aderet, and the aderet always speaks of greatness. So your calling will be too big for you. It won't fit. It won't match who you are. And there will be times when you'll struggle with that, with its magnitude in comparison to who you are...It will always be greater, more powerful, more noble, more excellent, and more glorious than the one who wears it and to whom it was given."

"But why? Why does God give us mantles that are too big and don't fit?"

"Your mantle is not meant to fit who you are. It's meant to fit who you are to be, who you are to become. So when you were a little child, your parents bought you clothes that didn't fit, that were too big. It wasn't to fit who you were; it was to fit who you were to become. So too your mantle must be beyond you, that you can grow into it, that you can rise to it. So never be discouraged at the difference in size. It must be that way...that you might become greater, more excellent, more noble, more powerful, and more glorious than you are now."

The Mission: Today, embrace the aderet, your mantle. Accept its greatness and that it's over and above you. Believe it, and, by God, rise to it.

1 Kings 19:19; 1 Corinthians 1:26–31; 2 Corinthians 3:5–6;
Ephesians 4:1

Don the Mantle

YARDEN: THE DESCENDER

HE LED ME to the edge of a small valley. "Look," he said, pointing to a rocky slope on the other side of the valley down which a stream of water was cascading.

"It comes from a nearby spring," he said, "and descends the slope to a pool at the bottom of the valley...similar to the river that flows through the Promised Land."

"The Jordan River?"

"Yes. The Jordan flows from one end of Zion to the other and, as it flows, gives life to the land. It begins its course in the north at Mount Hermon and flows down to Galilee, then through the Jordan Valley to the wilderness of Judea, and finally into the Dead Sea where it comes to its end. In Hebrew, the *Jordan* is the *Yarden*. Do you know it means?"

"No."

"It comes from the Hebrew word *yarad*. *Yarad* means to go down, to descend. So the Jordan means the descender. All rivers descend," he said, "but no river descends as much as does the Jordan. It descends so far that it ends its journey in the lowest place on earth, the Dead Sea. And yet it is in the Jordan's descent that it gives life to the Promised Land...What is the revelation of the Yarden?"

"It is through a descent," I said, "that life is given."

"Yes," said the teacher. "And who is the Descender?"

"God. God is the Descender."

"Yes," said the teacher. "God is the Yarden. It is the Most High who is the Descender. Only He can fully descend. And so the Descender humbled Himself, descending from the heights to come into the world, and taking the form of man. And as the Jordan descends to Galilee, so the Descender came to the land of Galilee, and there gave life to those in need. And in the same way that the Jordan descends from Galilee to the Dead Sea, the lowest point on earth, so from Galilee the Descender went down to the lowest of depths, to death and judgment. For God is love. And the nature of love is to descend that it might give of itself, and that we, in its descent, might find life. And those who have received the life of this Yarden must likewise descend to give of that life to others. For God is the Yarden...and the Yarden is love."

The Mission: As God descended in Messiah the Descender in order to bless us, so today descend, go lower, pour out your life that you might bless others.

Ephesians 4:8–10; Philippians 2:3–9; James 4:10

THE DANCE OF THE CIRCLES

IT WAS EVENING. There was, in the tent village below the hill from which we watched, a celebration. The camp was aglow with the light of torches. "Come," said the teacher as he led me down the hill and into the midst of the celebration. They didn't mind our presence. Before us were men, women, and children, old and young together, all taking part in a circle dance. One of the girls in the circle motioned for the teacher to join in. So he did. I was content to watch.

"Come," he called. "Join in the dance."

So, with great reluctance, I did as well. I had no idea what I was doing, but I did my best to follow the steps of the teacher and of those around me. After a time, it began to almost flow and even became a joy. At the end of the dance and before the next one began, the teacher and I stepped back from the circle and watched the others as they continued in the circle dances.

"You would have seen this in ancient Israel, the dance of circles," he said, "in the days of their celebrations, in the holy festivals that God gave them. And you know what they were called, the feasts and celebrations of the Lord?"

"No."

"*Khag* . . . a feast or festival. And do you know what *khag* really means?"

"No."

"*Khag* actually means a dance, and specifically, the dance of circles. God named His holy days, His sacred gatherings, after the dance of circles."

"So God ordained that His people take part in the khag, the festival, but also the dance of circles."

"And not just His people," he said, "but another."

"What another?"

"The world," he said. "God ordained that the earth also take part in the *khag*, in the dance of circles. So the earth performs the circle dance around the sun. And so our entire world is part of a khag. And so our entire lives have taken place and are taking place within a cosmic circle dance. And the circle dance is the khag. Therefore, if you dwell on earth, you must live your life as part of the khag . . . as a celebration of the Lord, a manifestation of worship, a festival of His love, a sacred expression of joy and thanksgiving . . . You must live your life as a sacred dance of circles."

The Mission: Take part in the khag. Live your life today as an act of worship, a flowing of His love, a dance of joy.

Psalm 149:1–3; Jeremiah 31:13; 1 Corinthians 10:31

The Dance of the Heavenly Circles

THE CHRYSALIS

WE WERE SITTING outside under an olive tree. The teacher's attention was drawn downward to a small dark object slowly moving along the ground.

"It looks like a worm," he said, "but different from the worm…a caterpillar, a fascinating creature…the child of a butterfly…an ugly crawling wormlike creature born of a beautiful winged creature. And it has no idea of its origins or who its parent is. It goes through life crawling on the ground. The only life it knows is a wormlike life."

He picked up the caterpillar and placed it on the olive tree.

"But one day the caterpillar climbs up a tree, hangs itself upside down, and begins to form around its body a hard protective shell, a chrysalis. In the chrysalis, that which was the caterpillar comes to its end. Only in its dying as a caterpillar can the creature undergo a metamorphosis. And when the metamorphosis is complete, a new being emerges from the shell of the chrysalis. The new creature no longer has anything wormlike about it. It is now winged and beautiful. It will never again crawl through the earth and never again be earthbound. It will live in the image of the one who gave it life…as the winged creature it was always meant to become."

"It is an amazing phenomenon," I said.

"Yes, within it a shadow."

"Of…?"

"The caterpillar is given life by the butterfly. We are given life by God. As the caterpillar crawls through life, earthbound and unaware of the purpose for which it was born, so man goes through life earthbound and unaware of the purpose for which he was born. We see with wormlike eyes, think wormlike thoughts, and live wormlike lives. But to some of these earthbound creatures a miracle happens…They allow themselves to die to the old, to the earthbound wormlike life. And yet in their dying to their old self they begin a metamorphosis. The earthbound life dies. But what emerges in its place is a different life, a new creation, beautiful and no longer earthbound but now heavenly and made to dwell in heavenly realms…and what it was always meant to be…a heavenly being in the image of Him from whom it was given life in the first place."

"The new birth, the new creation."

"Yes, the metamorphosis of the children of God, born as earthly creatures, but reborn as the children of heaven…the Gospel of the butterfly."

The Mission: Move away from the earthbound—everything in your life that is tied to the world, to the flesh, and sin. Move into the realm of the heavenly. Start flying.

Romans 6:4–8; 2 Corinthians 5:17; Galatians 2:20; Ephesians 4:22–32

The Gospel of the Butterfly

ZICHARYAH, ELISHEVAH, AND YOCHANAN

THERE HAD BEEN centuries of silence," said the teacher, "in between the Hebrew Scriptures and the New Testament. To many, it seemed as if God had forgotten His promises to Israel. Do you know what ended that silence? The first earthly event recorded in the New Testament?"

"The birth of Messiah?"

"No," he said. "It was an event concerning a priest named Zachariah. When Zachariah was young, he married a woman named Elizabeth. Undoubtedly they had dreamed of having a child, but were never able to. They were both now old. Time had taken away their youth and their dream. But while Zachariah was performing his priestly service in the Temple of Jerusalem, an angel of God appeared to him and told him that Elizabeth would, in her old age, give birth to a child. So God would fulfill the ancient hopes of Israel through the fulfilling of an old couple's long lost hopes for a baby. But behind it was a mystery. Zachariah's real name was *Zicharyah*. *Zicharyah* means God has remembered. Elizabeth's real name was *Elishevah*. *Elishevah* means the oath of God. Zicharyah and Elishevah were joined together in marriage. So *God has remembered* was joined to the *oath of God*. The very joining of the two lives created a prophetic message, *God has remembered the oath of God*. A sign to Israel that God had not forgotten His promise, but was about to fulfill it. And when God remembers His oath, then the oath bears life. So Elishevah will bear a child who will be known as John the Baptist. But his real name was *Yochanan*."

"And what does *Yochanan* mean?"

"The grace of God. God's remembrance of His oath causes to be born the grace of God."

"The grace of salvation, the very thing that would come forth out of God's fulfilling of His oath."

"And when Zicharyah gave praise to God, he would declare that God had performed the miracle 'to remember His holy covenant, *the oath* which *He swore* to our father Abraham.' Never forget this," said the teacher. "No matter how long it takes, whether centuries or moments, God will never forget His promise and never break His Word. And out of the broken, the barren, and the impossible, the grace of God will be born."

The Mission: The Scriptures are filled with promises for His people. Take one today. Hold to it. Live in light of it.

Leviticus 26:40–42; Luke 1:4–17, 72–73

THE MYSTERY OF EUROPA

HE LED ME into a room of varied ancient artifacts and to a table on which rested a black vase. He lifted it up to show me. Against the black was an image, a robed woman riding a large, white bull.

"It's from Greece," he said, "a depiction of an ancient pagan myth. The woman was a princess. The white bull is the Greek god Zeus in disguise. According to the myth, Zeus became enamored with the princess and disguised himself as a white bull. When she saw the bull, she was fascinated and got on his back. He then carried her away and seduced her."

He set the vase back down on the table.

"The Scriptures prophesy that in the end times there will be a world civilization characterized by godlessness and evil. They also foretell that in the last days will be a great falling away, a great apostasy from the ways of God. How do the two go together? And what does an apostasy require?"

"It requires that one has once known God. Otherwise there could be no falling away."

"So a civilization that once knew God ends up as a civilization of evil. How does that happen? In the case of the princess, it was a matter of abduction and seduction. Could that happen as well to a civilization? The princess had a name. She was called *Europa*...as in Europe. Think about it, a whole continent, an entire civilization bearing the name of a woman seduced by a pagan god. Europe was once the center in the sending forth of God's Word. But as it turned away from God, it was seduced by other gods and carried off by other gospels, the gospel of communism, the gods of humanism, fascism, Nazism. In the ancient myth the god who seduces Europa takes the form of a bull. So too in the apostasy of ancient Israel, the god to which the nation turned, Baal, assumed the form of a bull. In the end, it's all the same god...the same satanic principality, the enemy, seeking destruction. Never forget the warning of Europa: a civilization that once knew God, which, in its turning away from God, produced more destruction than any civilization in human history. For when you depart from the light, the darkness will abduct you. And when you turn away from God, you'll end up seduced by the god of your turning. So guard your heart. Stay far from all gods and idols. Love the Lord with all your heart and strength...and you'll never be touched by the seduction of Europa."

The Mission: See behind the temptation to the destruction that awaits. Turn from all temptations, gods, idols, and sins. Love God with all your heart.

2 Timothy 3:1–5, 12; 4:1–5

The Woman, the Beast, and the Saints: The Maccabee Blueprint

HEAVEN'S LADDER

WE STOOD AT the bottom of an empty cistern. I had asked the teacher to show me as I had never seen one before. We were now ready to leave.

"Look," said the teacher, "right now that's our only hope."

He was pointing to a wooden ladder, the same ladder we had climbed down to get to where we were. "Without that ladder," he said, "we'd be stuck here at the bottom. And what if it only went halfway up to the top?"

"If it didn't reach the top, it wouldn't do us any good."

"And if the latter started from the top but only went halfway down?"

"If it didn't reach the bottom, it wouldn't do us any good either. We'd be stuck here either way."

"What about getting into heaven?" he asked. "How high is heaven above the earth? How great is the distance that separates man from God, and sin from the Most Holy? How long would that ladder have to be...to get you into heaven?"

"As high and as long as the distance that separates man from God, a ladder between heaven and earth."

"It was that ladder that Jacob saw in his dream, a ladder from heaven to earth. It was the shadow of Messiah, that which joins heaven to earth, and God to man. It can only work if the ladder touches both ends, the highest height with the lowest depth. So the Most High had to descend to the most low of depths so that those in the lowest depths could ascend to the highest heights. The Most Heavenly had to become earthly so that those who were earthly could become heavenly. And the Most Holy had to join Himself to the most unholy, the Holy One joined to the lowest of sins, the Most Sacred to the most profane...So God descended to the deepest depths of darkness, to the lowest rung of degradation and judgment."

"The bottom of Jacob's ladder," I said, "that which joins earth to heaven..."

"Therefore," said the teacher, "no matter how low you find yourself, no matter how lost you are, no matter how sinful, no matter how hopeless, no matter how far from God you are...no matter how deep the pit you find yourself in...look for the ladder...and it will be there to take you out. The ladder will be there with its one end touching the bottom of your lowest depths, and the other end touching the Most High."

The Mission: Wherever you are there is a ladder connecting you to the Most High. Find the first rung of heaven's ladder and take it.

Genesis 28:10–17; John 1:51

The Heaven and Earth Continuum

ANI LO

ANI LO," SAID the teacher, as we walked through the garden. "It's from the Song of Solomon. It's what the bride says of the bridegroom. Those two Hebrew words sum up everything you're called to be and do in God...every good work, every prayer, every act of repentance, every overcoming of sin and evil, every manifestation of love, every decision of righteousness...everything. It's all summed up in *Ani Lo*."

"What does it mean?"

"*Ani Lo* means I am His."

"How does it sum up everything we're called to do?"

"If you live an Ani Lo life, if you're His, then you can't give yourself to anything else. Therefore you can turn down sin and its temptation. And if you're His, then what is it to give of yourself, or of what you have? It's nothing. Even self-sacrifice is nothing. And if you're His, then you have nothing to worry about, or to be offended over, or to be weighed down about. Your burdens are His. Your life is His concern. You're free."

"But you said that in Hebrew there's no true verb for having, for his or hers. So there has to be something else that the bride is saying."

"There is," he said. "*Ani Lo* literally means I am *to Him*. So if you belong to God, you must be 'to Him.' In other words, you can't just belong to God, any more than a bride could just belong to a bridegroom. The bride is only his if she gives herself to him. It's her choice. So to belong to God, you must choose to give yourself to Him, your desires to Him, your heart to Him, your burdens to Him, your everything to Him. And you must do this freely and every day of your life. You must live an Ani Lo life, a life that is *to Him*, in which everything you do has one aim and direction...to Him. And you must do this as does the bride."

"And how is that?"

"The bride isn't a theologian. When she says 'Ani Lo,' 'I am His,' or 'I am to Him,' she's not making a doctrinal statement. She's overflowing with the joy of love. It's her joy to be His and her joy to give herself to Him. To give yourself is not a burden when you're filled with love—it's a joy. Live your life this way, giving yourself in love to Him in the joy of Ani Lo."

The Mission: Today live out the words Ani Lo. Live as one totally belonging to your Beloved. Make Him the aim and purpose of all you do. Give yourself to Him.

Song of Solomon 2:16; Romans 14:7–8; 1 Corinthians 6:19–20; Colossians 3:17

Ani Lo

THE SCARLET REDEMPTION

HE LED ME into the Chamber of Books where he retrieved one of the large reddish books of the Talmud, the writings of the rabbis. He then took out from his pocket a scarlet cord.

"It is recorded by the rabbis," said the teacher, "that in the time of the second Temple, on Yom Kippur, the Day of Atonement, a scarlet cord, representing the sins of the people, was tied to the Temple doors. When the ordinances of Yom Kippur were completed, the cord on the Temple doors would turn from scarlet to white...as in the Scripture, 'Though your sins are like scarlet, they shall be as white as snow....'"

"Every year?"

"Yes," he said, "that's what they record. The phenomenon would take place every year on the Day of Atonement to signify that the atonement had been completed and accepted. But then something happened. The rabbis write that at a certain point in the first century a sign appeared in the Temple signifying a change of cosmic proportions. The cord stopped changing from scarlet to white."

"A sign that the sacrifices were no longer accepted?"

"Or that they were no longer central to the forgiveness of sins."

"Because..."

"Because the final atonement had been offered up...the final sacrifice for sin."

"When do the rabbis say that this happened, that the change took place?"

"They record it beginning about forty years before the destruction of the Temple."

"The Temple was destroyed in the year AD 70," I said. "Therefore, the cosmic change took place around the year AD 30."

"Which just happens to be the same time in history when Messiah came to Jerusalem to die as the final sacrifice for sin, as the final atonement. So too the Book of Hebrews declares we are no longer saved by the sacrifices of the Temple or of Yom Kippur, but by the atonement of Messiah. And the rabbis pinpoint the time of the cosmic change to the time of Messiah's death...a sign of history written in scarlet that the final atonement has absolutely taken place, that the guilty have actually become innocent, that God has indeed cleansed us of the past, and that our sins which were as scarlet...have for real become white as snow."

The Mission: See all the sins and errors of your life as turning from scarlet to white. Seek now to live a scarlet-free life, in the white of your cleansing.

Isaiah 1:18; Hebrews 10:10–14, 18–22

The Yoma Mysteries

GALILEE OF THE BROKEN

WE WERE WATCHING the sunset from the ridge of a low hill. "Did you ever wonder why Messiah first appeared in Galilee? Why He made Galilee the center of His ministry?"

"Because it was unlikely?"

"Yes," said the teacher. "It *was* unlikely, but there was another reason. Centuries before Messiah's coming the people of Israel fell away from God and defied His ways. And then the judgment came as the armies of Assyria ravaged and depopulated the regions of the north, namely the land of Galilee. It was destroyed and left desolate. Galilee was the first of lands to suffer God's judgment. So too Galilee would be the first of lands to receive the comfort of God's mercy in the coming of Messiah. And it was of this land that Isaiah prophesied, 'There will be no more gloom for her who was in anguish. In earlier times He treated the land of Zebulun and the land of Naphtali with contempt, but later on He shall make it glorious, by the way of the sea, on the other side of Jordan, Galilee of the Gentiles. The people who walk in darkness will see a great light. Those who live in a dark land, the light will shine on them.'"

"So Galilee was the first land to be broken," I said, "and therefore, the first to see the power of God to bind up the broken and heal the crippled."

"Yes," said the teacher. "Galilee, the broken land...and the land of the broken. And who do you find in Galilee being drawn to Messiah? The crippled, the leprous, the sick, the outcast, the sinful, the defiled, the broken. Galilee is the land where the broken find Him who came for the broken, to be touched by His hands, and healed by His touch. The people who walked in darkness saw a great light, Messiah, and in a dark land the light of God lit up their lives. What is Galilee all about? It's about mercy, God's mercy and compassion for the broken and crippled of man."

"And even for those who are broken because they fell into sin and rebellion."

"Yes," he said, "even those...especially those.

"And that's all of us," I said. "Isn't it?"

"Yes," said the teacher. "We are all of Galilee."

The Mission: What in your life is broken or not whole? Bring it to the Messiah of Galilee. Let Him see it. Let Him touch it. And let Him heal it.

Isaiah 9:1–2; Matthew 4:13–16; Mark 2:16–17

Galilee

THE NINTH OF AV MYSTERY

WHAT IS THIS?" I asked. "Or rather what *was* it?"

"It was a great house," said the teacher, "a great house of ancient times."

We walked through the wreckage, stones, broken pillars, and fragments of ancient pottery. He sat down in the midst of the ruins. I joined him. He took out a scroll and began to read, "'How lonely sits the city that was full of people...Zion spreads out her hands, but no one comforts her...' The Book of Lamentations. The Jewish people read it every year to commemorate the destruction of Jerusalem in 586 BC, as the armies of Babylon razed the Temple to the ground on the ninth day of the Hebrew month of Av. Centuries later Messiah foretold that Jerusalem would be destroyed again and the people of Israel taken captive into the nations. His prophecy would come true in AD 70 when the Temple of Jerusalem was destroyed by the armies of Rome and the Jewish people again exiled from the land. And it all happened on the same day, the Ninth of Av. Less than a century later came another calamity as the armies of Rome crushed the Bar Kochbah uprising, killing over a hundred thousand Jewish people, a calamity that culminated with the destruction of the city of Bethar—on the Ninth of Av. In the Middle Ages, the Crusades would wipe away thousands of Jewish people. The Crusades began on August 15, 1096—the Ninth of Av. In 1290 the Jews were expelled from England. The calamity began with the signing of the decree of expulsion on July 18—the Ninth of Av. In 1492, the Jews were expelled from Spain, with a final deadline of August 2—the Ninth of Av. The ancient mystery has manifested again and again from the fall of Jerusalem in 586 BC to the Final Solution of Nazi Germany."

"Wasn't all this foretold as far back as the Law at Mount Sinai?" I asked.

"It was," said the teacher. "And what does it reveal?"

"God is real," I said. "His Word is true. And we must pay it close attention."

"Yes," he said. "And Messiah not only warned that this would happen, but wept because of it...as a shepherd weeps for a scattered flock. But His tears will cease when they return to their Shepherd and the Ninth of Av mystery comes to its end."

The Mission: Messiah wept for His people. Share of His heart and pray for the Jewish people, for their redemption and their return to their Shepherd.

Lamentations 1:1, 17; Ezekiel 11:17; Luke 19:41–44; 21:24

THE RESISTANCE SECRET

IT WAS EARLY morning. The sun hadn't yet risen, and I would never have been up had the teacher not scheduled our time together for that hour. As we walked through the school grounds, we came to an open space in which several students were engaged in morning exercises.

"Notice that one," said the teacher, pointing to one of the students exercising with weights and straining under the pressure. "He's lifting weights. Why?"

"To become stronger," I said.

"The principle of resistance. The man resists the weight by exerting his strength against it. The resistance causes him to grow stronger. And so it is with God."

"What do you mean?"

"God calls each of us to grow...to grow in faith, in righteousness, in love, in joy, in hope, patience, peace, perseverance...in godliness. How do you do that?"

"Not by lifting weights."

"But you do," he said. "You grow stronger in these by doing just that."

"How?"

"What causes the weight lifter to grow stronger? Resistance. And what is it that makes you stronger in these things? Resistance. When you exercise the qualities of God against resistance, it causes you to grow stronger."

"But with what weights?"

"The weights are whatever goes against the motion of what must grow stronger. So that which goes against love is the weight, the resistance that enables love to grow stronger. When it's hardest to love, and you love regardless, your love grows stronger. When your circumstances are not conducive to joy, but you rejoice anyway, your joy increases. When it's hardest to do what is right, but you do it anyway, when it's hardest to hope, but you hope anyway, when it's hardest to be holy, but you turn down what is not holy, when you feel like giving up, but you keep going, and when all hell comes against you but you shine with the light of heaven, that's when you grow stronger in God and in all these things. So don't despise the resistance, but give thanks for it...and make the most of it. Use every measure of resistance to exercise the good. They are the weights of your training that you might become one of the mighty."

The Mission: Today, embrace the resistance. Seek out that which will challenge you, stretch you, grow you, and strengthen you in the Lord.

Romans 5:3–5; James 1:2–4

Pumping Spiritual Iron

THE MATRIX

WE WERE OUTSIDE at night and, as we often enjoyed doing, looking up at the stars.

"Your life began in darkness," he said, "in the darkness of the womb. It was once all you knew, your entire life, your entire world. If you had been asked then to describe life, you would describe it as being dark, warm, and wet. And if someone tried to tell you that there was more to life, another life, another world, outside the womb, a world of stars and grass, of flowers and faces, of sand castles and setting suns, what would you have thought?"

"I guess I wouldn't have believed it. I wouldn't have been able to fathom it."

"But would there be a way that you could have known that this other life, this world beyond the womb, actually existed? What evidence would you have had within the womb of that which was beyond the womb?"

"I don't know."

"You," said the teacher. "*You* would be the evidence...you, dwelling in darkness yet with eyes made to see color and light...with no ground to walk on, yet with feet made to run...with no air to breathe and yet with lungs made to breathe air and a voice box with which to speak into the air...with no one's hand to hold, yet with two hands made to hold and be held by the hand of another. You yourself would be the evidence of the life beyond your life in the womb and the world beyond your world. Your very being was the evidence of a world yet to come, and yet you were surrounded by a much smaller world that was unable to answer what was within you."

"And this reveals..."

"When you hear of a world beyond this world and a life beyond this life, when you hear of heaven, you're hearing of it as a child in the womb. You've never seen it or touched it. And yet everything within you was made to know this world and live within it...a heart made for a love that is perfect and without condition, a soul yearning for that which is eternal, a spirit longing to dwell in a place of no death, no fear, no tears, no darkness, and no evil. And yet you live in a world of imperfection, of corruption, of pain and evil, of darkness and the absence of love. And as it was in the womb, so too this world can never answer the longings of your heart or the purpose for which you came into existence. And every tear, every sorrow, every disappointment, every unfulfilled longing is just a reminder that you're not home, and that you were made for something more, to be a child of heaven...and that this life is only the beginning of real life and the matrix of the world to come."

The Mission: Take all the unfulfilled longings, needs, and desires of your life and turn them away from the worldly and to the heavenly.

Psalm 139:13–16; Romans 8:22

The Matrix World

THE GREEK REDEMPTION

HE LED ME into the Chamber of Scrolls. He removed a scroll from its shelf, opened it to its beginning, and gave me a few moments to look it over.

"Do you remember what I shared with you about the Abrahamic covenant?"

"Those nations or civilizations that bless the Jewish people will be blessed. And those that curse them will be cursed."

"And the law of reciprocity," said the teacher. "That which they do to Israel will be done to them. It was Greek civilization that waged an all-out war against God, the Bible, the Law of Moses, the covenant, and everything that was biblical and Jewish. They set up idols of the Greek gods in the Temple of Jerusalem and throughout the land of Israel and commanded all the Jews to worship them. Any Jewish person caught observing the Law of Moses was to be put to death. Scrolls containing the Word of God were burned. It looked as if the biblical faith would be destroyed. But against all odds, the Jewish people drove out the Greek invaders and the Temple of Jerusalem was restored."

"Chanukah," I said.

"Yes, Chanukah. But the Abrahamic covenant decrees that what you do to Israel will be done to you. In the first century AD, the message of the Jewish Messiah and salvation went forth from Israel to the nations...and especially to the Greeks. As Greek civilization had once attempted to eradicate Jewish civilization, it was now Jewish civilization that transformed Greek civilization. As Greek paganism was used to replace the biblical faith, it was now the biblical faith that would replace Greek paganism. As the Greeks had left the Temple of Jerusalem desolate, now the temples of the Greeks and their gods would be abandoned as Greek men and women turned to faith in the God of Israel. And as the Greek language was used to erase the revelation of Scripture, now the Greek language would be used to bring forth the revelation of Scripture to the world." At that, he began reading from the scroll: "'*Biblos Genesis Iesous Christos Huios Dahvid Huios Abraham.*'"

"What does it mean?" I asked.

"'The Book of the Genealogy of Jesus Christ Son of David, Son of Abraham.' The very fact that the New Covenant Scriptures are written in Greek bears witness of this truth: All that the enemy has used for evil and to destroy, God will use for good, and to preserve, and to save...in this world...in Jewish history...and in your life...everything. Therefore...do likewise."

The Mission: What part of your life has the darkness attacked? Take that very thing and use it to for the purposes, the salvation, and the glory of God.

Genesis 12:1–3; Matthew 1:1; Romans 8:28

The Chaldean Secret of World History I–III

GOD IN THE IMAGE OF MAN

O N THE DAY of His death," said the teacher, "Messiah was arrested, beaten, bound, scourged, abused, mocked, humiliated, degraded, stripped naked, nailed to a cross, put on display as a blasphemer and a criminal, cursed, judged guilty, and condemned to death. It all happened on Friday, the sixth day. It was on the sixth day that God made man in His own image. Now it was again the sixth day. And it all happened in reverse."

"What do you mean, 'in reverse'?"

"On the sixth day God made man in His image. So on the sixth day...man made God in *his* image."

"How?"

"On the sixth day, the day of man's creation, God caused man to bear the image of God, an image of glory and perfection. So on the sixth day, the day of man's redemption, man caused God to bear the image of fallen man, as one who had fallen, as one found guilty, and as one cast out. All that was the image of man's fall. So God was judged as a blasphemer because blasphemy was the sin of man. Man passed judgment on God, because man himself was under judgment. As God had made man in the image of God's glory, man now made God in the image of man's guilt and degradation. As God had made Adam in His image, it was now Adam making God in the image of Adam, as one who had transgressed, under judgment and condemned to death, cursed, and separated from God. When you look at the cross, you are beholding God in the image of man."

"Why did God allow Himself to be so abused and degraded?"

"God allowed Himself to bear the image of man, that man might again be allowed to bear the image of God. God allowed Himself to bear the image of fallen man, that man might bear the image of the risen God. So make it your aim that your life would become a reflection of His life, your nature a reflection of His nature, your works a reflection of His works, and your heart a reflection of His heart. Allow Him to make you and form you into His image. For God bore *your image* in His death, that you, in your life, could bear the image of God."

The Mission: Messiah, in His death, took upon Himself your image. Now take upon yourself His image. Live today in the image and nature of God.

Genesis 1:26–27; Matthew 27:27–37; 2 Corinthians 5:21; Galatians 3:13

The Sixth Day Revelation Mystery

DODEKHA: THE DIVINE LOVES

WE SAT ON a low stone wall encircling one of the school's vineyards.

"In the Song of Solomon," said the teacher, "the bride compares the love of her beloved to wine. Wine was a symbol of earthly pleasure. Yet when the bride speaks of her beloved, she says this: 'Your love is better than wine.'"

"And the Song of Solomon is ultimately about God and us; the bride represents us and the beloved represents God."

"That's correct," he said. "So what is it saying?"

"That the love of God is better than any earthly pleasure."

"Yes, and something more than that. Behind the translation is a revelation one can only find in the original language. The Hebrew reads this way: *Kee tovim dodekha me yayin*. It is translated as 'Your love is better than wine.' But in the original language, the bride says, 'Your *dodekha* is better than wine.'"

"And what does *dodekha* mean?"

"Not 'your love.' *Doekha* means *your loves*...'*Your loves* are better than wine.' What does that reveal?"

"The love of God is not just the love of God...but the *loves* of God."

"*Dodekha* means that God loves you so much that it can't even be described or contained without breaking out of the language. It means the word *love* cannot adequately express it. It means that God doesn't just have love for you, but many loves. When you need His mercy, He loves you with a merciful love. When you need His strength, He loves you with an encouraging love. When you've been wounded, He loves you with a tender love. When you need the love of a friend, He loves you as a friend. When you need to be lifted up in His arms, He loves you with the compassion of a loving Father. His love for you is many. He loves you today, not with yesterday's love, but with a love for today, a love that is new every morning. Therefore, you must seek not only to know the love of God, but to know the *loves* of God. You can never rest on knowing yesterday's love or the love you have known before. You must seek each day to know the *loves* He has for you, the new love, the fresh love, the surprising love, the never-ending love. It is that love, His love, that is better, much better, than any earthly joy...for His loves are better than wine."

The Mission: Seek this day to know not only the love but the *loves* of God—the always new and never-ending loves of your Beloved for you.

Psalm 63:3–6; Song of Solomon 1:2; Ephesians 3:18–19

The Dodekha Mystery

STARWOMAN

HE LED ME up a hill at night. At its summit was a tree.

"A myrtle," said the teacher. "You can find it growing on mountains and hills. It prospers in high places. Now look up from the myrtle. What do you see?"

"Stars."

"A myrtle grows under the heavens. A star exists as part of the heavens. A star is certainly much higher than a myrtle." He paused for a moment, then continued. "There once was a woman who was lifted up from obscurity and set on a high place, like a myrtle. But she feared losing her high position...Look at the stars," he said, as if forgetting the story. "They do what myrtles cannot do. They shine. And do you know how they shine? They burn, they expend themselves, as does a candle. They give up their essence...and, by that, they shine. So their shining is an act of self-sacrifice. They must sacrifice themselves to shine, to become stars."

"The story," I said, "the woman who was like a myrtle..."

"Oh yes," he replied, as if having forgotten his point, "the woman. It was not only that she was like a myrtle—that was her name. She was called *Hadassah*. *Hadassah* is Hebrew for myrtle. Hadassah, an orphan girl, was lifted up to the throne of Persia; she was a myrtle set on high places. But the day came when she had to make a choice, hold on to her high position...or risk it all, even her life, to do what is right, to save her people. She ended up choosing do what is right, saying, 'If I perish, I perish.' And it is that moment, when she offers up her life, that her life becomes one of greatness."

"Like a star," I said.

"Hadassah had another name," said the teacher. "She was called *Esther*. Do you know what *Esther* means? It means Star. She was born for that moment. But it was only then, when she was willing to sacrifice her life to do what was right, to save others, that her life became a light and she became the star she was born and named to be. Learn from her," said the teacher. "And learn from the stars. Live to keep your life, and you'll dwell in darkness. But live to give your life, and your life will become one of greatness, a light that shines in the darkness...a star above the myrtles."

The Mission: Live this day as a heavenly light. Live as a living sacrifice, a gift given for the purposes of God. And you'll shine as the stars.

Esther 2:7; 4:16; Daniel 12:3; Matthew 10:39; Philippians 2:16

The Power of Perishing

THE PIDYON HA BEN

HE LED ME into the Chamber of Vessels where he retrieved a small cloth bag. It was filled with ancient coins. He emptied them onto the wooden table and began to explain.

"In the days of the Temple, these were used in a ceremony called the *Pidyon Ha Ben*."

"What was it?"

"It means *The Redemption of the Son*. The firstfruits or firstborn of the womb were considered holy and belonging to the Lord. The firstborn lambs were offered as sacrifices. The firstborn sons of Israel were to belong to the Temple and the priesthood. They were to minister for God—unless they were redeemed back by the father paying a redemption price of silver coins to the priests of the Temple—the *Pidyon Ha Ben*. In practice, every firstborn son of Israel was redeemed back. Otherwise they would have belonged to the priests and to the Temple ministry...Two thousand years ago, as the Passover drew near, the priests of the Temple plotted Messiah's death. They would get one of His disciples to turn Him over at the set time. How? By paying him thirty pieces of silver. Where did the silver pieces come from? From the Temple treasury, the treasury that for ages had received the silver coins for the *Pidyon Ha Ben*. Now, for the first and only time in history, the priesthood was giving the money back to purchase a human life. And Messiah was a firstborn son of Israel. The priests were, in effect, returning the ransom money of the Pidyon Ha Ben. They were taking back the firstborn son...and the Firstborn Son of God."

"And so Messiah now becomes the possession of the priests."

"Yes. And what else did the Pidyon Ha Ben do? It released the firstborn son from ministry. So if the priests return the silver pieces, it means that the son now assumes his ministry...So the Son of God now assumes His priesthood. Thus He now will offer up the final sacrifice."

"And if the firstborn male is a lamb," I said, "then there's no redeeming. The lamb must be sacrificed. And Messiah is the Lamb. So the redemption money is returned and the Lamb of God is sacrificed."

"Yes," said the teacher, "for the Pidyon, for the Redemption, of all who will be redeemed."

The Mission: Messiah is your Pidyon Ha Ben, the redemption and ransom for your life. Live as one ransomed, redeemed, free, and indebted to love.

Numbers 3:44–48; Matthew 26:14–16

The Pidyon Mystery

FROM THE DAYS OF FOREVER

IT WAS DAWN. We had spent the night on top of a desert mountain. Though the sun was not yet visible, we could now see its red-orange glow in the distance.

"Do you ever wonder about God's love," asked the teacher, "if His love for you will endure...if it will outlast your sins, or if your sins will exhaust it? Have you ever wondered about His faithfulness to you, if it will always be there...if it will always keep you no matter what?"

"I guess I have," I said.

"It is written in the Psalms: 'The lovingkindness of the Lord is from everlasting to everlasting upon those who reverence Him.' The word translated as *lovingkindness* is the Hebrew word *khesed*. *Khesed* speaks not only of God's merciful, tender love, but of His *faithful* love, the love of God that doesn't let go. But what it goes on to say about that love is amazing: 'The faithful love of the Lord is from *everlasting* to *everlasting* upon those who reverence Him.' Do you realize what it's saying? His tender and faithful love for you is *from everlasting*. In other words, He doesn't only love you now. He loved you before you were."

"How?" I asked.

"He's God. Did He not know you before you existed? A year before you existed? Ten years before you existed? He has always known you. For ages before you existed, He has known you. And if He loves you now, it could not have been any different then. God has loved you, tenderly, mercifully, and faithfully...from everlasting. How long has He loved you? For an eternity! He's loved you from forever. His love for you has already lasted an eternity! It has already traveled an eternity to reach you."

"But then how could it ever have reached me?"

"You can't fathom eternity," said the teacher, "nor can you fathom His love, except to know that His love for you is greater than eternity...and to know the answer to the question...Will God's love for you ever cease or give up? The answer is no. God's love for you has already spanned the length of eternity. It has already lasted forever. For the love of God is, to you who reverence Him...from everlasting to everlasting...from forever to forever."

The Mission: Ponder the love that God has for you that has already endured for an eternity, and will not cease or fail you now. Live accordingly.

Psalm 103:17; Jeremiah 31:3; Micah 5:2

The From Forever Redemption

THE DAY OF THE MATTAN

HE TOOK ME into a room adorned with veil-like curtains that served as partitions to divide the space into several smaller chambers. On the floor were cushions and carpets covered in what appeared to be Middle Eastern designs. We sat down in one of the chambers in which was a small, metallic, and ornate chest. Opening the chest, he took out a necklace-like object of precious stones of a variety of colors, all joined together in a golden netting.

"In ancient times," said the teacher, "in the days of betrothal, when a bride and groom dwelt in their separate homes, preparing for their wedding, the groom could send to the bride a gift. It was called the *mattan*."

"And *mattan* means..."

"The gift," he said. "The mattan was a sign of the bridegroom's love for the bride. It was to encourage her in their days of separation and to assure her of his pledge, a guarantee of his faithfulness, a promise of things to come. And in the case of a mattan consisting of jewelry, like this one, it was also to beautify her and prepare her for her wedding day."

He handed me the mattan that I might examine it.

"Once a year on the biblical calendar, Israel celebrated the giving of the Law at Mount Sinai. The Law was considered a gift from God to His people. The celebration was known as the Day of the Mattan, or the Day of the Gift. What was the Day of the Mattan? It was the Feast of Shavuot."

"Pentecost!"

"Yes. Pentecost, the Day of the Mattan, the Day of the Giving of the Gift. And so it was on Shavuot, Pentecost, the Day of the Gift, that God gave the gift of the Spirit. And it wasn't just the Day of the Gift, but in Hebrew, the Day of the Mattan. What does that mean?"

"It means the Spirit is the Mattan," I said, "the gift that the Bridegroom gives to the bride."

"Yes," he said, "the Spirit is given as the sign of the Bridegroom's love for the bride, to encourage us in the days of our betrothal and separation, to assure us of His pledge, to bless us, strengthen us, and beautify us...the guarantee of His faithfulness, and the promise of things to come. The Spirit is the Mattan of the Bridegroom's love for the bride."

The Mission: Today, practice living in the power of the Mattan, moving in the Spirit, becoming more beautiful, strong, and ready for your Wedding Day.

Genesis 34:12; Luke 11:13; Acts 2:1–4; 2 Corinthians 1:22; 5:5

The Mattan Revelation

THE HOUSE OF THE DISPOSSESSED

WE WERE WATCHING the workers begin construction on one of the school's new buildings, setting in place its foundation stones.

"The Jewish people," said the teacher, "were called to build God's house and kingdom. They are the builders of houses and kingdoms. Whether with God or without Him, they were anointed as the builders. And so they have played a central role in the building of the great houses and kingdoms of man. In the modern age, most of the world's peoples have dwelt in two houses: the house of capitalism and the house of communism. The Jewish people were central in the building of each of the two houses. So too were they central in the building of the great houses and kingdoms of man, the houses of nations, economies, culture, and sciences, the house of the modern world itself. And yet over and over again, another mystery has manifested. The builders have been driven out from the very houses they built, dispossessed by others. They've been driven out of their places in the house of nations, out of their places in the house of capitalism and the house of communism, and in whatever house they've built."

"Why?" I asked.

"Thousands of years ago the Book of Deuteronomy gave a warning and a prophecy of what would happen to the children of Israel if they turned away from God and His ways: 'You shall build a house, but you shall not dwell in it.'"

"But then what house are they meant to dwell in?"

"There is one," said the teacher. "They began building it two thousand years ago. But then they removed themselves from dwelling there. And ever since leaving that house, they've never found another."

"What house?"

"The most universal and wide-spanning house in human history...the greatest house the Jewish people ever built...that which is called the church, the *kehilah*, the house that God built through them and into which people of all nations have come to dwell. When they return to that house, they will find themselves at home at last, and in a house from which they will never be dispossessed. And so it is for all of us. It is the only house in which we can dwell forever...and from which we will never be dispossessed."

The Mission: Seek, today, to dwell all the more in God's perfect will, that from which you cannot be dispossessed. And pray for the children of Israel.

Deuteronomy 28:30; Luke 13:34–35; 2 Corinthians 5:1

The Anguish of the Jews

THE MYSTERY OF KHAVAH

I T WAS THE middle of the afternoon. The teacher and I were sitting inside one of the school's gardens that possessed an especially wide variety of fruit trees.

"In Genesis, it is written that God said it was not good for man to be alone and that He would make a helper suitable for him. So He caused Adam to fall into a deep sleep. While he was sleeping, God opened up his side and removed a rib. From the rib He created woman."

"Eve," I said.

"Yes, but her real name was Khavah. She was created to be Adam's helpmate, to help him in the work of the garden and to be his companion. But Adam fell...and Messiah came to undo his fall, to bring redemption. To do so, He had to come in Adam's likeness...as a second Adam. So a question: If Messiah is the second Adam, then where's the second Eve? Where, in the redemption, is Khavah?"

"I don't know of any Khavah in the New Testament account," I said.

"God caused a deep sleep to fall on Adam. In the Scriptures, sleep is a symbol of death. So God caused the second Adam to fall into a deep sleep as well...a sleep of death. And in the death of Messiah, in the sleep of the second Adam, one is born. Who is born in the sleep of the second Adam, the death of Messiah?"

"We are," I said. "Through His death we are born again."

"And how was Khavah born?"

"Through the opening of Adam's side."

"And so too in Messiah's death, His side was opened, His heart was pierced through His ribs...And so, as with Khavah, so too the church was born through His side. And what is the church? The bride of Messiah...His Khavah. And therein lies the mystery. You were born again to be Khavah, the helpmate of God, to assist Him in accomplishing His work and purposes on the earth."

"And what does the name *Khavah* mean?"

"It comes from the Hebrew word for life. It means the life giver, the one who brings life. It was Khavah who bore Adam's children, his life, into the world. So, it is to be through the second Khavah that God's life, the love of God, the salvation of God, is now born into the world. It's the mystery of us...For we are His Khavah."

The Mission: Live today as Khavah, as the helpmate of God to accomplish His purposes on earth—and as the one who bears the life of God into the world.

Genesis 2:18–24; Ephesians 5:31–32

The Khavah Mystery of Existence

THE MOMENTUM KEY

WE WERE STANDING in the middle of a small plain when he gave me an unexpected directive.

"Jump," said the teacher. "Not up and down, but forward. Jump forward as far as you can."

So I did. It was nothing impressive, just a few feet. The teacher drew two lines, the first where I started, and the second where I landed.

"Now, go back as far as you want, run as fast as you're able, and jump as far as you can." So I did. The second jump was far more impressive than the first. "Why was your last jump so much farther than your first? One word: momentum. When an archer wants to shoot an arrow, he must first pull the arrow back on his bow. When an angry mob wants to force open a castle door with a battering ram, they must first back away from the door and then run into it. They all, in some way, move back in order to gain momentum. Without momentum the jumper won't jump, the arrow won't shoot, and the castle doors won't open. And what is true in the physical realm is also true in the spiritual. If you are going to have breakthroughs in the physical realm, you need physical momentum. And if you are going to have breakthroughs in the spiritual realm, you need spiritual momentum."

"But how do you translate a physical law into the spiritual realm?"

"In order to build physical momentum you need continuous consistent motion. If the angry mob stops on the way to the castle door, then starts up again, they lose their momentum, and the door won't open. In the same way, if you're not consistent in your walk with God, if you waver back and forth, if you stop and start and stop and start again, if you have no continuous motion, you'll lose spiritual momentum, and you'll never accomplish what you were called to do or see the blessings and breakthroughs you were meant to see. So make it your aim now to become all the more consistent, continuous, and unwavering in your walk, in your righteousness, in your purity, in your prayers, in your worship, in your joy, in your love, and in your holiness. This will give you spiritual momentum. Then go with that momentum, and increase it. Allow it to bring you to higher ground. And the doors will open, the walls will come down, and you will live the life of victory, power, and breakthrough you were always called to live."

The Mission: Today, apply the momentum key. Avoid wavering. Avoid stopping. Move in consistent godly motion—and to the breakthrough.

1 Corinthians 9:24–27; Philippians 3:13–14; Hebrews 12:1–2

The Momentum Secret

JACOB'S PARADOX

JACOB'S PARADOX," SAID the teacher. "Jacob was blessed for doing everything he could to receive the blessing. And yet because of the way he went about receiving the blessing, the blessing could never be received...until later. When his father, Isaac, was about to give his blessing to whom he thought was his first-born son Esau, he said, 'Who are you...?' Jacob replied, 'I am Esau.' So Jacob didn't say who he *was,* Jacob, but who he *wasn't,* Esau. And by doing so, he supplanted his brother, and thus became 'the one who supplants.'"

"Why is that a paradox?"

"Because the name Jacob, or Yakov, means the one who supplants. So by *not* being Jacob, the supplanter, he *became* the supplanter, Jacob. By not confessing his name, he became the very thing his name confessed he was: the supplanter. Now if he received the blessing intended for someone else, how could the blessing ever truly be received? He would spend the next part of his life struggling, striving, and running away...until finally coming face-to-face with the truth...on the night he wrestled with God and begged God to give him the blessing."

"In the same way he sought his father's blessing years before."

"Yes. And it was then that God asked him, 'What is your name?'"

"Just as his father, before blessing him, had asked him the same thing."

"But this time was different. This time he answered, 'I am Jacob.'"

"Which is to say, 'I am the supplanter.'...But now he wasn't the supplanter."

"The second paradox," said the teacher, "the reverse paradox. By coming as who he was, Jacob, the supplanter, he ceased to be the supplanter, Jacob. And it's only then that God said, 'Your name shall no longer be called Jacob but Israel...' Only when Jacob comes as Jacob can he cease to be Jacob and become Israel...and the blessing be complete. You see, you can never be blessed by coming as what you are not, but only as what you are, even when what you are is not what you were meant to be. God cannot bless a false saint. But He *can* bless a real sinner. So if you would receive your blessing, you must come to Him as you are, with all your sins and failings, with no pretense or covering. Then you'll be free...and no longer bound to who you were. And your blessing will be given, and your name...and your name shall no longer be called Jacob."

The Mission: Today, come to God as you are, with no covering or pretense, confess what you must confess. Then receive your blessing.

Genesis 27:18–19; 32:27–28; Psalm 32:1–6; Hebrews 4:16; James 4:8

THE BRIT HADDASHAH

WE WERE STANDING in the middle of one of the gardens. The teacher walked up to one of the trees and picked a fruit from one of its branches. It was round, red, and had something of a crown on its top. I knew I had seen it before, but I couldn't identify it.

"It's a pomegranate," he said, placing it in my hands, "fresh off the tree.

"Do you know where the new covenant comes from? From the Hebrew Scriptures, from the Book of Jeremiah, when God says to Israel: 'Behold, the days are coming...when I will make a new covenant with the house of Israel and with the house of Judah...' So why is the new covenant called the '*new* covenant'?"

"Because it came after the old covenant. So it's the newer covenant."

"But that was a long time ago," he said. "If it's only the new covenant because of when it came, then by now, thousands of years later, it would no longer be new. So it has to be more than that. The answer is in your hands."

"It's because of a pomegranate?"

"The original Hebrew doesn't say 'new covenant.' It says 'brit haddashah.' And the word *haddashah* doesn't speak of a position in time, but a state of being. *Haddashah* means new and fresh, as the fruit in your hand is fresh.

"It could be translated as 'the covenant of newness' or 'the covenant of freshness.' The new covenant is new not primarily because of *when it came*, but because of *what it is*. Its nature is to be new...to be fresh."

"So then the new covenant is just as new now as it was when it first began thousands of years ago."

"Exactly" he said. "No matter how long you've been in the new covenant, it never grows old. It stays just as new as the day you first entered it."

"But what if, for a believer, it's no longer something new?"

"If it's no longer new, then it's not the new covenant. The only way to know the new covenant is to know it newly, freshly, every day of your life. It must always be to you new. And if it is, then it will always renew your life, and you'll always walk in the newness of life, always young, always in the freshness of His presence. For the new covenant is the covenant of newness...the always fresh covenant...the covenant of haddashah."

The Mission: Come back to the haddashah. Receive anew the love, the grace, the truth, and the salvation that is always new—and be made new.

Jeremiah 31:31–32; Ephesians 4:24; Revelation 21:5

The Brit Haddashah

HEAVEN'S COOKING POTS

THE TEACHER TOOK me into the kitchen where all the meals served in the school were prepared. I thought it was only a stop on the way to the site of the teaching.

"Today, this is our classroom," he said. "It wouldn't appear likely. One wouldn't expect anything profound to come out of a school kitchen."

At that, he walked over to one of the cabinets, took out a cooking pot, and placed it on the table. "Just a cooking pot," he said. "But look." He turned it around so I could see its other side. On its outer surface were letters engraved in the metal. "It's Hebrew," said the teacher.

"What does it say?"

"*Kadosh L'YHVH*. It means Holy to the Lord, the same words that were inscribed on the golden crown of the high priest."

"Couldn't that be considered sacrilegious?"

"At the end of the Hebrew Scriptures," he said, "is a vision of what life will be like in the days when the kingdom of God is on earth. It is written: 'In that day "Holy to the Lord" shall be engraved on the bells of the horses....Every pot in Jerusalem and Judah shall be holy to the Lord of Hosts.' Do you realize how radical this is? The holy vessels could only be found inside the Temple. Outside the Temple was the mundane or unholy. But in the kingdom of God the sacred words of the high priest's crown will be written on the bells of horses. The sacred glory of the Temple will be in every kitchen and on every cooking pot. Everything will be filled with God's holiness and overflowing with His glory. And therein is the secret of living a heavenly life."

"Which is what?"

"Make every part of your life holy to the Lord...your work, your daily job, perform it as ministry...your house, dwell in it as if you were in the Temple. When you take out the garbage, do it as if you were a priest performing the sacred ministry in the holy place. And when you lie down to sleep, lie down as if you were in heaven's throne room, surrounded by the presence of God...and you will be. Bring every part of your life into the presence, the holiness, and the glory of God—and let the presence, the holiness, and the glory of God come into every part of your life. And you will live even now in the glory of the kingdom. And even your cooking pots will become holy to the Lord."

The Mission: Live this day as if you were in the kingdom. Let every act be a holy act, sacred in the presence and glory of God.

Zechariah 14:20–21; Colossians 3:23–24

Holy Bells

TAMIM: THE UNBLEMISHED

OOK," SAID THE teacher. It was a lamb grazing under its shepherd's care, a lamb of pure white, of radiant white, all the more radiant as it stood bathed in a shaft of bright sunlight...radiant white. "It could have been the Passover lamb," he said.

"Why do you say that?" I asked. "Any lamb could have been."

"No, only a certain kind of lamb."

"Which kind?"

"A *tamim* lamb. The ordinance states it must be tamim."

"And what does *tamim* mean?"

"It means without spot, unblemished, undefiled, whole, innocent, and perfect. The Passover lamb had to be tamim in order to set the Hebrews free from their bondage. And Messiah is the Passover Lamb. And if He's the Passover Lamb, then He must also be the tamim Lamb. Therefore, what must He be?"

"He must be perfect," I said.

"And without spot, blemish, or defilement, innocent and whole. The Passover Lamb had to be tamim, without spot or blemish because we've all been blemished and stained. It had to be unblemished so that the blemishes of our past could be removed. He had to be spotless that the stains of our past could be undone. And He had to be innocent and undefiled to take away all the defilements from our lives. And so it is from the Passover Lamb, Messiah, that we are given the power of tamim, the miracle of tamim, by which the guilty can become again innocent, that the defiled can live an unblemished life, with an unblemished record, and an unblemished conscience...and with unstained memories."

"And each had to apply the blood of the Passover Lamb to one's life."

"Yes. So you must likewise apply the power of tamim, to every shame and defilement of your past, your memory, your conscience, and your life...that as He is spotless, undefiled, untouched, innocent, and whole, you now have the power to become likewise...tamim."

The Mission: Today, apply the power of tamim to every defilement in your life, past or present. Be complete, spotless, and tamim—just as He is tamim.

Exodus 12:5; 1 Corinthians 5:7; Ephesians 5:27

Tamim

THE BRIDE AND GROOM PROCESSION

COME," SAID THE teacher. "It's time for the wedding to begin!"

We journeyed to one of the tent villages, which we reached just after sunset.

"We've been to this one before," I said, "several times."

"Yes," he said. "This is the camp of the bridegroom."

"It was from here that we went with him on the journey to the bride."

"That was for the betrothal," he said. "They haven't seen each other since then. They've been preparing for this day ever since. And now the day has come. Come."

He led me to the other side of the camp where everyone was gathered together around the bridegroom. He was adorned with a festive robe, with a garland around his head. And then the procession began, the groom and his men leading, the rest of the camp following behind, many with torches in their hands. We journeyed for some time before arriving at the camp of the bride where she was waiting, adorned with robes and precious stones, her maidens at her side, and the rest of the camp gathered around them. The bridegroom's men lifted the bride and the groom on a sedan chair and carried them away in a great and festive procession, with singing, shouting, and dancing. We followed along.

"The bridegroom's bringing the bride home," he said. "He came first to make the covenant, but he comes the second time to take her home, to the place he prepared for her. So too it is with the other Bridegroom."

"God."

"Yes," said the teacher, "the Bridegroom of bridegrooms. He came first to make the covenant. But He comes the second time to take us home. The next time we see Him, whether on that day, or on the day we finish this life, it will be to take us home . . . to the place He's prepared for us . . . of no more tears, no more pain, no more sorrow."

It was a few minutes along the procession before he spoke again.

"Look back," he said. "The bride's home . . . it's fading away. Soon she won't be able to see it any more . . . So too will it be with the old creation, and all its sorrows. But then the bride will see . . . and then we all will see . . . the Bridegroom's house . . . the place of our hearts' longings."

"Heaven?"

"Home."

The Mission: This world is only the first house. It is destined to fade away with all its issues and concerns. Live this day in light of that reality.

Jeremiah 33:11; Matthew 25:6; John 14:2–3; Revelation 19:6–9; 21:1–2

The Blessing of the Bridegroom

THE WAY TO THE MOUNTAINTOP

IT WAS ALMOST sundown. We were standing at the bottom of a high mountain. But the ascent was very gradual as the mountain was spread out over a vast area and connected to other mountains, part of a chain. At its base were the beginnings of several mountain paths, each diverging from the others.

"At the top of this mountain," said the teacher, "is a flat, white, circular stone. Find it. When you get there, you'll be standing on the summit. Find that stone, and then return to me."

"But which of the paths do I take?" I asked.

"That's the challenge," he said. "I'll be waiting here until you return."

So I chose one of the many paths and began following it. It wasn't long before the sky grew dark, and it became apparent that I was on the wrong path. I chose another, and another, until finally I realized I was heading downward. At that point I began shouting in the dark for the teacher. He shouted back. Following his voice, I made my way back to him at the base.

"So," said the teacher, "I imagine you didn't get there."

"How could I have?" I replied. "I didn't know which path to take."

"You didn't have to know," he said. "You didn't have to know anything...except one thing. You were too focused on which path to take, but that wasn't the key. Remember when I shared with you about the Hebrew word *aliyah*? Had you applied that here, you would have succeeded. The key was the direction...up. The white stone was at the pinnacle. All you had to was to choose the higher path, continuously. And if the path stopped ascending, then you choose the higher ground. And it would make no difference where you started from or on which side of the mountain. If you just followed this simple law, it would have led to the exact place at the pinnacle. Don't forget this. It's one of the most important secrets in your walk with God. The pinnacle of the mountain represents God's calling on your life, His specific will and exact purpose and plan for your life. How do you get there? You don't have to know where it is. All you have to do is continually ascend, continually choose the higher path, the higher ground, the higher footstep. And no matter where you started from and no matter where you are now, you will end up in the exact, specific, appointed, and perfect will of God, at the summit, the pinnacle of God's purposes for your life."

The Mission: Today, focus only on one course, one path, one journey, one destination, and one direction—up. Aim to go higher with every step.

Psalms 24:3–6; 122; Proverbs 3:6; Philippians 3:14

Secrets of the Mountaintop Walker

SUNERGOS

I'M SURE THE teacher had a different sharing planned for that day, but I was the one who initiated the lesson.

"I have a question," I said. "How does one live up to the standards of God? How does one attain such high standards?"

"One doesn't," he said.

"What do you mean?"

"One doesn't do it . . . as you think. How could you?"

"I don't understand."

"Who can live up to the standards of God?"

"The godly?"

"No," said the teacher. "The only one who can live up to the standards of God . . . is God. And the only one who can live the life of Messiah is the Messiah. So how you do you live up to His standards? How do you live the godly life?"

I didn't answer.

"There's only one way—you let Him live it. You let God meet the standards of God. You let Messiah live the life of Messiah through you."

"So it's Him and not me."

"It's Him *through* you. It's Him living His life . . . through your living your life in Him. In the Book of First Corinthians it is written, 'We are God's fellow workers.' But in the original language the words *fellow workers* are just one word—*sunergos*."

"And what does it mean?"

"*Ergos*," said the teacher, "means to act, to work, or to do. And *sun* means with or together. So *sunergos* means to act together, to work with, to move together, or to do as one. That's the key. It's impossible for you to live the life of God. But it's impossible for God *not* to live the life of God. So the key is not to live up to the standards of God, but to let God live *out* His life through you. It means to let God live in your living . . . as, in His living, you live. It means to let God love in your loving . . . as, in His loving, you love. It is from *sunergos* that we get the word *synergy*. That's the energy of salvation, the energy of God, and the energy of you flowing together as one . . . one energy, one motion, one life. As it is written, 'Be strong . . . in the power of His might' . . . sunergos."

The Mission: Today, discover and practice the sunergos, the synergy of God. Move in His moving, act in His acting, and live in His living—as one.

1 Corinthians 3:9; Ephesians 6:10; 1 John 4:9

The Two Shall Be One

THE SOLDIERS OF DARKNESS AND LIGHT

H E LED ME across a large valley and toward a mountain on its other side.

"Imagine," said the teacher, "you had to make your way across this valley, to get to that mountain as fast as you could. But the valley is filled with soldiers, half of them dressed in white and half in black. As you try to make your way across the valley, you discover the soldiers in white are there to help you across and to get you to the mountain as quickly as possible. But you soon discover that the soldiers in black are there for the opposite purpose. They battle the soldiers in white, resisting every step of advance. Finally, after a long an arduous battle, you make it across to the base of the mountain on the other side. The battle is over. It is then that you notice a strange thing—the soldiers in black begin removing their outer garments to reveal garments of white underneath. The soldiers in black were really soldiers in white. The soldiers were all of the same side. And the ultimate goal wasn't to bring you to the other side as fast as possible but to get you there at the exact right time. And for that to happen, both the soldiers in white and the soldiers in black had to fulfill their mission. And though it looked like war, both sides were actually working together for your good. So then which side was against you?"

"Neither," I said. "Both were battling for my benefit."

"Exactly," he said. "And so it is written in the Book of Romans that 'God causes all things to work together for good to those who love God, to those who are called according to His purpose.' So if you love God and belong to Him, He will work all things in your life together for good and the evil, the beautiful and the ugly, the joyous and the sorrowful, the problems and the triumphs, all for your blessing and good. Now if both the good and the bad are working for your good, then in the end, was there any bad?"

"No, if even the bad is working for my good, then it's ultimately good."

"And so for the child of God, for you, there are only two realities…blessings…and blessings in disguise. Sometimes the blessings are very well disguised, but they remain blessings nevertheless. Hold on to this. And learn to see and believe through the disguises. And remember, it only looks like a battlefield. But in the end, you will see it as it always was, a field of blessings where even your darkest enemies—your greatest adversities—were, in the end, your blessings in disguise."

The Mission: Give thanks today for all your blessings, and for all your blessings in disguise—those of the past and the still-disguised blessings of the present.

Jeremiah 29:11; Romans 8:28

All Things

THE ROSH PINAH

THE TEACHER LED me over a great distance to the ruins of an ancient building. He pointed to one of the stones in its foundation.

"The cornerstone," he said. "The stone that begins the building. Do you remember when we spoke of it?"

"Psalm 118," I said, "the song of Passover. 'The stone which the builders rejected has become the chief cornerstone.' Messiah the Cornerstone."

"Yes," said the teacher. "But the Hebrew word for *cornerstone* is *rosh pinah*. And *rosh pinah* not only means the cornerstone—but the capstone."

He pointed to a stone that rested above the building's entranceway, on its pinnacle. "The capstone," he said, "the final stone, the stone that completes the building, the stone to which every other stone leads and converges. So Messiah is not only the Cornerstone but also the Capstone."

"How so?"

"The rosh pinah prophecy is read on Passover. And it was then, on Passover, in His death, that Messiah became the Capstone...the stone that brings completion. It was on the cross that Messiah became the Capstone on a fallen world, the Capstone of the curse, the Capstone of the Law, the Capstone of the old covenant, and the Capstone of every sin. And as every stone leads and points to the Capstone, so everything led up to Messiah and to that moment, all the prophecies, all the shadows, all the guilt, and every longing for redemption. And as every stone converges upon the capstone, so upon Messiah everything converged, the burden of the world, the weight of all sin, the brunt of all evil, and the judgment of God. The capstone is the stone by which the work is finished. So it was then, at the moment of His death, that He said, 'It is finished.' And for every life that comes to Him, He becomes the Capstone...the end of one's sins, the finishing of one's past, and the completion of everything that was lacking."

"But how is He both the Cornerstone and the Capstone?"

"Only after the old is ended, can there be a new beginning. After the Capstone event, His death, comes the Cornerstone event, the resurrection. So let all that must be ended find its ending in that Capstone...and you will find on its other side the Cornerstone of new beginnings."

The Mission: Whatever is incomplete in your life and must be completed, and whatever must be ended, finish it, cap it, with the power of the Capstone.

Psalm 118:22–23; John 19:28–30

The Rosh Pinah

KHATAAH: THE NAME ON YOUR SIN

D O YOU REMEMBER," asked the teacher, "when I told you about the Asham?"
"The sacrifice that took away guilt...but which also *was* the guilt?"

"Yes," he said. "But there was another sacrifice of a parallel nature and containing a parallel mystery. It was called the sin offering, the sacrifice that took away sin. On the Day of Atonement, it was this sacrifice that took away the sins of the entire nation."

"And Messiah," I said, "is the sacrifice that 'takes away the sin of the world.' So the sin offering is a shadow of Him."

"Yes. But the Scriptures concerning the sin offering are written in Hebrew. And in Hebrew the sin offering is called the *Khataah*. So Messiah is the Khataah. But the word has a double meaning. On one hand it means the sin offering. But on the other hand, it means the sin."

"The same as in the mystery of the Asham...the sacrifice becomes the very thing it takes away. So in order for Messiah to take away sin, He had to *become* sin itself."

"Yes," said the teacher, "and the mystery of the Khataah also appears in the New Testament, 'He made Him who knew no sin to become sin for us ...' And yet there's more to it. Both the sacrifice and the sin bear the same name, the Khataah. What that means is not only does the sacrifice bear the name of the sin—the sin bears the name of the sacrifice that takes away the sin. Every sin bears the name of the sin offering. And Messiah is the sin offering, the Khataah. So what does that mean?"

"If every sin bears the name of the sacrifice...then every sin bears His Name."

"Yes," he said. "In the sacred tongue, every one of your sins bears the name of the sacrifice. On every one of your sins is written His Name. And what does *that* mean?"

"I don't know."

"It means that all of your sins belong to Him. It means they don't belong to you anymore. And to keep what doesn't belong to you is to be in possession of stolen property. It constitutes an act of theft. So give to Him that which belongs to Him, and that which already has His Name on it. Give Him your sins, every one of them. Let them go. They don't belong to you. And thus to keep your sins is a sin."

"Yes," I replied, "And even that sin would have His Name on it."

The Mission: Take every sin, guilt, shame, failure, regret, and mistake in your life, and put His name on each one. Then give to Him that which is His.

Matthew 1:21; 2 Corinthians 5:21

The Sacrifice Mysteries I–V

SECRET OF THE GROGGER

HE TOOK ME into what appeared to be some sort of storage room where he removed a strange-looking object from a cabinet drawer. It appeared to be an ornate wooden box, but too thin to hold anything, and with a wooden handle sticking out of its underside. Holding it by its handle, he whirled the box around and around, causing it to make a loud grinding noise.

"In Hebrew," he said, "this is called a *rashan*, which means noise maker. But it's more commonly known as a *grogger*. It has a very unique and specific purpose. During the Feast of Purim, when the name of Haman, the man who tried to exterminate the Jewish people in ancient Persia, is read, the grogger is turned like this." Again he whirled the wooden box around its handle, to make again the loud grinding noise. "By using the grogger, they would drown out the name of Haman. And in this strange-looking instrument of noise is a profound principle that you must learn and apply to your life. Haman is a symbol of evil. So how do you overcome evil?"

"By fighting it?"

"How?" asked the teacher. "Someone hurts you and you hurt them back. Someone hates you and you hate them back. You become bitter over what they did. Is that how you overcome evil? No. That's how you echo evil and perpetuate it. All you're doing is repeating the name of Haman. But the grogger holds the secret."

"So when someone sins against you, you use the grogger?" I asked flippantly.

"In a sense, yes," he said. "The secret of the grogger is that it deals with the sound of evil by producing its own sound, a different sound, and by doing so, it drowns out the sound of evil. So how do you overcome evil in your life? By producing a different sound, that which is not a reaction to evil, that which has an entirely other origin, an entirely different essence, and an entirely opposite spirit. You overcome evil by bringing forth its opposite. You bring forth the good. You overcome hatred by bringing forth love. You overcome despair by bringing forth hope. And you overcome that which is negative by bringing forth the positive. You overcome the sound of darkness by the sound of light, and by so doing you drown it out. Learn the secret of the grogger...and drown out your Haman."

The Mission: What problem, evil, or wrong are you dealing with? Don't dwell on it. Don't react. Dwell on its opposite. Overcome the dark with the light.

Joshua 6:5; Psalm 95:1–2; Matthew 5:44; Romans 12:21

The Grogger

THE VALLEY OF HINNOM

SOMETHING THAT'S BEEN troubling me," I said. "Hell. If God is love . . ."

"Why would there be a hell," said the teacher. "Come." He led me into the Chamber of Scrolls, removed one of the scrolls from its shelf, unrolled it, and began to read.

"'Thus says the Lord, "Go out to the Valley of the Sons of Hinnom . . . proclaim there the words I will tell you . . . Behold, I will bring . . . a catastrophe on this place . . ."' Look at these words here," he said, pointing to the text on the scroll. "God told Jeremiah to go to the Valley of Hinnom. Why? Why was that important? The answer is it was in the Valley of Hinnom that those of Israel who had turned away from God would sacrifice their children in fire to the foreign gods of Baal and Molech. So the Valley of Hinnom was a place of evil, of bloodshed and fire. When Messiah spoke of hell, He would often refer to it as Gehenna. Do you know why? The *Geh* of *Gehenna* means valley. And the *henna* means Hinnom. So *Gehenna* means the *Valley of Hinnom*. The Valley of Hinnom was an earthly revelation of hell. And what does it reveal? Did the Valley of Hinnom represent the heart of God or the heart of man?"

"The heart of man," I said, "the heart of evil men."

"Yes," said the teacher. "And so Gehenna, hell, represents not the heart or will of God, but the heart and will of those who reject the heart and will of God, the heart and will of heaven. God must judge evil. It is His necessity. But His heart is salvation, to save all who would come to be saved. You have a problem with hell. God has an even bigger problem with it. He hates it much more than you do. In fact, He hates it so much so He would even give His own life to save you from it. And what was it that He said through Jeremiah concerning the Valley of Hinnom?"

"That He would destroy it," I said. "So would God destroy hell if He could?"

"He would destroy the *power* of hell . . . and He did. He destroyed its power by giving His life in our place to bear our judgment . . . to bear our hell."

"The power of hell is destroyed?"

"For everyone who receives it . . . the power of hell is destroyed by the power of His love. For the love of God is greater than hell and deeper than the Valley of Hinnom."

The Mission: Take part in undoing the power of hell. Share the love of God and His salvation with someone who needs to be saved.

Jeremiah 19:1–3; John 3:16; 2 Peter 3:9

The Harvest of Heaven and Hell

BLUEPRINTS OF THE SPIRIT

THE TEACHER TOOK me into the Chamber of Vessels and to its only bookcase. Inside its shelves were large bound volumes of plans, instructions, and diagrams. He removed one of them from the top shelf, laid it on the wooden table, and opened it up.

"It looks like a mechanical drawing," I said.

"It *is* a blueprint of sorts," he said. "These are the plans based on the instructions given by God for the building of the Tabernacle. Note the precision. Everything had to be made exactly according to the pattern, to the exact measurements and specifications. And it all came about through a man named Bezalel. God had filled him with His Spirit. And through Bezalel, the Spirit of God built the Tabernacle. What does that reveal?"

"The Spirit," I said, "fulfills the plans of God."

"Exactly. And the building of the Tabernacle was part of the Law of Moses. And the day that marks the giving of the Law is the Feast of Shavuot. And on that same day, the Feast of Shavuot, also known as Pentecost, the Spirit of God was given to the first followers of Messiah...the same Spirit that translated all these plans and blueprints and measurements into reality...That same Spirit was given to His people...given to you...Why? To do the same work, to translate the purposes of God into reality. As it is written, 'I will put My Spirit within you and cause you to walk in My statutes...' Behind the word *statutes* is a Hebrew word that speaks of appointed times and measures. You see, God's purposes, God's will and plans for your life, are just as detailed, specific, and precise as the plans and measurements of the Tabernacle. His plans are perfect and not only for your life but for every day of your life, for every moment. That's why He gives you the Spirit. The Spirit gives you the power to fulfill God's plan, to move in His perfect will, and to walk in the exact footsteps, down to the exact measurements and specifications of His appointed purposes for your life. Make it your aim to find and fulfill the perfect and precise plan God has for your life. Live by the Spirit, move in His leading, and you will walk into your appointed footsteps...footsteps as real and as exact as the diagrams in this book. They're already there...in the blueprints of the Spirit."

The Mission: Seek to live this day in the heavenly pattern. Walk, speak, and move by the impulse and leading of the Spirit into the divine blueprint.

Exodus 25:40; 31:2–5; Ezekiel 36:27; Ephesians 2:10; Hebrews 13:21

THE MISHKAN

WE WERE LOOKING into the distance at a solitary brown tent. It sat in the middle of an open expanse in the foreground of a range of desert mountains. I thought he would say something about the tent, but instead he spoke of prayer.

"How would you define *prayer*?"

"*Prayer* is to talk to God," I said, "to bring to Him your needs and requests."

"That's a part of prayer," he said. "But it's more than that. The Tabernacle was Israel's central place of prayer. But it was never called the Tabernacle."

"What then was it called?"

"The *mishkan*."

"What's a mishkan?"

"It comes from the Hebrew root word *shakan*. *Shakan* means to dwell. So *mishkan* means the dwelling. The mishkan was the tent or tabernacle that would allow God *to dwell* in the midst of His people. It was also the central place of prayer. So prayer is linked to..."

"The dwelling of God."

"But the mishkan wasn't only the dwelling place of God. It was also called *the Tent of Meeting*. It's where God and man met together. You see, prayer is not just an action; it's a meeting, an encounter. The mishkan was not only where God dwelt, but man. Prayer is not primarily about saying words or performing an act. Prayer is a mishkan. Prayer is about dwelling. It's the dwelling of God and man together. So the deepest part of prayer is that of dwelling in the dwelling of God...being present in the presence of God. And to dwell is more than just saying the words of a prayer or singing the words of a song and then being finished with it. Prayer is to dwell in the presence of God. And the word *mishkan* also means *the remaining, the continuing, the abiding,* and *the inhabiting*. What then is the heart of prayer? It is to abide in His abiding."

"And to rest in His resting."

"To remain in His remaining."

"To dwell in His dwelling."

"And to inhabit His habitation. To know what prayer truly is, you must go deeper...you must enter the mishkan."

The Mission: Today, seek to practice the secret of shakan, to dwell in His dwelling, to remain in His remaining, and to abide in His inhabitation.

Exodus 33:9–10; Psalms 16:11; 61:4

Into the Tent of Glory

THE PASSOVER DIP

WE WERE IN one of the chambers in the building where meals were served for the students. He had me sit down by a wooden table on which was a small bowl. Inside the bowl was some sort of mixture I had never seen before.

"This," said the teacher, "is called *kharoset*. It's one of the foods unique to the Passover Seder. On the night of Passover, the Jewish people eat the kharoset with bitter herbs as they commemorate their deliverance from Egypt."

He paused to take out a piece of matzah, the unleavened bread, then continued.

"On the night before He died, Messiah partook in the Last Supper. The Last Supper was a Passover Seder. In the middle of the meal He began to speak of His death. 'One of you will betray Me,' He said. Then He gave them a sign. 'He who dips his hand with Me into the dish will betray Me.' It was then that the disciple named Yehudah or Judas dipped his hand in the dish. Why do you think that Messiah gave that particular act as the sign of His betrayal to death?"

"I don't know."

"On Passover, the Jewish people dip a piece of matzah into the kharoset. Undoubtedly it was into a cup such as this that Messiah and Judas dipped their bread that night."

"Why is that significant?"

"The kharoset and bitter herbs represent bondage and suffering. And what was the betrayal? It was the delivering of Messiah over to bondage and suffering. So the sign revealed that it would be Judas who would deliver Him to His suffering. And yet Messiah also dipped into the cup. So the sign also revealed that it would be Messiah who freely gave Himself over to suffering and death. And why dipping? The word in Greek is linked to the word *baptism*, which means to submerge or to overwhelm. So Messiah's life would be submerged in suffering, in *our* suffering, submerged in the cup of *our* judgment. And in the process, He would be overwhelmed. So He submerged Himself in the cup of our judgment, in the cup of suffering and bitterness, so that our judgment, our tears, and our hell would be taken away."

The teacher then dipped the matzah into the cup.

"He bore our hell," said the teacher, "so that we would never have to."

The Mission: Ponder the love that takes all your sorrows, sufferings, and judgment upon Himself. Live, accordingly, a life worthy of that love.

Exodus 12:8; Matthew 26:20–25; Isaiah 53:4

THE PROPHECY BOY

I SAT IN FRONT of the teacher's desk as he thumbed through an old book. I could tell by the pictures that it was a book of history. He stared, for a time, at an old photograph of what appeared to be a military man.

"Which is more powerful," he said, "an empire or the prayers of a little boy?"

I didn't know how to answer.

"There was once a little English boy who ended his prayers every night with the words, 'Lord, we would not forget Your ancient people, Israel. Hasten the day when Israel shall again be Your people and shall be restored to Your favor and to their land.' At the time of his prayers, the Jewish people had been living in exile from their homeland for nearly eighteen centuries. The land of Israel was in the hands of the Ottoman Turkish Empire, an Islamic power that had occupied it for nearly four centuries and had no intention of giving it back to its original owners. But the Scriptures contained a clear promise and prophecy that God would one day bring His ancient people back to their homeland. So that's what the little boy prayed for."

"And what happened?"

"The First World War happened, and the Ottoman Empire began to collapse. The British army under General Edmund Allenby gained the land of Israel and the Holy City of Jerusalem. The British Empire decreed that the land should again become a homeland for the Jewish people."

"The little boy's prayer was answered," I said. "And what became of the boy?"

"He grew up and ended up in the British army. He was ultimately elevated to the rank of general—General Edmund Allenby, the man who defeated the Ottoman Empire and won the land of Israel. God fulfilled the little boy's prayer and His ancient promise through the little boy himself. What does that reveal?"

"Sometimes God will answer your prayer by using you to answer it."

"Yes," said the teacher. "And as to the question of the prayers of little boys and empires..."

"In God's hand, the prayers of little boys are stronger than empires."

"And the power of prayer," said the teacher, "is greater than kingdoms. It not only changes lives, but history itself. The story of man is filled with such accounts...nations turning on a single prayer. And the one who prays in the will of God can end up the chosen vessel of long-waiting ancient prophecies...and the changer of world history."

The Mission: What do you need to lift up to God? Lift it up—even if it's impossible. Lift up even the course of nations and history.

Daniel 9:1–25; James 5:16; 1 John 5:14

The Resurrection of Zion

THE DIVINE LAW OF ADJECTIVES

THE TEACHER HELD up a pomegranate.

"In English," he said, "and in many other languages, you would call this a 'red fruit.' The adjective comes first, and then the noun. But in other languages it would be described as a 'fruit, red.' The noun comes first, and then the adjective. In Hebrew, the language used for most of Scripture, and in the tongue of Messiah, it's not a 'red fruit,' only a 'fruit, red.'"

"I'm not getting it."

"In the sacred tongue there's no such thing as an evil man...only a 'man, evil.' Rather there exists a man. The man is a creation of God. Evil is the state he's in. So too in the sacred tongue, there's no such thing as a sinful woman. Rather there exists a woman, a creation of God, who happens to be sinful. Messiah spoke in this way and knew God's Word this way, with the noun first and the adjective second, and thus with no evil men and no sinful women. He saw men, in Hebrew, in the image of God, and who were now in a fallen state. He saw the adulterous woman not as an adulterous woman but as a woman caught in the state of adultery. And thus she could be saved out of it. He saw the possessed man as a man who happened to be possessed and thus who could be set free. He saw the sick not as sick people but as people who happened to be sick or oppressed and so who could be healed. He saw through the evil, through imperfection, and through the fall, to the perfect that God created and to the perfect to be redeemed. He died to separate adjectives from nouns, people from their evil, their sinfulness, and their fallenness."

"By joining their adjectives, their sins, to another noun, Himself."

"Yes. And to join His adjective, His holiness, to us. Learn the secret of the sacred tongue. When you see the sinful, the fallen, the crippled, the defiled, the broken, the hateful, the perverse, the ravaged, don't see first the adjective. See first the noun, the one whom God made in His image, the one God made them to be, and the one God redeemed them to become. And that includes you. When you look at yourself, your sinfulness, your fallenness, don't see the adjective first, but the noun. Bring the adjectives to the cross. And see yourself first as the one God made you to be and live your life as the person He redeemed you to become."

"That we," I said, "might become a people...holy."

The Mission: Today, apply the divine law of adjectives to others and to yourself, see first the noun God created, then give to Him the adjective.

Luke 13:11–16; Acts 9:11–15; 1 Corinthians 6:11

The Hebrew Mysteries I–IV

THE REBEGOTTEN

A QUESTION," SAID THE teacher. "Who was the first person to be born again?"
"The disciples?" I said.

"No," said the teacher.

"Then who?"

"Messiah."

"That doesn't sound right," I replied.

"But it is," said the teacher. "Who was He before the incarnation?"

"The Son of God."

"And how could He be the Son of God if He wasn't born? What did God give to the world? His only begotten Son. *Begotten* means born. So when He was born in Bethlehem, was that His first birth?"

"I guess it wasn't," I said. "It was His second."

"It was His second birth. He was already begotten, born, before Bethlehem. The incarnation was His second birth. The nativity was His new birth. In Bethlehem He was born again."

"So then the new birth is connected to incarnation?"

"He who was born of spirit was born again of the flesh so that we who were born of the flesh could be born again of the Spirit. He who was born of heaven was born again of earth so that we who were born of earth could be born again of heaven. And He who was born of God was born again of man so that we who were born of man could be born again of God."

"He was born again," I said, "to partake of our life, that we could be born again to partake of His life."

"Yes," said the teacher. "He who was *rebegotten* in Bethlehem had to learn how to live in His new birth, His new life, and His new nature, that of flesh and blood. He had to learn how to walk on the earth, how to see with physical eyes, and how to touch with physical hands. For the rebegotten are born into a life they had not previously known, and in which they must now learn to live. So you who are rebegotten of God must now learn how to live in your new birth, in your new life, and your new nature, that of the Spirit. Learn how to see in the Spirit, live in the Spirit, and walk in heavenly places. That is the journey and the mystery of the rebegotten."

The Mission: As God took on your nature and life, so today, take on His nature, live His life, and walk in the footsteps of the heavenly.

1 Corinthians 15:48–49; Colossians 3:9–10; 1 Peter 1:23

ALTARS ON THE HIGH PLACES

WE WERE STANDING on top of what was less than a mountain and more than a hill, and not quite either. The teacher led me over a stone platform or, rather, to the remains of what had once been a stone platform.

"What is it?" I asked.

"It's the ruins of an altar," he said. "It was one of the many altars erected on the high places."

"Altars to..."

"Baal, Molech, Ashtoreth, Zeus, and a multitude of other gods and idols."

"Altars for..."

"Sacrifices. You see, they not only set up idols on the high places—but altars. Every god had an altar and every altar required a sacrifice."

"How does this relate?" I asked. "The altars are gone or they lie in ruins."

"No," he said. "The altars are very much here, just as are the gods and idols. Remember what we spoke of. Whether or not people call the gods they worship 'gods' or the idols they serve 'idols' doesn't change the fact that they're worshipping gods and serving idols. Whatever you put first, above everything else, that's your god. Whatever you serve, whatever you live for, whatever it is that drives you, that's your idol...whether your idol is money or pleasure, success, beauty, comfort, power, possessions, a career, an object, a goal, or your own self...whatever you put first and serve, that's your god and idol. But here's what you must always remember—every god and idol has an altar."

"What does that mean?"

"There is always a cost to serving them, there's a price to the idols and gods. There's always an altar. And the altar will always require a sacrifice. Some will require the sacrifice of your peace; others will require the sacrifice of your health, your marriage, your time, your family, your integrity, your well-being...And the more you serve them, the more you must sacrifice."

"But doesn't God also have an altar and require a sacrifice?"

"Yes," said the teacher, "God *does* have an altar, but not like any other. You see, on all the other altars of this world, man sacrifices for his gods. But on God's altar, it is God who sacrifices Himself for man. It is God Himself who *is* the sacrifice. Therefore, you must no longer sacrifice and give yourself to any of the gods...except for One, the one and only God who gave Himself as a sacrifice for you."

The Mission: Are there any idols or gods in your life, anything you're following above God? Smash the altars of those gods. And live free, wholly to Him who gave Himself wholly to you.

Jeremiah 32:35; Romans 12:1; Ephesians 5:2

Altars on the High Places

HEAVEN'S LOOM

THE TEACHER TOOK me inside one of the tent camps of the desert dwellers. No one seemed to mind. We sat down beside a woman who was working on a loom made of sticks and strings. Into the loom she wove threads of red, black, purple, and yellow into a pattern that appeared both ancient and elaborate.

"Notice how carefully she goes about her weaving," he said, "how meticulously she works...how intricate the pattern."

We continued to watch as more and more of the pattern emerged.

"When judgment came on Israel in 586 BC, it seemed as if the plans God had for the Jewish people were finished. The Promised Land was in ruins and God's people in exile. It was then that God gave this word to His fallen and broken people: 'I know the plans I have for you, plans of shalom and not of calamity, to give you a future and a hope.'"

"A beautiful word," I said. "After everything, after all their failures and sins, and after all their calamities, it must have been a beautiful thing for them to hear."

"Yes," said the teacher. "Even though He should have been finished with them, He was not finished. His love was greater."

"Is there a reason," I asked, "that you're telling me this as we watch the woman weave?"

"There is," he said. "You wouldn't see it in the translation, but in the original language is a Hebrew word that appears in one form or another no less than three times in that promise. The word is *makhashabah*. It's translated as plan. But it means much more than plan. *Makhashabah* speaks of the careful, skillful, intricate weaving of a fabric. Thus it could be translated as, 'I know the meticulously woven purposes that I am skillfully, carefully, and intricately weaving together for your future.' You see, God is the Master Weaver, not only of the cosmos but of the lives of His children. And the plans He has for your life are not only good and beautiful, but intricately woven plans, already worked out. And He will take every thread of your life...every joy, every mistake, every failing, every victory, every defeat, every gain, every loss, every regret, every wound, and every question—every thread—and will knit them all together carefully, skillfully, and meticulously to become a perfect tapestry of woven love."

The Mission: Consider how God has woven the threads of your life together for good. Take confidence that with the present threads, He will do the same.

Jeremiah 29:11; Ephesians 1:4; 2 Timothy 1:9

I Know the Plans

THE MYSTERY OF THE GOEL

O NE OF THE most unique commandments God gave Israel," said the teacher, "concerned what was called the 'goel.' When a woman was left a widow and with no children, the law of the goel decreed that if a nearby relative could redeem her house by marrying her, providing for her, and giving her children, he would be called the *goel*. The Bible records the fulfillment of this law more than once. These fulfillments or redemptions are all focused on one specific tribe, the tribe of Judah, and one specific line, the line of David. The man Judah became the goel of the widow Tamar and fathered her child. From that child and line was born the man Boaz. Boaz, in turn, became the goel of the widow Ruth and fathered her child Obed. From Obed came King David."

"So King David only existed because of the law of the goel."

"Yes. He was born of a genealogy that saw the goel's intervention, a substitute fathering—not once, but twice. And it would be his line that would see one more intervention, one more substitute fathering...and one more goel. And it would happen in the same place where Boaz redeemed Ruth...Bethlehem."

"The nativity?"

"Yes," said the teacher. "It was at the nativity that God Himself became the Goel. It was now God Himself intervening in that same line, God Himself becoming the substitute father...the virgin birth.

"But Mary wasn't a widow," I said.

"No," said the teacher, "the widow was Israel, humanity, and the creation itself. The creation was barren, cut off from the Creator and unable to bear the fruit it was meant to bear. So God Himself became the Goel. For only the intervention of God in this world could cause the barren to bear its fruit and be redeemed. Listen to these words from Isaiah: 'For your Creator is your Husband. The Lord of hosts is His Name. And the Holy One of Israel is your Redeemer.' But in Hebrew, it doesn't say 'your Redeemer.' It says 'the Holy One of Israel is *your Goel*.' So the mystery is this...We've all become barren, unable to bear the fruit that our lives were called to bear, unable to become what we were created to become. So God intervenes...into our lives. And if you will receive it, God will become...your Goel."

The Mission: What in your life has never borne the promise and purpose you were meant to bear? Give it to God today. Let Him become your Goel.

Ruth 3:9; Psalm 103:4; Isaiah 54:5

The Goel Redemption

THE WAY OF BREADLESSNESS

THE TEACHER WAS seated on top of a hill with the sun behind him partially silhouetting his form. In front of him at the beginning of the slope sat the students. He was holding in his hand a loaf of bread.

"Messiah," he said, "taught His disciples to pray, 'Give us this day our daily bread.' Why?"

"Because we need to eat," said one of the students.

"But why should that be part of a prayer to God?" asked the teacher.

"Because God wants us to bring Him our most basic needs," said another.

"Yes," said the teacher. "Messiah was teaching us to bring our most basic needs to God. But how many of you is it that don't have bread for the day ... or food for today? Raise your hands."

No one raised their hand.

"Then why did He tell you to ask for bread you already have? How can He give you what is already yours? And how could you receive what you already possess?"

"If we have it," said one of the students, "then we can't receive it."

"Then we must not have it," said the teacher.

At that, he began breaking the loaf into small pieces and passing them to the students. When he finished, he continued with the teaching.

"You can't ask for what you already have. Yet we are told to ask for our bread every day. So what does it mean to pray that prayer? To pray that prayer you must relinquish your ownership. You must let go even of your daily bread. But it is in that relinquishing that you open yourself up to a miracle ... It is only what you don't have that you can receive from God. And if you don't even own your daily bread, then what do you have? And if you don't have anything, then God can bless you with everything ... every day. Then the possessions you once took for granted are freed up to undergo a transformation, to be turned into blessings given and blessings received from heaven. For when you take no blessing for granted, then everything in your life is transformed into a gift. Learn the power of this prayer and the blessings that come in the letting go even of your daily bread. It is then that your life will be filled with miracles and blessings ... the inheritance of those who have attained the state of *breadlessness*."

The Mission: Practice the state of breadlessness. Empty yourself of all possessions—even the most basic of things—and receive it all anew as a gift from God.

Deuteronomy 8:3; Joshua 13:33; Matthew 6:9–11

Our Daily Bread

THE SPECTRAL MESSIAHS

WE WERE IN his study. The teacher had placed a glass prism near the window causing a rainbow of light to appear on the opposite wall.

"The prism causes the light to break up into its individual parts, the colors of the spectrum."

We walked over to his desk and sat down.

"Have you ever heard of the two Messiahs?" he asked.

"No," I replied, "never."

"In the books of the rabbis are writings that speak of two different Messiahs. The one is called Mashiach Ben David or the Messiah Son of David. This Messiah, they write, will fight for and deliver His people, sit on David's throne, and reign over Israel and all the earth in the age of peace on earth, the kingdom of God. The other is called Mashiach Ben Yosef or Messiah Son of Joseph. This is the Messiah of sorrows…who suffers and dies for the redemption of His people."

"Where did the two Messiahs come from?"

"From the prophecies of Messiah in the Scriptures. The prophecies only speak of one Messiah. But they couldn't put it together, a Messiah who reigns victoriously and a Messiah who suffers and dies. So as the prism breaks up the light into the colors of the spectrum, the rabbis broke up the Messiah into differing images. But what happens if we put Mashiach Ben David and Mashiach Ben Yosef back together again?"

"One Messiah, two works, two appearings…two comings."

"And which work," asked the teacher, "and which coming would have to be first?"

"He can't reign victoriously forever and then suffer and die. So the second appearance and coming would have to be that of the reigning Messiah. And the first would have to be of the suffering, dying Messiah."

"It would have to be that way. And peace on earth can only come after making peace with God. But how can Messiah die and then reign forever?"

"By one thing only," I said. "By resurrection."

"Even the rabbis implied that the suffering Messiah would rise from death."

"So the two Messiahs of the rabbis are really two witnesses of the two works and appearings of the one Messiah."

"The one Messiah, Yeshua of Nazareth…who alone is true and all in one."

The Mission: Messiah is the light in which all the colors of the spectrum become one. Bring everything in your life into Him—and it will become light.

Psalm 2; Luke 24:26–27; Revelation 5:11–12

The Rabbinic Mysteries I–VI

THE DOUBLE CALENDAR PARADOX

WE WERE IN the Chamber of Books. The teacher placed a large book on the table and opened it to what looked to me like an old diagram, spread out over two pages.

"It's the Hebrew calendar," he said. "It lies behind every event in Scripture. This," he said, pointing to part of the calendar, "is the month of Tishri. And this, at the beginning of Tishri, is called *Rosh Ha Shannah,* and means *The Beginning of the Year.*"

"So the year begins with the month of Tishri," I said. "And when is that?"

"At the start of autumn. Now look over here," he said, pointing to the opposite page. "This is the month of Nisan in the spring. *Nisan* also means The Beginning. So they both are identified as the beginning. The Hebrew year has two beginnings, two calendars."

"How can that be?"

"The year that begins in the autumn with Tishri is considered the *civil* or *secular year.* But the year that begins in the spring with Nisan is considered the *sacred year.* So the people of Israel lived by two calendars...So do all of the children of God."

"What does that mean?"

"Every child of God has two calendars and two beginnings. The first calendar begins at their conception. The second begins at the moment of their new birth. The first calendar is natural. But the second is supernatural. The second is the sacred. When you're born again, you begin living in the second calendar, the calendar of the sacred. And when does the sacred calendar of Israel begin? In the spring time, the time of Passover. And so it is for all the children of God. The sacred calendar is always ushered in at the time of Passover. So it is the death of Messiah, the Passover Lamb, that ushers in the springtime of your life, your new beginning, your second and sacred calendar."

"So how do we live with two calendars?"

"Each day you will be given a choice, to live in the old calendar or the new, in the old identity or the new, the old life or the new, the natural or the supernatural. And so every day you must choose not to live in the old calendar, or walk in the old life, but to live every moment in your new identity and life, in the supernatural, in His grace...in the calendar of the sacred."

The Mission: Live this day, not by the old calendar and not according to the old course, but by the calendar in which every day and every moment is new.

Isaiah 43:18–19; John 3:1–8; Colossians 3:5–10

The Mixed Up New Year

THE ANATOLAY MAN

IN ONE OF the smaller rooms within the Chamber of Scrolls was shelving filled with scrolls of varying sizes and a wooden stand in the center. The teacher retrieved one of them, placed it on the stand, and began to unroll it.

"It's not Hebrew," I said.

"No," he said. "It's Greek, the Hebrew Scriptures in Greek. It's called the *Septuagint*, the ancient translation of the Old Testament made by Jewish scholars centuries before the New Testament. And this is the Book of Zechariah and the prophecy of Messiah as the *Tzemach*, the Branch. Look at this word," he said. "It's what they used in Greek to translate *tzemach*. But it doesn't mean branch. It's the Greek word *anatolay*."

"What does it mean?"

"It means the rising or the sunrise. And this same Greek word appears in the New Testament to speak of Messiah."

"So Messiah is 'the rising.'"

"Yes," he said. "Messiah is the rising, the resurrection."

"And so He could be called the Sunrise."

"Yes, and what does a sunrise do? It ends the night. Why is Messiah the Sunrise?" asked the teacher. "Because He ends the night."

"And the sunrise," I said, "is the light that breaks *through* the darkness."

"Yes. And so the light of Messiah is that which breaks through the darkness of this world, through the darkness of history, and through the darkness of our lives."

"And the sunrise," I said, "brings a new beginning...the dawn."

"Yes. And so Messiah is the One who brings a new beginning to history and a new beginning to every life that receives Him. He even alters the world's calendar. His light is the light of dawn."

"And the light of sunrise grows continually brighter."

"Yes," said the teacher. "And to have Him in your life is to have the Sunrise in your life. That means you must let that light continually grow and grow always brighter until it lights up every part of your life. For to those who know Him, He is not only the Light of the World...He's the Dawn...He's the Sunrise."

The Mission: Let the light of Messiah shine brighter in your life today. Believe the Sunrise. Live in the power of the Sunrise. Begin today.

Zechariah 3:8; Luke 1:78; 2 Peter 3:18; Revelation 21:23

The Dayspring

THE MYSTERY OF ASENATH

WE WERE STANDING by the wooden table in the Chamber of Books. Resting on the table was an old oversized volume bound in amber. The teacher had opened it up to a page showing a highly stylized image of an Egyptian woman, something one might have expected to find on the wall of ancient Egyptian tomb.

"Do you know who Asenath is?" he asked.

"No," I replied.

"A woman of ancient Egypt, the daughter of a pagan priest. The name *Asenath* is believed to mean belonging to and a worshipper of the god Neith. Neith was the Egyptian goddess of war. So Asenath grew up in the heart of the pagan world, far removed from the God of Israel. But she would end up marrying a Hebrew, Joseph, the son of Jacob. Through Joseph Asenath would become part of Israel, an Israelite woman. She would give birth to two sons, Ephraim and Manasseh, and thus she was the mother of two of Israel's tribes...Asenath, a pagan Egyptian woman who became joined forever to the nation of Israel, to its covenant, and to its destiny."

He closed the book. "Joseph was the shadow of whom?"

"Messiah," I replied. "The Suffering Redeemer."

"But then what is the revelation of Asenath?"

"Messiah has an Egyptian bride?" I said.

"Who is the bride of Messiah? The church. So the mystery of Asenath is the mystery of the church. Asenath was an Egyptian, far removed from the God of Israel and His ways. And who is the church? Those who once dwelt in darkness, foreigners, strangers, those who walked far removed from God's ways, and, overwhelmingly, those born not of Israel but of the nations. And yet though spiritually Egyptian, they become married to a Hebrew, Messiah. And through Him they become joined to God. And though outwardly they may still appear as foreigners, they have now, by marriage, become Hebrews. They are now joined forever to the nation of Israel and to its destiny. That is the grace and the glory of God's kingdom. It belongs to those who are the least likely to belong to it, those farthest away. Asenath is the mystery of the church, Messiah's Egyptian bride...and yet secretly Hebrew...We are Asenath."

The Mission: Ponder the grace that brought you from far away into the kingdom of Israel. And help bring near those still far away.

Genesis 41:45; Galatians 3:14; Ephesians 2:12, 19

The Shadow Man I–VI

THE STRANGER AT THE WELL

WE WERE SITTING on the same hill and overlooking the same camp where we had previously seen several women converge on a well in the late afternoon. But it was now midday. And there was no one at the well but a single woman with a clay pitcher in her hand. She was standing there as if lost in thought.

"Did you ever wonder why Rebekah met Abraham's servant at the well?" asked the teacher.

"It would make sense," I replied. "The women would go there to draw water, as would Abraham's servant to draw water for his camels."

"Yes, but God planned the encounter from the beginning. And did you know that meeting the bride at a well is a theme in Scripture? Isaac's wife was found at the well, Isaac's son Jacob would find his wife Rachel also at a well, and even Moses would find his wife, Zipporah, at a well. The bride is found at the well."

"And why is that?"

"A well is the place where the thirsty come to drink, a place where needs are fulfilled. Remember what Abraham's servant represented, the Spirit of God, the Servant of the Father. Why at a well? Because the Father's Servant always meets the bride at a well. That's where the Spirit of God meets us, at a well, in our place of need, thirst, and emptiness. It's in our need that we're most open. That's when most people meet God, receive the Spirit, and become the bride. You see, need is not a bad thing, nor is emptiness. It's what you do with it. Everyone has needs, everyone thirsts, and every heart knows emptiness. But that's where the Spirit will meet you, at the well, in your place of need and emptiness. And so it becomes a holy place. And He will meet you there not just once, but all the days of your life. So don't despise your needs. Don't try to extinguish the thirst of your soul or fight the emptiness of your heart. In God, such things become sacred. Let them instead fulfill their purpose, to bring you closer, to the Bridegroom, and to the filling up of those needs with the waters of the Spirit. So the next time you find yourself thirsting, longing, and feeling the pangs of emptiness, bring your thirst to His waters. And there you will find a stranger, a sacred Guest, and a holy Visitor who will meet you at the well."

The Mission: Take every need, want, emptiness, desire, or longing and direct it away from the world, to the Spirit and the heavenly.

Genesis 24:11–28; Isaiah 12:3; 55:1; John 4:7–14

The Isaac Rebekah Wedding Mystery I–III

THE MIRACLE WORLD

IT WAS LATE into the night and especially dark. The moon was nowhere to be seen. The teacher and I were sitting in an open expanse not far from the school while everyone else was asleep.

"Imagine," he said, "if we lived in a world where everything was night, a world where we could never see the blue of the sky, the yellow of the sun, the green of grass and trees. Imagine we could barely see each other. Now imagine that something takes place in this world that has never happened before...a sunrise. What would it be like?"

"I would imagine it would be amazing to them," I said. "Indescribable."

"Yes," said the teacher, "for the first time in our lives, the black sky begins to transform, subtly changing its color, the first hints of dawn. Then come the first orange yellow rays of daybreak...and then the circle of blazing light rising up from the horizon as if floating on nothing, and our entire world is transformed. For the first time we see everything in vivid color and clarity...It would be a miracle, a miracle as dramatic and as amazing to our world as the parting of the Red Sea..." The teacher paused, turned to me, and said, "But the miracle *has* happened...The miracle happens every day. Should we not then be living in the miraculous all the time? And why don't we? It would be as if the Red Sea parted at about six in the morning every day. We would no longer be amazed by it. And yet was there ever a vision given to any prophet as vivid, as full of detail and brilliance as the vision we see every day of this world? But when the miracle happens every day, we no longer see it. We become blind...and blind to the fact that there is nothing as supernatural as existence itself...that existence came into existence...and that it could have only come into existence from nothing...and that the natural world is the witness of the supernatural."

"The sun," I said. "It's beginning to rise."

"Behold the miracle," said the teacher. "This life, this universe, everything you see and touch, everything you hear and have known...it's all a miracle...a vision come to life. Open your eyes and see the world as if for the first time, as if your first sunrise and your first Red Sea, as the miracle it is...Live in the miraculous...For you are already living...in a miracle world."

The Mission: Today, live as if you were in a "miracle world," as if everything you see and hear is miraculous—because it is. Live in the miraculous.

Psalms 8; 19:1–6; Isaiah 6:3

The Miracle World

THE MYSTERY OF THE WOLF

WE WATCHED A shepherd tend his flock at sunset. Eventually he led them on and out of our sight. It was then that I noticed an animal following in their path.

"It's a wolf," said the teacher. "It's trailing the flock, looking for a chance to attack. The Scriptures speak of wolves. Messiah spoke of them. They symbolized evil and particularly those who seek to destroy God's people, His people. Ultimately they symbolize the one who seeks the destruction of all of God's people...the enemy...the devourer."

"The devil?"

"The ultimate wolf...the predator of God's flock. The Jewish people are spoken of in Scripture as a flock that would wander the earth and be attacked by their predators."

"It came true," I said. "That's the history of the Jewish people."

"So who," asked the teacher, "of all their enemies, of all the predators, were the most evil?"

"It would have to be the Nazis...Hitler."

"And what did they do to the Jewish people? They hunted them down, herded them together, and led them as sheep to the slaughter. They were driven by evil, by the spirit of the wolf, by the enemy...And do you know what he named his military headquarters?"

"No."

"*Wolfsschanze*. It means the wolf's lair. And another he called *Wolfsschluct*, the wolf's gorge. And another he named *Werewolf*. And the mystery goes even deeper. Do you know what his closest friends called him? *Wolf*. And do you know the name he was given from birth?"

"Adolf?"

"Yes, but do you know what *Adolf* means?...*The wolf*. The greatest enemy of the Jewish people, God's flock, was named *the wolf*...That's how real this is...and how real is the Messiah."

"How?"

"If there's a flock, and a wolf, there must be a shepherd. And if the flock is without its shepherd, then it must be a shepherd from whom the flock was separated. Messiah said, 'I am the Good Shepherd...who lays down His life for the sheep.' For two thousand years they've been without their Shepherd, and the wolf has devoured them. And we too are as sheep. All the more we must walk as close as possible to the Shepherd, and as far as possible from the wolf."

The Mission: Today, stay as far away from temptation as you can, and as close as you can to the Lord. Far from the wolf and near to the Shepherd.

Psalm 23; Ezekiel 34:6–8; Matthew 10:16; John 10:11–14

The Kingdom of Broken Crosses

REBUILDING THE RUINS

WE WALKED TO a ruin that lay alone and abandoned in the desert sand.

"Imagine," said the teacher, "standing in the midst of ruins extending as far as you could see. So it was in the land of Israel after the armies of Rome had laid it waste. And in the ages since then it was said that God was finished with the Jewish people. But the words of the prophets recorded a promise: In the latter days God would gather the Jewish people from the ends of the earth back to the land of Israel. And when they returned there, it was prophesied that they would 'rebuild the ancient ruins. They shall raise up the former desolations. And they shall repair the ruined cities, the desolations of many generations.' And the words of the ancient prophecies would come true. The Jewish people were gathered back from the nations to their ancient homeland. Once there, they began rebuilding the ancient cities and repairing the ancient ruins. What revelation does this give us?"

"The Word of God is true."

"Yes," said the teacher, "and something else. After centuries of rebellion, it would have been easier for God to have ended His dealings with them and to have chosen another people. But He chose instead to restore the destroyed, rebuild the ruins, and raise up His fallen nation. He chose to heal the broken, to take the scattered pieces of His fallen nation and put them back together, one by one, piece by broken piece. Why is that? It's because when you love something, and that something breaks, you don't abandon it, you put it back together, piece by piece...So with the nation Israel...And so with us. Israel is a sign to all people, a picture of God's redemption for all who will receive it. And what is that redemption? It's the restoring of what was broken. He doesn't abandon us in our sins. He doesn't give up on us in our fallen and broken state. Instead, He rebuilds the ruins. He takes the broken pieces of our lives, of our mistakes, and puts them back together, piece by piece. And as God has done for us, so we must do the same to those who are fallen and to that which is broken. For when you love something and it breaks...you don't abandon it. You put it back together...piece by piece."

The Mission: Is there something broken that you've abandoned or given up on? Pray for its redemption and, if you can, put it back together in God's love.

Isaiah 61:4; Amos 9:14; Luke 4:18; Acts 15:16–17

Dry Bones Rising

DODI LI

HE LED ME into one of the vineyards in the middle of which was a rock on which we rested.

"It was in another garden," said the teacher, "that I shared with you a Hebrew phrase spoken by the bride in the Song of Solomon, *Ani Lo*. Do you remember what it means?"

"It means I am His, or I am to Him. And it's at the foundation of everything we are to be and do in God, our consecration, our works and sacrifices, our ministry and our calling."

"Yes. And for the revelation to be complete, you need to know one more Hebrew phrase. It is this: *Dodi Li*. Before the bride says *Ani Lo*, she says *Dodi Li*."

"And what does *Dodi Li* it mean?"

"*My beloved is mine. Dodi Li V'Ani Lo, My beloved is mine, and I am his*. *Ani Lo, I am His*, sums up everything required of you in God. But *Dodi Li* is the secret to fulfilling it. Before the bride can say *Ani Lo, I am his*, she must say *Dodi Li, My beloved is mine*. The more she realizes that her beloved belongs to her, the more she will give herself to her beloved. If she receives his love for her, she will give her love to him. The more her heart can comprehend *Dodi Li*, the more her life will become *Ani Lo*. If he is hers, she will be his. And that's the secret to your life in God. It is your Dodi Li that brings about your Ani Lo."

"What does that mean?"

"All that you are to be and do in God begins with Dodi Li, My Beloved is mine. The more you fathom what it means that God belongs to you, the more you will give yourself to Him. The more you receive His love for you, the more you will give your love to Him. The more your heart comprehends '*My Beloved is mine*,' the more your life will become '*I am His*.' And you won't have to struggle to live a life of righteousness and holiness or to do what is good. You'll just do it, freely, flowingly, out of love, out of His love. For it is the Dodi Li heart that produces the Ani Lo life. So make it your aim to fill your heart with the knowledge of Dodi Li—and your life will become Ani Lo. It's as simple as Dodi Li V'Ani Lo. My Beloved is to me, and I am to Him."

"My Beloved is mine," I said, "and I am His."

The Mission: Make today a Dodi Li day. Live as if God belonged to you—as He does. Receive His life as your gift. And make your life His gift.

Song of Solomon 2:16; Titus 2:14; 1 John 4:10–19

Dodi Li

THE MASTERWORK

THE TEACHER TOOK me around the back of the common hall where there was a blank canvas on a wooden easel and, to its right, a second wooden easel on which rested a beautiful and intricate painting of a landscape.

"Your assignment," he said, "is to copy this painting."

"But I don't know how to paint."

"That's the challenge," he replied. "I'll be back in a few hours."

For the rest of the afternoon I tried my best to reproduce what I saw on the canvas. But for all my efforts, the result looked like something a preschooler would have done. When the teacher returned, there was a long silence as we both stared at my work.

"You won't forget this lesson," he said. "You were trying to reproduce the work of a master. Most of those in the kingdom do the same thing."

"Copy paintings?"

"Try to reproduce the righteousness of God. They know what's right and good and holy. They know what a godly life looks like. And they try to live it. The goal is worthy. But the way they go about achieving that goal is wrong. They're doing what you just did, trying by their own abilities to reproduce the work of the Master. And to do that is to compete with God. And if you *could* do that, you wouldn't need God. Only God can do the works of God. And a holy life is the work of God."

"Then how can we do it," I asked, "if God is the only one who can?"

"Then that's the key. God must do it. And you must let Him. Imagine if, instead of trying to copy this painting, you were given the artist's heart and mind, his skills, and his spirit. Then it wouldn't be a struggle, nor would it be a copy. It would be as if the master was painting through you. Therein lies the key. Don't compete with God by trying to copy His works. But learn the secret of letting God work His works in everything you do. If you live with the heart of God, you'll do the works of God. If you live by the Spirit of God, you fulfill the will of God. Move in His moving. Love in His loving. Live in His living, and be in His being. As for that painting you did..."

"It's a mess," I said. "And I think I'll keep it...as a reminder."

"Live by the Spirit of the Master," said the teacher, "and that which you do will be a masterpiece."

The Mission: Today, instead of focusing on the works of God, seek to live in the heart and Spirit of God—and you will accomplish the works of God.

Ezekiel 36:27; Galatians 5:16, 22–25; Philippians 1:6; Hebrews 13:21

The Poem of God

THE ZYGOTE MYSTERY

WE WERE STANDING in the middle of a garden of flowers of every color and type. The teacher removed from his pocket a tiny object and handed it to me.

"It's a seed," he said. "And the Scriptures have much to say about them. Messiah even spoke of His own life as a seed. "'The hour has come,' He said, "that the Son of Man should be glorified. Truly, I say to you, unless a seed of wheat falls into the ground and dies, it remains alone; but if it dies, it produces much fruit.'" He was speaking of His death, and the fruit it would bear...the resurrection, salvation, eternal life. But what Messiah referred to when He spoke of His life and death is called a *zygote*. The word *zygote* literally means the joined. A zygote is the new life that comes from the joining of two lives, that of the two parents. So the zygote is the union of two natures in one life. That's what a seed is. And He spoke of His life as a seed, a zygote."

"That's what His life was," I said, "the union of two natures, the joining of God and man, the uniting of the Spirit and the flesh, deity in bodily form, the union of heaven and earth in one life, a joining...the zygote."

"But then what happens," asked the teacher, "to the seed, the zygote? It falls to the ground as if dying. And its outward form undergoes a type of death. But only then does the life inside the zygote bear its fruit. So Messiah's life falls to the ground and dies, and by His death, bears new life into the world...And so it is with others."

"How could there be others?" I asked. "Only He was of two natures."

"But there are others," said the teacher. "The moment one is born again, one's life in this world becomes a union, a union of two natures, earth and heaven, the flesh and the Spirit, the temporary and the eternal, God in man. Every child of God is a union, a joining of two natures, a zygote. But if the zygote falls to the ground and dies, it brings forth much fruit, it bears its life."

The teacher bent down and buried the seed in the soil between us.

"Every time you die to the self, every time you crucify the flesh, every time you surrender your will to God's will...the power of God and of new life will be released, and you will bear much fruit, and your life will bring forth the life it was always meant to bear. Do this, and the purposes of God in your life will bear much fruit...It is the law of the zygote."

The Mission: Learn the secret of the zygote. Let the old self die, crucify the flesh, surrender your will. And the power of life will be released.

Matthew 10:39; John 12:23–24; 15:13; 2 Corinthians 4:10–11

The Mystery of the Zygote

PRUNE THYSELF

WE RETURNED TO the garden where we first saw the man who was trimming the branches.

"Do you remember what you saw here?" asked the teacher.

"The man trimming the branches," I answered. "The pruning."

"And what is the purpose of pruning?"

"Pruning removes the branches from a tree that hinder its fruitfulness or its well-being, to allow it to become as fruitful as possible."

"Pruning, therefore, is critical to living a fruitful life in God, so God prunes the lives of His children. But in order to live a fruitful life, you must also be part of the process. You must learn also how to prune yourself."

At that, he led me over to a tree in need of trimming. He handed me two of the gardener's tools, a pruning hook and a pair of pruning shears.

"Do you see this?" he said. "It's a diseased branch. If it's not cut off, it will harm the tree. Any action, course, or habit of sin in your life is a diseased branch and will hinder you from living a fruitful life in God. Prune it off."

So I did.

"And this here is a dead branch, once fruitful but now detrimental to the tree's health. Any action or expenditure of energy in your life that produces no fruit, even if it once did, is a dead branch. You must prune it off."

So I did.

"And these branches here are hindering the tree by blocking sunlight from the tree's most fruitful branches. So in your life, anything you do that keeps you from receiving from God, from dwelling in His presence and His Word, is a hindering branch." He pointed downward. "And these branches here are too low. They stand for all the low pursuits, indulgences, and actions that drain away your time and energy from the higher things to which God has called you. Cut them off. Cut them all off," he said.

"From my life?"

"Absolutely. But from the tree as well, as an object lesson. Cut them all off. It will not harm the tree, but help it. So it is with your life. By giving up, you will gain. Make it a continual practice, and you will become spiritually healthy, strong, great, and fruitful. Prune thyself...and you will bear much fruit."

The Mission: Today, identify in your life the dead branches, the diseased, the hindering, the wasteful, and the low—and cut them off. Prune thyself.

Mark 1:35; 10:29–30; John 15:1–5

The Secrets of Pruning I–III

THE POWER OF AS

IN THE BOOK of Ephesians it is written, 'Therefore, be imitators of God, as beloved children.' How would you understand and apply that?" asked the teacher.

"Beloved children would imitate their fathers. So since you are beloved children, imitate your heavenly Father, God."

"That's good," he said. "'Be imitators of God as beloved children.' You *could* take that to mean since you are beloved children, imitate God. And that would be correct. But it doesn't exactly say that. It says *as,* the Greek word *hoce. Hoce* can be translated as in the same way as, or just like. So it could be translated as 'Be imitators of God *in the same way as*, or *just like* beloved children.' How do you carry out *that* command? First you must have an idea of what beloved children are, how they act, how they react, how they live. Then you live as if you were one of them. So as you believe they would act, so act in that same way. As a child of God, you are not bound by what you've been or even by what you are now. In God you have the power to live as you are *not*...or rather as you are *not yet*...but to live *as you are yet to be*. And toward that end, the word *as* is a very powerful thing. When the angel came to Gideon, he found a man living in fear. Yet he said to him, 'The Lord is with you, you mighty man of valor.' A mighty man of valor was not who Gideon was, but who Gideon was to become. But the angel greeted him *as if* he was a mighty man of valor. Gideon now had live by faith *as if* he was that mighty man of valor. And that's what he became. That's the secret of *as*. Do not be bound by what you are. Rather, live *as if* you were that which you are to become. Be as Gideon, the one whose life was changed when an angel greeted him. And do you know what the angel called him...in Hebrew? He called him *gibbor. Gibbor* literally means champion. Now imagine how a champion in God would live, a person of righteousness, purity, holiness, godliness, and power. Imagine how a champion of faith would live. Then live *as* that champion. Live *as if* you could do great and mighty things for God...even if it's far beyond anything you've known, or been, or done. Live by faith *as if* you could, *as if* that champion was you and, as it was with Gideon, it will become so. It will become you in the power of *as*."

The Mission: Live now not according to who you are but as you are to be. Live this day in the power of *as*—as a victorious, mighty champion!

Judges 6:11–12; Ephesians 5:1, 21–29

The Perfect Bowler

THE YAD

ABOUT TWENTY OF the students were gathered in a circle. They were singing a song of worship. I had never heard it before. It was in another language. They had to have learned the song while in the school. Many of them lifted their hands as they sang. I just watched. When it was over, the teacher, who had been observing their worship from outside the circle, approached me.

"Was that strange to you?" he asked.

"I've just never seen them sing like that."

"Or lift their hands?"

"Is that important?"

"You are free here to sing and worship however you like, but yes, the lifting of hands is of significance. Do you remember when we spoke of the mystery of the word *Jew*, how it comes from the words *Yehudim* or *Yehudah*?"

"Yes."

"But it goes deeper," he said. "The word *Yehudah* comes from *yadah*. *Yadah* means to praise, to give thanks, and to worship. But it's specifically linked to holding out one's hand."

"As in, they held out their hands in worship?"

"Yes. And *yadah*, in turn, comes from the word *yad*. And *yad* means hand."

"So the word *Jew* comes from the word *hand?*"

"Ultimately, yes," he said. "But not just from the word *hand*—but from one particular kind of hand."

"What particular kind of hand?"

"An open hand. The word specifically speaks of an *open* hand. For the hand of worship is an open hand. The hand of praise is an open hand. The hand of thanksgiving is an open hand."

"So to live a life of praise and thanksgiving," I said, "is to live a life of the open hand."

"Yes, and an open hand is the only hand that is able to receive blessings from heaven. So the more you live a life of praise, worship, and thanksgiving—a life of yadah—the more your life will become an open hand to receive the blessings of heaven—the yad. The more you praise and give thanks without condition, the more you will have to praise and give thanks for."

The Mission: Live this day giving thanks and worship at all times, no matter what. Open your life to blessings through the power of the yad.

Psalms 63:4–7; 150; Ephesians 1:12

The Yad People

THE ALPHA COMMANDMENT

WHAT," ASKED THE teacher, "was the first perpetual commandment God gave to the nation of Israel?"

"The first of the Ten Commandments?"

"No," he said, "the first continuous command given to the nation of Israel was this: 'On the tenth day of this month everyone shall take for himself a lamb...' This was the command that established the Tenth of Nisan as the day when the Passover lamb had to be taken to the house...the Tenth of Nisan, the same day that Messiah, the Lamb of God was taken to Jerusalem on the day we know as Palm Sunday."

"So the first command God gave Israel is take the lamb."

"Yes, but in Hebrew, the word for *take* is *lakakh*. *Lakakh* also means to bring. So it can be translated as bring the lamb. So they brought the Lamb, Messiah, on a donkey into Jerusalem. But *lakakh* can also mean to purchase and thus, purchase the lamb. It was this that the priests of Israel fulfilled as they paid for the life of Messiah. So they purchased the Lamb. And *lakakh* can also mean seize, and thus seize the lamb. So Messiah would be seized, arrested, and taken captive. And there's one more thing that *lakakh* means."

"What?"

"'Receive.'"

"Receive the lamb."

"Yes," said the teacher. "This is Alpha commandment, the first perpetual commandment given to Israel by God: 'Receive the lamb.' Or 'Receive for yourself the lamb'...the Alpha commandment...and the Omega commandment."

"Why the Omega?

"Because all of Jewish history, all of world history, is waiting for that commandment to be fulfilled. When the children of Israel finally fulfill their first commandment, when they receive the Lamb for themselves, then the Lamb will come, then Messiah will come, then the kingdom will come. Thus it is the first and last command—and not just for Israel, but for every life. It is the commandment which, when fulfilled, brings salvation to everyone who obeys it. Everything begins and ends with that...Receive the Lamb."

The Mission: Is there something in your life that God has called you to do, that you haven't yet done? Open up the blessing. Do it today.

Exodus 12:3; Matthew 23:39; John 1:12; Colossians 2:6–7

THE GRAPES OF HEAVEN

WE WERE STANDING inside of one of the vineyards. The teacher broke off a cluster of grapes from the vines and placed it in my hand.

"A most important fruit," he said. "Upon it once hung the future of a nation."

"On grapes?"

"Yes," he replied. "When the children of Israel came to what should have been the end of their journey in the wilderness, on the verge of the Promised Land, Moses sent twelve men into the land to spy it out. They returned with a cluster of grapes from the Valley of Eshcol. The grapes were the firstfruits of the Promised Land, the first evidence they possessed that it was all real, the first taste of what up to that point they had only heard about and believed by faith. It should have been an encouragement for them to press on and take the land. But they refused the encouragement. They believed their fears over the grapes. And because they lost sight of the grapes, they lost the Promised Land...a most critical key," he said.

"What?"

"Never lose sight of the grapes.

"The grapes of the Promised Land?"

"The grapes of *your* Promised Land," he said.

"Heaven?"

"Throughout your journey God will give you grapes from the Promised Land."

"What do you mean?"

"He will give you the firstfruits of heaven and of heavenly life, signs and evidences of that which you believe by faith, the first taste of the age to come. Every answered prayer, every moving of His hand in your life, every whispering of His voice, every providing for your needs...these are the grapes, the clusters of the Promised Land. Every encouragement that you know came from Him, every guiding of your steps, every provision, every measure of unexplainable peace, every moment of heavenly joy, and every touch of His Spirit...these are the firstfruits given to you as an encouragement so that you won't give up or give in to fear, but press on, to fight the good fight, to take your inheritance. And all these things are just a taste of the blessings yet to come...the firstfruits of your Promised Land...the grape clusters of heaven."

The Mission: Gather the clusters of the Promised Land—every answered prayer and blessing from God. Take strength from the grapes of heaven and take new ground for God.

Numbers 13:23–28; Romans 8:23; Hebrews 11:1

Clusters of Your Promised Land

THE FEAST OF TRUMPETS

WE STOOD ON the ridge of a high mountain. The teacher had in one hand a tallit, the Hebrew prayer shawl, and in the other, a shofar, the ram's horn. The sun was just about to set. It was the Feast of Trumpets.

"Later on," he said, "we'll observe it with the rest. But I wanted to share of it now with you. It is written: 'You shall have...a reminder by the sounding of trumpets, a holy convocation...' the Feast of Trumpets."

"I have a question about that," I said. "Why is it that the holy days of Israel appear, in one form or another, in the New Testament...except for one, the Feast of Trumpets? Why is the Feast of Trumpets missing?"

"It's not," he said. "You just didn't see it. When in the sacred Hebrew year does the Feast of Trumpets take place, at the beginning or the end? At the end. So then its mystery doesn't focus on the beginning of the age, but the end. The Feast of Trumpets announces the closing of the sacred cycle. So too it will announce the closing of the age. And what is it that you find in Scripture when you look at the prophecies concerning the end of the age? Trumpets. The trumpets of Israel announced the coming of kings and kingdoms, the approaching of armies. So it is prophesied that when the trumpet sounds, the kingdom of God will come. The trumpets called the people of Israel to gather before God. So it is prophesied that at the sound of the trumpet, God's people will be gathered up to His presence. The sound of the trumpet was a wake-up call. So it is foretold that when the trumpets sound, the dead in Messiah will be awoken. And lastly, it was the sound of the trumpet that announced the beginning of a king's reign. So it is foretold that when the trumpet sounds, the reign of the King will begin, the kingdom of this world will become the kingdom of the Lord. The Feast of Trumpets and the holy days of autumn are just as much a part of the new covenant as are the holy days of spring. They tell us that our faith is not only in what was, but in what is yet to come...as is Messiah. We live *from* salvation and yet *to* redemption, and we are, above all, a people of hope."

At that he covered his head with the tallit, lifted the shofar to his mouth, and blew. The sound echoed throughout the wilderness. He then turned to me.

"So live confident and in hope of what is yet to come...and ready for that day...the Day of Trumpets."

The Mission: Live this day in confidence and hope, looking to the future, knowing He is already there, Lord of the future, and awaiting you to arrive.

Leviticus 23:24; Matthew 24:31; 1 Corinthians 15:52;
1 Thessalonians 4:16

Yom Teruah

THE WARS OF THE HOLY

HE OPENED ONE of the drawers in his study and took out a thin rectangular wooden box. Inside was a collection of ancient coins, most of them badly worn, but some well preserved. He gave me time to examine them.

"Of the entire surface of this planet," said the teacher, "what plot of earth do you think has been the most fought over plot of earth?"

"I wasn't a history major," I answered. "I really have no idea."

"The answer is Jerusalem. All these coins are from that plot of land, each representing a kingdom or empire that approached its walls. Jerusalem, the City of God, the City of Peace, yet it's been reduced to ashes more than once and been laid siege to over twenty times. It's been the ground of over a hundred conflicts. From ancient times to the modern world, no city on earth has been so fought over or the focus of so much warfare. Why? It has no great military or strategic value, and no great resources. If we were visiting this planet for the first time, it would tell us that there's something about that city, something that sets it apart from all other places, and beyond natural explanation. What conflict would there be from that which is beyond the natural...to war against the City of Peace?"

"A conflict in the spiritual realm. The conflict of the enemy."

"And why?" asked the teacher.

"Because Jerusalem is at the center of God's purposes?"

"Yes," he said, "at the center of His purposes, past, present, and future, the place where His feet will touch the earth, and the throne from which the kingdom of God will go forth. Thus it must be the most warred over of grounds. So all the conflict, the controversy, and the warfare itself is a testimony to Jerusalem, to what Jerusalem is—the central ground of God's purposes on earth. And why is the conflict so great? Because the purposes God has for Jerusalem are so great...And so too in your life, and in the lives of all God's children.... as you do the will of God, there must be conflict, and warfare, and attacks. But don't ever let that discourage you. Be encouraged. It's a sign of revelation by default, that you're on the right path and what you're doing will be of great effect and reward. Don't stop. But press on all the more. For the greatness of the battle is only because of the greatness of God's purposes for His holy place—you!"

The Mission: Don't fear the battles. Embrace them. What is of God will be opposed. And that which is good is worth fighting for. Fight the good fight. And you will prevail.

Isaiah 52:1–2; 2 Corinthians 6:4–10; 10:3–5

Jerusalem Besieged

THE SECRET OF THE THIRD PRINCE

WE WERE WALKING through a large open plain covered with loose sand. "Walk on," said the teacher. "And seek to walk in a straight line."

So I kept walking as he watched. He let me go on for a few minutes.

"Stop," he yelled from the distance. "Now turn around and look." I was sure I had been walking a straight line. But the footprints in the sand revealed that I had veered markedly off to the right. The teacher then approached me.

"Let me tell you a story," he said. "There was once a king who issued a challenge to the princes of a neighboring land that whoever among them could, over a long journey of varying landscapes, walk in a straight line to the king's castle would have the right to ask for his daughter's hand in marriage.

"The first prince embarked on the journey, looking to his right and left to make sure he was not veering off in either direction. But, like you, despite his best efforts, the farther he journeyed, the more off course he veered.

"The second prince determined to look down, to keep his eyes on his feet, making sure that every footstep followed in the same path as the footstep before it. But he too ended badly off course.

"But the third prince embarked on the journey, looking neither to the right nor the left, nor down at his footsteps. And yet at the end, it was determined that he had walked in a straight line. No one could figure out how he did it. So he told them his secret: 'All I did was look into the far distance to the light on the crown of the castle tower. I didn't look at my path or the landscape to my right and left. I just kept my eyes on that light, and kept pressing forward to that light until I arrived there.' And this," said the teacher, "is the secret to your walk in God. We are all called to walk a straight path in God. But how does one do that over the course of a lifetime and over a long journey of varying landscapes and changing circumstances? Not by focusing on your circumstances or even on your own walk. Rather, you fix your eyes on your destination, despite your surroundings, despite the mountains and the valleys, despite the highs and the lows, despite even your own walk and footsteps. You fix your eyes on the Eternal, on Him...and you press forward, always onward and closer to that goal...and you will end up there...and straight will be your footprints in the sand."

The Mission: Practice today the secret of the third prince. In all things, in all situations, fix your eyes on your goal, on Him, and draw continually closer.

Psalm 25:15; Jeremiah 31:9; Hebrews 12:1–2

To Finish the Race

THE DAYS OF TESHUVAH

HE LED ME into the Chamber of Garments and over to an assortment of white prayer shawls.

"These," he said, "are for the Days of Teshuvah, the holiest time of the Hebrew year."

"What is *teshuvah*?" I asked.

"It comes from the root word *shuv* and means to return."

"So *teshuvah* would mean the return?"

"Yes," he said, "the Days of Teshuvah are the Days of Return. But it's a particular kind of return, a return to God. And to return to God is to repent. So *teshuvah* also means repentance. So during the Days of Teshuvah the Jewish people are called to turn away from wrongdoing, to confess their sins, to repent, to return to the Lord, and to seek His mercy."

"When exactly are the Days of Teshuvah?"

"Late summer and early autumn, the time of the High Holy Days, the Feast of Trumpets, the Days of Awe, and the Day of Atonement, the days ordained for returning to God..."

He paused for a moment, then asked, "When do you think the Days of Teshuvah fall, in the beginning of the sacred year, the middle, or in the end?"

"The beginning?" I said.

"No," said the teacher. "The Days of Teshuvah fall at the end of the sacred year. And therein lies a prophetic mystery. Every year the Jewish people return to the Lord, not at the beginning of the sacred cycle but at the end. And here is the mystery it bears: The Jewish people will not, as a whole, come to the Lord at the beginning of the age—but at the end. The time of their Teshuvah will be at the end. They will only return to the Lord as a nation at the end of the age. Their return will be linked to the end. But *teshuvah* has a double meaning. It can also mean a *physical* return. And so the Days of Teshuvah contain another revelation, which is this: Before the end of the age, the Jewish people must return to their land, to the land of Israel, and to the city of Jerusalem."

"As they have," I said. "And it was all there from ancient times in their calendar. They return at the end."

"Yes, they will return to the land...and to their God, all at the appointed time...in the Days of Teshuvah."

The Mission: Repentance is an entire life. Live your life in the days of teshuvah. The greater your repentance, the greater will be your return.

Isaiah 30:15; Jeremiah 3:22; Hosea 3:4–5

The Three End-Time Teshuvahs

THE HEAVEN SCENARIO

IT WAS LATE at night. The teacher and I were sitting around the dying embers of the campfire when I heard a noise. It sounded as if someone or something was walking over a bunch of broken branches.

"What do you think that was?" I asked.

"An animal," he said, "or the wind." We stopped talking for a few moments, waiting to see if the noise would resume, but it didn't.

"What would be the worst case scenario?" he asked.

"Right now?" I asked. "With the noise? If it turned out to be that of a lion or a bear...or a murderer. I would say any of those would qualify."

"And what would be the worst case scenario after that?"

"We'd get killed."

"What if it was a less extreme scenario," he said. "You get sick. What's the worst thing that can happen?"

"The sickness turns out to be fatal."

"And the worst case scenario after that?"

"I die."

"You have a job," he said. "You get fired."

"I can't find another job. I sink into poverty and starve to death."

"Notice," said the teacher, "each of our worst case scenarios end with the same thing—death. Now if you're a child of God, if you're saved, what happens after your worst scenarios?"

I paused for a moment. "I go to heaven."

"Heaven," he said, "with no more pain and no more sorrows. Your worst case scenario...is heaven! All your anxieties, all your fears...are ultimately based on heaven...streets of gold...perfect peace...unending joy...That's what you have to be afraid of? Think about that. All your fears and anxieties end up in the most beautiful and joyous place you could ever imagine; then once you've resolved that, what do you have to be afraid of ever again? Look to the end. Look to heaven. And live a life of confidence that is beyond fear. For the truth of the matter is, for a child of God, the worst case scenario...is heaven!"

The Mission: Take your fear, your worry, your anxiety to its end—heaven. And with heaven as your worst scenario, overcome to a fear-free life.

1 Corinthians 2:9; Philippians 1:21–23; Colossians 1:5;
2 Timothy 4:6–8

FIRSTFRUITFULNESS

THE TEACHER LED me into a garden filled with laborers hard at work harvesting the olive trees and over to a low stone wall where we both sat down. The laborers then approached the teacher with a basket full of olives they had just harvested from the trees.

"God commanded man to be fruitful," he said. "Beyond physical fruit, we were to have brought forth the fruits of love, righteousness, truth, joy, peace, godliness, and much more. But with the fall of man and the beginning of sin, we lost the ability to bear the fruit we were called to bear."

He looked down at the basket of olives.

"On what Hebrew holy day did Messiah rise from death?"

"The Day of the Firstfruits."

"It had to do with fruit. So the resurrection has to do with the power of fruitfulness, that we might bear the fruits we were created to bear. But it wasn't just about fruit. And this is not just a basket of fruit. This is a basket of *firstfruits*. Messiah rose on the Day of the *First*fruits. So the resurrection not only has to do with fruitfulness, but with *firstfruitfulness*. And so the power it gives us is not only the power of fruitfulness, but the power of *firstfruitfulness*."

"And what is the power of *firstfruitfulness*?" I asked.

"It's the power to bear the fruits of God in circumstances where those fruits have never been borne, and from the ground that has never before been able to bring them forth. It's the power to produce the firstfruits of love, the firstfruits of joy, the firstfruits of hope, the firstfruits of repentance, the firstfruits of forgiveness, the firstfruits of life. It's the power to bring forth hope where there is no hope, and love where there is no love, joy where there is no joy, forgiveness where there has been no forgiveness, victory where there has been no victory, and life where there is no life. It was from just such a ground that the miracle of the resurrection took place...a ground of darkness, hopelessness, and death. And yet from that came forth the firstfruits of new life. It was so you could do likewise. And now you have a new command: Be ye not only fruitful...from now on...be ye firstfruitful."

The Mission: Today, be not only fruitful, but be firstfruitful. Where there is no fruit of love, or hope, forgiveness, or joy, be the first one to bear them.

2 Chronicles 31:5; Matthew 5:44; 1 Corinthians 15:20

The Power of the Bikoreem

THE DEATH OF THE ZACHAR

MOST OF THE students had gone to bed. Only the teacher and I were left sitting around the fire.

"The Passover lamb," he said, "was the first sacrifice offered by the nation of Israel and the archetype of all sacrifices. What do we know of it?"

"The Hebrews were told to kill the lamb and put its blood on their doors."

"But what kind of lamb?" he asked. "The lamb had to be spotless, a year old...And it had to be a male."

"Is that significant?" I asked.

"It's the Passover lamb," he said. "Every detail is significant. And in this one detail is a mystery. The word for *male* is the Hebrew *zachar*. *Zachar* also means the remembrance, the recounting, the mention, and the record. So when the Passover Lamb was killed, the zachar was killed. And to kill the zachar is to end the remembrance, to destroy the record, to wipe out the memory." The teacher got up to place some small sticks on the fire, then sat back down and continued. "Messiah died on Passover as the Passover Lamb. Thus He was also the Zachar...the Zachar of our sins. And when He died, it was the death of the Zachar. And when the Zachar dies, the remembrance of our sins also dies. The record of our guilt is destroyed. And the memory of our shame is no more. In the Book of Jeremiah, God promised to make a new covenant. In the new covenant He said, 'I will remember their sins no more,' or in Hebrew, 'I will *zachar no more their sins*.' Messiah became the Zachar of our sins...and then was killed...So the Zachar was no more...that God's zachar, God's remembrance, of our sins would be no more."

"When the zachar died in Egypt, the Hebrews were released from their bondage and set free to fulfill their calling."

"Yes," said the teacher. "In the death of Messiah, the Zachar, is the end of God's remembrance of sin, but it's also the power to end your own remembrance of your own sin and of the sins of others. So if you believe in the death of the Zachar, you must end the remembrances of sin in your life. It is then that you'll be released, and leave the old, and enter the fullness of your calling...when the Zachar is no more."

The Mission: Take all your sins and all that haunts you and cast it onto the Zachar. Reckon it dead in His death. Do likewise with the sins of others.

Exodus 12:3; Jeremiah 31:31–34; 1 Corinthians 5:7; Hebrews 10:14–17

The Nisan Lamb

THE PRIEST KING

I N THE CHAMBER of Garments were two wooden boxes. The teacher placed them each on the wooden table, then carefully removed their contents.

"This," he said, "was the crown of the king, the descendant of David. And this," he said, as he placed the second object on the table, something of a mix between a crown and a turban, "was the crown of the high priest, the descendant of Aaron. These are the two crowns representing the two offices and the two houses of Israel. No man could wear them both. The king could never minister as priest, and the high priest could never reign as king. The Temple and the palace were separated by an unbridgeable chasm."

"Why was the separation so important?" I asked.

"The true king of Israel was not man but God. So the king represented the kingship of God. On the other hand, the high priest represented the people in fallenness and sin. It was his ministry to reconcile a sinful people to God, to their King and Judge."

"So then the King of Israel...God, was the Judge. And the high priest was something of a defense attorney before the Judge. So the two offices had to be kept separate."

"Exactly," said the teacher. "And yet there came a word to the prophet Zechariah that one day the two offices would become one. Messiah would be both King and High Priest. Yeshua, Jesus, the Messiah, was born of the royal line of David, the line of kings. And yet His ministry was to offer up the sacrifice of atonement, the act not of the king but the priest. Only the high priest could offer up the sacrifice of Messiah. The only other one who could do it is Messiah...as the Priest King."

"Is it crucial," I asked, "that He was both Priest and King?"

"It is. Think about it. What would happen if the judge deciding your case could become your defense attorney and still remain the judge—your case is over. So if the King of the universe, the Judge of all existence, God, the Almighty...becomes your Priest, your Defense Attorney...then your case is over, your guilt is over, your judgment is gone. And there's no more condemnation."

"So if the Judge of all becomes your defense, then all judgment is gone."

"Yes. And He has...and it is. The Almighty has become your Defense Attorney. That means you're free...in the miracle of the Priest King."

The Mission: The Judge of all has become your Defense Attorney. Therefore, start living today a judgment- and condemnation-free life.

Psalm 110:4; Zechariah 6:12–13; Romans 8:31–34

The Priest King

THE APOSTASIA

THE TEACHER PLACED an old brown book on the wooden table in the Chamber of Books and turned to a page so faded one could barely make out the words on the right side or the image on the left.

"It looks like a worn-away image of Adam and Eve," I said, "in the garden."

"It is," he said. "But we speak now not of the creation but the apostasia."

"What's an apostasia?"

"In the Book of Second Thessalonians it is written that the age will not end until first comes a falling away. The words *falling away* are a translation of the Greek word *apostasia. Apostasia* comes from two Greek root words. The first, *apo,* means to depart from. The second, *stasis*, means the stand or state of. So *apostasia* means to depart from one's stand and from one's state. Thus, before the end of the age there will be a mass departing, a moving away from the stand of faith, from the Word of God, and from truth. So the first meaning of *apostasia* has to do with faith and the Word. But the second concerns the departure from the state of being."

"Why is that?" I asked. "How do the two go together?"

"The creation came from the Word. From the Word comes the creation. So the departure from the Word will lead to a departure from the state of being."

"What does that mean?"

"Look at the book," he said. "On one side is the fading away of the Word. On the other is the fading away of the image of creation. An age that witnesses the falling away from faith and the Word will also witness a falling away from the image of creation, from the state of being. It means that before the end of the age, there will not only be a falling away from faith, but a falling away from being...the departure of men from the stasis or state of manhood, the departure of women from the stasis or state of womanhood, of fathers from the state of fatherhood, of mothers from the state of motherhood, and of man from the stasis and state of humanity."

"So what does one do in the days of apostasy?"

"In the age of departure from the Word, you must hold all the stronger. You must commit to hold all the more strongly to the Word, the faith, and the stand. And the more you hold the Word, the more you will find your stasis, the person you were created to be...And you will stand."

The Mission: Take a command from the New Testament and fully carry it out today. Commit to live your life all the more by the Word of God.

Ephesians 6:13; Philippians 2:15; 2 Thessalonians 2:3;
2 Timothy 3:1–4

The Stasis

THE YOM

THE TEACHER HAD asked me to meet him in the Chamber of Vessels. He was wearing a white linen robe and standing in front of the Temple veil.

"Is that the robe of the priest?" I asked.

"No," he said, "it's a robe worn on 'the Yom,' 'the Day,' the holiest day of the year, Yom Kippur. It's what observant Jews wear on the Day of Atonement. It's called the *kittel*. It's actually a burial shroud."

"A burial shroud? Why would they wear that on Yom Kippur?"

"Because Yom Kippur is a shadow of the Day of Judgment, when all is sealed, when we will all stand before God face-to-face beyond the veil, and when all sin is dealt with and all evil separated from God forever."

He was silent for a few moments as if lost in thought. Then he spoke. "And those who have chosen the darkness and to reject the salvation given them will have chosen separation from God, which is hell. For, in the end, there are only two destinies: heaven and hell...heaven and God's mercy for those who have chosen salvation. And the key is there on Yom Kippur, as the high priest enters the presence of God, bringing with him the blood of the sacrifice, the atonement. Of what does that speak?"

"The blood of Messiah, the sacrifice, the atonement."

"Yes. But note, the high priest must take the blood from outside the holy place, from the altar in the court, *before* he passes beyond the veil into God's presence. So too it is here, outside the holy place of God's dwelling, that we must each partake of the atonement, on this side of the veil, in this life, and in this world, where the altar of Messiah is...while we still have breath and before we pass beyond the veil to the other side. And what then comes after that day?"

"The Day of Atonement leads into the Feast of Tabernacles."

"Yes, the last and greatest of celebrations, the shadow of heaven. You see, God's will is not hell, but heaven...so much so that He would even give up His own life and bear hell and judgment in our place. And I am convinced that if it was only you or me who needed to be saved, if it was only one person, He still would have done it. It is Yom Kippur's ultimate mystery, that it is God Himself who becomes our Kippur, our sacrifice on the altar...and the greatest love we could ever fathom...the love we must come to know and take part in...before we pass beyond the veil...on that Day."

The Mission: No one knows when they will pass beyond the final veil. Live this day as if it were your last. What must you do?

Romans 14:11–12; 2 Corinthians 5:10, 20–6:2; 1 John 4:17–18

The Mystery of the Three Yom Kippurs

THE SECRET OF THE DESMIOS

ARE YOU WILLING," he asked, "to be part of an experiment?"

"OK," I replied.

He led me to a dimly lit chamber. There was some sunlight streaming in from a small open window and a wooden stool on which he asked me to sit. So I did.

"You need to stay here," said the teacher, "until I get back."

So I sat there in the darkness, trying to keep my mind occupied with things unrelated to my surroundings. But I ended up spending most of my time thinking about how slowly time was elapsing in that room. Finally he returned.

"How was it?" he asked.

"Taking into account the circumstances," I said, "pretty bad."

"And yet Paul the apostle went through the same thing, but not as an experiment, but as a major part of his ministry and life."

"Imprisoned in something like this?"

"Imprisoned often in something much worse than this. In such circumstances it would have been natural to grow angry, frustrated, depressed, bitter, and hopeless, to let one's heart be darkened by the darkness of his circumstances. But Paul never did. From one of his prison cells he sang praises, from another he ministered God's love in hope of bringing salvation to his captors, and from yet another he wrote the sacred words of Scripture. Out of his imprisonment came forth the Word of God. He was called a *desmios*, a prisoner. *Desmios* speaks of one who is bound, shackled, impeded, even disabled. But the desmios Paul, even in prison, was never bound. Even in chains, he was never shackled. And even confined to the walls of a dungeon, he was never disabled or impeded. In fact, it was as a desmios that Paul, from prison, would minister to millions of lives throughout the ages. Paul refused to be defined by any circumstance, bound by any chain, hindered by any impediment, or limited by any set of walls. He knew that no chain can bind the will of God. Therefore, if you live your life to the fullest of God's will, you will live unshackled and unstoppable. Live in the secret of desmios . . . and you will walk unbound."

The Mission: Nothing can stop the one who walks fully in the will of God. Be that person and break every chain and obstacle to the contrary.

Ephesians 3:1; 4:1; 6:19; Philippians 4:13; 2 Timothy 2:9

Ambassador in Chains

THE TZIPPURIM

IN THE BOOK of Leviticus," he said, "a unique sacrifice is performed on the day of a leper's healing—the sacrifice of the *tzippurim*, the birds, specifically two birds. The priest takes the first bird and sacrifices it over running water. Then he dips the second bird in the water and blood of the first. Then, with that blood and water, the leper is sprinkled seven times and pronounced clean. Centuries after the giving of the ordinance, a leper named Naaman is told by the prophet Elisha to dip himself seven times in the running waters of the Jordan River. He obeys. And as he does, he is healed of his leprosy. Note the reappearance of the ancient elements: the leper, the running water, the dipping, the number seven, the healing. But the difference is it's not a bird in the waters, but a man."

"And the other life," I said, "the sacrifice. And if it's a bird for a bird, then the sacrifice would have to be a man for a man...and it would have to be brought to the same running waters, the Jordan River."

"Centuries later, the other life appears. Messiah, the sacrifice, comes to the same running waters, to the Jordan River. And who is waiting there? John the Baptist, of the line of Aaron, a priest, the very one given charge concerning the sacrifice by running waters. The sacrifice must be joined to the running waters. So John dips Messiah in the running waters of the Jordan. And what is the baptism? The symbol of Messiah's sacrifice. So a priest symbolically performs the sacrifice in the running waters where the leper was cleansed and healed."

"But that priest dipped, baptized, multitudes of others in those same waters."

"Yes, just as the second bird was saved by being dipped into the waters and blood of the first. So they were baptized, for the forgiveness of sins, to be cleansed. They were the spiritual lepers. In fact, hidden in the ancient Greek translation of the ordinance, when the priest dips the bird in the water, the word used is *baptize*. As it is written, 'We are baptized, dipped, into His death.' We all come as lepers, the unclean and the cursed. But the sacrifice for the cursed has been offered. 'Thus we are no longer outcasts or unclean.' For the unclean becomes clean, the cursed become blessed, and the leper is no more...in the miracle of the sacrifice by the running waters."

The Mission: Immerse every part of your life in Him. Then walk in the power of freedom, cleansing, restoration, and the breaking of curses.

Leviticus 14:1–9; Matthew 8:1–3; Romans 6:3–4; 1 John 1:7

The Mystery of the Tzippurim

THE STATE OF THROUGHNESS

WE WERE SITTING in the same sandy plain where the teacher had previously drawn symbols and letters in the sand. He now drew two symbols. I remembered them from an earlier lesson.

"The Alpha and the Omega," I said. "The symbols of God."

"Yes," said the teacher. "The Alpha is the first letter in the Greek alphabet. So God is the Alpha, the Beginning of all things and the Reason all things exist. And the Omega is the last letter. So God is the Omega, the End of all things and the Purpose for which all things exist."

The teacher then drew a horizontal line connecting to the two symbols.

"And this," he said, "is everything else...including you."

"Me?"

"If God is the Beginning and the End, then what does that make you?"

"I guess it makes me *not* the Beginning and the End."

"But it's human nature *not* to know that. If you live *from* yourself, you've become your own Alpha. If you live as if you yourself are the reason and motive for everything you do, then you've made yourself your own Alpha. And if the reason for your living is yourself, then your living has no reason. The line becomes a circle...On the other hand," he said, "if you live *for* yourself, to serve yourself, with yourself as your own goal and end, then you've become your own Omega...which is to have no real purpose...another circle."

"I guess then most people live as their own Alphas and Omegas," I said. "So how then should we live?"

"As this line. You live as that which is neither the Reason nor the Purpose, not the Beginning, nor the End...but the middle...Your life becomes the vessel for His purposes, the instrument for His end. You live for a Reason and a Purpose greater than yourself. And that's when you find the Reason and Purpose for your existence. You make Him your Beginning and your End, the Reason and Purpose for everything you do. You do everything *from* Him and everything *for* and *to* Him. You become the vessel through which flow His love, His power, His purposes, His Spirit, His life, and His blessings. It is the state of *throughness*. Discover it, and your life will be filled with the blessings of the Alpha and the Omega, the Beginning and the End."

The Mission: Live today in the state of throughness. Make Him your Alpha, the reason for everything you do, and your Omega, the One for whom you live.

2 Corinthians 4:7; 2 Timothy 2:21; Revelation 1:8

The Omega Stone

LORD OF THE TWO VANISHING POINTS

WE WERE STANDING in what had to be the largest open expanse I had yet seen in that desert. It was late in the day. The western sky had grown orange with the setting of the sun.

"It's as if you can almost see forever," said the teacher. "Do you know how to say *forever* in Hebrew?"

"How?" I replied.

"*L'olam*," he said. "It means forever and yet more. It means *that*," he said, pointing to the sunset. "*L'olam* literally means to the vanishing point. God is forever. God is l'olam, to the vanishing point. So if God takes our sins on the cross, where does He take them to?"

"To the vanishing point," I said.

"Yes, and so God took our sins *to* the vanishing point and vanished with them...l'olam, to forever away, an eternity away, and beyond."

"Beyond forever?"

"It could be said. You see, God is not only *to* forever. God is *from* forever, in Hebrew, *m'olam*. So He not only takes our sins from here to eternity, but from eternity to eternity...the distance *from* forever and *to* forever."

"As far as the east is from the west," I said.

"Yes, just as the scapegoat carried away the sins of the people on the holiest day of the year...It was from the west to the east, the plane of infinity..."

"To the vanishing point."

"How far," he asked, "is the distance between God and us, between His holiness and our sinfulness?"

"It's infinite," I replied.

"And that's why we could never save ourselves. That's why it had to be God Himself...as He alone is from the vanishing point and to the vanishing point, m'olam l'olam, from forever and to forever. It's the distance of God...and the distance of His love for you. And in the prayers of Israel He is called *Melekh Ha Olam*, the King of the Universe. But it also means King, the Sovereign of the Vanishing Point. As it is written, 'From the rising of the sun, to the setting of the same, the name of the Lord is to be praised.'"

"From everlasting to everlasting, forever...and forever."

The Mission: Ponder the length of God, the breadth of your salvation, and the love God has for you that spans from everlasting to everlasting.

Psalms 103:12; 113:3; Ephesians 3:18–19; 1 John 1:9

The Days of Eternity

THE PRICE OF THE PRICELESS

IMAGINE," SAID THE teacher, "if there was a treasure hidden in that field. Imagine it was worth a hundred times the value of everything you owned. But the field was for sale. And the asking price was equal to everything you owned. So you sell everything you have and purchase the field. The treasure is now yours. How much did it cost you to buy the treasure?"

"Everything I had."

"No," said the teacher. "It didn't cost you anything."

"But I had to pay for it with everything I had."

"For the field," he said, "but not for the treasure. The treasure was beyond your ability to buy, even with all your possessions. It was, in effect, priceless. And yet it was free. What I just told you was the parable Messiah gave of a man who buys a field in order to gain the treasure hidden within it. What do you think the treasure represents?"

"Salvation? Eternal life? The blessings of God?"

"All correct," he said. "You can never earn or warrant God's blessings, or His salvation, or eternal life. A million years of perfect works couldn't purchase it. It's priceless. And yet it's given freely, apart from any work, undeserved, and solely by the grace of God. That's the treasure. But there's another side to the story. Though the treasure is free, it causes the man to go out and do everything he can, use everything he has, let go of everything he can let go of, and give everything he can give in response to having found the treasure. Salvation is the treasure beyond price and yet given freely to all who freely receive it. But the treasure is so great, that if you truly receive it, if you realize what you have, it will lead you to do everything you can, to use everything you have, and to give everything you can give in response to having found it. If you've truly found this treasure, then it must lead you to love God with all your heart, mind, soul, and strength, and to love others as yourself, to forgive as you have been forgiven, to give as you have been given to, to make your life a gift of love, and to do all this in joy in light of the treasure that has now come into your life. If you've found the treasure that is beyond price and freely given, then live a life that is of the utmost of value and the greatest of worth, and do so freely. This is the way you possess the priceless."

The Mission: In view of the treasure freely given, pay the price of the priceless. Give all you have and are. Live all-out. Apprehend the field.

Matthew 13:44; Luke 18:22; Philippians 3:7–8; 2 Peter 1:4

The Heavenly Exchange

CAMPING IN HEAVEN

IT WAS SUKKOT, the Feast of Tabernacles. The students were sleeping outside in sukkahs—tabernacles of branches, wood, and fruit. I was one of them. During the night, the teacher paid me a visit. We sat and talked through the night in the light of the full moon that penetrated the branches.

"This is how it looked," he said, "in Jerusalem, in the days of the Temple. The Holy City was filled with tabernacles inside of which the people of Israel lived for the seven days of the festival. They were to dwell as they did when they journeyed through the wilderness to the Promised Land, as a commemoration. Is there anything strange about that?"

"They were camping out in their homeland, living in the Promised Land as if they were still living in the wilderness."

"And what does the Promised Land ultimately represent? Heaven. And what does the wilderness represent? The journey to heaven ... our days on earth. So if those in the Promised Land are living in tabernacles to remember how God kept them when they journeyed in the wilderness, will not we in heaven remember our days on earth and give thanks to God for His keeping us through our journeying there? You see, in the Feast of Tabernacles, the two realms, the Promised Land and the wilderness, come together. And that joining bears witness of a mystery: The realm of heaven and the realm of earth are joined. What you do in the earthly realm touches the realm of the heavenly. And what is done in the heavenly realm touches the earthly. While on earth, you are to store up treasures in heaven. And what you bind on earth is bound in heaven. When you pray, you are to pray that as it is in heaven, it will be on earth. And as you pray on earth, you are to enter the heavenly throne of God. Messiah is the joining of the heavenly and the earthly. So those who live in Messiah are to live in both realms, in the joining together of the two realms. You see, in the realm of salvation, heaven is not only there and then, but here and now. Learn the mystery of the Feast of Tabernacles and the secret of living in the realm of the heavenly even now. For if those in the Promised Land can dwell in the tabernacles of the wilderness, then we on the wilderness journey can dwell even now ... in the tabernacles of heaven."

The Mission: Learn the secret, while living in the earthly realm, to dwell in the heavenly realm. Live in the realm of heaven and earth as one.

Leviticus 23:40–43; Ephesians 2:6; Revelation 7:9

Camping in Heaven

THE SHEPHERD AND THE FISHERMEN

IT WAS IN a place like this," said the teacher, "far into the wilderness, where an old shepherd was tending his flock by a mountain and a desert bush. He had no idea he would become the deliverer of an entire nation."

"Moses," I said.

"And then there were the fishermen casting their nets into the waters, having no idea they would one day become some of the most famous people who ever walked the earth...the disciples. There's a pattern," he said. "Moses, in his former life, was a shepherd who led his flock through the desert. God would then use him to shepherd a nation and lead the flock of Israel through that same wilderness. The disciples in their former lives were fishermen. God would use them to become messengers of Messiah...fishers of men. Their former lives corresponded with their redeemed lives."

"So God takes the former life and redeems it to use for His purposes."

"He does," said the teacher. "But the mystery is deeper. God created and purposed them from the beginning to become what they would become. So it wasn't that Moses became the shepherd of Israel because he was a shepherd of sheep. It was that Moses became a shepherd of sheep...because he was to become the shepherd of Israel. And it wasn't that the disciples became fishers of men because they were fishermen. Rather, they became fishermen...because they were to one day become fishers of men. So it is for all of God's children. And so it is for you. When you look back at your life, you will find hidden within it this mystery. You'll find a Moses in the wilderness...a fisherman in a boat. Your life was a mystery waiting to be redeemed...a mystery in which was embedded the seeds of His purposes to be used for His glory. It wasn't that He happened to discover your life and then decided to use it for His purposes. It was that you were what you were because God had purposed from the beginning what you would one day become. Your life was a shadow of that which it was made to become. So commit every part of your life, all that you have and all that you are, to the will and purposes of God. And your life will become that of a fisherman become an apostle, a shepherd become a deliverer...all that it was created and called and formed to become, all it was *waiting* to become...from the beginning."

The Mission: Look back at your life. What is it that you were meant to do and be? Take steps today to all the more fulfill your calling.

Exodus 3:1–8; Jeremiah 1:5; Matthew 4:18–20; Galatians 1:15;
2 Timothy 1:9

The Heavenly Pattern I–IV

ALTAR OF THE HEAVENLIES

HE TOOK ME back into the chamber that housed the stone replica of the Temple. "That," he said, pointing to his right, "is the brazen altar, the altar on which the sacrifices were offered up and by which the people were reconciled to God. On the Day of Atonement, after the sacrifice was complete, the high priest would take the blood and enter through those two golden doors into the holy place. He would then go beyond the veil into the holy of holies where he would sprinkle the blood on the ark of the covenant in between the wings of the golden cherubim. Everything begins with the altar. What does it foretell, the altar of sacrifice?"

"The offering of the final sacrifice," I said, "the sacrifice of Messiah."

"On what altar?" he asked.

"On the altar of the cross."

"Yes," he said. "The cross is the ultimate and cosmic altar of the ultimate and cosmic sacrifice, the Lamb of God. But the altar of sacrifice was only one part of the Temple. What about the rest?"

"What do you mean?"

"People see the cross as if it was the end of salvation. But the altar of sacrifice was never the end, but the beginning. It is the altar of sacrifice that gives access, the ability to enter through the Temple doors, to walk beyond the veil, and to stand in the holy of holies. The altar begins the journey. So then, the cosmic altar must give you cosmic access...that you might begin a cosmic journey. The altar of Messiah's sacrifice gives you access to go where you never could go before, to open doors you never before could open, to enter into that which you never before could enter, and to walk a path you never before could walk. This cosmic altar gives you the power to enter the realm of the holy and, in the Spirit, to stand in the heavenly places, in the holy of holies, in the actual dwelling place of God. Learn the mystery and the magnitude of this altar and enter beyond the veil...For if the altar of sacrifice opened the way that one might dwell in the holy place, then the altar of Messiah's sacrifice has opened the way for you to dwell in the heavenlies...and the realms of glory."

The Mission: Bring your life totally inside the cross. It is a doorway. Use its access to go where you never could before.

Exodus 40:6; Leviticus 16:12–14; Hebrews 4:14–16; 10:19–23

THE MYSTERY OF AUTUMN

HE LED ME into the Chamber of Vessels and to a room within it that had several platforms built into its walls. It was almost identical to the room he had taken me to months earlier when he shared of the spring holy days. But its contents were different. On one of the platforms was a shofar, the ram's horn; on another, a brass laver for washing; on another, fruit; and on another, three large scrolls.

"Tell me the theme," said the teacher, "that binds all these things together."

"The autumn holy days," I said.

"Very good. Do you remember what I shared with you about the cycles of the biblical calendar?"

"That the sacred Hebrew year has two cycles or clusters of holy days, the spring cycle and the autumn cycle. And in each cycle, the holidays are joined together not only in their timing but in their themes."

"And what is the theme of the spring cycle?" he asked.

"The beginning, salvation, freedom, rebirth, new life, Passover, the Lamb."

"And now we move to the autumn cycle and to the mystery it holds. In the natural realm, as the spring is about beginning, the autumn is about ending. So it is in the biblical year. As the spring cycle opens the sacred year, the autumn closes it. So the autumn holy days are all about the ending, and closing up that which began in the spring."

"And what are their themes?" I asked.

"The end," he said, "the end of the harvest, the return, the sounding of the trumpets, the regathering, the repentance, man and God face-to-face, the judgment, the redemption, the kingdom of God, and all things returning to Him...the closing."

"If the spring cycle speaks of the beginning and Messiah's first coming, then the autumn cycle would speak of His second coming...and the end."

"Yes. And what will the end of the age be? It will see the end of the harvest, the regathering and return of His people, the trumpets of His coming, man and God face-to-face, the judgment, the kingdom of God, and all things returning to Him. The spring cycle reminds us that Messiah is the Lamb. But the autumn cycle reminds us that He is also the Lion, the King, the Almighty, and the Lord of all. Remember that. And live your life accordingly...just as we now live between the Lion and the Lamb."

The Mission: Dwell on the Lion of Judah, the coming King. Live in the power of the Almighty, strong in that which is good, and bold as the Lion.

Daniel 7:13–14; Matthew 24:14; Revelation 11:5; 14:15; 19:16

The Holy Day Finale

THE TENTH OF AV REDEMPTION

H E LED ME back to the ruins of the ancient house in which he had read aloud from the Book of Lamentations. We sat down. He reached into his pocket, pulled out a coin, and gave it to me. It was dark and worn, with an image of what appeared to be three towers enclosed by an ornamental circle.

"Did that come from this place?" I asked.

"No," said the teacher, "far from this place. It's a coin from the Spanish Empire...coins that altered history and fulfilled an ancient mystery. It was here," he said, "that I shared with you of the day of calamity in Jewish history, the Ninth of Av." He set the coin down on a stone. "Centuries ago the land of Spain constituted one of the greatest of refuges the Jewish people had ever known. But in the late fifteenth century it all ended as the Spanish monarchs gave the Jews until August 2 to flee the land or be killed. August 2 was the Ninth of Av, the Hebrew date on which calamities have befallen the Jewish people through the ages. On that day the Spanish harbors were filled with ships carrying Jews fleeing for their lives. But there was more to the story. Three of the ships waiting to sail from the harbors of Spain had a different purpose. The year was 1492."

"Christopher Columbus!"

"Two momentous events of world history, taking place in the same year, the same land, the same week, the same harbors...happening one day apart."

"Why?" I asked.

"What would come from the journey of those three ships?"

"The discovery of America."

"Yes," said the teacher. "So in the midst of the calamity of 1492, when the Jewish people lost their greatest land of refuge, God was working through those same events for redemption. On the very day after the calamity, on the Tenth of Av, from the very same land and harbors, three other ships would set sail to discover the New World. America would become the greatest refuge the Jewish people would ever know outside of Israel. And so every child of God's kingdom has this promise: He will turn every sorrow into joy and work every calamity into redemption. And even in the midst of calamity, the seeds of redemption will already be there...a redemption that begins on the Tenth of Av."

The Mission: Remember the Tenth of Av times of your life, how God turned your sorrows into blessing. And know that for every Ninth of Av in your life, God will always give you a Tenth.

Psalm 126; Jeremiah 31:1–16; Joel 2:25; Revelation 7:16–17

The Ninth of Av Mystery

INTO THE GARDEN

I T WAS LATE afternoon. We were sitting inside one of the gardens of fruit trees.
"A question," said the teacher. "What was God's first act toward man after the creation?"

"To create woman?"

"Before that?"

"I don't know."

"It was to take him somewhere."

"Into the garden."

"'The Lord God took the man and placed him in the Garden of Eden.' God's first act toward man was to bring him to a place of life, fruitfulness, and blessing. And when did God bring him into the garden?"

"On the sixth day."

"Messiah died on the sixth day, Friday. And what happened to Him that day after the crucifixion, the work of redemption, was finished?"

"They took Him down from the cross and laid Him in the tomb."

"But it wasn't just any tomb," said the teacher. "What do the Scriptures say of that place? 'In the place where He was crucified there was a garden, and in the garden, a new tomb.' It wasn't just a tomb...It was a *garden* tomb...a tomb in a *garden*. On the sixth day God brought man into a garden. So on the sixth day man brought God into a garden, into a garden tomb. A garden is a place of life, but a garden tomb is a place of death. So God brought man into a place of life. But man brought God into a place of death. The Garden of Eden was a place of blessing. But the Garden Tomb was a place of sorrow. The Garden of Eden was the place of God's creation. The Garden Tomb was the place of man's creation. So God brought man into the place of God's blessings. But man brought God into the place of man's curse. Why? God allowed Himself to be brought to the place of our curse to give us the power to leave that place, that He might once more bring us to a place of life, and to a life of His blessings."

The Mission: It is the way of the sacrifice and dying to self that leads into the garden. Choose to walk in that way and enter the blessings of the garden.

Genesis 2:15; Song of Solomon 6:2; Luke 23:43; John 19:41–42

The Sixth Day Revelation Mystery

THE END OF THE SCROLL

E TOOK ME into the Chamber of Scrolls. There on the table was the scroll of the Torah rolled out to its end.

"Do you remember," said the teacher, "what I told you about the most mysterious day of the Hebrew year, *Shemini Atzeret*, the Gathering of the Eighth Day?"

"The last day of the sacred year, the day after the end...the day that represents the beginning of eternity."

"Yes. And do you know what is done on that day? The Torah scroll, which has been continually unrolled and read on every Sabbath of the year, comes to its end. Then begins the sacred rolling back of all that has been unrolled throughout the year...A fascinating thing," said the teacher. "When you read the prophecies concerning the end of ages, you find the image of the scroll and the act of rolling it up. In Isaiah it is written, 'The heavens shall be rolled up like a scroll.' And in the Book of Revelation, the same imagery reappears, 'And the sky departed as a scroll when it is rolled up.' And then at the end of Revelation concerning the end of the present order, it is written that before eternity, 'earth and the heaven fled away.' Heaven and earth depart; the old creation is gone. The scroll is finished, the story is ended, and the day after the end, Shemini Atzeret, the Eighth Day, the day of forever, begins."

The teacher paused to look down at the scroll.

"And do you know what is read at the end of the scroll before it is rolled up?"

"No."

"The last words written on this scroll are about the journey's end. Moses goes up the mountain to catch his first glimpse of the Promised Land, to leave his earthly existence, and to be with God. And the Israelites finish their journey through the wilderness. So Shemini Atzeret speaks of the day when our journeying through the wilderness will end, the completion of our earthly existence, and the passing away of this world. It tells us that we must always leave the old before we can enter into the new. And it reminds us that this life is not the destination, but the journey to the destination. So live your life and every moment of your life in light of that, in light of the end, in light of the day when the old will flee away, and of your first glimpse of that of which you had only dreamed...as the scroll is rolled up together."

The Mission: What is it in your life that you must bring to an end in order to enter the new that God has for you? Roll up the scroll today.

Deuteronomy 34; Isaiah 34:4; Revelation 6:14; 20:11; 22

The Alpha and Omega Scroll

THE CHILDREN OF LEAH

WE WERE SITTING on the ridge of a hill overlooking one of the tent villages of the desert dwellers, watching the women going about their daily tasks and breaking to talk and sometimes laugh.

"Do you know who Leah was?" asked the teacher.

"I've heard of her," I replied. "One of the matriarchs of Israel?"

"Yes. Leah was married to Jacob. Jacob's true love was Rachel. But he had been tricked into marrying Leah instead. In the end, he married both. But of all the matriarchs of Israel, Leah had the unhappy distinction of being unloved. And she knew it. It was the deep wound she always carried, the unceasing sorrow of her life. We have no idea how many tears she cried because of it, but undoubtedly they were many. But then something happened...Leah became fruitful, even more fruitful than Rachel. And when Leah bore her third son, she named him *Levi*. From Levi came the priesthood of Israel, and from Levi was born Moses. Through Moses came the Passover, the Exodus, the Ten Commandments, the Law, the sacrifices, the holy days, and the Tabernacle...the priesthood, the high priests, and the Temple. Through Moses, the children of Israel would enter the Promised Land. And through Moses would begin the writing of the Word of God, the Bible."

"Who else did Leah bear?" I asked.

"Judah," said the teacher. "From Judah came David. And from David came the royal house of Israel, the kings and princes of God's nation. From Judah came the kingdom of Israel and the words *Jew* and *Jewish*. And from Judah came Yeshua, Jesus, the Messiah, the hope and salvation of the world...all this from the Leah's womb. God chooses the children of Leah...even to this day."

"And who are the children of Leah to this day?"

"Those who, through sorrows, wounds, rejection, emptiness, broken dreams, broken hearts, frustration, discontentment, pain, tears, emptiness, or simply the longing for something more than they have on earth...become born into the kingdom, born of God...and chosen for great and mighty things, the vessels through which His love and redemption come to the world...For God especially loves the unloved and the unlikely...the children of Leah."

The Mission: Commit any sorrow, rejection, frustration, or broken dream into His hands. Believe Him to bring out of it the blessings of Leah.

Genesis 29:31–35; Isaiah 54:1, 4–8; Revelation 5:5

THE LAW OF CHANGE

THE TEACHER WAS standing to the side of a large circular stone, an upright wheel of sorts.

"What is it?" I asked.

"A stone in the form of a wheel," he said. "In ancient times it could be used to seal the entrance of a tomb. Try moving it."

So I did, but the stone didn't budge.

"Try harder," he said. I tried again, but still there was no movement.

"Just a little bit more."

I pushed with all my strength. Finally, the stone began to roll just a little. "What did that show you?" asked the teacher.

"I'm out of shape?"

"You were seeking to move an object at rest. It was a new action. It required new momentum. In order to begin that momentum, you had to concentrate all your strength into moving it just a few inches. That's physics. The universe resists new motion, change. So with an object at rest, and with new momentum, you have to concentrate the power into a smaller space in order to get things moving—the law of new momentum."

"So that's how to get the ball rolling," I said. "But how does it ..."

"Apply to you?" he said. "The same law applies to the spiritual realm. God calls us to change. *Change* means new action, new motion, and new momentum. The universe resists new momentum. The universe resists change. So in order to initiate change in your life, you must concentrate as much power and energy, as much decision, thought, focus, and resolve, into the smallest of motions. The bigger the change, the greater the concentration of power needed. That's why, when dealing with change, it is wisdom to take first one small step, but to put everything into it, and then the next step and the next. When Moses was called by God, the first thing he did was to take off his sandals—the first step, the smallest of motions—but it changed the world. The first thing the apostles had to do was to drop their fishing nets—the first step and the smallest of motions— but it would as well change the world. Apply the law of change, and the power of God to the first step, and you'll get the ball rolling ... and you might even end up changing the world."

The Mission: What is the change, the new course God is calling for your life? Focus your energy into the first step and apply the law of new momentum.

Exodus 3:5; Mark 1:17–20; Mark 2:11–12

Spiritual Gear Shifting & the Secret of True Change

THE TISHRI REVELATION

THE TEACHER LED me into one of the smaller rooms within the Chamber of Scrolls.

"Tishri," he said, "is the most intense of Hebrew months...the month that closes the sacred Hebrew year. And if the sacred Hebrew year holds the mystery of the age, then the closing month of the sacred year, Tishri, will hold the mystery to the closing of the age. And could it be that Tishri also holds the mystery to the closing of God's Word itself?"

"The closing of the Bible? The Book of Revelation?"

"Yes, could the month of Tishri hold the mystery of Revelation?"

At that he retrieved one of the scrolls and unrolled it on the wooden stand.

The Book of Revelation," he said, pointing to the scroll. "Tishri is the seventh month of the sacred year, seven, the number of completion. And what do we find in the Book of Revelation? It's saturated with the number seven. And how does Tishri, the seventh month, open up?"

"With the Feast of Trumpets?"

"'And I saw the seven angels,' said the teacher as he read from the scroll, 'who stand before God, and to them were given seven trumpets.' What do we see in the Book of Revelation? The Feast of Trumpets. And what else is Tishri? Yom Kippur, the Day of Judgment. And what do we see in Revelation? 'The hour of His judgment has come.' And as man and God stand face-to-face on Yom Kippur, so too in the Book of Revelation. In the month of Tishri, God is proclaimed King. So too in Revelation. And in Tishri comes the Feast of Tabernacles, the greatest of celebrations, the kingdom feast, and the time of tabernacling with God in Holy City. So Revelation closes with God's kingdom on earth, celebration, and God tabernacling with His people in the Holy City, as it is written, 'Behold the tabernacle of God is with men.'"

"You forgot one," I said. "Tishri closes with Shemini Atzeret, the mystery day."

"Yes," said the teacher, "the day that speaks of eternity. And so Revelation closes with the same day, the day of eternity... 'and they shall reign forever and ever.' You see," he said, "God's purposes have only perfect endings. And so for those who let Him write their story, the ending is the same... perfect. Their ending... is heaven."

The Mission: In the end, we will appear in the light of God with nothing hidden. Prepare for that day. Remove all darkness. Live now in total light.

Leviticus 23:23–44; Revelation 8:2; 14:7; 19:16; 20:4; 21:3; 22:5

The Lion of Tishri

IMAGINE

I MAGINE," SAID THE teacher, "that there existed a world where people wore jewelry in the shape of an electric chair...where models of electric chairs crowned the pinnacles of sacred buildings, where people sang songs about one particular electric chair. Imagine a world where people found in this electric chair hope, mercy, love, forgiveness, restoration, redemption, and new life. What would you think?"

"I would think," I replied, "that it was crazy."

"Yes, but with one slight change, what I just described was *this* world. Just replace one instrument of capital punishment with another and you have earth."

"Replace it with what?

"Replace the electric chair...with the cross. The cross is as much an instrument of execution as is the electric chair, the gallows, or the guillotine. But what makes it different from every other instrument of execution is that Messiah, the Son of God, died on it. And that changes everything. We live in a world where people wear jewelry in the shape of an instrument of capital punishment, where sacred buildings are crowned with reproductions of this instrument of death, where people sing songs about it, and where multitudes find in it love, hope, mercy, and new life. What does this reveal?"

"How radical it is."

"Yes, and how radical is the power of God in Messiah. To take an instrument of execution and transform it into an object of love and mercy, in which people find hope, grace, and new life—only the Messiah, only the Son of God, could make such a thing a reality. An instrument made to bring death now brings life...now causes us to come alive...an instrument of judgment now causes us to be released from judgment...the most evil object of ancient times now transforms into the most powerful sign of love the world has ever seen—that's the power of God. And so in that same object is the power to turn every darkness in your life into light, every sorrow into joy, every evil into good, every sin as white as snow, every failure into victory, and every death into resurrection. That's the miraculous and radical power of the execution stake that has become the sign...of everlasting love."

The Mission: Apply today this most radical power to turn darkness into light, defeat into victory, and death to life. Start turning things upside down.

Isaiah 52:13–15; John 3:14; 1 Corinthians 1:18–28; Ephesians 1:6–7

The Radical Love

THE DAYS OF ONE-ETERNITIETH

WHICH IS MORE valuable," asked the teacher, "that which is common or that which is rare?"

"That which is rare," I replied.

"And which is more valuable: that which is rare or that which is extremely rare?"

"That which is extremely rare," I said.

"How valuable is this life?" he asked. "How valuable is your time on earth?"

"I don't know."

"Is it rare or is it common?" he asked.

"I would say it's common as it's what everybody has. And it's made up of countless moments, every day, every year."

"So then it wouldn't be especially valuable," he said. "Now let's say your time on earth is one hundred years. But time goes on for a thousand years. Your time on earth becomes rare, one-tenth of time. And what happens after a million years have gone by? How long was your time on earth?"

"One ten-thousandth."

"One ten-thousandth of time, one in ten thousand...very rare. Now what happens when we consider eternity? What happens to your time on earth in light of eternity?"

"It becomes once in eternity."

"So your life on earth becomes one-eternitieth," he said. "How rare is that?"

"Very," I answered.

"Infinitely rare," he said. "So how valuable is your time on earth?"

"Of infinite value."

"That's correct. Your days on earth come around only once in an eternity...only once. Every moment you have, comes around only once in an eternity...and never again. Every moment is a once-in-eternity moment, a one-eternitieth moment. Therefore, every moment is of infinite value...infinitely priceless. Then how must you live?"

"Appreciating every moment."

"Therefore make the most of every moment. For it will never come again. Whatever good you would do, do it now. Treat every moment as if it was infinitely rare and of infinite value...because it is. For every moment, and your life itself, comes around only once in an eternity."

The Mission: Whatever good you would do, do it now. Treat this day as if it comes around only once in an eternity—because it does.

Psalm 90:10–12; Romans 13:11–14; 2 Corinthians 6:1–2; Ephesians 5:16

I Shall Not Pass This Way Again

THE PURPLE MYSTERY

THE TEACHER WAS holding a purple cloth and running it through his fingers as if inspecting it. He then placed it in my hands.

"The color purple," he said. "It was woven throughout the Tabernacle, on the veils and curtains, even in the garments of the priests. Now look at the cloth I gave you. It's purple. It should be made up of purple threads, but it's not. If you look closely, you won't find any."

So I examined it. And as he had said, I was unable to find in the cloth a single purple thread. Instead, it was made up of tiny blue and red threads finely woven together.

"Purple is the joining of blue and red. And if you looked at the veils of the Tabernacle, you would find the colors blue, purple, and red. The colors appear in the instructions for building the Tabernacle over and over, the same three colors and in the same order 'blue, purple, and scarlet.'"

"Why?"

"The Tent of Meeting was the place of the joining, the reconciliation, the meeting of two realities, God and man."

"And so the colors represented God and man?"

"Blue is the color of the sky, the heavens...representing the heavenly, God. So the blue is first."

"And the color red...scarlet?"

"In Hebrew, the word for *man* is *Adam. Adam* comes from Hebrew word for red. Red is the color of the Middle Eastern earth from which man came. And scarlet red is the symbol of sin and guilt. Red is the color of man...So then what is purple? Purple is the joining of blue and red. And so it speaks of the joining of God to man, heaven joined to earth. But for there to be purple, it must be a total joining...the joining of all that is holy to all that is not, all of God to all that is us...to all that is *you*...so totally joined that God will appear as sin. And as that total joining drew near, the Heavenly One was beaten and mocked and made to wear a crown of thorns...And then He was covered with a robe. And do you know what kind of robe it was? It was a purple robe...a purple robe to cover the One in whom heaven and earth, God and man, blue and red...become completely one...purple."

The Mission: Today, join all that is red to all that is blue. Join all that is ungodly to God and God to the ungodly—so much so, it becomes purple.

Exodus 26:31; John 19:1–6; Philippians 4:5–7; 1 Timothy 1:15

The Purple Mystery I–IV

THE SABBATH OF AGES

THE TEACHER HAD invited me and a handful of students to join him in his living quarters for a Sabbath meal. The sun had just set. We sat around a table filled with food as one of the students lit the two Sabbath candles and the teacher gave thanks for the meal. We began to eat.

"What is the Shabbat," asked the teacher, "the Sabbath day?"

"It's the day set apart from all other days of the week," said one student.

"Yes," said the teacher. "And what else?"

"The last day of the week," said another. "It's what comes at the end."

"And what else?" he asked.

"The day of the Lord," I said, "the day of rest, the holy day."

"And what do the Jewish people do on the Sabbath?" asked the teacher.

"They rest from all their weekly labors," said one of the students, "and devote the day to prayer, to the Word, to worship...and to God."

"The Sabbath holds a mystery," said the teacher, "a shadow of what lies ahead. The age to come is the age of Shabbat, the Sabbath age. For as the Sabbath day comes at the end of the week, so the Sabbath age will come at the end of history. And as the Sabbath day is set apart from all the other days of the week, so the Sabbath age will be set apart from all other ages. It will be the Sabbath of ages, the age of the Lord, the age of rest. It is then that the nations will rest from war, and the Jewish people will rest from their burdens, and peace will cover the earth, and the lion will lie down with the calf. And as the Sabbath is Israel's day, so the Sabbath age will be Israel's age...a holy age, an age wholly consecrated to God and blessed. When Messiah spoke of the Sabbath and His relationship to it, what was it that He said?"

"He said, 'The Son of Man is Lord of the Sabbath,'" I replied.

"Yes," said the teacher. "And so with the Sabbath age, the Son of Man, Messiah, will be Lord over it. And therein lies the key. Even before the coming of the Sabbath age, you can live in its blessings now. If Messiah is Lord of the Sabbath, then if you will truly make Him the Lord over every part of your life, then the Sabbath age will begin for you now. For where Messiah is Lord...there is the kingdom...and the age of Shabbat."

The Mission: Make the Lord of the Sabbath all the more the Lord of your life. And learn the secret of dwelling in the Sabbath age even now.

Exodus 20:8–11; Isaiah 11:1–9; Mark 2:27–28

The Age of Shabbat

THE DAY OF TIME AND TIMELESSNESS

THIS TIME IT was I who led the teacher into the Chamber of Scrolls, or rather, he allowed me to go in first. I had asked him to take me there to the scroll of Isaiah. I had a feeling about something, and a question. Together we unrolled the scroll to Isaiah 53.

"Please translate it," I said, "literally."

So he began reading Isaiah's prophecy of the Messiah who dies for the sins of others.

"'For He shall grow up before Him as a tender plant,'" he said.

"In the Hebrew, it's written in the future tense?"

"It is," he said.

"Read more."

"'He is despised and rejected of men, a man of sorrows and acquainted with grief.'"

"What tense?" I asked.

"The present tense," he said, and then continued reading. "'Surely He has borne our griefs and carried our sorrows.'"

"The tense?"

"It's in the past tense."

"How can that be?" I asked. "It was a prophecy, written before the events took place. How could it be written in the past tense as if it already happened, before it happened? And how can the same event be written in all three tenses, the past, the present, and the future?"

"Because," said the teacher, "it is the event of God's redemption...an event in which are contained the past, the present, and the future, every event of every sin...in the past tense and covering all the sins of the past...in the present tense and covering every present sin...and in the future tense and covering all sin that is not yet but which will be...It is the event of tenses and times, of past, present, and future, that no sin and no event is beyond its power to touch and redeem. For the love of God is not bound by time...It is time that is bound by the love of God. What happened two thousand years ago on an execution stake in the land of Judea is a mystery...the day of time and timelessness and yet containing all time and times in the love of God."

The Mission: Your future is already contained by your salvation and covered by it. Ponder this fact and, by it, be at peace and live in confidence.

Isaiah 1:18; 53; 1 John 1:7; Revelation 13:8

Divine Hebrew Time Travel

THE PROMISED LAND WILDERNESS

WE STOOD AT the edge of a precipice overlooking a vast desert panorama.

"The Israelites wandered for forty years in a wilderness like this to get to the Promised Land. One can only imagine their relief and joy when they finally reached their destination, when their days in the wilderness were over. What does the Promised Land represent?"

"The place God brings you to...your destiny, the goal of your calling, the place of joy, blessing, completion, where His promises are fulfilled...a shadow of heaven."

"And what then does the wilderness represent?"

"The place you go through to get to the place God is calling you to—the place of the journey to the place where God's promises are fulfilled."

"So the wilderness and the Promised Land are two very different places, a land of hardship and a land of rest and blessing. But here's what you need to know: The wilderness is also *part of the Promised Land*. In the Promised Land is the Wilderness of Judea...the Wilderness of the Arabah...the Wilderness of the Negev, which alone makes up more than half the land of Israel. Most of the Promised Land is the wilderness. The wilderness is also part of the Promised Land. Now listen," he said. "In your life you will have wilderness, times of hardships, losses, challenges, tears, as well as times of waiting, or of simply not being in the place you want to be. Remember then this truth: In God, even the wilderness can be part of the Promised Land. In other words, the wilderness is not outside the purposes of God, nor outside His promises. It's the place God brought you to. And God will use it to accomplish His purposes and to fulfill the calling and promise of your life. In God, even the wilderness becomes a place of blessing. And if God is with you, then your journey is also part of your destination. And your life on earth is also part of heaven's domain. And so even while you journey on earth, you can live a heavenly life. Therefore, no matter where you find yourself, no matter what your circumstance, no matter what your surroundings, rejoice, press forward...and choose to live in victory even now...For in the end you will see it...that your wilderness was part of the Promised Land."

The Mission: Heaven is not only after this life, but within it. Live this day as the commencement of heavenly life, the beginning of heaven.

Isaiah 35:1–10; 40:3–4; 51:3; Hebrews 11:9–10

The Midbar

THE RUSSIAN CASE

WE WERE GAZING up at the night sky when I brought up something I had been pondering.

"I was thinking," I said, "of the Abrahamic covenant. And I was wondering about the case of Russia, and the Soviet Union. The Soviet Union didn't bless the Jewish people. Yet it was one of the world's two greatest powers."

"It's not a mechanical formula" he said, "or one in which every repercussion must be instantly manifested. But let's look at it. In the late nineteenth century the Russian czars and the czarist government embarked on an all-out war against the Jewish people living in Russian lands. They instigated mass uprisings of violence against them called *pogroms*. They sought to drive the Jews out of the land or else murder them. But the Abrahamic covenant decrees that what you do to the Jewish people shall be done to you. And as it had been done to the Jewish people...mass uprisings began in Russia against the czar and the czarist government, and overthrew them. Russia was now communist, the Soviet Union. But under Soviet rule, antisemitism continued, and the Jews of Russia were oppressed and treated as a captive people. So the Soviet Union was itself as a captive civilization. Then in the Second World War, the Soviet Union warred against Hitler, the enemy and destroyer of the Jewish people and was critical in his defeat and in liberating the Jewish people from the concentration camps. So it had blessed the Jewish people militarily..."

"So the Soviet Union was blessed militarily...to become a superpower."

"Yes, but within its borders, the Jewish people were still oppressed..."

"So according to the Abrahamic covenant they would be blessed militarily and yet cursed and oppressed domestically."

"And that is exactly what happened. But then, in the late 1980s, the Soviet Union ended its oppression of the Jewish people and granted them freedom to leave. And it just so happened that at that very same time Russia and Eastern Europe were released from the oppression of communism. 'I will bless those who bless you and curse those who curse you.'"

"Amazing," I said, "a promise given to a Middle Eastern tent dweller determining the rise and fall of superpowers."

"Because the God of that tent dweller is real...and faithful. And when He gives His Word, you can depend on it. It is stronger, much stronger, than kings and superpowers."

The Mission: Ponder this fact: the Word of God is stronger than powers, even superpowers. Today, live accordingly, and use that power for victory.

Genesis 12:3; Deuteronomy 7:9; Jeremiah 16:15

The Chaldean Secret of World History I–III

THE INEXPLICABLE EQUATION

USING A STICK, the teacher began drawing letters and symbols in the sand, first a zero, then a plus sign, then an X, then an equal sign, and then the letter A. $0+X=A$. "It's an equation," he said. "The zero will stand for a life and a movement brought to nothingness, that of the Jewish Rabbi Yeshua. His followers had believed that their leader was the Messiah. But it all came to a traumatic end with His public execution on the cross. They were demoralized, traumatized, in mourning, broken, and fearing for their lives. If ever a movement was crushed, it was this one. But then something happened. The crushed and broken followers of the crucified Rabbi were transformed into the most confident, unbowed, unafraid, and overcoming people the world has ever witnessed. Their despair was replaced by hope and their mourning by an unconquerable joy. Their fear of persecution entirely vanished, as did their fear of death. They became unstoppable, and they changed the course of world history."

He pointed to the A and continued, "The A represents all that took place after that transformation, an Alpha, for the new beginning. So what happened? How do you go from 0 to A, from death and total crushing devastation to the overcoming of the world? From mourning to joy? 0 plus X equals A. It is X that changes everything. So, what is X?"

He paused for my answer. I remained silent, so he continued. "Let's do the math: X must be the opposite of 0. 0 is death. And the power of X must be greater than the power of 0. So the power of X must be greater than death. And as 0 was a real and historical event, so X must be an equally real and historical event. It is X that turns mourning into joy and nullifies the fear of death. And it is X that is the overcoming of 0. So X must equal nothing less than the overcoming of death. So what is X?"

"The resurrection," I said.

"Yes, X can only equal the resurrection. For only the resurrection could bring them from 0 to A, from death and from the tomb to the new beginning so powerful it changes the history of the world. There can be only one answer. X equals the empty tomb, the risen Messiah. And if you're in Messiah, then you have the same equation over your life, and the same power, the power to turn the end into the beginning, death into life, despair into hope, and mourning into joy. And when you find yourself broken and at your end, it will be that power by which you rise up...and overcome the world. It is that power alone that explains the equation of your life and that will bring about the equation of your victory—the power of X."

The Mission: Apply today the power of X. Do what you could not have done and live what you could not have lived except by the power of X.

Acts 4:7–33; Romans 8:10–15; 1 Corinthians 15:3–8; 1 John 1:1–4

The Resurrection Factor

THE SECRET NAME OF GOD

WE SAT ON the bottom ledge of my window looking out at the star-filled night.

"God has a name," said the teacher, "a name that has to do with you, and you only, a secret name that only you know the meaning of."

"I don't understand."

"When Jacob wrestled with God, God asked him for his name. And when he spoke it, God changed his name from Jacob to Israel. But did you know that Jacob also asked God for *His* Name that night?"

"And what was the answer?"

"It doesn't say. But soon after the encounter, Jacob would reveal the Name of God. He would build an altar and call it El Elohai Yisrael. *El Elohai Yisrael* means God, the God of Israel. What was he saying?"

"Israel was Jacob's own name. So for Jacob to call Him 'the God of Israel' is the same as naming Him 'the God of me.'"

"Exactly. And throughout the Scriptures, God would refer Himself as the God of Israel. You see, it is God's will to join His Name to the name of His people. And the Scriptures say that if you're born again, you are also Israel. So you must also join your name to the Name of God. It means it's not enough to call Him God. You must give Him a new name."

"How can I give God a name?"

"He must become the God of you, the God of..." he paused, "your name. The one named John must know Him as the God of John. The one named Mary must know Him as the God of Mary. It is His will that your name be in His Name and that His Name be joined to yours, just as His life is joined to your life and His identity to your identity. His secret Name is as sacred as all His other Names. It means He's the God of your existence, your life, the God of your past, the God of your needs, the God of your wounds, the God of your heart. It means He's the God of you and all you are...So it is the Name that only you and He fully know the meaning of. So Jacob asked God for His Name and then discovered it. And for those who truly know Him, this is the name they too discovered...the sacred Name: the God of you."

The teacher left my room. I was now alone, gazing out the window at the star-filled sky and pondering the love of the One who bore a secret Name...the God of me.

The Mission: Speak God's secret name—the God of you, the God of your name. Ponder what that means: He's the God of all you are and has chosen your name in His.

Genesis 32:29–33:20; Psalm 18:2; Isaiah 48:1

Yeshuati

THE ISHMAEL MYSTERY

WE WERE OBSERVING one of the encampments, where a group of children were at play, darting in and out of the tents, hiding, laughing, and running after and away from each other.

"It was in a camp of tents like this," said the teacher, "a camp with children, that an event took place upon which has hung the peace of the entire world...a mystery of two children in a desert tent camp."

"Which camp was that?" I asked.

"The camp of Abraham. It was there, because of an ongoing conflict, that Ishmael, Abraham's firstborn son and the son of his maid Hagar, was, in effect, exiled from the rest of the family. Isaac, Abraham's son by his wife Sarah, remained. Imagine being Ishmael. To him, it was the end of a world, the loss of everything he had known, his father, his birthright, his inheritance, the promises of God, the covenant, the land of Israel, everything. It would be enough for the boy to grow embittered, jealous, and angry. And yet God blessed Ishmael and made of him a great nation. His descendants would end up far more numerous than those of Isaac and with far more land. But the conflict between Ishmael and Isaac would continue through the ages. From Isaac would come the nation of Israel and the Jewish people, to whom was given the land of Israel and the covenant."

"And who," I asked, "are the children of Ishmael?"

"They were called the *Ishmaelites* and from ancient times were identified with the Arabs, even by ancient and pre-Islamic Arab tribes. Mohammed himself claimed to be Ishmael's direct descendant and, in the Koran, exalted him. The blood of Ishmael undoubtedly flows throughout the Arab world, and it is there that his identity and mantle have been taken up. Ishmael's fury has, more than once, shaken the world, and continues to rage against his brother Isaac, the nation of Israel, and over what? Over the birthright, over the land, over Abraham's legacy, and over Isaac's inheritance. And so the fate of the world has rested on this ancient mystery that began in the tents of Abraham. What does the mystery of Ishmael tell you? Never let bitterness take root. Never allow yourself to live as a victim. Never dwell on the blessings you don't have and miss all the blessings you do. And the one who is most blessed is not the one who has been given the most, but the one who has most received and most dwells on the blessings he's been given."

The Mission: Live today not focusing on the blessings you don't have, but dwelling on all the blessings you do.

Genesis 17:20–21; 21:12–21; Ephesians 4:30–5:21

The Ishmael Mystery

THE SEASONS OF THE HARVEST

WE WERE SITTING under an olive tree inside one of the school's gardens. The teacher bent down, picked up one of the olives that had fallen to the ground, and held it in his hand.

"The harvest is great, but the laborers are few," he said. "That's what Messiah told His disciples about the harvest of salvation, a harvest that every child of God must reap. On what harvest was He basing this?"

"The harvest of Israel, I would guess."

"That's correct. But the harvest of Israel was not only one but many. Its harvest was made up of many harvests. First came the barley harvest in the spring, then the wheat harvest, then the fruit harvests, the fig harvest, the date harvest, the pomegranate harvest, the olive harvest, and the grape harvest into the autumn. Every harvest had a season. If you didn't reap the harvest in the appointed time of that harvest, you missed your one chance."

He let the olive fall back to the ground.

"And so too it is with the harvest of salvation. It is not only one but many. The harvest of salvation are many harvests. And every harvest has its appointed season and time. If you don't reap the harvest in its appointed time, its season will pass, and the time and chance you had to reap it will be gone."

"What harvests?"

"The harvest of your loved ones. You have only a limited time to share with them of God's love. If you don't reap, the season will pass. The harvest of your friends. The harvests of those in other lands who need to hear the word of salvation. The harvest of acquaintances and those you will only see for a short time. To each person in your life there is a specific time and season. They won't always be in your life...and you won't always be in theirs. Every season passes. People will pass in and out of your life...and then from this world, and the season is over. And then you yourself will pass from this world. And whatever you didn't reap will be forever gone. So make the most of your time in this world. Lift up your eyes and see the fields that are all around you. Don't miss the harvests given to you or the appointed times in which to reap them. Don't wait to give the word of salvation to those who need to hear it. Don't delay in showing your love, or to forgive or to ask to be forgiven. Don't wait to bear the fruit your life was called to bear. Every season must pass. And only that which was reaped in its season will remain forever. And these are the seasons of your harvest."

The Mission: Today is the day of the harvest. Share the good news. Show your love. Forgive. Bless. Don't wait. The time of your harvest is only now.

Ecclesiastes 3:1; Jeremiah 8:20; Matthew 9:37; Luke 10:2

Seasons of the Harvest

THE FACES OF GOD

IT WAS A sunny day. We were standing next to a pool of water formed of the desert rains. I was looking at my reflection in the water when I noticed the reflection of another. It was the face of the teacher. He was standing over my shoulder.

"Imagine," he said, as I watched him speak through the waters, "imagine seeing the face of God. In Hebrew the word for *face* is *panim*. Do you notice anything about it?"

"It has *im* at the end," I said. "So that would make it plural?"

"It would," he said. "So the word *face* is not really face but *faces*. So to speak of the face of God in Hebrew is to speak of the faces of God. And what is a face? It's not the essence of the person or being, but the appearance. It's how you know and recognize another. And how do you see the face of God? By the panim…through His many faces. You see them in His blessings, in His provisions, in every good thing that has blessed your life, in the love He wove into those who once cared for you, in every kindness shown to you in your time of need, in every good given to you by His people. In their loving you, He was loving you. In their helping you, it was He who was helping you. And in their encouragements, it was He who was encouraging you. In their panim, in their faces, was the panim, the face of God. And as Mary Magdalene looked into the face of God but didn't realize it was His face, so too in your life you have looked into His face and not realized it was the face of God. But if you look, you'll see it. For 'blessed are the pure in heart, for they shall see God.' Look always for the good, for the holy, and the beautiful, and you'll find, and you'll see the face of God."

He turned from the waters. I did likewise. We were now face-to-face.

"And one more thing," he said. "When you allow your life to be used as a vessel of His love and your heart to be moved by His Spirit, then when people look at you, they will see the face of God. Now look back at the waters. Do you know what you're looking at?"

"What?"

"A face," he said. "You're looking at…one of the faces of God."

The Mission: Today make it your aim to see the faces of God in all their appearances. And be one of them.

Genesis 32:30; Numbers 6:24–27; Matthew 5:8; 2 Corinthians 3:7, 13, 18

The Face of Messiah

BAAL ZEVUV

HE LED ME inside a cave about halfway up the side of a relatively small mountain. Inside the cave was a chamber that appeared to be a storage place for varied archaeological artifacts. He bent down, picked up one of the objects, and carried it to the cave's entrance, where we examined it in the light. It was a strange metal figurine, a man wearing a long conical hat with his right arm raised as if to throw something.

"This is Baal," he said, "an idol of Baal."

"They sacrificed their children for that..." I said.

"Baal was Israel's substitute god, their anti-god, the god of their turning away from God. For whenever they turned away, Baal was always there to meet them and fill in the gap. So Baal was the god of whatever it was they chose in place of God. And thus he appeared to them in many different forms and with many different names. Baal was the god of their apostasy. To him they sacrificed their children, and because of him, in the end, they would be destroyed. One of the names by which he was known was *Baal Zevuv*."

"What does it mean?" I asked.

"*Zevuv* means flies," said the teacher. "So *Baal Zevuv* means Lord of the Flies. Baal Zevuv was later translated into Greek and became a name you might be more familiar with."

"What name?

"Beelzebub."

"Beelzebub? Isn't that the name of the devil?"

"It is."

"Baal is the devil?"

"The devil has many masks. Baal is one of them. Baal is the substitute god, and the devil is Baal. So if one turns from God, the devil is always there to fill in the gap. He's the god of one's turning away from God. Whatever one would choose in place of God, that's the form in which he will appear. That's why when a nation turns away from God, it moves not to the neutral—but to the satanic. The Baal of Russia was communism. The Baal of Germany was Nazism. The manifestations were different, but the end was the same. The enemy destroys those who worship him. So it is with all who worship Baal. So beware of idols. Beware of serving other gods, even the gods of your desires. Guard your heart, that God be your only God. For in the end, every other is Baal Zevuv. And Baal Zevuv is Beelzebub."

The Mission: Is there anything you're living for, serving, putting first, above God? See it for what it is—Baal Zevuv. Flee from it today like the devil.

1 Kings 18:21; 1 Thessalonians 1:9; James 4:7; 1 John 2:15–17; 5:21

The God of a Thousand Faces

THE DAY OF NEOGENESIS

HE HAD REMOVED the Torah scroll from the ark, laid it on the table, and opened it up to its beginning.

"Look," said the teacher, "the very first word of Scripture...*B'Resheet*. In Hebrew, the entire book is named after that word. It's the Book of B'Resheet."

He paused to look up from the scroll, then continued.

"The resurrection took place on a Hebrew holy day."

"The Day of the Firstfruits," I said.

"Yes. As the resurrection was the firstfruits of the new creation."

He turned his attention back to the scroll.

"The *B* in *B'Resheet* is just a preposition to indicate 'in.' The first word of the Bible is *Resheet*. When the ancient rabbis translated the Bible into Greek, the word *Resheet* became a word known throughout the world."

"Which word?"

"*Genesis. Genesis* is the translation of *Resheet*. And the book is the Book of Genesis. Now," said the teacher, "do you remember what the Day of the Firstfruits was called in Hebrew?"

"*Yom Resheet*," I said, "the Day of the Resheet...It's the same word! So He didn't only rise on a Hebrew holy day, but on the Hebrew holy day that's called the Day of the Beginning!"

"Yes," said the teacher. "The day on which Messiah rose contains the exact same word that begins the Scriptures, the universe, and the creation. And in Greek, the day Messiah rose was ..."

"The Day of Genesis! The resurrection is the new Genesis!"

"It's the Neogenesis," he said. "And what happened on the first day of creation? It was dark and void. And God said, 'Let there be light!' and there was light. So too on the Day of Neogenesis, it was dark and void in the tomb. And God said, 'Let there be light!' and there was light and new life. And from that empty tomb comes the power of Genesis, the power of Neogenesis to all who will receive it. In the deepest darkness of this world and of this life, it's the power of 'Let there be light!' and there is light. And in every ending, it's the power to call forth a new beginning, the power of Genesis, the power of a new creation. It is, for all who enter it, the power to be born again. For Messiah is our Neogenesis."

The Mission: Where in your life do you need a genesis? Take the power of the resurrection, the Resheet, and declare into your life, "Let there be Light!"

Genesis 1:1–3; Luke 24:4–7; 2 Corinthians 4:6; 5:17

The Genesis Day

LIVING FROM THE FUTURE

WE WERE STANDING in an open expanse. In the distance before us was a cluster of date palm trees.

"Imagine your goal is to get to those trees," said the teacher. "So you set your mind on going from here to there. But what if you did the opposite? What if you set your heart on getting from there to here? What if you did it backward, proceeding not from the starting line, but from the finish line?"

"I'm not getting it."

"If you do get it," he replied, "it can change your life. Messiah said, 'On earth as it is in heaven,' the heaven-to-earth principle. Do you remember what it was?"

"The direction of God and His blessings proceed from heaven to earth. Therefore, we must live our lives from heaven to earth."

"Yes. But what happens if we take it from the realm of space to the realm of time? Heaven is not just what's above us, but what's ahead of us. Heaven, in one sense, is that which comes at the end, at the end of earthly history and earthly life. So heaven is also what is yet to come, the future. So to live from heaven to earth, you must also learn the secret of living, not from the past, and not from the present...*but from the future*...from God's future."

"How does one live from the future?"

"Every problem you have will be answered, either in heaven or before. So the secret is to live not from the problem, but from the problem solved, from the answer, before the answer. You must choose to live not from your present crisis, but from its future overcoming, not from your present obstacle, but from its future breakthrough. You're in a battle. In the future that battle will be won. So don't live from the battle. Live from its future victory. As it is written, when you ask in prayer, believe you have received it, and in your asking, give thanks to God. Live from heaven, from the kingdom yet to come, from the life yet to be, even from the *you* you are yet to become. Fight the won battle, run the run race, accomplish the finished work, start from the finish line, begin from the victory, rejoice now from the joy at the end. Live now from what will one day be, and you'll live a life of blessing, and victory, on earth as it is in heaven."

The Mission: Learn the secret today of living from the future, fight your won battle, accomplish your done work, and live from the finished you.

Matthew 6:10; 16:18; Mark 11:24; Ephesians 4:1

As It Is in Heaven

THE MYSTERY SCROLL

WE WERE IN the Chamber of Scrolls when he gave me an assignment.

"There exists a scroll," said the teacher, "in this chamber unlike the rest."

"How is it different?"

"It doesn't look like the other scrolls, or much like a scroll at all."

"What does it contain?"

"The Scriptures, the Word of God, the divine revelation. It is, in essence, like the other scrolls, but possessing unique properties. It was made to be read by those who will never study and have never read the other scrolls. Even those who have no interest in reading anything, they will read this one. They will read it without even realizing they're reading it."

"Sounds like a pretty amazing scroll."

"It is," he said. "And this is your assignment: Find it."

"What does it look like?"

"It's covered in cloth of blue, brown, and white."

So I went searching throughout the Chamber of Scrolls to find the mystery scroll, going through every platform, every corner and recess, and every shelf of every case. But I couldn't find anything matching the description given me.

"Are you sure it's in this chamber?" I asked.

"Absolutely," he answered, with much assurance.

I searched again, but with no more success than before.

"I give up," I said. "It's definitely not here. If it was, it's not anymore."

"But it *is* here," he said. "I'm looking at it right now."

"Where?"

"Right in front of me," he said. "It's you. You are the scroll of God. You are the vessel on which He has now written His Word, His message of salvation, and His divine revelation. Your life is the translation of His Word, the translation of His love, the translation of His nature and His salvation. And it will be the best translation many will ever see, and the only translation some will ever read. Whenever they see His work in your life, His grace in your actions, and His love in your love, they will be reading the scroll. And now that you know where it is, you never have to lose sight of it again. Make your life the scroll of God...and His Word will reach the lost."

The Mission: Today, translate the Scripture into thought, action, reality, life. Make your life a scroll, a living translation of the Word of God.

Jeremiah 31:33; Matthew 5:16; 2 Corinthians 3:2–3

THE LOGOS CRUCIFIED

IT WAS A cool desert night. The sky above us was stunning in its clarity. Its deep black background made visible a vast multitude of stars, which in some places were so small and many that they fused into a white mist.

The teacher was gazing upward as he spoke: "'In the beginning,'" he said, "'was the Word...and the Word was with God...and the Word was God. He was in the beginning with God. All things came into being through Him, and apart from Him nothing came into being that has come into being.' Imagine that," he said. "All things came into existence through the Word   the earth, the oceans, the moon, the sun, the stars, the galaxies, and the universe itself, all came into being through the Word. And what is the Word?" he asked.

"The Word of God," I replied.

"Yes, but in the original language, the word for *word* is *logos*. And *logos* also means the cause."

"All things came into being through Him...the Cause of all things."

"The Logos caused the universe to come into existence. Therefore, the existence of the universe rests on the existence of the Logos."

The teacher gazed at the ground, then up again at the sky.

"But the cosmos is fallen," he said. "The world is darkened by evil, and this life by sin. 'And the Logos became flesh and dwelt among us...' The Logos *became* flesh and blood. Why? Because only that which is of flesh can die for our sins. Who died on the cross?"

"The Messiah."

"Messiah is the Logos. It was the Logos that died on the cross. The Logos was crucified. That means the Word was crucified. The Cause of everything was crucified. And if the Cause is crucified, nullified, then so too is the effect. The effect is nullified. It disappears. If the Logos dies, the cosmos is nullified...the old world dies...the old life dies, the fallen past dies...the old you dies. And if the Cause of existence is removed, then all the sins of your life are brought out of existence, as if they never existed in the first place. So for all who are in Messiah, the old is gone. And they become new, as it is written, 'If anyone is in Messiah, he is a new creation; the old has passed away, behold the new is come!' For the Logos has been crucified."

The Mission: The Logos has died, and with it, your old life. So stop letting the past affect you. Live free today in the newness of having no past.

Isaiah 43:18–19; 44:22–23; John 1:1–14; 2 Corinthians 5:14–17;
Revelation 21:1–5

The Keburah

THE POWER OF APOLUO

IT WAS A hard lesson, and hard to forget. The teacher had me go through the entire day wearing a cloth backpack filled with stones. Everything I did became a burden and a strain. At the end of the day he approached me and asked, "Would you like to keep carrying it or let it go?"

"Is that a serious question?" I replied.

"Release it," he said. So I did.

"I know," he said, "it was not a pleasant experience for you. But that's how many go through life...for years. In the Gospel of Luke, Messiah told His disciples to forgive. But behind the word *forgive* is the Greek word *apoluo*. When Pilate decided to release Barabbas from prison, behind the word *release* is the same word: *apoluo*. When Messiah saw a woman suffering from a condition that caused her to be crippled for eighteen years, He said to her, 'Woman, you are loosed from your affliction.' Then He touched her, and after eighteen years, she was healed. But when He said to her, 'You are loosed,' it was again the same word: *apoluo*. And when the believers of Antioch sent forth Barnabas and Paul to begin their ministry to the world, behind the phrase *sent forth* was again the word: *apoluo*."

"That's a lot of meaning for one word," I said. "What's the connection?"

"The connection and the key is this: *apoluo* means to forgive, but it also means to be released. If you don't forgive, you won't be released. You'll stay bound and imprisoned. But the same word speaks of healing. So forgiveness is linked to healing and the lack of forgiveness to the lack of healing. Those who cannot forgive cripple themselves. And the same word speaks of moving on and being sent forth for the purposes of God. If you don't forgive, you won't be able to move on or to let go of the old. Nor will you be able to be sent forth and fulfill God's calling for your life. So it is written: 'Forgive and you shall be forgiven.' But the word is *apoluo*. So it can also be translated as: 'Forgive and you shall be released.' 'Forgive and you shall be healed.'"

"Let it go," I said, "and you'll be set free."

"Yes," he said, "release it, and you yourself shall be released. Then you'll be free to move on with your life...and free to fulfill the calling for which you were born."

The Mission: Today, apply the power of apoluo. Release and you shall be released, loosed, freed, made whole, and sent forth.

Leviticus 25:10; Matthew 27:26; Luke 6:37; 13:12; Galatians 5:1

Notes on Forgiveness

UNDER THE HUPPAH

HE TOOK ME into an olive grove in which, in the midst of the trees, was a canopy, a large white cloth embroidered with decorations and held up by four long poles.

"It's called a *huppah*," said the teacher.

"What's a huppah?"

"The huppah is the wedding canopy. In the Hebrew marriage, the bride and groom exchange their vows and pledges under the huppah. And under the huppah, they become husband and wife."

"And what does it signify?"

"The covering of the bridegroom over the bride, and the covering of God over both of them. In the fourth chapter of Isaiah it speaks of the last days and the coming of God's kingdom on earth. It describes Jerusalem as filled with God's glory. And 'over all the glory there will be a covering.' Imagine, a covering from heaven over the glory of Jerusalem. But what covering?" he asked. "The mystery is revealed in the original language. The word translated as 'covering' or 'canopy' or 'defense' is much more than that. It's the Hebrew word *huppah*. In other words, in the days of the kingdom, the Holy City of Jerusalem will be covered by a..."

"Wedding canopy!"

"Yes, a wedding canopy, a huppah over all Jerusalem. And what will that mean? It will mean that Jerusalem will be married to God. And through Jerusalem, the world itself will be married to God. In that day everything will be joined to God. Every part of life, every earthly thing, will be married to the heavenly. And that which is married to God will become holy and glorious. And there's a secret here."

"Which is..."

"You don't have to wait for the kingdom to come in order to live in the blessings of the kingdom...even now. The key to living in the kingdom is to live under the huppah, under the wedding canopy. Spread the huppah of His covering over everything in your life. Bring everything in your life under His huppah. Marry every part of your life to God...and everything in your life will become holy and glorious...under the huppah."

The Mission: Spread today God's huppah over your life. Bring every part of your life under His covering and pronounce it "married."

Psalm 91:1–4; Song of Solomon 2:3–4; Isaiah 4:2–6

Under the Huppah

ADONAI

THE TEACHER BEGAN drawing letters in the sand.

"What is it?" I asked.

"It's the Hebrew word for *lord, adon. Adon* means the ruler, the owner, the master, and the one who's in charge."

"So *Adon* is the Name of God as Lord of the universe."

"Yes and no," said the teacher. "The word *adon* can be used for *any* ruler or master."

He lifted up his stick and added a small mark at the end of the word.

"Now," he said, "it's the Name of God, *Adonai.*"

"What's the difference?"

"*Adon* means lord. But *Adonai* means my Lord. And God's specific and sacred Name is Adonai, 'my Lord.' So in order to utter His Name, you can't just say 'Lord'; you have to say 'my Lord.' It means the only way to know God is to know Him personally, to know Him as your God."

"So then 'my Lord' is not just the One who rules, but The One who rules over me."

"Exactly. Adonai is the One to whom you submit your life, your will, and your heart. It means He's the One in charge of your life. If you call Him *Adonai,* 'my Lord,' then you have to follow His will above your own. But there's more to *Adonai.* To say 'my Lord' in Hebrew, should be *Adoni.* But God's Name is *Adonai.*"

"What's the difference between the two?"

"*Adonai* is 'my Lord' plural. Literally, to say *Adonai* is to say, 'My Lords.' What it means is that the reality behind the Name *Adonai* is so great that the Name can't contain it. So *Adonai* means my Lord followed by a multitude of exclamation points. It means He's my Lord!!!!!! And thus to use the sacred Name means you don't just follow Him and submit to Him, but you follow and submit to Him with a multitude of exclamation points, and with all your heart and zeal. The heart of *Adonai* is this: My Lord is so amazing that even saying Adonai, my Lord, cannot even begin to describe who He is. Let your heart learn what this one word truly means. And then live in light of it...and with exclamation points...For He is your Adonai!"

The Mission: Ponder and live the mystery of Adonai, make the Lord your "my Lord" whom you follow and submit to with endless exclamation points.

Ezekiel 36:22–23; Daniel 9:4; Zechariah 13:9; John 20:28

YHVH

THE CHILDREN OF THE EIGHTH DAY

I T WAS A warm, breezy morning. We were sitting on the side of one of the hills that overlooked the school.

"I believe I made a discovery," I said.

"I'd love to hear it," said the teacher.

"Shemini Atzeret is the Eighth Day...but there's another Eighth Day."

"And what day is that?"

"The resurrection," I said, "the day of the resurrection. The resurrection happened on the first day of the week. Therefore, it was the Eighth Day."

"It *was* the Eighth Day. So what does that mean?"

"The Eighth Day is about leaving the old creation..."

"Yes, and the resurrection is also about leaving the old life."

"The Eighth Day," I said, "is the day of transcending, of breaking out of the limitations of the finite and into the realm of the infinite."

"And the resurrection is also the day of transcending the old, overcoming the ultimate limitation, death, and thus every limitation."

"And the Eighth Day is the day after the end..."

"As is the resurrection...the day after the end of the old life, the old existence, and the power to live beyond it."

"So the two days," I said, "the day of the resurrection and the day of eternity, are joined together."

"And on what Hebrew holy day was the resurrection?" he asked.

"The Day of the Firstfruits."

"Yes," said the teacher. "The resurrection is the firstfruits of the age to come, the first manifestation of the Eighth Day, heaven. And when in the week do most of Messiah's people gather?"

"On the first day."

"Which means they gather on the Eighth Day. They gather on the Eighth Day because they are *of* the Eighth Day. For all who are of Messiah are given the power of the Eighth Day, the power to leave the old life, to transcend this creation, to overcome all limitations, to live after the end, and in the realm of the heavenly. So do not be bound by this age. Live beyond it. For we are not of this world...We are children of the Eighth Day."

The Mission: Learn the secret of living in the Eighth Day—beyond the flesh, beyond the world, beyond the self, beyond the old—in the beyond of now.

John 20:1; Acts 20:7; Romans 6:5–11; 12:2; 1 John 4:4

The Mystery of the Eighth Day I–III

AWAKE THE DAWN

HE HAD IN his hand a parchment and was studying its text. "It's from the Book of Psalms," he said. "Some translations render the passage as if it was speaking about waking up early. But it can literally be translated as, 'I will awake the dawn.' Imagine that! Imagine if you had the power to wake the dawn! Would you like to know how?"

"To wake the dawn?" I asked.

"Tell me," said the teacher, "why is it dark?"

"Because it's nighttime," I replied.

"Not really," he replied. "It has nothing to do with the time. We think of night as a period of time. And, of course, in one sense, it is. But night is not so much a period of time as it is a state of being. It isn't dark because it's nighttime. It's nighttime because it's dark. Night is the effect of the earth's turning away from the light of the sun. Night is the earth dwelling in its own shadow. God is Light. So when you turn away from God, you create the night. When you turn away from His presence, night comes into your life. When you turn away from His truth and away from His love, darkness comes to your heart. And you end up dwelling in your own shadow, in the shadow of your turning."

He paused a few moments before continuing to speak.

"So is the night," said the teacher. "What about the dawn? What is the dawn?"

"Dawn is when the earth turns away from the darkness and back to the sun."

"So how do you bring about the dawn? How do you cause a sunrise? You turn away from the darkness. You turn away from your sins, away from substitutes and distractions and idols. You turn away even from focusing on yourself and your own shadow. And you turn back to the Light. You don't have to wait for the dawn. You can cause the dawn to come. You can make the sun to rise. Turn away from the darkness. Turn away from *all* darkness, and turn to the Light. Then the Light will break through your darkness. Then the sunrise will light up your life. Then the joy of the morning will replace the tears of night. Imagine if you had the power to cause a sunrise! In Him, you do . . . Now awake the dawn!"

The Mission: Today, turn your eyes away from darkness. Turn them back to the Light. Cause the sun to rise. Awake the dawn!

Psalms 57:8; 112:4; Acts 26:18; Romans 13:12

She Like the Dawn

THE CENTRALITY FACTOR

HE LED ME to an ancient monument. It was too badly worn to tell what it was. "What is it?" I asked, "Or what *was* it?"

"It was a testament," said the teacher, "a monument, a tribute to a civilization that once believed itself to be unconquerable and unending, but which now can only be found in ruins and history books. If we were to look at those kingdoms and powers that once stood at the center of world history over the course of ages, what would we find? Thousands of years ago, we would have found the center of history in Egypt and Babylonia, and then in Assyria, Persia, Greece, Rome, Byzantium, and then the great European empires, and then Russia, and America. Now what if we had come from another planet and we knew that God had intervened in the history of earth...where would we expect His intervention to have taken place, in the outer periphery of history or in its center?"

"In the center of history," I replied. "And if He did act on the outer periphery, it would end up, by His acting upon it, in the center of history."

"It would," said the teacher. "And yet if we look at the center of world history from the days of the pharaohs to the age of the superpowers, there's no common thread, no common kingdom or power. Those at the center of history in the ancient world are on the periphery in the modern world. There's no common nation or people...except for one—the nation of Israel, the Jewish people. When ancient Babylonia was the center of the world, they were there. When it was Rome, they were there. From the Egyptian Empire to the British Empire, they were there. From the Persian Empire to the Soviet Union, they were there. From streets of Ur of Chaldea to the streets of New York City, only one nation has always been there in the center. If God were to use a people through whom to bring forth His Word and His redemption to the world, that people would remain at the center of history. And so they have. And it just so happens to be the same people through whom came the Book of books, the Word of salvation, and the One known throughout the world as Salvation. If God were to intervene in the course of this world..."

"Then He already did."

"And His Name is carved into the witness of history...the God of all nations...the God of Israel."

The Mission: Whatever is of God is in the center. Put the things of God in the center of this day. And make God the center around which your life revolves.

Deuteronomy 4:34–35; 32:8; Zechariah 8:23; Isaiah 2:3

The D328 Secret of World History I–II

THE JOSIAH PRINCIPLE

WE SAT IN the shade of an olive tree on a warm breezy afternoon.

"Josiah," said the teacher, "was one of the most righteous kings ever to sit on the throne of David. In pursuing God's will, he went up to the high place of Beth El, to break down the altars of the pagan gods. While doing so, something caught his attention—a grave. It was then that a mystery of centuries was revealed. The grave was that of a prophet who, centuries earlier, had come to Beth El with a prophecy: A man named Josiah would, one day, come to that same place and do exactly as Josiah had just done. But Josiah had no idea of the prophecy. He came there that day simply to do the will of God. And yet he did exactly as was prophesied centuries before he existed...the outworking of destiny."

"How does that work?" I asked. "Without knowing the prophecy, he fulfilled it. How do you fulfill God's plan for your life...your destiny?"

"I would call it 'the Josiah Principle,'" he said.

"Which is what?"

"How did Josiah, without knowing the prophecy, end up fulfilling it?"

"By following the way of righteousness?"

"Yes," said the teacher. "By following the will of God that he knew from the Word of God."

"But except for the prophecy, which Josiah didn't know," I said, "the Word of God wouldn't have told him exactly where to go or when to go for him to end up at the exact right place and time."

"But it did," he said. "And it will in your life as well. The Word of God will give you the overall direction and leading for your life. As you follow the direction of the Word, you will be led to walk into the exact and specific will of God that is your destiny. You see, the Scriptures are not so much focused on finding the will of God that you don't know, but on obeying the will of God that you do. Obey the will of God you do know, and it will lead you to the will of God you don't. Follow, with all your heart, that which is revealed, and it will lead you into that which is not...and as it was with Josiah, you will find yourself standing on a high place in the exact place, and at the exact time that was appointed for your life before the foundation of the world."

The Mission: Take God's Word today and obey it. By obeying the revealed will of God, you will be led into the unrevealed will of God—your destiny.

2 Kings 23:15–17; Psalm 37:23; Proverbs 2:20–21; 3:5–6; Ephesians 2:10

Entering Your Prophetic Destiny

THE NIGHT CANDLE

THE TEACHER LED me outside his living quarters to a terrace where we sat down by a table. On the table was a lit candle. The sky began to darken.

"When we first sat down," he said, "the sun was still shining, even on the candle. The light of the candle blended in with the light of the day. The two lights were in harmony. But then what happened?"

"It grew dark," I said.

"So now the light of the candle was no longer in harmony with its surroundings. It no longer blended in. As the sky darkened, the candle stood out more and more dramatically. It was not the candle that changed, but everything around it. So now it was shining in marked contrast to its surroundings and against the darkness."

"And what does this reveal?" I asked.

"The candle in the day," he said, "represents the believer who shines in the midst of a Christian civilization. Its light blends in with the surrounding culture. The culture is in harmony with the light, at least on the outside, and appears to support it. But the candle in the night represents the believer who shines in the midst of a post-Christian civilization, an apostate civilization, an anti-Christian, anti-biblical, anti-God civilization. Now the cultural supports and the external props are removed. The light of the Gospel is no longer in harmony with the surrounding culture. The surrounding culture now stands increasingly in opposition to the light. The light cannot blend in. It must now increasingly stand out in contrast to its surroundings, and increasingly shine against the flow. So if you had a choice, which candle would you rather be, the candle of the day or the candle of the night?"

"The candle of the day."

"But it is the candle of the night that changes the world. The candle that shines in the daylight can hardly be seen. But the candle that shines in the darkness can be seen miles away. It is at the very time when it's hardest to shine the light, that it is most crucial that you do. It is then that the light is most needed. And that is when the light becomes its most powerful. So never fear the darkness. You're a light. Shine into it, especially into the night...and you'll light up the world."

The Mission: Live today as a candle in the night. Don't fear the darkness or be intimidated by it. But shine all the more brightly against the night.

Matthew 5:14–16; 13:43; John 1:5; Philippians 2:15; 1 Peter 4:14

The Stars

THE I AM REDEMPTION

DO YOU REMEMBER," said the teacher, "at the very beginning, when I told you that when you speak of your existence you must speak the Name of God?"

"I Am," I said.

"Yes," he said. "But there's another side to it. We've all fallen. So when we speak of our existence, we speak of a fallen existence. But how can the Name of God be linked to that which is fallen, sinful, defiled, broken, and marred? If you say, 'I am sinful,' you're telling the truth, but you're joining the sacred name I Am to sin. And if you say 'I am unholy,' you're joining I Am to unholiness...and defilement. You're bearing witness against God. It could be called blasphemy...the I Am of God and the I am of man now infinitely separated from each other."

"Then what's the answer?"

"When Messiah died for our sins, it was I Am. It was I Am joining Himself, rejoining Himself, to our I am...to our fallen, sinful, and unholy I am. It was I Am joining Himself to our sins...I Am becoming sin, I Am joining Himself to all that is not I Am...that by so doing all separations would be ended. So when you find yourself saying 'I am condemned,' then look at the cross, and what will you see there? You will see I Am condemned. When you find yourself saying, 'I am guilty,' look at the cross and you will see I Am guilty. When you're hurting, you will see there I Am hurting. When you're broken and crushed, you will see I Am broken and crushed. And when you're rejected, you will see on the cross I Am rejected. And when you find yourself at your end, you will see I Am at the end...I Am finished. What happened there is a mystery...the Holy One joining His I Am to your I am, that nothing, no sin, no shame, no darkness, not even death, could ever separate you from Him again...that even in those things He will be there with you...He who is I Am has joined His I Am to your I am that your I am would be joined to His I Am. And this is the other side of this mystery...For after His death comes the resurrection. And it is in the resurrection that we find our new I am. For what is it that we find there? We find I Am alive...I Am victorious...And we find...I Am risen!"

The Mission: Let your fallen I Am be finished in His death and let His risen and victorious I Am become the I am of your life.

Exodus 3:14; John 8:58; Colossians 2:9–12

The I Am Revelation

MOUNTAINS AND CAPSTONES

WHEN THE REMNANT of Israel," said the teacher, "returned to the land, after their exile in Babylon, they knew it was the will of God to rebuild the temple. The man in charge of the rebuilding was Zerubbabel, a descendant of King David. But as they began the undertaking, they encountered resistance and conflict. And because of it their work was brought to a standstill. Then God spoke through the prophet Zechariah saying 'Not by might nor by power, but by My Spirit. Who are you, O great mountain? Before Zerubbabel you shall become a plain! And he shall bring forth the capstone with shouts of "Grace, grace to it!"' So then what was God telling Zerubbabel?"

"God would remove the obstacles and cause the temple to be rebuilt. And Zerubbabel himself would complete the work by laying the capstone."

"That's right," said the teacher. "And the prophecy would come true. What was the symbol, in that word, of the obstacles to God's purposes?"

"The mountain," I replied.

"And what was the symbol of the fulfillment of God's purposes?"

"The capstone."

"Do you notice anything about that?"

"They're both stone."

"Yes," he said, "both the obstacle to God's purposes and the fulfillment of God's purposes are made of the same substance, the same material. But it's even more than that. Where do you think the capstone came from?"

"A mountain?"

"Yes," said the teacher. "The capstone came from a mountain. And what does this reveal? God never promises that our lives will be free of obstacles, problems, crises, and adversities. He promises something better. He will use every obstacle in your life to bring to fulfillment the very purposes He has planned for your life. Every problem, every crisis, every adversity, every setback, and every sorrow will be turned around to bring breakthrough, blessing, and triumph. And in God, every mountain, every obstacle that has hindered God's purposes in your life, will, in the end, be turned around and become a capstone to bring about the completion of those very purposes."

The Mission: Today, see every problem, obstacle, trouble, and adversity as a mountain to be turned into a capstone. Take part in turning it.

Genesis 50:15–21; Isaiah 60; Zechariah 4:6–9; James 1:2–4

THE GLORY INSIDE THE TENT

IN THE DISTANCE before us was an encampment of desert dwellers. Their tents were dark, mostly black, and a few of a very dark shade of brown.

"What do you think the Tent of Meeting, the Tabernacle, looked like?" asked the teacher.

"I would imagine very impressive," I replied.

"Not really," he replied. "More likely it looked like one of these...much larger, but of a similar appearance. Its outer covering was of badger's skin. So its appearance would have been dull, plain, and unattractive. But if you were able to step inside, then everything changed. The first of its chambers was called the holy place. Inside the holy place was the table of the presence, the altar of incense, and the seven-branched menorah, each of gold, each a treasure of inestimable value. And if you ventured even deeper, you would find yourself in the holy of holies with the ark of the covenant, within which were the Ten Commandments and on top of which rested the glory of God. All these things were hidden from the outside and could only be seen from within. So what looked plain, dull, unattractive, and of little worth on the outside turned out to contain the greatest of treasures on the inside. What does this reveal?"

"You can't judge a tent by its coverings?"

"Yes, and much more than that. In the world, most things appear more impressive and attractive on the outside and on the surface than on the inside. The reality is less than the appearance. But with God and the ways of righteousness, it's the opposite. On the outside and on the surface it tends to look hard and unattractive. So the way of the cross and of sacrifice, on the outside, looks hard. But the deeper you go, the more beautiful it becomes. The deeper you go, the more treasures you find. So too the deeper you go into prayer and worship, the more awesome it becomes. The deeper you go into His presence, the more glorious it becomes. And the deeper you go into the love of God, the more golden it becomes. Therefore, go deeper...and deeper...and deeper still. Go ever deeper...beyond the surface, beyond the appearance, and beyond the tent skins...to the treasures and the glory that await only those...who go inside."

The Mission: Go beyond the curtains today, deeper and deeper into the tent of meeting to the innermost sanctum, until you find His glory.

Exodus 40:34–36; Psalm 27:4; Ezekiel 44:16; Hebrews 4:16

The Glory in Your Tent

THE SECRET HEBREW PROPHECIES

THE TEACHER WAS giving a lesson before a gathering of students in the open-air tent. Reading from a scroll of the Prophets, he expounded on the Hebrew prophecies of Messiah's coming: the prophecy of Micah that Messiah would be born in Bethlehem; of Zechariah that He would ride into Jerusalem on a donkey; and of Isaiah that He would be despised and rejected of men, die for sin, and yet become the light of the Gentiles. At the end of the lesson he left the tent and invited me to join him for a walk.

"Consider the Messianic prophecies," he said. "Each one created by God, each one unique, each containing a different piece of the mystery, a different promise of Messiah's coming. Each existed for centuries waiting for the day of its fulfillment. Many of these prophecies are mentioned in the New Testament, along with a particular Greek word used to speak of their fulfillment. The word is *plero'o*. *Plero'o* has to do with the filling up of that which was empty, as in the filling up of a cup. It is recorded over and over again that an event took place so 'that what was spoken by the prophet might be fulfilled' or rather 'that what was spoken by the prophet might be plero'o.'"

"So a prophecy is like an empty cup to be filled up at the appointed time."

"Yes," said the teacher. "But there's more to it. In the second chapter of Colossians it is written 'in Him you are complete.' But behind the word translated as 'complete' is the Greek word *plero'o*. So the word used of Messiah fulfilling the ancient Hebrew prophecies is the exact same word used of Messiah fulfilling your life."

He stopped walking, turned to me, and said, "Do you understand? Your life is like a Hebrew prophecy. You came into existence by God's ordinance. And as a prophecy is unfulfilled and empty until its fulfillment, so too your life was unfulfilled until the day you found Him. Your life was a shadow of what it was created to become. So every life exists to find its plero'o. And only in Messiah can the plero'o be found. Your life is as a prophecy in waiting, a prophecy of Messiah, unique from all others, a promise waiting for its fulfillment, and that can only be fulfilled by Messiah's coming...into your life. Messiah is your Plero'o. So make Him the aim and purpose of all you are and all you do. And He will fill every part of your being. For He is the Plero'o of your life...and your life is the prophecy of Him."

The Mission: Live today as if your life was a prophecy, existing solely to be fulfilled by His presence and, in that fulfilling, to glorify Him.

Philippians 1:6; Colossians 2:9–10; 1 Thessalonians 5:24; 2 Thessalonians 1:11

YOUR PRESENT AFTERLIFE

WE WERE SITTING on the top of a high mountain, a vantage point from which we could see a multitude of other high mountain peaks far into the distance, into the increasingly orange horizon of the sunset.

"How do you enter heaven?" he asked.

"You get saved," I replied. "You become born again."

"Yes," said the teacher, "but assuming you are saved, how do you actually enter into heaven?"

"You die," I said. "You die and go to heaven."

"So that's the only way?" he asked. "You have to die to get into heaven?"

"No? It's not the only way?"

"It *is* the only way," he said, "but there's more to it. In the New Testament the kingdom of heaven is spoken of as that which is beyond and not yet, and yet also as that which is here and now and in our midst."

"But heaven is the afterlife," I said.

"Heaven *is* the afterlife," he said. "It has to be. One must leave the old world to enter the new, and that which is of the flesh, to enter that which is of the Spirit. One must leave the imperfect of the earthly to enter the perfect of the heavenly. So heaven must be the afterlife. But..."

"But there's a *but*?"

"For the child of God, the heavenly life cannot be limited to the afterlife. It is too great to be contained in that which is not yet and not here. For the child of God, heaven has to be known and lived in this life as well."

"Then how do you enter it?"

"You have to die to get to heaven."

"But I thought you just said..."

"You have to die go to heaven," he said again. "So the key is to die. But the secret is, don't wait until you die in order to die. If you do, you'll never know the heavenly life until this life is over. But there's a way to die now even while you live. In Messiah you have that power...to depart from this realm, from the old and the earthly, even now. Die to your old life, and you will enter the new. Die to the flesh, and you'll live in the Spirit. Die to the earthly, and you'll enter the heavenly. Learn the secret of living in your afterlife now. It's as simple as dying and going to heaven."

The Mission: Today, live as if your life was over. Then enter your afterlife, beyond the flesh and the earthly, to live in the Spirit, in the heavenly.

Romans 6:4–11; 8:10–14; Galatians 2:20; Colossians 3:1–9

How to Enter Your Afterlife Now

THE GUARDIAN

COME," SAID THE teacher. "Let's go for a camel ride."

"To where?" I asked.

"To nowhere in particular," he said. "Just for a ride."

So we embarked on a desert journey to nowhere in particular. It was late afternoon when we began. We rode parallel to each other, slow enough and close enough to be able to carry on a continuous conversation.

"Many journeys in the Bible were made with camels. So it was with Rebekah. When she said yes to marrying Isaac, Abraham's servant immediately prepared to take her and her maidens on a long journey through a Middle Eastern desert. That was the mission for which he had been sent, to find a bride for Isaac and to bring her back to the groom. Imagine seeing it...a caravan of camels carrying on their backs a bride, her maiden, and all their possessions across the desert landscape. Rebekah was being led by a man she had never seen before, a stranger, the servant of Abraham. She was in his care. She was now his responsibility. He was her guardian for the journey. It was his responsibility to bring her safely through the desert and home to the tents of Abraham. Only he knew the way. Rebekah had no idea. So what did she have to do?"

"She just had to trust...trust his intentions, his knowledge, his leading, and his commitment to bring her where she had to go. And she had to let him bring her there."

"Now let's open up the mystery," he said. "Rebekah represents the bride. And Abraham's servant, the servant of the father, represents the Holy Spirit. And the servant's mission is to bring the bride to the Bridegroom. Thus it is the Spirit's mission and responsibility to lead you, to keep you, to protect you, to guard against your going off the path, and to bring you safely home. And since He alone knows the way, what must you do?"

"Trust Him to lead me where I need to go...and let Him lead."

"Yes," said the teacher, "the bride must be guided by the leading of the Spirit every day of her life. Each day she must let Him lead her and go where He leads. She doesn't need to know every detail of the journey or the path. She just needs to know Him who journeys with her, and to allow herself to be moved by His moving. And as she stays close to Him and goes as He leads, she will end up dwelling in the tents of the Father."

The Mission: Live today in the leading of the Spirit. Go only where He goes. Move as He moves. Let your every step be guided by His.

Genesis 24:51–61; John 16:13; Romans 8:14

The Isaac Rebekah Wedding Mystery I–III

THE MOSES PARADIGM

I T WAS A breezy and hot afternoon. We were sitting at a table in the shade just outside the Chamber of Books.

"I call it 'the Moses paradigm,'" said the teacher. "It's one of the most important keys of your calling. Moses led the children of Israel out of Egypt. But what happened before he did that? Years before the Exodus, God caused Moses to undertake his own exodus out of Egypt. Only after Moses's own exodus did Moses lead the Exodus of the Israelites out of Egypt. Moses brought Israel to Mount Sinai. But years before that event, God brought Moses to the same mountain, Mount Sinai. When Moses fled from Egypt, he came to the land of Midian and there entered into the covenant of marriage. Forty years later, Moses would bring Israel to the same land to enter into a covenant of marriage to God. Do you see the pattern?"

"Everything happened to Moses first, then to Israel."

"Yes. But it goes back even further. When Moses was a baby, God caused Pharaoh's daughter to draw him out of the Nile River and thus save his life. It was because of that that he was given the name *Mosheh*, or *Moses*, which means *drawn out*. And what was Moses's calling and destiny? It was to *draw out* his people from the land and ways of Egypt. So his entire life and calling, his destiny, was to do that which was done to him, to save others by drawing them out. The Moses Paradigm is this: The key of your calling and life is found in what God has done for you. In the same way that God has touched your life, so touch the lives of others. The disciples fulfilled their calling when they made disciples of others, as they themselves had been made disciples by Messiah. Paul fulfilled his calling when he imparted to others the revelations that God had imparted to him, and when he ministered grace to the lives of others as God had first ministered that grace to him. As God has given Himself to you, so give yourself to others. As God has saved you, so save others. And deeper than that, love others not only *as* God has loved you, but with the same love with which He has loved you. For all that God has called you to do and fulfill, you already have. God has already done for you...Now go and do likewise."

The Mission: How has God saved you, loved you, and touched your life? Use your life to do the same for others. Begin today.

Exodus 2:1–10; Matthew 10:8; John 15:9; Ephesians 3:7–8

THE UNENDING BOOK

HE LED ME into the Chamber of Scrolls and to one of its rooms where a solitary scroll was resting on a wooden stand, unrolled to its end.

"The Book of Acts," he said. "Tell me about it."

"It begins where the Gospel accounts end," I replied. "It's the sequel, the account of what happened to the disciples, how they went forth in the power of the Spirit and spread salvation to the world."

"Yes," said the teacher. "It's the account of miracles, healings, and the spreading of the Gospel to foreign lands. It's the account of a people who could not be stopped, who overcame all odds, all barriers, all opposition, and the world."

"They were an amazing people."

"And this is how it ends," he said. He began reading from the last words at the end of the scroll. "'Then Paul dwelt two whole years in his own rented house, and received all who came to him, preaching the kingdom of God and teaching the things which concern the Lord Yeshua, Jesus, the Messiah with all confidence, no one forbidding him.'" He paused for a few moments of silence, then asked, "Did you notice anything strange?"

"Like what?"

"There's no ending. There's no closure, no finality, nothing. It's as if the book was cut short in the middle of two paragraphs. God was obviously overseeing its writing, and yet it has no ending. Why?"

"Tell me."

"Because the Book of Acts has no ending. The Book of Acts never ended. How could it? The Gospel is still here. The Spirit is still here. The disciples are still here. The acts of God are still here. The Book of Acts is still here. And we're in it. You're in it. And what they did back then, you are to do now. As they spread the Gospel to the multitudes then, you are to do so now. As they could not be stopped then, you are to become unstoppable now. As miracles followed them then, miracles are to follow to you now. As they overcame all odds, all barriers, and all opposition then, you are to overcome the same, all things now. And as they changed their world then, you, by that same power, are to change your world now. The Book of Acts never ended, so that you could be part of it. So be part of it. Write your own chapter. Live as if you were actually living in the Book of Acts...because you are."

The Mission: Live today as if you lived in the Book of Acts and as if your life and your acts were being recorded in Scripture.

Acts 1:7–8; 2:39; 28:30–31

The Book of Acts

THE KARAT

IT WAS EVENING. We sat at opposite ends of a small wooden table in the center of a mostly empty chamber. Resting on the table in front of the teacher were two small parchments. "This," he said, pointing to one of them, "is from the Book of Jeremiah, the promise of the new covenant. The prophecy begins, "'Behold, the days are coming,' says the Lord, "when I will make a new covenant with the house of Israel and with the house of Judah."' It ends with the words, 'I will forgive their iniquity, and their sin I will remember no more."'" He turned the parchment around and moved it across the table so I could see the text. "But in Hebrew," he said as he pointed to the bottom of the parchment, "it doesn't say, 'I will make a new covenant.' The word is *karat*. It means to cut, as in offering up a sacrifice. The prophecy literally says, 'I will cut a covenant' or 'I will make a new covenant through the cutting of a sacrifice.' So according to the Hebrew prophecies, the new covenant can only begin with a sacrifice. Only then can sin be forgiven."

He lifted up the second parchment. "This is from the Book of Daniel...the prophecy of the event that will 'finish the transgression, make an end of sins, and make atonement for iniquity,'—the same thing promised in the new covenant. But Daniel's prophecy will reveal the nature of the sacrifice...and its timing."

He now moved the parchment of Daniel across the table so I could see.

"Do you know what this says?" he asked, "It says 'Messiah shall be cut off.' And do you know what it says in Hebrew? *Karat*. It's the same word. It means the new covenant will begin with the cutting of a sacrifice. So Messiah will be the sacrifice that is offered up to begin the new covenant. Daniel's prophecy goes on to reveal the timing. Messiah would be killed and then Jerusalem would be destroyed. Jerusalem was destroyed in AD 70. That means..."

"The Messiah has definitely come. The sacrifice has definitely been offered up. And the new covenant has been *cut* and has definitely begun."

"Yes," said the teacher, "and just as definitely that means that your iniquities are, without question, forgiven, and your sins are absolutely and conclusively remembered no more."

The Mission: The karat is the sign and assurance that your sins are absolutely remembered no more. Live in the confidence and repercussions of that fact.

Jeremiah 31:31–34; Daniel 9:24–26; Hebrews 9:14; 13:20–21

A Most Holy Verse

THE NAME IN WHICH YOU ARE

WE WERE SITTING in the sandy plain, in the same place where the teacher had in the past drawn symbols in the sand. But this time he handed me the stick and asked me to draw. So I did, slowly, as he directed. When I was finished, he told me what it was that I inscribed in the sand.

"Each of the symbols you drew," he said, "is a Hebrew letter. The first is the *yud*. The second is the *shin*. The third is the *vav*. And the last is the *ayin*. Do you recognize it?" he asked. "It's how the name *Yeshua* looks in Hebrew, which was then translated into 'Jesus.'"

"Yeshua," I replied, "Messiah's real name."

"Yes," said the teacher, "but think about it. He wasn't always Yeshua or Jesus."

"What do you mean?"

"Before the creation, the *Son* was with the Father and the *Word* was with God. He was the Son. And He was the Word. But He wasn't called *Yeshua*. In view of eternity, He has only borne the name Yeshua for a very short time. Why was it that He was given that name?"

"Because He was to save His people from their sins."

"Do you remember what *Yeshua* actually means?"

"God is salvation."

"Yes. So it wasn't His inherent name nor His Name from the beginning. In the beginning there was no sin, no darkness, no fall, no crisis, no brokenness, no judgment, no death, no need for salvation. For His Name to be *Yeshua* from the beginning would make no sense. Think about it. His Name is *Yeshua* because of us...because of *our* need to be saved. So every time His Name is spoken, it proclaims His being joined to us. And He chose to bear that name forever. And do you know what else that name means? It means we're actually *in* His Name. It's the salvation of us that His Name is declaring. It's the salvation of *you*. His Name declares *your* salvation. *You're* in His Name. And when you receive Yeshua, when He becomes your salvation...then it's all complete."

"It's as if His Name is a prophecy...a prophecy that comes true when you receive it."

"His Name is a mystery in which we are part. And when you receive the name, then the name is fulfilled. God becomes your salvation. And all who receive the name...are already in it...Yeshua."

The Mission: Ponder this mystery: You are in His Name. He was named for you. You are joined forever. Seek what that means. And live this day in that joining.

Isaiah 12:1–3; Jeremiah 23:5–7; 33:16; Matthew 1:21; John 1:1–2

Yeshuati

THE SCEPTER OF JUDAH

HE REMOVED THE scroll from the ark and read from the Book of Genesis: "'The scepter shall not depart from Judah, nor a lawgiver from between his feet...until Shiloh comes.' This," he said, "was a prophecy given by the patriarch Jacob to the tribe of Judah. What was Shiloh?"

"I have no idea."

"Listen," said the teacher, "to what the rabbis wrote in the Book of Sanhedrin in the Talmud, concerning Jacob's prophecy: 'What is Messiah's name?...His Name is Shiloh, for it is written: "Until Shiloh comes."' What are they saying?"

"They're identifying Shiloh as Messiah," I said. "So then the scepter won't depart from Judah until Messiah comes. But then what is the scepter?"

"A scepter is what a king holds. It denotes power, rule, dominion, and sovereignty. So the rabbis understood it this way: The power of dominion would not be removed from Judah, or the Jewish people, until the coming of the Messiah. And the crux of that dominion, they said, was the power of life and death, the power to decide cases involving capital punishment."

"So then the Messiah would have to come before the power of life and death, capital punishment, was removed from Judah."

"Yes. And the rabbis went further. They actually identified the moment in time when it happened. They wrote that when the members of the Sanhedrin found themselves deprived of the right over life and death, they cried out, 'Woe to us, for the scepter has departed from Judah and Messiah has not come.' When did that take place? The Book of Sanhedrin gives the answer: The scepter departed from Judah forty years before the destruction of the Temple, thus forty years before the year AD 70. Therefore, according to the rabbis, the year the scepter departed from Judah and thus the year by which Messiah had to have come was AD 30. Do you realize what that means? Of all the years of Jewish history, in all the years of human history, the Book of Sanhedrin itself marks the year by which Messiah had to appear...as AD 30—which just happens to be the very same time in human history when a man appears in Israel who will change the course of human history and be known throughout the earth as Messiah...Yeshua, Jesus of Nazareth!"

"So according to the rabbis, the time of Messiah's coming...is AD 30."

The Mission: Even the Book of Sanhedrin bears witness that Messiah has come. Live this day and beyond a life that manifests that fact.

Genesis 49:10; Matthew 26:63–64; Ephesians 1:20–22; Colossians 15:24–28

THE GARDEN OF MIRACLES

DURING ONE OF our walks by the gardens I asked him a question I had been pondering.

"You shared with me how on the day of man's creation, on the sixth day, God brought man into a garden of life. Then, on the day of man's redemption, on the sixth day, man brought God into a garden of death, a garden tomb."

"That's correct," he said.

"But when God placed man in the garden, it wasn't the end of the story, but the beginning. God put man in the garden to work the garden, to tend to it. The garden was a real functioning garden. It was an ongoing work. So when man placed God in the garden of death, wouldn't it also be an ongoing work? And, if so, what is the ongoing work of the Garden Tomb?"

"A garden tomb," said the teacher, "the most radical of places. A tomb is a place of ending, but a garden is a place of beginnings. Tombs are where life ends, but gardens are where life begins. So a garden tomb is the place of death and life, the end and the beginning."

"A place of life after death," I said, "resurrection."

"Yes. And how does life begin in a garden?" he asked. "It rises. It rises up from the earth."

"The rising of Messiah from the earth."

"And what rises in a garden? That which has descended to the earth. The seed. And what did Messiah liken His death to?"

"A seed falling into the earth and dying."

"And what happened to the seed of Messiah's life as it was buried in the Garden Tomb?"

"It bore life. It rose."

"And so," said the teacher, "it *is* an ongoing work. Just as the Garden of Eden was to be. Whatever is brought into *this* garden, whatever is planted in the Garden Tomb will bear a miracle. Whatever you plant here, your past, your broken dreams, your old life, your failures, your losses, your tears, whatever you let go of here, your treasures, your life, whatever it is that you plant in this garden will come alive again and blossom and bring forth life, a miracle more beautiful than what you planted. For this tomb is now the Garden of God . . . and the ground of miracles."

The Mission: Take all in your life that failed, that was taken or lost, that was broken, or that came to an end, all your sorrows. Come to the Tomb and plant them in the Garden of Miracles.

Genesis 1:27–29; Isaiah 61:3; John 19:31–20:16; 1 Corinthians 15:36–37, 42–44

The Gardener

THE RETURN OF THE PROTOTYPE

IT WAS AT the beginning of the age," said the teacher, "that the new covenant faith was in its original and most natural state."

"And what was its original and most natural state?"

"Revolutionary," he said, "set against the status quo of the world...underground, miraculous, countercultural, distinct, radical, powerful, overcoming, and world-changing...And it was also something else."

"What?"

"Jewish. What the world knows as Christianity, in its original and prototypical form, is a Jewish faith. But something happened in those first centuries. The more embedded and established the faith became in the mainstream of Western civilization, the more it lost its original and natural identity. What was a countercultural faith became a cultural faith, what was a radical faith became an established faith, what was a revolutionary faith became the faith of the status quo...and what was a Jewish faith became a non-Jewish faith. As the faith became joined to a non-Jewish Western culture...its Jewish disciples, messengers, and apostles began to disappear." He paused at that point as if to delineate a change.

"But now we've come to the other side of the phenomenon. We are now witnessing the separation, the dislodging, and the disestablishing of the faith from Western civilization."

"That's not a good thing," I said.

"And yet in one sense it is. The reverse of the phenomenon means that the faith will return to its original and natural state. From a cultural faith to a countercultural faith, from an established faith to a radical one, and from a faith of the status quo to a revolutionary faith."

"But then there must be one more transformation," I said. "The faith must change from its non-Jewish identity and form and return to its original Jewish form and identity.

"Yes," said the teacher, "and we might also expect the return of Jewish disciples. So notice what this reveals. The more established and of the world this faith becomes, the weaker its spiritual power. But the more separate from the world it becomes, the greater its spiritual power. Apply this to your life. Disentangle yourself from all compromise, from worldliness, and from the status quo. And you will grow stronger in spiritual power. Remember, this faith, in its truest and natural form, is always radical and revolutionary. Live your life accordingly."

The Mission: Divest yourself today from worldly attachments, that you might gain spiritual power. Exchange a comfortable walk for a revolutionary one.

Zechariah 8:3–8; Matthew 23:37–39; Acts 2:16–18, 39; Romans 11

The Mystery of the Rains

DOWN THE MOUNTAIN

HE TOOK ME up one of the desert's high mountains. Only upon reaching the summit did he tell me why we had come there.

"We have no other purpose here," said the teacher, "but to spend time in His presence."

We spent hours there, each of us alone with God, in prayer, in the Word, in worship, in silence. The experience was exhilarating. I could have stayed into the night. But that wasn't the plan.

"We must go down now," he said.

As we began our descent I said, "I thought you brought me up the mountain to give me a revelation."

"I did," he said.

"Then why didn't you give it?"

"Because this one's not about the mountaintop...but about leaving the mountaintop."

We continued our descent.

"The disciples spent more than three years in Messiah's presence. But then He sent them out from Jerusalem to the world. In what direction did He send them?"

"Out from Jerusalem."

"Down," said the teacher. "Jerusalem is a city built on the mountains. So to go out from Jerusalem, they had to go down. They had to go down the mountain. So to send them out from Jerusalem was to send them *down* from Jerusalem. Just as important as it is to ascend the mountain is to descend it. In fact, that's the direction of ministry...down the mountain."

"What do you mean?"

"When you receive from God—His blessings, His love, His revelations, His Spirit, His joy, His salvation—you're on the mountaintop. But you can't stay on the mountaintop. Nor can the blessings of God stay on the mountaintop. You have to go down the mountain. That's where your ministry is...at the bottom of the mountain...where the cities are, and the towns, and their marketplaces, and the fields, and the rest of the world. That's where they are, at the bottom of the mountain. So you have to go down. You have to bring down His love to the unloved. Bring down His blessings to the cursed, His riches to the poor, His presence to the godless, and His salvation to the lost. Your calling was given in the Great Commission. And the Great Commission begins on the mountaintop. So there's only way to fulfill it...by going down the mountain."

The Mission: Dwell today on the mountaintop with God. Receive His blessings. Then bring them down the mountain to touch your world.

Exodus 34:28–31; Psalm 96:1–3; Isaiah 58:5–11; Acts 1:8

Down the Mountain

THE UNCAUSED CAUSE

DO YOU REMEMBER when we spoke of the necessity of the Uncaused Cause?"

"God."

"Yes," said the teacher. "And what does it mean that God is the Uncaused Cause?"

"It means that nothing is the cause of His existence, but He is the cause of all existence."

"Yes, and what else is He? He's love. God is love. Put it together. If God is love and God is uncaused, then ..."

"Love is uncaused?"

"Love, pure, absolute, divine love, is uncaused. It exists as God exists, of its own. And understanding what this means can change your life."

"How?"

"It's one thing to believe God's love when you believe you've given Him cause and reason to love you. But it's something else entirely when you've given Him no cause and no reason. But love needs no cause or reason. And God needs no reason to love you. He loves you because He is, and because love is. You can't cause God to love you anymore than you could cause God Himself. Love loves without cause, except for the cause of love. So in your darkest pit, in your most unworthy, undeserving, sinful, and ungodly state, when you've given God absolutely no cause or reason to love you, He will love you still. And it is then, when you receive that uncaused love, that amazing grace, that it will change your life ... and allow you to manifest the miracle to others."

"How?"

"When others give you no cause or reason to love them and yet you love them anyway ... you're manifesting the miracle. When you love the unloving and the unlovable ... you're manifesting the miracle of His uncaused love."

"Then love is not only uncaused ... but the Uncaused Cause."

"Yes," he said. "So love is that which needs no reason, but gives reason to all things. So when you receive God's love when there's no reason for God's love or for you to receive it, then the love of God will give reason to your life. For it is the love of God without cause and that makes no sense that, once received, causes our lives to make sense. For God is the Uncaused Cause. And God is love ... So the Uncaused Cause is love."

The Mission: Today, make it your aim to receive the love of God with no reason or cause. And love others the same way, with no reason or cause.

Luke 6:27–36; 23:33–34; 1 Corinthians 13; 1 John 4:7–12

The Unknowable Love

THE SEVEN MYSTERIES OF THE AGE

THE TEACHER LED me into one of the chambers in the main building in which stood seven pillars of light golden stone. Each pillar was capped with a square stone slab, on top of which rested an object or group of objects.

"The seven mysteries of the age," he said. "We've looked at them separately, but now we bring them all together to see the mystery of the age itself."

He led me to the first pillar on which was a cup and a piece of matzah.

"God has set up the present age according to the pattern of the sacred Hebrew year. The sacred year begins with Passover. Its mystery foreshadows the death of the Lamb that begins the age with salvation."

He led me to the second pillar, on top of which was a sheaf of barley.

"The second mystery," he said, "Yom Resheet, the day the firstfruits of the spring harvest is lifted up to God. Its mystery foreshadows the second appointed event of the age, the Day of the Firstfruits. Messiah is lifted up from the dead, the raising up of the firstfruits of new life, the resurrection."

On the third pillar rested sheaves of wheat and two loaves of bread.

"The third mystery, the Feast of Shavuot, the launching of the summer harvest. Its mystery foreshadows the third appointed event, the Feast of Pentecost, Shavuot, the giving of the Spirit, launching the harvest of the age."

On the fourth pillar were grains, figs, grapes, and olives.

"The fourth mystery. The great summer harvest, the time of reaping the fields. Its mystery speaks of the harvest of nations, the time of the Gospel, of sowing, and reaping, and going to the ends of the earth with the word of salvation, the time that is now."

On the fifth pillar was a shofar.

"The fifth mystery, the Feast of Trumpets, what is next to come. Its mystery foretells the sounding of the trumpets at the end of the age to herald the coming of the King."

On the sixth pillar were a cloth, a piece of veil, embroidered with cherubim.

"The sixth mystery, Yom Kippur, the Day of Atonement, man and God, face-to-face. Its mystery foreshadows the Day of Judgment and salvation, of man and God, standing face-to-face."

On the seventh pillar were the branches of the lulav and a citrus fruit.

"The seventh mystery, the Feast of Tabernacles, the Feast of Dwellings. Its mystery foretells the age of the kingdom, when God will tabernacle among us and we with Him...And the mystery of the age will be fulfilled."

The Mission: Time is framed by the holy days of God. Live today as a holy day, a sacred day, centered in the presence of God. And it will be so.

Leviticus 23

The Seven Mysteries of the Age I–VII

THE SUNRISE REDEMPTION

THE TEACHER HAD asked me to sleep out in the open, on the sand of a small plain from which one could see a vast panorama that included the school. While it was still night, he woke me. Once I realized where I was, he began to share.

"Do you remember what I told you about the sunset and Messiah's death?"

"How He died and was buried as the sun was going down," I replied.

"And why?" he asked.

"In the sunset we see the light of the world descending to the earth. At the same time, Messiah, the Light of the World, was descending to the earth."

"So the sunset," he said, "was a sign, a picture in the physical realm of what was taking place in the spiritual realm...the Light of the World was descending into the earth...a cosmic sunset. So as Messiah descends to the earth, He becomes the Sunset on our old lives, the Sunset on our sins, on our past, and on the old. And when a sunset is finished, everything fades away to black and disappears. And in Messiah's Sunset, the past fades to black, the old life disappears, and the old creation is brought out of existence into nothingness. But what happened next?"

"The resurrection."

"Each of the four accounts of Messiah's resurrection contains a word that speaks of the dawn, the sunrise. And what is a sunrise?"

"It's when the sun, the light of the world, rises up from the earth."

"And what is the resurrection?"

"It's the Light of the World rising up from the earth."

We sat for some time in silence as it began to dawn.

"What do you see?" asked the teacher.

"From the darkness, everything's beginning to appear."

"And so the power of the Sunrise is the power to *bring into existence* that which did not exist, to bring forth, out of nothing, a new creation, a new being, a new identity...to bring hope from hopelessness, love from lovelessness, life from the death, and a way where there was no way...light from darkness. That's why His rising is linked to the sunrise, because that's what it was...the Sunrise of the new creation. It's the miracle of bringing into existence that which was not...a new life out of nothing...And that is the power given and to be received by those who live in the light of the cosmic dawn."

The Mission: Believe in God's power to bring into existence that which is not. Live this day in that power. Speak that which is not as if it was.

Isaiah 60:1; Matthew 27:57–60; 28:1–6; Ephesians 5:14;
1 Thessalonians 5:5

The Divine Good Morning

PERFORMING YOUR SEMIKHAH

WE RETURN ONE last time," said the teacher, "to the Semikhah. Tell me what it was."

"The placing of sin on the sacrifice by laying hands on its head and confessing your sins over it...that which the priests of Israel performed on Messiah before they delivered Him to His death."

"That's correct," he said. "But it wasn't only the priests who performed the Semikhah. It was performed by whoever needed to be forgiven of their sins. In order to offer up a sin offering, you had to perform the Semikhah over it. You had to touch it with your hands and confess your sins over it. And by doing so, you became one with the sacrifice. Only with that total identification could the sacrifice die for your sins. Now if we've all sinned, and Messiah is the offering for our sin, what must there also be?"

"The Semikhah?"

"Yes. The one who needs their sins to be forgiven must perform the Semikhah. So how does one perform it? The same way it was performed in ancient times. You must touch the sacrifice and become one with it."

"But how?" I asked. "The sacrifice of Messiah took places ages ago."

"But remember, it is the one sacrifice that transcends time, that touches all time, past, present, and future. So the time doesn't matter. The Semikhah can still be performed. You reach out your hands across time and space to touch Messiah on the cross...You confess your sins upon Him. You become one with Him there just as He was one with you in His sacrifice. That's when it's complete, when the two moments are joined together. That's when your sins are forgiven and washed away."

"It sounds like salvation."

"It is," said the teacher. "How do you become saved? You confess your sins, you bring them to the sacrifice, and you become one with the sacrifice as the sacrifice has become one with you on the altar. What is that? It's the Semikhah. The act of salvation is the act of the Semikhah. You're performing a cosmic Semikhah across time and space. Perform your Semikhah, and not only once. Touch the head of the sacrifice, place your sins upon Him, your burdens, your fears, your shame, your cares, join every part of your life to the sacrifice, and the sacrifice to every part of your life...that the two moments and the two lives be lived as one."

The Mission: Perform the sacred Semikhah. Place your hands on His head. Lay your life upon His life. Release what must be released. And be released.

Leviticus 16:21; Galatians 2:20; 1 Peter 5:7; 1 John 1:8–9

Footsteps on the Altar

HEAVENLY NOSTALGIA

WE WERE SITTING on a ridge on one of the highest mountains in the desert, overlooking a vast landscape of distant mountains and plains, more than one tent encampment, the school, and several shepherds tending their flocks.

"Imagine," said the teacher, "that your life is over. You're in heaven, paradise, seeing and experiencing things which before you couldn't begin to imagine. If you were able, would you go back to earth?"

"No."

"But there are things you'll never be able to do again, even in heaven, things you could have only done in the time you had on earth."

"Like what?"

"Faith. You'll never again be able to live by faith."

"But in heaven…"

"In heaven you'll see what you believed in. But you'll never again be able to stand in faith or choose to believe God. Earth, not heaven, is the place of faith. And in heaven you'll never again be able to choose to stand with God in the face of opposition. That too can only be done on earth. In heaven you'll never again be able to repent, or to bless God by turning down sin. In heaven you'll never again have the chance to share salvation with the unsaved, or to bring a life out of darkness and into the light. They all know Him there. In heaven you'll never again be able to help someone in need or to bless God by doing so. Heaven has no needs. In heaven you'll never again have the honor of standing with God when it costs you to do so, or to share in His reproach. In heaven you'll never again be able to sacrifice for God. There's no loss there. And in heaven you'll never again be able to overcome or become victorious. There's nothing there to overcome. The place for victory is here. The place for all these things is not heaven—but earth. And the time for these things is not then, but now. You see, earth is a most awesome place. And every moment you have here is a most precious gift, one you will never have again, even in the eternity of heaven."

"Let's go down the mountain," I said.

"Why?" asked the teacher.

"There are things I want to do…I'm not yet ready for heaven."

The Mission: Live this day as if your life was over, but you were given a second chance to go back. Do now what, in heaven, you can never do again.

Psalm 90:9–12; John 4:35–36; 1 Thessalonians 5:16–18; James 1:17

THE JUBILEE MAN

H E WAS HOLDING a small shofar. "The sign and sound of the Jubilee," he said, "the year of restoration. What do you remember of it?"

"It was the year in which the land would return to its original owners," I said, "So if your family had lost its ancestral land, they would return home."

"Yes," said the teacher, "now think about it...Two thousand years ago, the Jewish people lost their homeland and their Holy City, Israel and Jerusalem, their ancestral possessions. But it was prophesied that they would return. In other words, it would be a prophetic Jubilee, a restoration to their ancient possession. So could the Jubilee hold the key to the mystery of that restoration?"

He placed the shofar in my hands. "In 1917, in the midst of the First World War, the British Empire issued the Balfour Declaration to give the land of Israel to the Jewish people. So the land would be restored to its original owners. But still missing was the restoration of the Holy City, Jerusalem. The Jubilee comes every fifty years. If we count to the fiftieth year from that first restoration, it brings us to 1967. It was in 1967 that the Holy City, Jerusalem, was restored to the Jewish people, to its original owners...the Jubilee. And in the same moment that Israel was restored to its ancient city, the sign of the Jubilee was manifested—the rabbi who accompanied the soldiers to the Temple Mount sounded the shofar. And do you know what the Temple Mount was when Israel first obtained it three thousand years before? A threshing floor...in Hebrew, a *goren*. And the man who sounded the shofar there in the day of restoration was named 'Goren,' Rabbi Goren. And do you know when he was born? In 1917, the year of the first restoration, the first Jubilee. So he who sounded the shofar of Israel's Jubilee, the fiftieth year, was, himself, fifty years old, the living sign of the Jubilee. It had all happened in the exact place at the exact time. You see, God is the God of restoration. And to those who are His, He will restore all things...all that was lost will be found again...in their Jerusalem...and in their appointed time of Jubilee."

The Mission: If you belong to Messiah, you have the power of Jubilee, the power to restore the lost and the broken. Today, live, speak, and use that power.

Leviticus 25:10–11; Joel 2:25–27; Zechariah 8:7–8; Luke 4:18–19; Acts 1:6

The Prophetic Jubilee

THE FOUR CORNERS OF THE ALTAR

THE TEACHER LED me into something of a hidden valley, small and hedged in by low-lying mountains on all sides. In the middle of the valley was a rectangular object, about seven feet across and about four feet high.

"What is it?" I asked.

"It's an altar," he replied, "an altar of sacrifice, a model of the brazen altar that stood in the Temple courts. Note the horns at its corners. The sacrifice would be tied to the horns, bound to the four directions of the four corners of the altar...as it is written in Psalm 118: 'Bind the sacrifice with cords to the horns of the altar.' It's from the same song that Messiah and His disciples sang at the end of the Last Supper."

"So they sang a song about the sacrifice on the altar the night before He would be offered up...as a sacrifice...but not on the altar."

"But it was on the altar," he said. "In Hebrew, the word for *altar* is *mizbayakh*. It means an instrument of slaughter by which a sacrifice was lifted up. Come." He led me to the other side of the valley on which there stood another object behind a ridge in the mountain that obscured it. It was a large wooden cross, looking less like a religious object than an instrument of execution.

"Another altar," he said, "of another sacrifice. The altar in the Temple was an object of four directions. So too the altar of Messiah was an object of four directions."

"But the altar had four corners. I don't see any corners on the cross."

"Yes," said the teacher, "the altar of sacrifice must have four corners. And it does. You're just not seeing it. You're looking for four corners pointing outward and framing the space inside, as on the rectangle of the brazen altar. But this is heaven's sacrifice and heaven's altar. The four corners of this altar are the opposite. They point inward and frame the space outside."

And that's when it hit me as I stared at the beams. "I see it now! The four corners are that of a rectangle turned inside out, converging on Him. And the space they frame...is the sky."

"The four corners of the Temple altar contained a finite space. But the space contained by these four corners is infinite...it frames the universe...to cover every ground, every circumstance, every sin, every burden, every problem, every guilt, every pain, every tear, every shame, every heart, and every moment of every life...just as the life it sheds and the love it bears are infinite...It's the altar of infinity."

The Mission: Ponder this truth: The love of God is bigger than the universe, stronger than evil, and longer than time. In that, overcome all that you must overcome.

Exodus 40:6; Psalm 118:27; Galatians 6:14; Hebrews 13:10

The Lamb and the Altar

ENTERING THE HEAVENLY DIMENSION

THE TEACHER LED me into the Chamber of Vessels and to a section within it in which was a large reproduction of the Temple veil, that which marked the entrance to the holy of holies.

"What do you see," he asked, "on the veil?"

"The cherubim."

"An *image* of the cherubim embroidered on the veil...a two-dimensional representation of the cherubim...with height and width but with a missing dimension—depth. The reality represented by the image has, of course, more than two dimensions. But on a veil, one is limited to representing three-dimensional realities on a two-dimensional plane. Now let's go behind the veil."

So we passed through the veil and into a reproduction of the holy of holies.

"Now, what do you see?"

"The ark of the covenant," I replied.

"And what do you see on top of the ark of the covenant?"

"Figures...of the cherubim...in gold."

"And how many dimensions do they have?"

"Three."

"So from outside of the veil, one sees the cherubim in two dimensions. But from inside the veil, one sees them now in three dimensions.

"So as we passed through the veil, another dimension was added. And where are you when you pass through the veil?"

"In the holy of holies."

"Which represents the dwelling place of God, the heavenlies, and the secret place, the place you dwell in prayer and worship before God's presence. Outside of that place you see the cherubim in two dimensions, but inside, you find another dimension. There are realities," said the teacher, "that you can never know until you go beyond the veil and dwell in the presence of God, realities waiting in the depth of God's presence, the depth of faith, and the depth of prayer and worship. Compared to that which lies in the presence of God, everything you've known in the world is like a two-dimensional drawing on a piece of parchment, and all your ideas of God are like two-dimensional images embroidered on a veil. Make it your aim to go beyond the veil, into the secret place of the holy of holies and dwelling of His presence...beyond the woven images of cherubim and into the reality of the Most High."

The Mission: Enter this day beyond the veil, into the deep and deeper and deeper of His presence, to dwell in the dimension of the heavenlies.

Psalm 100; Hebrews 9:3–5; 10:19–20; 2 Corinthians 12:1–4

SPECIFICITY

FROM OUR VANTAGE point on a small hill near the school, we observed a young family of tent dwellers, a father, a mother, and their newborn baby, sitting outside a solitary tent in the middle of a large plain in the desert night.

"A poor family," said the teacher, "holding their newborn baby out in the elements, under the stars. It could almost be a scene from Scripture, from Bethlehem. Can you fathom the miracle of it? The God who created the universe, now a helpless baby inside the universe He created...the Almighty become the weakest of beings...the hands that stretched out the heavens now too weak to even grasp the hand of His mother...the eyes that see all things now can barely focus...the mouth that spoke the universe into existence now can only offer up the cry of a helpless baby. How amazing is that? It is the miracle of love...the humility of love...and the miracle of specificity."

"Specificity?"

"God is omnipresent, everywhere at once. But in the incarnation He becomes specific to time and space, to only one point of space and to only one moment of time. God is universal, the Light of the World, the spring of all existence. Yet now He becomes specific to one culture, one people, one tribe, one house, one genealogy, one family, one life. The universal God of all existence becomes a Jewish baby, a Jewish boy, then a Jewish rabbi, walking in sandals on the ground and dust of first-century Judea. Everything He does is now contained in one specific place and one specific moment of time. He forgives specific sinners, embraces specific outcasts, multiplies specific loaves of bread, and touches specific people and heals them of their infirmities."

"How does one apply that?" I asked.

"In order to know the power of God's love, you have to receive it in its specificity, as specifically from Him and specifically to you, His sacrifice as specifically given for you, His Word specifically to your life, His blood and forgiveness poured out specifically for your specific sins. And so too you must live your life in God in specificity. Your love must manifest in specificity...in specific actions to the specific people who are here and now in your life...You must love and bless and live out your faith on earth...in specificity."

The Mission: Manifest the love of God in specificity. Bless specific people with specific actions of love—specifically today.

Matthew 25:31–46; Luke 2:1–20; Galatians 4:4–5; 1 John 4:20–21

God With Us

DESERT RAINS

THERE HAD BEEN several rains in recent days, mostly during the night. The most recent night was no exception. But in the morning the sun came out, and the teacher invited me to join him on a hike through the desert, which I did. He brought me to a mountain ridge that overlooked a vast expanse of valleys, hills, and other mountains.

"Do you remember this?" he asked. "I've brought you here before."

"But it looks completely different now," I replied.

"What's different?"

"When we were last here," I said, "except for a few scattered desert plants, it was dry and barren. But now the valleys are green, the hills are green, and there are plants everywhere. And over there. That was a dry riverbed. Now it's a river. It's kind of miraculous."

"It is," said the teacher. "It's what happens when the rain comes to the desert. And so God gave the prophet Isaiah this word: 'The wilderness and the wasteland shall be glad for them, and the desert shall rejoice and blossom as the rose; it shall blossom abundantly and rejoice...For waters shall burst forth in the wilderness, and streams in the desert...There shall be grass with reeds and rushes...' It's a prophecy of what would happen when the Jewish people return to the land of Israel. The barren land would blossom. And that's exactly what happened. When they came back to the land, it was almost entirely barren. But then the barren land blossomed as a rose."

"As did this desert," I replied.

"Do you know why this desert blossomed so quickly? Because it was all there waiting to blossom, the seeds, the dry riverbeds, the potential was there waiting. Remember what you see here. It's a picture of redemption. The barren wilderness represents our lives without God. And the rain is His Spirit, and the outpouring of His love and grace upon our lives. And the blossoming of this wilderness tells us this: it doesn't matter how barren our lives have become or how hopeless any situation in our lives has become. It doesn't matter how dry and lifeless. All it takes are the rains of heaven. And that which is dormant and that which is dead and that which is hopeless will blossom again. And the seeds that He planted will spring up, and our valleys will again be covered with green, and our riverbeds will again flow with rivers of living waters. The most barren of deserts is but a miracle waiting to happen...under the outpouring of the desert rains."

The Mission: Your entire life is as a desert waiting for the desert rains to blossom, to flow, and to produce miracles. Seek today the desert rains.

Isaiah 35:1–2, 6–7; 43:19; 44:3–4

The Arabah

THE CALAH

WE JOURNEYED TO one of the desert's tent villages with which the teacher was very familiar, but one I had never been to before.

"Do you see the woman there," said the teacher, "with long wavy hair, dressed in brown and black? She's the bride."

"But she's not the same as the other."

"There's more than one bride among these villages. And this one is at the end of her wait. Soon will be her wedding day. Do you remember how to say *bride* in Hebrew?"

"Calah," I replied.

"Yes," said the teacher, "but I never told you what it meant. The word *calah* contains a mystery. It doesn't only mean bride."

"What else then?"

"*Calah* also means the perfect one."

"The perfect one? But if, in the mystery, we're the bride and the Bridegroom is God, shouldn't it be the Bridegroom who is called the perfect one?"

"That's the point," he said. "We're born *to be* the bride, but we're not born *as* the bride. We're born imperfect and subject to imperfection throughout our lives. But we're to become the calah, the perfect one...when we say yes to the Bridegroom...in the new birth."

"And we become perfect?"

"Becoming a bride is about being joined to a bridegroom. So becoming the calah is about being joined to God. The more we join our hearts and lives to God, the more we become the calah...the perfect one. In Him and in our joining to Him is found our perfection. And do you know what else *calah* means? It means the completed one. To be completed is to be perfect."

"But then how can we ever be perfect, if we can only be completed at the end?"

"The Bridegroom looks at the bride and sees her as she will be. God looks at you and sees what He made you to become, and as you will become. And the bride must see herself in the eyes of the Bridegroom. You must see yourself in the eyes of God, and then God compete His work. For the works of God are perfect...even the *calah*."

The Mission: Marry every imperfect part of your life to the Bridegroom. Let Him fill in all that is missing. See yourself in the eyes of His love—as the calah—the perfect one.

Isaiah 62:5; Matthew 5:48; Ephesians 5:25–27; Revelation 19:7–8

GOD ON THE BLUE PLANET

IT WAS EVENING. We sat on a hill overlooking the school. The stars appeared particularly bright and clear that night.

"Imagine," said the teacher, "that we came from somewhere out there in the universe. And we heard that the God of the universe had visited this one particular planet, this blue planet...earth. Imagine we heard it reported that He walked among its people as one of them. And so we came to find out which life it was that He lived. How would we find that Person?"

"He would have the nature of God," I said. "He would be the epitome of goodness. He would be holy, righteous, loving. And He would be humble, because humility is part of goodness. And He would exist to *do* good. His life would be about giving of Himself. His life would be a gift. It would answer the needs of man and give life to everyone it touched."

"What else would it be?" he asked.

"It would have to be a unique life, the *most* unique life. It would have the greatest impact on this world of any life. It would be like a rock thrown onto the waters of a lake. It would cause reverberations throughout the world...throughout time. It would change the course of history and the world."

"And would everyone love and praise this life?" he asked.

"No," I replied. "Since it was a fallen world, He would be both loved and hated. The forces of darkness would be against Him. He would become the focal point of all evil. And being the incarnation of good, He would have to come against evil. And being God, He would have to overcome it...If God came down to earth, then His life would have to become the most central life ever lived on this planet."

"So," said the teacher, "if God were to come down to this planet...then God has already come down to this planet. That's something to celebrate. And how incredible that we could even come to know such a One...and that such a One would call us friend. And if we should have the life of that One inside of us, then..."

"What kind of lives should we be living?" I said. "Lives of goodness and holiness, lives of giving and selflessness, that answers the needs of those around us, that goes against the flow of this world, that overcomes evil, and that makes a difference for having been lived."

"Yes," said the teacher. "So live that life...as if the life of God was, through your life, walking among us on the blue planet...and it will be so."

The Mission: Make it your aim this day to live the life of God in this world. Live to bless, to fill, to save, to overcome, and to change the world.

John 15:14–16; Ephesians 1:20–21; Colossians 1:10–11; Hebrews 13:8

God on the Blue Planet

THE ATZERET

IT WAS THE late afternoon of a beautiful sunny day. We watched as the children of the tent village below us played in a warm gentle wind.

"All this passes away?" I asked. "In eternity is everything gone, the good as well as the bad?"

"Do you remember the day that foretells all that, the ending of the present order and the beginning of eternity?"

"Shemini Atzeret."

"That's right," said the teacher. "And do you remember what it means?"

"The Gathering of the Eighth Day," I answered.

"The word for *Gathering* is *Atzeret*. But *Atzeret* is a mystery word. It can be used to speak of gatherings, but it's especially joined to this particular and mysterious last day of the Hebrew year. The word *Atzeret* comes from the Hebrew verb *atzar*. *Atzar* means to keep, to maintain, to hold back, to recover, and to retain. So *Atzeret* literally means the Keeping, the Maintaining, the Holding Back, the Recovery, and the Retaining. So the day that foreshadows the passing away of heaven and earth and the dawning of eternity could be called 'the Keeping.' The day that speaks of the last day of earthly existence is called '*Atzeret*,' 'the Retaining.'

"What does that mean?" I asked.

"Heaven and earth will pass away. The sorrows of this world, its pains and its evils will all pass away. But there will be an Atzeret. There will be a Keeping, a Retaining. All the good of this life that came from Him will be kept. All the good that was done for Him and for His purposes will be preserved. Every work of faith, of love, of purity, of redemption, of salvation...these will be kept. All that was birthed of God, all that was sacrificed and given up for God, these will be restored. All the labors of the righteous, all the prayers of the holy, and all the praises of His children, all that which was of born of His love, all this will be retained and brought across the Jordan as a treasure to be kept forever. The old will pass away. There will be no more darkness or tears or mourning or death. But the good...the good will be kept in the keeping of heaven's Atzeret."

The Mission: In heaven, the good of this life will be retained. Do not retain anything of this day that is not good. Retain only what is.

Matthew 6:20; 19:21; Revelation 7:9–17; 21:12–14

The Mystery of the Eighth Day I–III

THE INVISIBLE HARP

THE TEACHER WAS sitting in one of the gardens as I approached him. Cushioned between his legs and abdomen was a harp on which he was playing soft, gentle, beautiful music. I waited until the piece was finished before I spoke.

"I had no idea you knew how to play," I said.

"It's very scriptural," he said. "The Bible's praises are called psalms. The word *psalm* is a translation of the Hebrew word *mizmor*. A *mizmor* is a musical piece, in this case, a praise to God played with an instrument."

"A piece played with *any* instrument?"

"The word is specifically linked to the music of a harp. It was when the ancient Jewish scholars translated the Scriptures into Greek that *mizmor* became *psalmos*, from which we get the word *psalm*. *Psalmos* comes from the word *psallo*. And *psallo* specifically speaks of making music on the strings of a harp. So if you want to praise God, you must play a musical instrument."

"But I don't play a musical instrument...I've never even owned one."

"But you do own one," he said. "There is an instrument that makes music to the Lord...and you own it."

"What instrument?"

"It is written in the Scriptures, 'Make melody in your heart to the Lord.' The instrument that produces music to the Lord...is the heart. So your heart is a musical instrument. And what is the heart? It's the center of your being, the deepest part of your existence. That's what makes the music of God's praise, the deepest part of your being. Your heart was never made to produce bitterness, hatred, anxiety, or gloom. It was made to be an instrument that makes melody to the One who created it, the melody of praise and thanksgiving, the music of love, worship, and joy. And when the Scriptures say, 'Make melody in your heart,' do you know what's behind it? The word is *psallo,* which literally means to pluck the strings. You see, you have always had a secret harp. And as a harp has highs and lows, so too does your life and your heart. And you're to praise Him in all of it and with all of it. The very center of your being was made as an instrument to praise God. Therefore, praise Him in all things, at all times, and from your heart, and your life itself will become a psalm...a song of praise to God."

The Mission: Today, learn to make music from the instrument of your heart—from the deepest part of your being—the melody of praise, joy, and worship.

Psalm 33:1–5; Ephesians 5:19–20

Melody in Your Heart

THE SHABBAT MYSTERY CODE

THE TEACHER AND I were returning to the school after a long journey. Before we arrived, the sun began to set. It was the Sabbath. The teacher sat down on the sand and motioned for me to join him.

"Do you remember what I shared about the Sabbath of ages?" he asked.

"That the Sabbath is a shadow of the age to come? Yes."

"A shadow of the kingdom, the millennium. There's more to that mystery," he said. "Who was it that was commanded to keep the Sabbath?"

"The Jewish people," I replied, "the children of Israel."

"And so each week, as the Jewish people keep the Sabbath, we have a prophetic shadow of the Sabbath age. So could it be that what they do on that day, in the liturgy of their Sabbath observance, holds the mystery of what will happen in the age to come, the age of the Sabbath? As the Sabbath liturgy begins, proclamations are made of the Lord's coming: 'The Lord is coming...to judge the earth,' 'The Lord reigns. Let the earth rejoice,' 'In His Temple all cry out "Glory!"' In the same way, the age to come will begin with the coming of the Lord to earth, to judge and reign from the Temple of Jerusalem. The Sabbath liturgy then speaks of the coming of the bride. So too does the Book of Revelation. Then it is proclaimed that 'the Word of God shall go forth from Jerusalem.' So too, in the age to come, the Word of God will go forth from Jerusalem to all the earth. The liturgy continues with the speaking of ancient blessings, one of which blesses God 'who revives the dead.' Thus, the age to come will see the resurrection of the dead. Then comes the proclamation that every knee will bow and every tongue confess that the kingdom belongs to the Lord, 'the King of kings.'"

"That's exactly what it says of the age to come in the Book of Revelation. It's amazing how it all lines up. The age of the Sabbath, the Messianic age, would correspond to the millennium. At the end of the Book of Revelation, the millennium ends with the beginning of eternity. Is there anything in the Sabbath observance that speaks of that...perhaps at the end of the liturgy?"

"There is," said the teacher, "and it comes at the end. "It's called *Adon Olam*, which is translated as 'the Lord of eternity.' And these words are then proclaimed: 'After all has ceased to be, He alone will reign, the Awesome One...without beginning and without end.' And so," said the teacher, "as the Jewish people look forward to the Sabbath day and prepare to enter it...so live your life looking forward to and in preparation...for the Sabbath of ages."

The Mission: In God, the best comes at the end. Live this day in full confidence of that fact, looking forward, and preparing in hope for that day.

Exodus 31:16–17; Isaiah 2:1–5; 66:22–23; Matthew 12:8

The Shabbat Mystery Code I–II

THE OTHER THROUGH THE ONE

THE DAY WAS sunny with a cool afternoon breeze. We were walking through a garden of olive trees, the leaves of which were rustling in the wind.

"A mystery," said the teacher. "Listen to these words written by the apostle: 'For as woman came from man, even so man comes through woman.' What does it mean?"

"'As woman came from man'...So from Adam came Eve. But after that, every man comes into the world through a woman...'so man comes through woman.'"

"It's a circle of love," he said, "a circle of being. The one comes from the other and the other comes through the one. They each come through the other. And yet it contains an even deeper mystery. Adam was created in the image of God, the visible reflection of the invisible realities of God. So if from Adam came Eve, if from the man came the woman, then what is this a reflection of? What then came from God?"

"The creation came from God," I replied.

"So the one came from the other," said the teacher, "but the mystery, then the other must come through the one. So if the creation came from God, then..."

"Then God...must come through the creation." "Yes," said the teacher. "As man comes through woman who came from man, so God must come through the creation that came from Him...And so God is born among us. And the circle is complete."

"Israel," I said. "Israel also came from God. So as the man comes through the woman, so the God of Israel must come through Israel...God must be born of Israel."

He paused, looked into my eyes, and said, "And what else comes from God?"

"We do," I said. "We came into existence from God."

"The one from the other and the other from the one. So what about you?"

"I came into existence from God. Therefore, it's only complete if God is born through me."

"You exist from Him...that He might exist through you. And what is salvation? It is exactly that. It is this mystery. It is God come through you who came from Him...His life now born through your life. And that is the purpose of your life. So make this your aim: Let God come through you. Let His love, His goodness, His nature, His presence, let His life come through your life...the one from the other and the other through the one. And then the circle...is complete."

The Mission: Take part in the mystery today. Let the life, the love, the goodness, the power, and the presence of God, through your life, be born.

Genesis 2:21–23; 1 Corinthians 11:11–12; Ephesians 5:25–32

Male and Female

THE RESURRECTION LAND

I WAS SITTING IN his study by his desk when he showed me an ancient coin.

"What do you see on it?" asked the teacher.

"A man standing by a palm tree," I said. "And under the tree is a woman sitting down."

"The man is a Roman soldier," he said. "And the woman represents Israel weeping. It's called *Judaea Capta,* a commemorative coin issued by the Romans to celebrate their destruction of Israel. Now look at this."

He handed me another coin, silver and not ancient but modern.

"What do you see?"

"The palm tree, the woman, and a man...but it's different. The woman is standing up and holding a baby, and the man is planting a tree."

"It's called *Israel Liberata.* It's the coin issued by Israel after it came back into the world. It's based on the Roman coin, but the image of death and sorrow has turned into one of resurrection and joy. Nations are born and grow. But Israel is different. Israel is a resurrection. And what is a resurrection? It's a restoring of what once was. So the coins of Israel are the resurrections of its ancient coins. Its language is the resurrection of its ancient language; its cities, the resurrections of its ancient cities. Even its trees and forests, are the resurrections of its ancient trees and forests. And much of these resurrections came through translating what was in the Bible into reality. Through the Word came the nation. The resurrection of Israel is a sign, a picture of salvation. You see, our salvation is not only a new birth. It's a resurrection. It's a restoration."

"But we've never been anything else but fallen," I said. "How can we be restored or resurrected to whatever we've never been?"

"If this is the fallen version, then there has to be another version, the person God made you to be. That is the resurrection of salvation. It is that you become the you that you were always meant to become...God's holy creation...the you as you would be if you were never fallen. And how do you take part in that resurrection? You do as in the resurrection of Israel. You translate the Word of God into your life, in every area and realm. Make your goal resurrection...that you might become that which, in Him, you are...and are to be."

The Mission: Your life is a resurrection. Follow, in the Word of God, the pattern for life and become the person you were created to become.

Jeremiah 30–31; Hosea 6:2; Amos 9:14–15; Ephesians 2:6

The Resurrection of Zion

THE END OF THE STORY

WHAT IS IT," asked the teacher, "that makes a story good or bad, happy or sad? What if I told you the story of a man hated by his own family, sold into slavery, taken to a foreign land, thrown into a prison for a crime he didn't commit, and forgotten by man and, it seems, by God. What kind of story would you say it is?"

"A sad story. A story of injustice and oppression...a tragedy."

"But the story is from the Book of Genesis. And the man is Joseph. And He will end up being released from prison, given a position of great honor, saving Egypt from famine, and being reconciled to his family.

"Now would you still say the story is sad and tragic?"

"No. I would say the story is one of triumph."

"And you would be right," he said. "The parts of a story are not all of equal weight. A happy story with a tragic end is not a happy story, but a tragic one. A tragic story with a triumphant ending is not a tragic story, but a triumphant one. You can never judge a story by its beginning or middle, or by any of its parts before its ending. It is the ending of the story that determines everything that went before it. Always remember that. The nature of the story is determined by its end...so too the story of your life. You can never judge your story by your current circumstances or problems. And as long as you're on earth, you haven't seen the end of the story."

"So then one can never know what kind of story you're in."

"Not so," said the teacher. "If you're a child of God, the end of the story is revealed."

"Which is..."

"Victory, restoration, triumph, blessing, joy, and glory. And it is that end that makes your life a good story, a wonderful story. Therefore, when you look at your life, see everything in the light of that ending...every problem, every defeat, every sorrow, every failure, every evil...they're only the components of a story of triumph and glory. Fix your eyes on the end of the story. And press on to that end. For it is that end that makes your story and your life...a great one."

The Mission: No matter what you're going through today or in your life, believe, look to, and live in confidence to the end of the story.

Job 42:10–17; Luke 24:46–53; 2 Corinthians 2:14; Hebrews 12:1–2

The End of the Story

THE RUNNER'S RIDDLE

A RIDDLE," SAID THE teacher. "Two men in a race. The first is a perfect runner, fast, strong, skilled, and confident, one who only runs perfect races. The second is slow, clumsy, weak, and unsteady. He's never been in a race where he didn't stumble and fall multiple times before the race was over. The two compete in a marathon of widely varying and, at times, dangerous terrain. The second runner finds himself far behind and falling continuously for the entire length of the race. The first runner performs with great speed and skill. In the most treacherous of terrain he falls only once and, apart from that, runs perfectly. So who wins the race?"

"The first runner," I answered, "From everything you told me, he has to win."

"But he loses," said the teacher, "It is the second runner who wins."

"But how?"

"The first runner runs only perfect races. Once he falls, it's no longer a perfect race. His race is over. He's finished. But the second runner isn't running a perfect race. So when he falls, the race isn't over."

"But how do we know he wins?"

"If he keeps falling for the length of the race, it means he also keeps getting up for the length of the race, until he crosses the finish line. So the winner is not the best runner, but the one who crosses the finish line. Never forget that. For you too are in a race. Do everything you can to avoid falling. But you won't win this race by running it perfectly. No one does. But when you fall, remember the runner's riddle. Get up and get on with it. No matter how great your fall, get up and keep going. And if you fall again, get up again. And if you keep falling, keep getting up again. And if you keep falling and getting up again, you'll end up crossing the finish line, and you'll win the race. For this race and this faith are not to those who run perfectly or never fall. Rather, those who win are those who get up after having fallen, and those who fall and get up…are those who win."

The Mission: Commit today that no matter what, even if you fall, you'll keep running until you cross the finish line. And if you've fallen, make today the day you get up and get going.

Proverbs 24:16; 1 Corinthians 9:24; Hebrews 12:1

To Finish the Race

THE MACCABEAN BLUEPRINT

THE TEACHER LED me through the darkness to the golden menorah, which stood in the center of its chamber. He lit the first of its seven lights.

"We've spoken of Chanukah," said the teacher, "the Festival of Lights, how it commemorates the victory of God's people over evil...But there's more to it. Chanukah contains a mystery. It's not only a commemoration but a prophetic shadow. It begins when an evil king sets up an idol in the holy place, the desecration of the Temple, the 'Abomination Desolation.' And yet Messiah speaks of an Abomination Desolation yet to come in the last days. So Chanukah contains a template, a prophetic blueprint of that which will take place at the end of the age."

"Beyond the abomination, what else does it foretell?"

"The account begins with the apostasy of God's people. The people who know God and who were to keep His ways, even His ministers, apostatized, turned away from God, and embraced the ways of the godless and the current spirit of the age. And so it will be in the last days...There will be a great falling away, a great apostasy. The account goes on to document the rise of a world culture that seeks to merge all cultures into one and to compel everyone to abandon their faith. Any culture, faith, people, or person that stands in its way, it seeks to stamp out. So it will be at the end of the age...a global culture...and the persecution of God's people...a civilization that criminalizes the ways of God, abolishes the Word of God, overturns the order of God, blasphemes the Name of God, desecrates the sacred things of God, and wars against the people of God. So it will be at the end."

"Is there any hope in the blueprint?" I asked.

"Always," he said. "Though most went along with the apostasy and the darkness, there was a remnant who would not go along, who held strong, and who became the resistance...the Maccabees. And God anointed them and empowered them to overcome the darkness and to usher in the light, thus, the Festival of Lights. Learn of the Maccabean Blueprint and follow its keys." Then he handed me the oil lamp. "Go ahead," he said, motioning for me to light the remainder of the lights of the menorah. So I did. "And this is how you overcome," he said. "You fight the darkness by shining into it the light of God."

The Mission: Live today by the Maccabean Blueprint. Stand with God and don't be moved. Go against the odds. Fight the fight. Light up the darkness.

Daniel 11:32; Zechariah 9:13–14; Ephesians 6:10–20; Revelation 12:11

The Maccabee Blueprint I–IV

HEAVEN'S WOMB

WE HAD BEEN observing one of the tent villages when suddenly the stillness was suddenly broken by a burst of high-pitched cries of excitement.

"Birth," said the teacher. "Do you remember when we saw the woman sitting by the tent door, the one who was expecting? That's the sound of celebration for her newborn baby."

It was some time before people began emerging from the tent, first a middle-aged woman, a friend or relative of the mother, cradling the newborn baby boy.

"Do you remember when I spoke of the child in the womb...how that child would never be able to make sense of his life in the womb, because the womb was not the world he was made for, but the place of preparation for the world he was made for? It wasn't just a revelation about heaven. It was a revelation about this world...and about your life. When Messiah spoke of what comes after this world, He spoke of it as the day we 'enter life.' Think about it...to enter life. If we will enter life then, then what is this present life?"

"It must be pre-life," I said.

"Yes," he said. "Pre life...pre-birth. In fact, it is written in the Scriptures that 'the whole creation groans and labors with birth pains together until now.' This entire life is prenatal. Do you know what this life really is?"

"What?"

"The womb of heaven," he said. "This life is heaven's womb. It's not what you're destined for. It's not your home. It's the place of your preparation for the place you are destined for. As the womb was to prepare you for this life...this life is to prepare you for what is yet to come. As an unborn child can never understand or judge his life by the womb, neither can you understand or judge your life by your present circumstances...but only by that which they are preparing you for...heaven. And God will use everything of this world, and everything in your life, the joys and the sorrows, the victories and the losses, the mountains and the valleys, all of it, to prepare you, to grow you, and to form you into the child of heaven you are yet to become. From here on, see this world and your life as it actually is, and let it prepare you for the life beyond this life, and the world beyond this world, that you would be ready on that day...when you leave this word...and are born to eternity. For everything you've known of this world and of your life on earth...was none other than heaven's womb."

The Mission: Take part in a new revelation—see everything in your life, as your preparation for eternal life. See this life as the womb of heaven. And live your life accordingly.

Psalm 139:13–16; Matthew 18:3; 19:7; John 16:21–22; Romans 8:22–23, 29

THE MASK OF THE EGYPTIAN

HE LED ME into the Chamber of Books and to a large volume bound in blue and much less ancient-looking than most of the other books in that room. It was a book of cathedral art, depictions of Messiah in paintings, sculptures, and stained-glass windows.

"Do you think He looks Jewish?" asked the teacher.

"Not in there," I said.

"Tell me of Joseph as the shadow of Messiah."

"He was despised and rejected by his brothers, separated from his family, exiled to a foreign land, falsely accused, and imprisoned. He suffered for the sins of others but was then raised up from his dungeon, exalted, and given a royal position from which he saved a nation."

"And all the while," said the teacher, "estranged from his family and they to him. He becomes the hope of a world beyond the world of his family. His brothers have no idea that the savior of Egypt is their rejected and long-lost brother Joseph. Then they go down to Egypt and stand in his presence, face-to-face. But they don't know it's him. Why?"

"He would have been dressed up as an Egyptian official."

"That's correct. They couldn't see past his Egyptian clothes and adornments. They could only see a lord of Egypt, a Gentile savior of a Gentile land. What does the mystery reveal?"

"For the last two thousand years Messiah has become the Savior to people of every nation and tongue...and yet, He's been estranged from His own family, Israel, the Jewish people. To them He's the Savior of the Gentiles. They can't see past the foreign clothing, the adornments..."

"The stained glass, the statues, the icons, the cathedrals of a culture cut off from its Jewish roots. But that's not the end of the story. What happens at the end?"

"Joseph's brothers finally realize that the Egyptian is their long-lost brother...and their hope as well."

"So too the story of Messiah and His people will end when they stand before Him face-to-face and finally see through the clothing, the adornments, and the mask of two thousand years. And then they will realize that the Savior of the Gentiles is their long-lost brother, Yeshua, their Joseph, and their hope as well. Pray for that day. For when it comes, it will be Messiah's joy, Israel's redemption, and, as it is written, riches for the world."

The Mission: Pray for the peace of Jerusalem and for His ancient people to see through the mask and behold Messiah, their long-lost brother, Yeshua.

Genesis 44:18; 45:1–2; Hosea 3:4–5; Zechariah 12:10–13:1; Matthew 23:37–39

The Shadow Man I–VI

AS A MAN CARRIES HIS SON

WE WATCHED FROM a mountain ridge as a family of nomads made their way across a barren plain. The father was carrying in his arms his infant son.

"As a man carries his son," said the teacher. "When is it that a man carries his son?"

"When his son is a baby," I replied.

"Yes, and when else?" he asked.

"When his son is too tired to continue walking, or when his son is sick or disabled."

"And when else?"

"When he holds his son...to embrace him."

"Did you know that it is written in the Scriptures that, as that father is to his infant son, so God is to His people? When the Israelites reached the end of their journeying, Moses told them, 'You saw how the Lord your God carried you, *as a man carries his son*, in all the way that you went until you came to this place.' Remember this image...a man carrying his son. It's a picture of God and His people...It's a picture of God and you. The wilderness journey is a symbol of our journey through this life. So in your journey through this life, there will be times when you'll find yourself too weary to go on. It will be then that He will carry you in His arms. And there will be times when you find yourself with infirmities, wounds, disabling wounds, brokenness, and in some way unable to go on. It is then that He will carry you. And when you find yourself in a valley, down, in the lowest times of your life, and unable to raise yourself, it will be then that His hand will grab hold of yours and lift you up. And there will be times when you feel alone and abandoned. And it will be then that the arms of your Father will hold you and embrace you. You will not see His arms with your eyes and only sometimes will you feel them. But they will be there, always lifting you up, always keeping you, always holding you, and always carrying you on, to bring you to the appointed place and day."

He was quiet as he stared at the family still making its way across the plain.

"And there is one other time," he said, "that a man will carry his son...when his son has died. And so when you close your eyes for the last time in this life, the arms of your Father will once more hold you and bring you from this wilderness into the Promised Land...as tenderly and as lovingly as a man carries his son."

The Mission: Thank God for the times in your life when you couldn't go on, but God carried you. Let those same arms carry you and your burdens now.

Deuteronomy 1:31; Song of Solomon 8:5; Isaiah 40:11; 46:3–4; John 10:27–29

As a Man Carries His Son

THE IMMANUEL PARADOX

SOMETHING I DON'T understand...When Messiah was dying, He said, 'My God, why have You forsaken Me?' Why would He have said that?"

"Would it have been better," said the teacher, "if He hadn't said that? Would it have been more fitting or more glorious if dying on the cross was easy for Him...if it was not excruciating...and if He was not overwhelmed? That's the point. It cost Him everything. It was the ultimate sacrifice even for God. It's all the more glorious...It's the love of God."

"But how could He be forsaken?"

"Remember, He was dying in our place. He *became* sin. He made Himself the focal point of all judgment. So He had to be separated...It's part of judgment—separation from God...And there's another reason, a beautiful reason. Did it ever occur to you, the paradox?"

"What do you mean?"

"He said, 'My God, My God, why have You forsaken Me?' But who is it that is saying those words? The One saying, 'My God, why have You forsaken Me'...is God. God is the One asking God why God has forsaken Him."

"God become God-forsaken...a colossal paradox."

"And He's speaking those words in our place. The One saying those words is Immanuel, 'God is with us.' So the One asking why God is not with Him is 'God is with us.' Why is that an awesome thing? Because it means this: When you come to the darkest moments of your life, when you feel God has forsaken you, even then He will be with you. When you cry out, 'My God, why have You forsaken me?,' God will be right there saying those words with you. When you feel infinitely far away and hopelessly separated from God, God will be there feeling just as infinitely far away and hopelessly separated from God with you. That it was God Himself saying those words in our place means that even if you were forsaken by God, God would choose to be forsaken with you...and so you will never be forsaken. If God was with us even when He was separated from God, then there is nothing in this world or beyond, nothing in this age or in the ages to come, that will ever separate you from the love of God in Him who is the love of God...and who will always be with you."

The Mission: Remember those times in your life when you felt farthest from God. Now ponder this: God was there feeling just as far from God with you. So nothing will ever separate you from the love of God.

Isaiah 43:2; Matthew 27:46; 28:19–20; Romans 8:35–39

Immanuel I–II

THE GREAT ASCENDING

THE TEACHER HAD given me a day's notice to prepare. We were to go hiking. I was to pack food and other necessities and get to bed early, as it would take the entire day. We left before dawn. Our hiking took us on a mostly level path surrounded by low-lying hills on both the right and the left. Because of the hills, for most of the journey our view of the surrounding landscape was limited. We talked for hours, stopped several times for breaks. By late afternoon the hills that flanked us began to recede. Finally we came to a ledge from which we were able to catch our first glimpse of the wider landscape. What I saw then stunned me, not just because of the view, which was breathtaking, but what it revealed about the journey we had just taken. We were standing at the edge of a high mountain. It had to be one of the highest mountains I had ever ascended during my days in the desert.

"Look over there," he said. "That's where we came from."

"I had no idea," I said. "The path seemed so level."

"It seemed level in the short run. But in the long run, over time, it was a colossal ascent. So how did we get here? We just walked...and continued to walk...and kept walking. You see," he said, "over the long run, continuance, consistency, and perseverance overcome everything else. And the small upward steps, taken every day, will end up lifting you to the heights. God has called you not only to love, but to keep loving; not only to believe, but to press on in believing; and not only to do right, but to persevere in doing it. When you do that, then the power of your love, your faith, and your righteousness will be multiplied...And something else...Don't ever judge your life or what God is doing in your life by how it appears in the moment on the journey. You'll rarely see it. But when you get to a vantage point like this one, and look back at your journey, at the big picture, at the long run, it is then that you'll see the magnitude of the miracle of what God has done in your life. Remember this day, and this journey. It's the journey you're on. Walk this good road, and no matter what...keep walking it. Never give up, but keep walking, and you will end up standing on heights you dreamed you could attained...and looking back at the magnitude of a miracle and a journey you never realized you were on."

The Mission: Take time today to look back at the big picture. See how far God has taken you. Press on in your journey step by step to the heights.

Psalms 18:36; 84:5–7; 122; Isaiah 2:1–2; Philippians 3:13–14

Higher Ground

THE GARDENER

HE ARRANGED FOR me to meet him in one of the school's gardens of fruit trees. I found him there wearing a large straw hat for shade and working the soil with a farming implement.

He laid down the implement, sat down on one of the garden's low stone walls, and motioned for me to join him. So I did.

"In the beginning," said the teacher, "God created man in His own image. And where was man?"

"In a garden."

"And what was man?" He waited for a response, but I couldn't think of any. "He was a gardener. God placed the man in Eden to till and keep the garden. Man was a gardener. So what would that mean?"

Again, I didn't know how to answer the question.

"Man," said the teacher, "was created in the image of God. And man was created specifically to be a gardener. Therefore..."

"God is a gardener?"

"Yes."

"But how?" I asked. "What's His garden?"

"The creation is His garden. He keeps it, He tends it, and He sows into it His seed...He sows into the creation His Word, and into His garden His life...that it might bear its fruit. But the garden didn't bear its fruit."

"Meaning," I said, "the creation never brought forth the life it was meant to bear?"

"Yes. So the Gardener came into the garden, that the garden might bear its fruit."

"God came into His creation that the creation might bring forth life."

"And when the creation bore the firstfruits of new life, when He first appeared outside the tomb, in what form did He appear? What was He mistaken for?"

"A gardener."

"And what kind of tomb was it that bore the firstfruits?"

"A garden tomb.

"He is the Gardener..."

"And we are His garden.

"So let the Gardener come into His garden. Let Him till its soil, sow its seed, and bring forth its new life. For every garden that is touched by the Gardener will bear the fruit it was meant to bear."

The Mission: Today, let the Gardener come into His garden, to every part of your life, especially the untouched soil, that every part would bear its fruit.

Genesis 1:29; 2:15; Song of Solomon 4:16; 5:1; 6:2; John 20:13–20

The Gardener

THE MISSION PLANET

HAD GONE WITH the teacher to the city to do some errands for the school. By the time we started our return journey, it was nightfall. Rather than travel the entire way back in the dark, we decided to sleep overnight on a nearby mountain. We talked late into the evening as we gazed at the darkness of the desert, the light of the city, and the stars in the night sky.

"Every child of God has a calling," said the teacher, "a mission to fulfill. What do you think is yours?"

"I don't know," I replied. "But I can't see myself as a missionary."

"Really?" he said. "Do you know who the greatest missionary was? The Messiah."

"How was He a missionary?"

"His mission was from heaven to earth, from God to man. His mission is this planet. In the Book of Hebrews, He is spoken of as the Apostle, meaning one sent as on a mission. So for Him, the world was not home or the place to live one's life. The world was the mission field. And so His life on earth was radically different from the lives of others. He didn't live *from* the world. He lived *to* the world. And if Messiah is now in you, what does that mean?"

"The world is no longer our native land...but our mission field?"

"That's correct."

"But that could be true for God, because He's not from this world. But we are."

"No," said the teacher, "you *were* from this world. But when you were born again, you were born from above. Therefore, from now on, you must see this world in a new way—not as your home—but as your place of mission. So you are not in this world to become rich or powerful or comfortable. You're not in this world to get anything from it. You are in this world to give to this world. So you are no longer to live *from* your circumstances, from your problems, or even from your life. You are now to live *to* them, from God and *to* the world. So it's not a question whether you're called to be a missionary to the mission field. You already *are* a missionary, and you're already *in* your mission field. So get on with your mission. Bring to the earth the Word, the truth, and the love of God. And live as an agent of heaven on earth, on a mission from God to bring the message of salvation to the natives of this planet—the mission world."

The Mission: You are already on the mission planet. Start living today not as one at home, but as one sent here on assignment. Fulfill your mission.

John 8:23; 17:16–18; Acts 13:3–5; 2 Corinthians 5:20; Hebrews 3:1

THE ANGELIC MEASURING ROD

HE BROUGHT ME into the Chamber of Measures and to a tall wooden cabinet attached to the wall in front of which we both stood. It had to be at least eight feet high.

"Open it," said the teacher. So I did. Inside the cabinet, leaning against its back wall, were several rod-like objects almost as tall as the cabinet itself. At the bottom of the cabinet were cords and ropes of various lengths.

"Measuring rods," he said, "and measuring lines. They were used as rulers and tape measures are used today."

He removed one of them and gave it to me to hold.

"But they weren't only used by men," he said. "They were used by angels. The prophets Ezekiel and Zechariah each saw an angel holding a measuring rod or line in his hand. In each case, the angel with the measuring vessel was a sign concerning God's future prophetic purposes, namely, the rebuilding of Jerusalem and the Temple. But God's prophetic purposes not only require building materials but events of human history. For Jerusalem to be rebuilt, human events had to conform to the measurements of angels."

"And in modern times," I said, "Israel was restored again, according to the biblical prophecy."

"Yes," said the teacher. "And in order for those prophecies to come true, world history and the lives and actions of individuals around the world had to all work together—acting, reacting, and interacting one upon the other at the exact place and time—for the plans of God and the measurements of angels to be fulfilled. You see, there exists a plan of precise measurements not only for the construction of temples but for human history and for your life. And even a world that wars against His purposes will, in the end, conform to the angelic measurements. He will use all things of this world and of its history—the good, the bad, the godly, and the ungodly—to bring about the fulfillment of His purposes. So whenever things appear out of control and you're tempted to fear, be at peace. Just remember this rod. It is a sign to you that, in the end, every evil will be overcome, every purpose of God will be fulfilled, the good will prevail, and the history of this world, and of our lives, will conform to the plans of heaven . . . and to the precise dimensions set forth by the angelic measuring rod."

The Mission: Take the Word of God today and follow its exact measurements and specifications and you will walk into the exact dimensions of God's will for your life.

Isaiah 46:10–13; Jeremiah 21:11; Ezekiel 40:1–5; Revelation 11:1; 21:15

The Heavenly Pattern I–IV

THE BOOK OF AGES

THE TEACHER LED me into the Chamber of Scrolls. There on two wooden stands rested two open scrolls, one next to the other. The scroll on the left was opened to its beginning and the scroll on the right, to its end. "This, on the left," said the teacher, "is the Book of Genesis. And on the right is the Book of Revelation. What do they have in common?"

"Genesis is the first book of Scripture and Revelation is the last."

"The beginning and the end," he said, "written over a millennium apart, one in Hebrew, the other in Greek. We're going to look at the beginning of the beginning and the end of the end, the first three chapters of Genesis and the last three last chapters of Revelation. It is here in the beginning, in Genesis, that the curse begins. And it's here at the end, in Revelation, that it's written, 'There shall be no more curse.' In Genesis, death begins. At the end of Revelation there is no more death. In Genesis, the tree of life is taken from man and disappears. In Revelation, the tree of life reappears and is given back to man. In Genesis, the first act of creation is God calling the light into being. In Revelation, God Himself becomes the light. And in Genesis God creates the heavens and the earth. In Revelation, He creates a new heaven and a new earth...That which begins at the beginning of Genesis only finds its resolution, and perfectly, at the end of Revelation. Think of it...The Bible was written in a span of ages, and not by one writer but by a multitude, each at a different point of time within those ages...No one person was alive to direct it or coordinate it...except one...God. Only He could have woven it all together from Genesis to Revelation, from the beginning to the end. So too perfectly does He work His plan of salvation from the creation to the New Jerusalem. And no less perfectly will He work the plan and story of your life. And as it is in the middle of His story, you can't quite see where it's all heading, so in the midst of yours. But at the end, it all comes home. In the end you'll see it all perfectly woven together from the beginning. Until then you must trust His perfect working in what you don't see and press on to the end when you will see. For as perfectly as He has written His story from Genesis to Revelation, so perfectly is He writing and will He write your story...from the beginning to the end."

The Mission: Don't try to understand your life from the middle. But know that as you follow His leading, your story will, in the end, become perfect.

Genesis 1–3; Hebrews 3:14; 12:2; Revelation 20:1–22:3

The Word

THE BRIDE AND GROOM IN THE MARRIAGE CHAMBER

WAS THINKING OF the wedding celebration," I said. "We left at the beginning...but it went on."

"Yes," said the teacher, "for seven days."

"I would have loved to have seen some of it."

"That celebration is long over," he said, "but there was another bride, the one you saw when I spoke of the calah. And right now she's in the midst of her seven days. Would you like to see it?"

My answer was, of course, yes. So we journeyed to the tent village where the celebration was still in full bloom. It was evening when we arrived. We followed the sound of laughter and singing and made our way to the celebration. The bride and groom were inside a festive-looking tent made of thin white fabrics. The light inside the tent caused their shadows to appear on the tent walls. There were others with them, their family and friends, but only the silhouette of the bride and groom could be seen through the tent wall from where we were standing.

"What's happening?" I asked.

"The bride and groom are surrounded by celebration and yet are also to themselves, alone in the midst of the celebration. Up to this point they've only seen each other in the midst of other things, mediators, rituals, families, villages, bridesmaids, and groomsmen. But now for the first time they're sitting in each other's presence, and everything around them fades into the background...It's a picture of the end."

"Of the end?"

"At the wedding celebration, when the bride and the Groom dwell in each other's presence. When the bride sees the Groom with no more mediation. Up to then we will have seen Him through other things, through His blessings, through His creation, His people, and His working in our lives...But then we will see Him with no more mediation. As it is written, in heaven there will be no temple. For God Himself will be our temple. And there will be no more need for the sun to give light, for God Himself will be our light. Then it will be as if it was only Him and us...only Him and you...Then you will see Him as He is...and always was...but now face-to-face...And everything else will fade away into the background...just the bride and the Bridegroom...you...and the One for whom you were brought into existence...alone together...as if for the first time...you and God...in the bridal chamber...and nothing else."

The Mission: Today, enter into the marital chamber and dwell there with your Beloved, you and God, alone, and nothing else.

Song of Solomon 1:4; 2:14; 1 Corinthians 13:12; Revelation 22:4

Under the Huppah

SHEMEN

THE TEACHER LED me into one of the olive gardens and to a stone vat filled with a brownish liquid. Sitting on the ridge of the vat was a clay pitcher. He dipped the pitcher into the liquid, lifted it up, and slowly poured back its contents, which glistened in the light of the afternoon sun.

"A sacred substance," he said. "Oil. The substance of anointing. And yet the true anointing comes from the Spirit of God. Oil is the symbol of God's Spirit. And it holds a mystery."

"What mystery?"

"The name for *oil* in Hebrew is *shemen*. The word for *eighth* in Hebrew is *shemini*. The two words are joined together. Oil is the symbol of the Spirit. And oil is linked to the number eight. So the power of the Spirit is linked to the number eight."

"I'm not understanding."

"Seven, in Scripture, is the number of completion. Then what is eight? That which is over and above completion, that which exceeds, that which surpasses, that which abounds and overflows. Thus the power of the Spirit is the power to go over and above, to exceed, to surpass, to not only be full, but to be filled up to the point of overflowing. The seventh day is the end of the week. Seven signifies the end. Thus eight signifies beyond the end, beyond the limit, beyond the finite, beyond all limitations. So the power of the Spirit is to go beyond the end, to transcend the finite, and to live beyond all limitations. And what is the eighth day of the week. It's the first day, the new beginning. So the power of the Spirit is the power of new beginnings, the power of newness. And lastly, eight is the number of the mystery day, *Shemini Atzeret,* the day that signifies what comes after the end, eternity...heaven. What will heaven be? Filled with the Spirit of God. So the power of the Spirit is the power of the age to come, the power of heaven. Therefore live in the Spirit, and you will have the power of shemen— the power to live over and above, beyond full and overflowing, exceeding, surpassing, going beyond the end, transcending the finite, breaking through all limitations, walking in newness and new beginnings, and living now, beyond this world, in the realm of heaven. That is the power of the Spirit...and the mystery of shemen."

The Mission: Discover the mystery of shemen. Live in the power of the Spirit, beyond your limitations, over and above, exceeding, transcending, overflowing, and dwelling in the heavenlies.

Exodus 30:30–31; John 7:37–39; Acts 1:8; Romans 15:19; Galatians 5:22–25

The Spirit-Filled Life

THE REBEGETTING

IT'S DRAWING NEAR," he said, "the end of our time together."

"And then what?" I asked.

"Then you'll go forth from here."

"It's kind of sad," I said.

"It's the way of life," said the teacher. "When you grow up, you leave the house of your childhood. From the parent comes the child, and from the child comoo a parent. Life reproduces itself. When you're a child, your purpose is to receive more than you give. But when you become an adult, your purpose is to give more than you receive, to give just as you were given as a child. So then those who live to take from this world have not attained completion. Only those who give have become complete. And when you give, then that which has been given to you has also become compete. And as it is in the natural realm, so too in the spiritual. Messiah made disciples of the fishermen. But the time then came for them to go out and make disciples of Messiah. So from the teacher comes the disciple, and from the disciple comes the teacher. It's the way of life...and the way of God. Whatever you have received from God, you must give to others. If you've been loved, you must love. And if you've been loved without having deserved that love, then you must love those who don't deserve your love. If you've been given joy, your life must bring joy to others. If you've been saved, then you must save others. And if you've been blessed, then your life must bring blessing into the lives of others."

"But God didn't only give," I said. "His life *was* the gift. And He didn't only bless. His life *was* the blessing."

"Yes, and therefore, if you've received that blessing, your life must *become* a blessing. And if you receive that gift, your life must *become* a gift."

"And He didn't just save," I said, "He became salvation. He became Yeshua."

"Yes," said the teacher. "And therefore, if you've received Yeshua, then your life must become Yeshua and Yeshua must become your life. Life begets life. Love begets love. So He made His life a gift to you, that your life would become a gift to the world. Only then is the circle complete...when your life becomes love."

The Mission: Life must beget life. Whatever you have received, you must give. Love others, bless others, give to others, and save others—as God has done to you.

Deuteronomy 3:14, 23; 34:9; Matthew 10:5–8; 28:19–20; John 14:12;
2 Timothy 4:1–2

Graduation I–II

THE PELEH

WE WERE SITTING on the plain where he had previously drawn words and letters in the sand. He now did so again.

"It's the word *Peleh*," said the teacher. "It means a wonder, something so amazing that you can't do anything but wonder about it. It's the word used in Isaiah's prophecy of Messiah's birth, a child will be born, and His Name will be *Peleh*, the Wonder. Messiah is the Peleh, the Wonder. His impact on the world defies natural explanation and, after all these ages, He still causes people around the world to wonder over Him. But *Peleh* also means the miracle. So Messiah is the Peleh, the Miracle of this world. His birth was a miracle, His ministry was a miracle, His resurrection was a miracle. Every moment of His life on earth was a miracle. And the word *Peleh* also means too high, too hard, too great, and too much. What does this tell you about salvation?"

"It's above us," I said. "It's above our ability to attain. We can't do it."

"But *He* can...because He's the Peleh. He can do that which is too hard for you, even what's impossible. And if He's in you, then you have the power to do that which is too hard for you to do, to attain what is too high for you to attain, and to live a life that's too great for you to live. If He's in you, then the Peleh is in you, and therefore you have the power of Peleh, the power to live a miraculous life, a life that causes those around you to wonder. But for that to happen, you must never forget the first meaning of Peleh."

"The Wonder?"

"The Wonder. He must be the One who always causes you to wonder...to wonder over His grace, to wonder over His mercy, to wonder over the fact that God loves you, and to wonder over the fact that you're saved. Never stop knowing Him as the wonder of your life. And never stop wondering over the wonder of being saved, the wonder of being forgiven, the wonder of knowing His love...the wonder of Him. If it doesn't cause you to wonder, then it's not the Peleh. Let Him be the Peleh, the Wonder, of your life...And your life will be full of miracles and wonders...Your life will become...a Peleh."

The Mission: Get back to the Peleh, the wonder of His love, the miracle of your salvation, and the power to do the impossible.

Exodus 15:11; Isaiah 9:6; Acts 2:43; Ephesians 3:19

THE SEVEN MYSTERIES OF YOUR LIFE

H E LED ME up one of the hills overlooking the school. Waiting for us there at the summit were seven stone pillars, the same seven pillars he had shown me at the school.

"The seven pillars," said the teacher, "representing the holy days and times of Israel. They hold the mystery of the age. But they also hold the mystery of your life. You see, God has ordained the lives of His children according to the sacred Hebrew year and the holy days of Israel."

"What do you mean?"

He led me to the first pillar, representing the Feast of Passover.

"Passover opens the sacred Hebrew year," he said. "So too Passover opens your life in God. Your salvation begins as you partake of the Passover Lamb...and its power begins changing your life, releasing you of bondage, ending the old, and setting you on a journey with God."

We came to the second pillar, representing Yom Resheet, the Day of Firstfruits.

"Then comes Firstfruits as you begin bearing the firstfruits of salvation, the firstfruits of repentance, of love, of godliness, and you begin walking in the power of resurrection and the newness of life."

He led me to the third pillar, representing the Feast of Shavuot.

"Then comes the Shavuot, the Pentecost, the power and anointing of the Spirit to enable you to overcome, to do the works of God, and to fulfill all you've been called to do and become."

We came to the fourth pillar, representing the summer harvest.

"Then comes the harvest of your salvation, as you go forth into His fields, as you reap new life, as you bless and give life to others, and fulfill your ministry and calling."

We came to the fifth pillar, representing the Feast of Trumpets.

"And then will come the time of Trumpets, the autumn of your salvation, the finishing up of your reaping, the completing of your harvest, and your readying to meet the Lord."

We came to the sixth pillar, representing the Day of Atonement.

"Then will come the day when you will stand before Him, beyond the veil...face-to-face."

He led me to the last pillar, representing the Feast of Tabernacles.

"And finally will come your Feast of Tabernacles, your days of dwelling in the presence of God, in His peace, His joy, His love, and His blessings...forever."

The Mission: God has ordained appointed times for your life—so too for your days. Seek and find His appointed times and moments of this day.

Leviticus 23; Psalm 139:16

The Moedeem and the Mystery of Your Life

THE LAND OF BEYOND

THE TEACHER LED me into the Chamber of Scrolls, but instead of unrolling a scroll and sharing, he began the sharing with no scroll.

"I've told you of the mystery of *Shemini Atzeret*," he said, "the last of the appointed holy days, when the scroll of the Torah reaches its end, and its last words are read...which are all about the end, the end of the wilderness journey. Of what does all this speak?"

"About the end," I replied, "the end of earthly existence, the end of this creation."

"Yes," said the teacher, "but Shemini Atzeret speaks also of what comes after the end. And there is another scroll. One scroll ends...but another begins."

He then led me over to one of the shelves, removed a scroll, laid it on the wooden table, and unrolled it to its beginning.

"This is the other scroll...the Book of Joshua. For the children of God, what comes after the end? When the wilderness journey ends, the Book of Joshua begins. And what is this book about? It's about leaving the wilderness, crossing the Jordan to the other side...to that which is beyond the wilderness...to the Promised Land...And so for the child of God, when the old is finished, a new book begins. When the old creation is no more, a new creation will come. And when the old life is finished, a new life begins. And we will cross over to the other side. Do you remember what the word *Hebrew* means in Hebrew?"

"One who crosses over."

"And so on that day you will cross the Jordan into the land beyond. And as it was for the children of Israel when they finally entered the Promised Land, so it will be for you...That which you had for so long hoped for, longed for, and believed in by faith, you will then see with your eyes and walk with your feet...the Promised Land. And who was with them in the Promised Land, who had walked among them in the wilderness? Joshua. And do you know what *Joshua* is in Hebrew?"

"What?"

"*Yeshua*...Jesus. And so when all has passed away, the old world and everything in it...He who led you through this life will lead you in...into the Promised Land. He who held you, who kept you, and who never left you...in every moment of your earthly journey...and who loved you before you were...will be with you every moment...to the end...and beyond the end...forever."

The Mission: Ponder the day you'll cross over into the Promised Land. And give thanks that He Who will be with you *then*, is with you right *now*.

Deuteronomy 8:7–9; 26:15; Joshua 1:1–4; 1 Peter 1:3–4; Revelation 21:1–4

The Mystery of the Eighth Day I–III

THE MYSTERY OF THE PLURALITIES

WE STOOD ON the flat top roof of one of the school buildings from which we took in a vast panorama of the surrounding desert landscape.

"Today," said the teacher, "we bring together the pluralities...those mystery words of Hebrew that can only be expressed in the plural. Tell me what you remember of them."

"*Elohim*," I said, "the word for *God*."

"God who transcends all things and all that we think He is."

"*Chayim*, the word for *life*."

"That life is more than this life and, in God, is unending."

"*Rachamim*, the love of God, His mercy and compassion."

"That there is no limiting of God's mercy and no end to His love."

"*Shamayim*, the word for heaven."

"That there's always more to heaven than you think there is."

"Jerusalem...*Yerushalayim*, the City of God."

"That there are always two Jerusalems, that which you see and that which is beyond seeing, that which is, and that which is yet to come.

"Do you see any pattern," he asked, "anything that binds them all together?"

"They all bear the property of transcendence."

"They do," he said. "And together they bear another revelation. Chayim, life everlasting. Where will we spend it? In Shamayim, heaven. Where specifically? Yerushalayim, in the New Jerusalem, the Jerusalem above, which is yet to come. And what will be flowing in that city? *Mayim*, yet another of the pluralities, the river of living waters. And what will fill up the New Jerusalem? The Panim, the Face of God. And what will be the essence of heaven and that which fills up its every moment? Rachamim, the infinite, overflowing, never-ending love of God. And what will it all center on? It will all center on Elohim...God. For what are all the pluralities about? That which is beyond. And so they will all be part of the beyond. And they tell us that the things of God are beyond containing and beyond the end. God is beyond all that is spoken of God, beyond all that is thought and imagined of Him, and beyond all the praises that are lifted to Him. He is beyond even the beyond. For His love to us...His love to you...has no limits and no end. It is beyond all things from everlasting to everlasting."

The Mission: Take time today to meditate and dwell on where you will dwell forever, and on all its never-ending and everlasting pluralities.

1 Corinthians 2:9; Ephesians 3:20–21; Revelation 22:1–5

The Hebrew Mysteries I–IV

THE TIME OF KNOWING

THE TEACHER LED me to the Chamber of Books and removed from one of the shelves a large ancient-looking book in a brown binding.

"Look through it," he said. So I did. "How long do you think it would take you to learn everything that's in this book in depth?"

"In depth? Maybe three months."

"And what about all the books on this shelf?"

There were many books. I did the calculation in my head. "Maybe ten years," I replied.

"And how long to learn what's in every volume in this bookcase?"

"I would guess eighty years."

"Now look at all the bookcases in this chamber. How long do you think it would take you to learn everything that's inside every one of these volumes?"

"Many lifetimes," I said.

"Do you know why God gives us eternity?"

"Why?"

"Because the purpose of our existence is to know God. And so it must be eternity. For eternity is the time it takes to know God...So never make the mistake of thinking that you know everything there is to know about Him. It's when you think you know, that you stop knowing. And if it takes an eternity to know God, then how much is a lifetime of knowledge next to how much there is yet to know?"

"One eternitieth," I said, "one infinitieth...next to nothing."

"No matter how much you know, there will always be more...there will always be so much more. No matter how much you know of Him, you've only just begun. And that's how you must always come, as one who doesn't know the half of it, which will always mathematically be the case. So you must come as a little child, as one who knows there's so much more to know, and for whom everything is new. Even the apostle Paul, who knew more of God than anyone else, even he wrote, 'That I might know Him.' If he could say that, how much more we. So never stop seeking Him. Never stop pressing on to know Him...and to know more of Him...and more than that. For eternity is the length of time it takes to know Him...and a lifetime is just the beginning of eternity."

The Mission: Since it will take an eternity for you to know God, there's so much for you to discover. Seek to know Him today as if for the first time.

Psalms 23:6; 27:4; 63; Matthew 18:3–4; Philippians 3:10

The Mystery of the Eighth Day I–III

THE BLESSING WITH NO END

WE WERE STANDING at the school's western border, beyond which was the rest of the desert. Just outside the border was one of the teachers surrounded by his students. His course had begun just before ours and so had now come to its end. The students were getting ready to depart, and the teacher was saying a blessing over them before they began their journey.

"That will be us," said the teacher, "not long from now. It reminds me of another teacher, another course, and another farewell."

"A teacher from the school?"

"The Messiah," he said, "and the students were the disciples. It is written, 'He led them out as far as Bethany, and He lifted up His hands and blessed them. And while He blessed them, He was parted from them and carried up into heaven.' It was the end of a course, and of Messiah's ministry on earth. So what exactly happened?"

"He blessed them and then ascended."

"No," said the teacher. "It doesn't say that. It says that He lifted up His hands and blessed them. And while He blessed them, He was parted from them."

"I thought that's what I said."

"No," said the teacher. "You said, He blessed them and then He left. But the Scripture says He blessed them, and *while* He blessed them, He was parted from them."

"Why is that significant?"

"He never ended the blessing...not on earth...His blessing never ended. You see, Messiah's blessing has no end...It has no limitation, no expiration, and no ceasing. It's an unending blessing. It's not limited to the first century, or to Jerusalem, or to the disciples, or even to the Book of Acts. He doesn't only bless *them*. He blesses *you*. And the blessing He gives you has no end. It doesn't stop because of your failures, your falling, and your sins. It has no end. There's just as much of it now as there was when He blessed them as He left. The blessing never runs out, never ages, and never fails. So receive it now, as new and as powerful as it was as on the day He gave it. And as the blessing keeps going, you do the same. All things of this world must end...except this...the blessing...it has no end."

The Mission: Receive this day the blessing Messiah gave His disciples. It was to you as well. Receive as much as you can. It has no end."

Psalms 21:6; 106; Luke 24:50–53; Revelation 22:21

The Unended

HOME

HOW STRANGE," SAID the teacher. "We're born into this world. We've never been anywhere else. And yet, we never feel at home here. It's the only place we've ever known, and yet still, we're never quite at home within it. We're never at home with its pain and sorrows, with its growing old and dying, with its losses, its death, its imperfections, its darkness, its evils...and where nothing lasts and everything passes away. Even in the best of times and circumstances, something's always missing. It can never fill our hearts. And the longer we're in this world, the less at home we are within it."

He paused to look up for a moment at the starlit sky above us.

"Where does the story of Passover begin?"

"In Egypt."

"The Israelites grew up in Egypt. It was the only home they knew. And yet they were never at home within it. And what was salvation about? Leaving Egypt and going to the Promised Land. They had never been to the Promised Land...and yet it was their home. Salvation is about coming home. From the Jewish people returning to the land of Israel to the prodigal son returning to his father, salvation is about coming home. And that's the mystery. That's why we're never at home in this world."

"Why aren't we at home in this world?"

"Because it's not home," he said. "Because it's not our home. Our hearts can never be at home in a world of imperfection and evil...of sorrows and dying and death...of seeing everything we know and love grow old and pass away. There is a home, but this world is not it. And our salvation begins on Passover. And Passover isn't only about being free...It's about coming home, coming home to God, and coming home to home."

"So home is..."

"The place for which our hearts were made...that place of no more sorrows and dying and death...and no evil or imperfection...and where nothing grows old anymore or passes away...the eternal...the Promised Land...heaven."

"But we've never been there before."

"Yes," said the teacher, "but when we get there, then for the first time in our lives...we'll be home."

The Mission: You are not yet home. Live today in light of that. Set your heart away from that which is not home, and toward that which is.

John 17:16; Psalm 46:4–5; Hebrews 13:14; John 14:1–3

THE TWO SHALL BE ONE

H E TOOK ME back to where the wedding had been. It was now sunset.

"We've been here several times," said the teacher, "from when we first saw the bridegroom alone until the wedding. This will be our last time here."

"What happened to the bride and groom?" I asked.

"Do you see that tent," he said, "over there...the light brown tent with the golden cord over the doorway? That's where they've been ever since the wedding. It was during the wedding celebration that they went off together to that tent and there the two became one. 'Therefore, a man shall leave his father and mother and be joined to his wife, and they shall become one flesh.' It's the completion of the circle," he said. "In the beginning, in the creation, the two were from one flesh. And from one flesh they become two. Now from two they become one. The woman came from the man. Now again she is joined to him, as in the miracle of creation, and from that joining comes the miracle of new creation. The two shall become one."

"But you're speaking of a mystery," I said, "more than of the man and the woman."

"Yes," he said, "I speak of a mystery. As the woman came from man..."

"So we came from God."

"And as the woman and the man must again become one..."

"So we must become one with the One from whom we came. We can only find the purpose for our existence in the One who is the reason for our existence. We must become one with God."

"And you do remember what the word *bridegroom* means in Hebrew?"

"The one who joins himself."

"And God is the Bridegroom, the One who joins Himself to us...to you. And if we are married to Him, then we must also become one with Him. The two become one. And of this it is written, 'The mystery is great....'"

"It's the mystery of love, isn't it? In the equation of love, one plus one equals one."

"Yes," said the teacher, "the mystery of love, and the final mystery. In that day, after the wedding, then the mystery of God and you will be complete. It is then that the two...shall be one."

The Mission: Join every part of your life to His life and let every part of His life be joined to yours. Unlock, experience, and live this mystery—the two shall become one.

Genesis 2:24; 1 Corinthians 6:17; Ephesians 5:31–32; The Song of Solomon

AFTER THE END

THE LAST MYSTERY had been given. It was now the day after, the day after the end. It was time to leave. I had spent the morning packing my belongings. The teacher came to my room and walked with me to the end of the school grounds. There we stopped and looked out at the vast expanse of plains and mountains of the desert wilderness.

"Do you know the way?" asked the teacher.

"Very much so," I answered.

"I mean through the wilderness."

"I do."

"What are you feeling?" he asked.

"Sad to leave."

"Are you glad you came?"

"I am. I can't imagine having not come. I wish it could go on."

"But leaving is part," he said. "You've been on a mountaintop. Now it's time to go down. Now you must take what you've learned and apply it to the world, to life. What you've received, you must now give. The disciple must become the teacher."

"The teacher?" I replied. "I could never be like you."

"But I was once just like you," he said, "a disciple, invited to come here by another teacher. And he, in turn, was once a disciple like me, invited by another. And so the mysteries have been passed down from teacher to disciple, from age to age. Remember what you were given here."

"I will. I wrote it all down. Every day, after every teaching, I wrote down everything I could remember. I have it all in a journal, a book."

"A book?" he said. "A book of mysteries. Good. Then you'll always have them. And every time you open up the mysteries, every time you ponder them, and every time you apply them to your life, you'll discover more revelations and more insights than you found at first."

There was a pause and a silence as we gazed out into the wilderness.

"Do you remember the fraction that represents our time on earth?"

"One-eternitieth," I said.

"Yes. That's how much you know so far, 'one-eternitieth,' 'one-infinitieth' of what there is to know. There's so much more to learn. So the course could never have ended here. And you must never stop seeking more of Him."

"So the course goes on for ..."

"Eternity."

"Because eternity is how long it takes to know God."

"Yes, and to know the final mystery."

"The final mystery?"

"God," he said. "The final mystery is God...God is the final and ultimate mystery...the mystery of all mysteries...and the mystery of you. And so the more you know Him, the more you'll know the answer to the mystery of you. And so the course goes on."

At that, we embraced, and then I left. I walked into the desert, then stopped to turn around.

"Teacher," I said.

"Yes."

"I never thanked you."

"For what?"

"For everything. For inviting a traveler who had no destination to find one."

"That *was* your destination," he said, "all of it. With God there are no accidents. It was He who invited you, He who called you, and He who taught you. And now it is He who goes with you."

Those were the last words I heard the teacher say. When, a little farther on, I turned around to look back, he was gone. And so ended the year of my dwelling in the desert, my days with the teacher.

And so with the writing of these words ends the record of those days and of the mysteries given therein.

I then resumed the journey, and the course of mysteries, as I walked through the wilderness in the presence of the Teacher.

And may the one who reads this book do likewise.

———◦———

THE RECEIVING

THE FOLLOWING TOOK place in the early days of my time in the desert. I include it here and not earlier as it wasn't one of the mysteries. But it was as important as anything else that happened that year and, in many ways, the point. It happened on a mountaintop after the teacher had finished sharing with me one of the mysteries.

"It's one thing to learn of the mysteries," he said. "But it's another to take part in them."

"What do you mean?"

"There's a difference between knowing about God and knowing God, hearing the truth, and receiving it. The mysteries cannot merely be learned. They must be partaken of, received."

"How do you receive and partake of the mysteries?"

"By receiving Him who is behind the mysteries, who is behind all mysteries. For behind all mysteries is the Truth. And the Truth cannot just be perceived with one's mind. It must be received with one's heart. The Truth is as a bridegroom. It cannot just be known of. It must be received. How do you receive the Truth? As a bride receives her bridegroom. You receive *Him*. As it is written, 'As many as received Him, to them He gave the right to become children of God...'"

"Born again."

"Yes," said the teacher. "In the end, it all comes down to that...and in the end, to one of two eternities—eternal life...heaven...or eternal separation from God...hell.... And there's only one way to enter heaven—not by good works and not by religion, but by the new birth. One can only enter heaven if one is born of heaven. And so you must be born again."

"How?"

"It can begin with a prayer."

"Which prayer?" I asked.

"It's not about which prayer," he said. "It's not a formula. It's the prayer of the heart that matters. It's when the bride says yes to the bridegroom...when she becomes his and he becomes hers. So all that is yours, your burdens and sins, becomes His. And all that is His, His salvation and His blessings, becomes yours."

The teacher then spoke in more detail about what it was to receive salvation and how to do so. It was then that I prayed. And it was then that everything changed. Soon after, I committed to writing the prayer I prayed that day, as best I could remember it. I include it here for one purpose, that all who read of the mysteries can truly know them and take part in them, that all who are not saved can become saved, that all who have not yet received can receive, and that all who have not yet become born again can become so. I include it not as a formula but as a guide, a guide for a prayer of the heart, a decision, a consecration, and a new beginning. For you who are not with absolute certainty sure where you will spend eternity, for you who have not yet received Him, and for you who have not yet partaken of the new birth, I include this now for your sake, that you might find eternal life:

> Lord God, I come to You now, and I open my heart and my life to Your calling. Thank You for loving me. Thank You for giving Your life, dying for my sins, rising again, and overcoming death that I could be forgiven and have eternal life. Forgive me of my sins. Wash me, cleanse me, and make me new. I turn away from my sins. I turn to You. From this moment on I make You the Lord of every part of my life. To You I place my faith and commit my life. I will follow You as Your disciple and go as You lead me. I receive Your love, Your forgiveness, Your cleansing, Your salvation, Your presence, Your power, and Your Spirit. I receive You into my heart and life. You are my God, and I am Your disciple. You are mine. And I am Yours. By Your Word and by this prayer, I can now say I am received. I'm forgiven. I'm new. I'm blessed. I'm free. I'm born again. I'm saved. And I have eternal life. Lead me on as I follow You from this moment forth and all the days of my life. I thank You, and I pray this prayer in the name above all names, the name of the Messiah, Yeshua, Jesus, the Light of the World, the Glory of Israel, my Hope, my Redeemer, and my Salvation.

For you who have prayed that prayer, the old is passed away and the new is come. Leave the old and walk in the power of newness, in the footsteps of the Teacher, ever higher, until you reach the mountaintop.

Begin the journey.

TO GO DEEPER, TO FIND MORE, TO CONTINUE THE JOURNEY...

A T THE BOTTOM of every mystery you'll find a title. The title identifies the full teaching or message from Jonathan Cahn that goes deeper into the mystery, or gives more than can be given on one page, or presents a complementary teaching or message that supplements the mystery given.

To receive these teachings, go to HopeOfTheWorld.org and to the list of all of Jonathan's messages, and search by the title or keyword.

Or you can write to Hope of the World, Box 1111, Lodi, NJ 07644, USA and request to order them by name.

Jonathan Cahn has been called the prophetic voice of our generation. He caused a stir throughout America and around the world starting with the release of his first book, *The Harbinger*, bringing him to national and international prominence. He's spoken at the United Nations, to Members of Congress on Capitol Hill, and has been interviewed on countless television, radio, and other media programs.

———•———

He leads Hope of the World ministries, an international outreach of Jew and Gentile committed to spreading God's Word to the nations and helping the world's most needy. He also leads the Jerusalem Center/Beth Israel, a worship center made up of Jews and Gentiles, people of all backgrounds, just outside New York City, in Wayne, New Jersey. He is a much sought-after speaker and appears throughout America and around the world. He is a Jewish follower of Jesus.

———•———

To get in touch with Jonathan Cahn's ministry, to get more and deeper into the mysteries, to receive free gifts, prophetic updates, other teachings, messages, or special communications from Jonathan, or to have a part in spreading God's Word, helping the needy across the world, and have a part in God's end-time work and purposes, here's how:

Write to:
Hope of the World, Box 1111, Lodi, NJ 07644
Or go to: hopeoftheworld.org and
www.facebook.com/Jonathan-Cahn-Official-Site-255143021176055

CONNECT WITH US!

CHARISMA HOUSE

(Spiritual Growth)

 Facebook.com/CharismaHouse

@CharismaHouse

Instagram.com/CharismaHouseBooks

SILOAM

(Health)

Pinterest.com/CharismaHouse

ReALMs

(Fiction)

Facebook.com/RealmsFiction